KATHLEEN O'BRIEN

"If you're looking for a fabulous read, reach for
a Katheleen O'Brien book. You can't go wrong."
—*New York Times* bestselling author Catherine Anderson

"Darkly gothic and disturbing, *Happily Never After* is a
thrill ride reminiscent of V.C. Andrews' *Flowers in the Attic*,
with the added appeal of a robust romance
and an unnerving mystery."
—Terri Clark, *Romantic Times BOOKclub*
on *Happily Never After*, 4½-Star Top Pick

"Any book written by the talented Ms. O'Brien
is a good excuse to leave all your troubles at the bathroom
door as you spend a couple of hours relaxing in your tub."
—Diana Tidlund, *Writers Unlimited*

"Ms. O'Brien has definitely made it to my 'must read' list."
—Bea Sigman, *The Best Reviews*

Dear Reader,

It's hard to believe that the Signature Select program is one year old—with seventy-two books already published by top Harlequin and Silhouette authors.

What an exciting and varied lineup we have in the year ahead! In the first quarter of the year, the Signature Spotlight program offers three very different reading experiences. Popular author Marie Ferrarella, well-known for her warm family-centered romances, has gone in quite a different direction to write a story that has been "haunting her" for years. Please check out *Sundays Are for Murder* in January. Hop aboard a Caribbean cruise with Joanne Rock in *The Pleasure Trip* for February, and don't miss a trademark romantic suspense from Debra Webb, *Vows of Silence* in March.

Our collections in the first quarter of the year explore a variety of contemporary themes. Our Valentine's collection—*Write It Up!*—homes in on the trend to online dating in three stories by Elizabeth Bevarly, Tracy Kelleher and Mary Leo. February is awards season, and Barbara Bretton, Isabel Sharpe and Emilie Rose join the fun and glamour in *And the Envelope, Please*.... And in March, Leslie Kelly, Heather MacAllister and Cindi Myers have penned novellas about women desperate enough to go to *Bootcamp* to learn how *not* to scare men away!

Three original sagas also come your way in the first quarter of this year. Silhouette author Gina Wilkins spins off her popular FAMILY FOUND miniseries in *Wealth Beyond Riches*. Janice Kay Johnson has written a powerful story of a tortured shared past in *Dead Wrong*, which is connected to her PATTON'S DAUGHTERS Superromance miniseries, and Kathleen O'Brien gives a haunting story of mysterious murder in *Quiet as the Grave*.

And don't forget there is original bonus material in every single Signature Select book to give you the inside scoop on the creative process of your favorite authors! We hope you enjoy all our new offerings!

Enjoy!

Marsha Zinberg

Marsha Zinberg
Executive Editor
The Signature Select Program

SAGA

KATHLEEN O'BRIEN

QUIET AS THE GRAVE

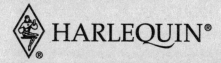

TORONTO • NEW YORK • LONDON
AMSTERDAM • PARIS • SYDNEY • HAMBURG
STOCKHOLM • ATHENS • TOKYO • MILAN • MADRID
PRAGUE • WARSAW • BUDAPEST • AUCKLAND

ISBN 0-373-83695-3

QUIET AS THE GRAVE

Dear Reader,

When you first met Mike Frome and Suzie Strickland, back in Firefly Glen, they were just impetuous teenagers, full of attitude and hopeless longing. They took foolish risks, as so many of us do when we're young, trading a sensible tomorrow for a thrilling today.

A special thanks to all the readers who wrote, asking for more. What happened to those two grouchy, mismatched kids? Did they ever find contentment? Did they ever find their way back to each other?

I know how you felt. They were special kids, and they deserved a happy ending. But, as we all know, happiness isn't handed out to the most deserving, like a merit badge. Sometimes you have to wait a long time, and trudge through a lot of tough times.

Quite simply, sometimes you have to fight for it, tooth and nail.

Now, ten years after their beginnings in Firefly Glen, Mike and Suzie are ready to meet that fight head-on. Mike's divorced from the glamorous Justine, sharing custody of his son, Gavin. Purple-haired, fiery-tempered Suzie has reinvented herself as a cool, collected beauty, and is even building a career as a portraitist.

But the calm is an illusion—the eye of the hurricane. Justine has turned up dead, and the authorities are only a heartbeat away from arresting Mike. If he's going to save himself, he's going to have to find out what really happened to his beautiful, toxic wife. He's surprised to learn that his strongest ally is the feisty girl he left behind in high school. The girl whose heart was too strong to be broken then—or daunted now.

I hope you enjoy their story.

Warmly,

Kathleen O'Brien

www.KathleenOBrien.net

CHAPTER ONE

EVEN AS THE DREAM played out, the man knew he was dreaming. Except...how could *dream* be the right word for anything so real? It was more like time travel. While his body lay there, helpless on the bed, twitching and whimpering and trying to wake up, his mind flew back to the cave and lived it all again.

Lived the stink. The air in the cave was wet. It had rained all day, and moisture clung to the slimy, pitted walls. Now and then a pocket of algae grew too heavy and popped from its secret pore. It slid across the gray rock slowly, an insect leaving behind a shining trail of ooze.

Everyone had come tonight, which was rare—but they must have heard that this would be special. Too many men crowded into the space, so the wet, stinking air was hot. He felt light-headed, as if the oxygen levels were too low. He wondered if they'd all die here, breathing foul air until they collapsed where they stood. How long would their bodies lie in their black robes before anyone discovered them?

Maybe they'd never be found, and they'd rot here. Poetic justice, surely. They were already rotted on the inside.

His mask was too tight. He couldn't breathe. He

adjusted the cloth so that the eye and mouth holes lined up better.

When the girl was brought in, it was obvious she'd been drugged. The man practically had to drag her through the opening. Her head kept dropping. She made small sounds that weren't quite human, more like a puppy whining in a cage.

From there the dream went black. No sight. All sounds. The sound of metal against metal. Metal against rock. Metal against skin.

And always the puppy sound, begging. Struggling to find its way out of the cage. Sometimes the noises escalated a little, but they never got very loud. The cage held. The puppy had almost given up hope.

The cave seemed to come alive then, as if it was being sucked into an auditory whirlwind. Weeping and low moans. Wet noises, as if someone gargled fear. Heavy breathing that rode the naked back of animal grunts. Babbling, strangely religious, from the blind trance of terror.

And then, finally, at the very end, one heartbreaking human word. The word to which everyone, even the dreamer, could be reduced, if things got bad enough.

"Mommy," the girl cried, though God only knew where her mother was. Not here, not in this wet stone room full of infected air and sweating men. The girl hadn't been more than a child when she came in, but she was a baby now. They had peeled fifteen years from her in fifteen minutes.

"Mommy, help me!"

And it was at that moment—every time, no matter how hard he prayed it wouldn't happen—that the dreamer felt his body jerk and release, spreading shame all over his pajamas, his sheets, his soul.

THE TUXEDO LAKE Country Day School Open House was the highlight of the elementary school season, and the Tuxedo Lake mothers knew it. They spent the entire morning getting ready. Manicures, pedicures, facials, eyebrow waxing and a hundred other little rituals Mike Frome had never known existed until he married Justine Millner.

Though he and Justine had been divorced two years now, he would never forget what an eye-opener the six years of their marriage had been. Her sunshine-colored hair, which used to mesmerize him the way a shiny bell on a string mesmerizes a cat, apparently was really an ordinary brown. Without its makeup, her face seemed to have different contours entirely. At home, he rarely saw that ivory skin. It was almost always buried beneath green cream and hot towels. Sometimes, when he turned to her at night—in the early days, when he still bothered to—he found her hands encased in gel-filled gloves that slid and squished when he touched them.

He would have been able to live with all that. It was called growing up, he supposed. Like discovering there's no such thing as Santa Claus. He could have coped, if only she hadn't been such a sick bitch. If he lived to be a million years old, he'd never understand why he hadn't seen sooner what a *bitch* she was.

Still, he'd put up with it for Gavin's sake. Gavin, who had been conceived when Mike and Justine were only teenagers—and who had been seven months old before his parents made things legal—loved his mother. So Mike had tried to love her, too.

He'd tried for six whole years that felt more like six hundred. Then he just couldn't pretend anymore. He had to get out, or he'd die. He figured Gavin was better off with a part-time dad than a dead one.

Since then, he'd worked hard to make this split-parenting thing a partnership. For the past two years, he and Justine had attended every single one of Gavin's Little League games together, and the kiddy birthday parties and, of course, the deadly dull PTA functions.

To attend this one, he'd stopped right in the most critical stage of a job. The Proctors' boathouse was almost finished, and he should be there. But he'd told the carpenters to take the afternoon off—which surprised the hell out of them, since ordinarily at the end of a job he was hyperfocused.

The Open House was more important. The fourthgraders were staging a musical play to welcome the parents to a new school year. *Learning Is Fun* featured historical characters who had demonstrated a love for education. Apparently Gavin's role was as the teacher in a one-room country school—a fact Justine had only this minute discovered.

"This *must* be a mistake," she was saying to Cicely Tillman, the mother of one of Gavin's friends. Cicely wore a small name tag shaped like a bow tie that read Cicely—Volunteer Mommy.

"No," Cicely, the Volunteer Mommy, said. "It's not a mistake."

"It *must* be," Justine said again, and Mike recognized that tone. Volunteer Mommy would be smart to back off. "Gavin was supposed to be the narrator. He was supposed to be *Abraham Lincoln.*"

"I know, I know, it's a shame, but he said he didn't want the part," Cicely explained, her voice brimming with the fakest sympathy Mike had ever heard, even from Cicely. "He wanted something smaller."

Justine scanned her program. "But this…this *farmer* isn't even a named part. What about Socrates? Or even Joseph Campbell?"

"We're five minutes from opening curtain, Justine." Judy Stott, who was the principal of Tuxedo Lake Country Day School, and also Justine's next-door neighbor, had noticed the fracas and joined the two ladies.

"But Judy—"

Judy reached out and patted Justine's arm. "Some children just aren't comfortable in the spotlight," she said. "I'm sure Gavin shines in other areas."

Oh, brother. Well, even if Cicely and Judy didn't have the sense to get away, Mike did. He found a folding chair fifth row center and claimed it. While the ladies' drama continued, he watched the stage. Someone new must be running the spotlight. The glowing circle lurched all over the blue curtain, leaped to the side and hit the American flag, then slid down the stairs, only to pop up again on the curtain.

When the overhead lights flickered, warning that the show was about to begin, Justine finally arranged herself next to him with a waft of Chanel. She hummed with fury.

"Did you hear that? Not comfortable in the limelight! Did you hear that? Can you believe how rude?"

Mike rolled his paper program into a cylinder and kept his eyes on the stage, where the curtains were now undulating with restless lumps. The kids, no doubt, trying to find their places.

"No, I didn't hear it." He didn't want to get into this. "I was too busy wondering what exactly it means to be a 'volunteer mommy.' Do you think they're implying that—"

But he should have known Justine wouldn't respond to any satirical attempt to change the subject. Justine didn't have a sense of humor at the best of times. And this was definitely not the best of times. She could really be like a dog with a bone, if she thought she'd been slighted.

"That self-important little pencil pusher," she whispered sharply, leaning her head toward his. "Just because she's the principal, she thinks she's God around here. She's a glorified babysitter. And her fool of a husband sells thumbtacks, for God's sake."

Mike set his jaw. He liked Phil Stott, who was kind of a wuss, but a damn nice guy.

"And she has the nerve to say Gavin isn't comfortable in the limelight. Right to my face."

Mike sighed and looked at his ex-wife. She was gorgeous, of course. She never ventured out of the house without looking perfect. But someone really should tell her that if she didn't stop disapproving of everything, her lousy temper was going to gouge furrows between those carefully waxed-and-dyed eyebrows before her thirtieth birthday.

"Gavin *isn't* comfortable in the limelight," he said, deciding to ignore the non sequitur about the thumbtacks. "Why would it be rude to say so?"

Justine glared at him a minute, then, flaring her elegant nostrils, turned her head toward the stage and tapped her program on the palm of her hand.

"For God's sake, Mike," she said under her breath. "Don't play stupid. Don't pretend you don't know what I'm talking about."

"I *don't* know what you're talking about. Frankly, that's the case about ninety percent of the time. No, make that ninety-nine."

She whipped her head around, but he got lucky. Taped music filled the air, the curtains began to open, two jerky feet at a time, and a pint-size Abraham Lincoln, complete with beard and top hat, stepped forward. It took the spotlight a few seconds to find him, and when it did Justine growled quietly.

"See? See what I mean? That's Hugh. Cecily took the part away from Gavin so she could give it to her *own* son. And Judy let her. You can't tell me it's not deliberate."

He didn't answer. He had spotted Gavin in the background, on the small risers that had been set up on either side of the stage. Mike had been to enough of these performances to know that, one at a time, the students would climb down and take center stage for their two or three lines. Ms. Hadley, the music teacher, was careful never to leave anyone out entirely. She knew all about Volunteer Mommy Syndrome.

Gavin looked nervous as hell. Mike stared at him, sending it'll-be-okay vibes. He hadn't liked this kind of thing much, either, when he'd been in school. He'd been tons happier on the football field, and he had a feeling his son was going to take after him. Which would, of course, piss Justine off in a big way.

About halfway through the play, her cell phone began to vibrate. These folding chairs were close enough together that, for a minute, he thought the rumbling against his thigh was his own phone. But he'd turned his off completely. He gave Justine a frown. Why hadn't she done the same?

To his surprise, she had stood up and was getting ready to edge her way down the aisle. She glanced back at him, holding her phone up as explanation.

God, she was absolutely unbelievable. Gavin was

due up any minute—he was one of only about two or three kids who hadn't performed yet. He reached out and grabbed her arm. He must have squeezed too hard, because she let out a cry loud enough to be heard up on stage.

"Sit down," he whispered. He jerked his head toward the stage. "Gavin."

He ought to let go of her forearm. He knew that. She was obviously strung out. She was humiliated because her son had a piddly part in the school play. She was mad at Mike for not caring. Plus, she'd had to repress all that resentment against Cicely Tillman, and self-control wasn't her strong suit.

She was probably as hot and high-pressure as a volcano ready to blow.

But he didn't let go. He was pretty damn angry, too. He knew who was on the other end of that cell phone. Her new boyfriend. The one she was going to be spending a month in Europe with, starting tonight. The guy was welcome to her, but, goddamn it, couldn't she at least pretend to put her son first, for once in her life?

"Let go of me, Michael," she said. Her whisper was so shrill it turned heads three rows away. "You're hurting me."

He hesitated one more second, and then he dropped his hand, aware that, in their section of the audience, they were now more fascinating than what was happening onstage. She rubbed her arm dramatically and then, with a hiccuping sob, made her way down the row.

Mike stared hard at the stage, ignoring the curious faces that were still turned in his direction. Gavin, who had just put on an old-fashioned hat, came forward.

"Our schoolroom is small, but it has to hold us all," he sang in a horribly off-key soprano. "My students walk for miles, and I greet them with a smile."

That was probably where Gavin was supposed to smile, but he didn't. He finished his tiny part, and then he scurried, head bowed, back to his spot on the risers. Mike felt his stomach clench. Was this just stage fright, or had Gavin actually heard his parents squabbling?

Justine didn't return even when the show was over, and Mike was fuming, though he managed to hide it fairly well, he thought. He ate cookies and drank fruit punch with the other parents until the kids joined them, enduring the awkward silences while everyone tried to figure out what to say about Justine's absence.

Finally Gavin came racing out, beaming. He barreled into Mike, trying to knock chests like the professional sports figures, but instead hitting Mike's ribs with his nose. Mike forgot Justine and his heart pounded a couple of heavy thumps of typical proud-daddy love. The kid was growing like crazy. In a year or two, that chest-bumping thing just might work.

Best of all, Gavin looked ecstatic now that his ordeal was over. He grinned up at Mike with those knockout blue eyes that were so like Justine's. "It's over!" He laughed. "I sucked, huh?"

Mike smiled back, relieved that the episode with Justine apparently hadn't reached the kids' ears. "Yep, you're pretty bad, pal. You're definitely no Pavarotti."

This was the kind of candor that would drive Justine nuts. She had the theory that admitting any inadequacies was bad for the boy's ego. But Mike knew that Gavin's ego was perfectly healthy. Maybe too healthy. Gavin was as gorgeous as his mother, he lived in a six-thousand-square-foot mansion with his own boat and plasma TV, he pulled down straight As, and he boasted the best batting average in his Little League conference.

It would do him good to face the facts: Hugh Tillman was a better singer.

"I know," Gavin agreed happily. "I can't ever get the tune. Mrs. Hadley hates me. Where's Mom?"

Mike felt the eyes of the other parents once again.

"She's outside," he said as casually as he could. "She got a phone call."

"Oh, well, tell her I love her, okay? I gotta go." Gavin and his buddies had plans to celebrate the success of the play with a pizza party at the Tillmans' house. "Hugh's mom is already waiting in the minivan for us."

"Go tell her yourself," Mike said. He knew if he let Gavin leave without saying goodbye, she'd carp about it all the way home.

The boy flew off, with Hugh and about four other boys trailing behind him like a pack of puppies. Mike grabbed a napkin, wiped cinnamon sugar off his hands and tossed his empty punch cup in the big trash bin.

"Three points," Phil Stott, Judy's husband, said with a smile. Mike appreciated that. He knew that Phil, a nice guy who didn't have kids but was here to support his wife's school, was trying to bridge the embarrassment gap.

Gavin was back in a flash. "Found her! She says to tell you she's waiting for you in the car." He held up his hand for Mike's goodbye slap. At home it would be a hug and a kiss, but with Hugh and the other "dudes" standing by, a high five would have to do.

Mike obliged, and then did the same for all the other boys, who were accustomed to parading by him

KATHLEEN O'BRIEN   17

this way after every Little League game. He'd coached these boys since they were in T-ball. They were good kids. But he couldn't help thinking his own smart, silly son was the best.

He wished Gavin were coming home with him right now, but he realized that was pretty cowardly. Yeah, the ride home would be a bummer, with Justine pouting or ranting, but he could handle it. He didn't need to use his son as a buffer.

By the time he got to the car, Justine wasn't speaking to him. Good. Pouting was ridiculous, but it was easier to ignore than the ranting.

She'd rolled back her silk sleeve and was rubbing conspicuously at the discoloration just above her wrist. He checked it out of the corner of his eye, just cynical enough to wonder which way the finger marks were facing. He was pretty damn sure he hadn't been rough enough to bruise anything. She'd probably done it herself, while she waited for him to come out.

He considered trying to make conversation, but it seemed like too much trouble. Woodcliff Road was kind of tricky, with a twenty-foot drop through wooded slopes on the passenger side. He needed to concentrate.

Let her sulk. She loved that anyhow.

Finally, though, her resentment simply had to bubble out in words. She swiveled in her seat and glared at him. "So? Don't you have a single thing to say for yourself? After what you did to my arm?"

Damn. He'd almost made it. They were only a couple of miles from Tuxedo Lake. He negotiated a curve through some overhanging elms, which were just beginning to go yellow. He glanced at her face, which looked slightly jaundiced in the glowing light.

The shadows of the trees passing over her made it seem as if her mouth were moving silently, though he knew it wasn't. It was a disagreeable sight.

He turned away and shrugged. "Sorry," he said. "I just couldn't believe you were actually going to leave right when Gavin's part was coming up."

She waved her hand. "You call that a part? I can't believe he dragged us all the way out there for that. He made a fool of me, that's for sure."

Clenching the steering wheel, Mike tried not to react. This was pointless, and he knew it. He'd tried for years to make Justine think about any situation, anywhere on this earth, without viewing it through the prism of her own self-interests, but she simply couldn't do it. He'd looked up *sociopath* once, and it fit perfectly. It was kind of scary, actually.

But, like an idiot, sometimes he just couldn't stop himself from responding. He accelerated, whipping the passing trees into a batter of lemony green.

"He made a fool of *you?* Sorry, but you're going to have to explain to me how Gavin's school play can possibly end up being all about *you*."

She didn't answer right away, and he knew that was a bad sign. She was lining up her ammunition, which meant this wasn't going to be just a skirmish. It was going to be war.

"That's just so like you," she said. "The perfect Mike Frome can't make mistakes. If anyone dares to point out that you've done something wrong, like rough up your own wife, you just launch a counterattack, trying to change the subject. Well, I won't be put on the defensive. You manhandled me, and I ought to go to the police."

"You're not my wife," he said. That was stupid,

too. That wasn't the point. But she did that to him. She made him so mad his brain shut off.

"I'm your son's mother. I think that is just as important, don't you?"

"No. I think it's tragic."

"God, you're so melodramatic." She narrowed her eyes. "Tragic? Because I took a call on my cell phone? I'm sorry to tell you, but that doesn't make me a bad mother."

He'd had enough. "No," he said. "What makes you a bad mother is that you're a raging bitch. You're the most self-centered, foul-tempered bitch in the state of New York. That's what makes you a bad mother."

He half expected her to slap him. He definitely expected her to start yelling epithets at him. But she didn't do either of those things. Instead, she did something that shocked the hell out of him.

She opened her car door.

"Justine—"

"Stop the car."

"Damn it, shut the door."

"No. Stop the car. I'm getting out."

He was already applying the brakes, but he had to be careful. She had one leg out. He didn't want to fishtail on these narrow, curving roads. He was mad as hell at her. He might wish he'd never met her, but he didn't want her to get hurt.

He maneuvered the car to a safe spot. His heart racing, he turned to her. "Are you insane? Do you want to kill yourself? Shut the damn door."

She didn't answer. She just picked up her purse and got out of the car, slamming the door shut behind her.

He rolled down the down the window. "Justine, for God's sake."

"Go to hell," she said without looking at him. "Just go straight to hell where you belong."

He looked at her, so messed up with contradictory, heart-racing emotions and adrenaline that he couldn't even decide what he felt. It was about five o'clock, and the trees behind her were already full of shadows. She had on high heels, the better to impress the other Volunteer Mommies with, but no damn good at all for walking along an uphill cliff road.

"Justine. Okay, look. I'm sorry. Get back in the car."

She didn't even answer. She just began to walk.

He trolled along behind her for a few yards, leaning over to beg her through the window and steering the car with one hand. He felt like a fool, which was bad enough, but when another car came up behind him and honked impatiently, the embarrassment of it was just too much.

"Justine, get in the car right now, or I'm going to drive away, and you're going to have to walk the rest of the way home. It's nearly a mile."

No response, except another short toot from the car behind.

"Justine, I mean it. It's getting cold. I'm not coming back to get you."

She didn't even turn her head. She shifted her purse to her other shoulder and kept walking. The people behind him probably thought he was a stalker, or a serial killer.

Honk…

Well, screw her, then. If she wanted to walk all the way home in a snit, fine. She logged about five miles on the treadmill in the home gym every single day of her life. He figured she could handle half a mile out here.

He rolled up the window and hit the gas. He watched her in the rearview mirror, getting smaller but never once looking his way or acknowledging her predicament by the slightest twitch of a muscle.

Finally he came to a curve, and when he looked in the mirror again she was gone.

That was the last time anyone—except perhaps her killer—ever saw Justine Millner Frome alive.

CHAPTER TWO

Two years later

"HOLD STILL. You've got a spot of green paint on your face."

Suzie Strickland waited while the man in front of her reached up and teased the bridge of her nose with his fingernail. She didn't believe for a minute that she had any paint there. Ben Kuspit just wanted to touch her. He'd been flirting with her ever since she arrived an hour ago to take pictures of his son.

He was paying her four-and-a-half thousand dollars for a painting of Kenny, the youngest of his four kids. It was the largest commission she'd landed yet, and she needed it. Still, if they'd been alone, she would have made it very clear that the price didn't include groping rights.

Unfortunately, nine-year-old Kenny was still in the room, and she was reluctant to embarrass Daddy in front of his kid.

And, to be fair, maybe Ben wasn't inventing the speck of paint. She had been using viridian paint this afternoon as she finished up her current project, a pair of adorable two-year-old twins with green eyes, green dresses and green ribbons in their hair.

She'd come a long way since the early years, when,

after a day's work, she'd find splattered color every-where. In her hair, under her fingernails, even on the soles of her shoes. She still painted with passion, but she'd learned how to harness that intensity. Today, her sunny workroom on the third floor of her Albany townhome was the cleanest, best-organized space in the house.

Still, paint was paint, and it had a way of insinuating itself into some pretty strange places.

"Thanks," she said, smiling politely at Ben, though her voice was tight. He needed to back up. He was se-riously violating her personal space. And that smile was gross. The man was fifty, for God's sake. His kid was staring right at him.

She lifted her camera up between them and moved to the far side of a gold chair, the kind of fragile, frilly thing Mrs. Kuspit apparently loved. The huge room was full of them.

"I'll just get two or three more shots, and then I think I'm done here."

"Great." Ben looked over at Kenny, who stood next to the living room mantel, where trophies were arrayed like a metallic rainbow, catching light from the overhead chandelier and tossing it onto the flocked ivory wallpaper in little oblongs of silver and gold. They didn't match the frilly gold chairs, but apparently Mrs. Kuspit didn't make *all* the decorating decisions.

"Hey, I've got an idea," Ben said, snapping his fingers. "Kenny, pick up the football. Make like you're getting ready to toss a long one."

Kenny grimaced, but he bent down and retrieved the football at his feet. He lifted his arm awkwardly, glancing sideways at his father. "Like this?"

Ben made a disgusted sound. "Damn it, Kenny,

why are you flashing us your armpit?" He strode over
to the boy and began twisting his skinny elbow into a
better position. "If you think I'm paying four-and-a-
half thousand dollars to have you look like a geek,
you've got another think coming."

The boy flushed, but he didn't protest. He just
stared at the floor while his father adjusted him like a
mannequin. Suzie lowered her camera and tried not to
hate the man. Throwing a football in the formal living
room? *Come on.* His ego had to have some limits,
didn't it?

She didn't say anything, though. She'd had weirder
requests, like the woman who wanted her parakeet's
picture painted as if he lived inside a genie's bottle.
She'd like to meet the psychiatrist who could figure
that one out.

She had taken that commission, too. She needed
every job she could get. If the Kuspits liked her painting—and she could already tell she'd have to add
about ten pounds of muscle to the little boy in order
to please Daddy—they would hang her picture where
their rich friends could see it.

Their rich friends would then decide that their own
little darlings deserved to be displayed in a big, beautiful rococo gold frame, too.

And voilà! Suzie could pay the mortgage on her
town house, and everyone was happy.

Except Kenny.

Poor kid.

Ben was big and beefy, a good-looking former
athlete. Kenny was scrawny and appeared to have
about as much athletic ability as a scarecrow. Most of
the trophies on the mantel were inscribed with phrases
like Most Improved or Best Sportsmanship.

"Okay, that's good, hold that. Don't move." Ben gestured impatiently toward Suzie. "Get one of him like that."

Suzie lifted the camera, although the image she saw in the viewfinder was hardly inspiring. Kenny looked like he was being tortured.

He must hate football, but Ben obviously didn't care. The three older Kuspit offspring were girls. Suzie would bet that, the minute Ben saw the little manly splotch on the ultrasound, he had scrawled *"live vicariously through my son, the awesome high school quarterback"* into his engagement calendar. He wasn't going to let the dream die easily.

If he only knew what a mistake he was making. Look at Mike Frome, the most "awesome" jock in Suzie's high school. At seventeen he'd landed Justine Millner, the prettiest girl in Firefly Glen. By eighteen, he'd been forced to marry Justine—because she'd had his kid—though he no longer even liked her. By twenty-five they were divorced.

Not that Suzie was keeping tabs on his life or anything. She knew all that only because, right after the divorce, Justine had hired Suzie to paint her son Gavin's portrait.

It had probably merely been Justine's way of spending Mike's money as fast as she could, but Suzie didn't care. She would have taken a commission from the devil himself to jump-start her career. And Gavin had actually been a pretty neat kid in spite of having been scooped out of a scummy gene pool.

"Suzie?"

She focused again, and saw both Ben and Kenny in her viewfinder. Ben was frowning. "Suzie? Is everything okay?"

Darn. It had been a long time since she'd let thoughts of Mike Frome distract her.

She pressed the camera's button automatically, forgetting that she'd now have both father and son in the picture. No big deal. She often picked up all kinds of extraneous people and things. She could drop them out with her photo program.

"Yeah, fine. I think that'll do it." She smiled at Kenny. "You did great."

Kenny looked skeptical, but he smiled back and shrugged. He turned to his father. "Okay if I go? I've got homework."

Ben patted him on the shoulder. "You bet. Gotta get those grades up."

God, could the jerk put any more pressure on this kid? Suzie began packing away her camera and supplies, reminding herself to schedule the sittings when Ben Kuspit was at work. He did go to work, didn't he? Surely plaguing the hell out of your family wasn't a full-time job.

"Ready?" Suddenly Ben Kuspit's voice was very close behind her.

Oh, *rats*. She'd forgotten that she'd agreed to let him drive her home. Her twelve-year-old Honda, which she'd named Flattery because it wouldn't get you anywhere, had hunkered down in her driveway and refused once again to start. She'd taken a cab over here, but Ben had insisted on driving her home.

Suddenly she didn't like that idea at all.

"You know," she said, turning, her camera still in her hand, "I think I should get a cab back. This took longer than I'd expected, and I know you have things to do."

"No, no," he said with a smile. *That* smile. He

caught his full lower lip between his teeth in a way that would have looked stupid even on a man half his age. "There's nothing I'd rather do than take you home. Honestly."

Oh, yeah? Well, honestly, *the idea of getting in a car with you makes my skin crawl.*

Somehow she kept the smile on her face, though she was getting downright sick of this guy.

She thought of the Sailor Sam's Fish and Chips uniform she'd hung above her easel as a reminder of what life used to be like. A reminder that she was always just a couple of blown commissions away from having to wear that blue sailor jacket, tight red short-shorts, kneesocks and jaunty red-ribboned cap.

She took a deep breath. "No, it's okay. I'd really rather take a cab."

"Don't be silly." He reached into his pocket and jingled his keys suggestively. "I insist."

"Mr. Kuspit, I don't think you understand. I want to take a cab." She smiled to soften it. "I'm *going* to take a cab."

He must be really rich, she thought. He looked as if he'd never heard the word *no* before. He gave her a playful scowl and came even closer, so close it made the hair on her arms stand up and tingle.

Cripes. Maybe she should go back to the Goth style she'd adopted in high school, the unflattering, chopped-off purple hair and the black, slouchy clothes. Passes from boy-men had never been such a nuisance back then.

"But I've been looking forward to it," he said in a throaty voice. "I'm eager to get to know you better, Suzie. You're such a talented young woman."

Oh, man, she really, really didn't like people

invading her space, and this guy was so close she could see the tiny broken veins around his nose. If she were painting his face, she'd need a whole tube of cadmium red.

A drinker. *Great.* She needed that.

She tried one last time to be smart, to remember the mortgage payments. Would it kill her to ride in the car with the guy one time? Her town house was only ten minutes away. She thought of the red short-shorts and the screaming kids who puked up tartar sauce on the tables. She thought of the way she had come dragging home every night, too tired and angry to paint.

He touched her arm. Still smiling, he ran his index finger slowly up, until it disappeared under the little cap sleeve of her T-shirt. She shivered in disgust, and she saw his gaze slip to her nipples.

Oh, no, you don't, buddy. Waaay over the line.

She narrowed her eyes.

"I'm sorry, Mr. Kuspit. I guess I didn't understand exactly what you wanted. The portrait is forty-five hundred. But if you're expecting to have a thing with me on the side, that's going to cost extra."

He blinked once, but then his grin twisted, and his fingers crept up another inch. They found her shoulder and cupped it. What an incredible sleazeball! He thought she was playing games.

"Oh, is that so?" He raised one eyebrow. "How much extra?"

She scrunched up her mouth and made a low hum of consideration. "Let's see," she said. "I'd say…oh, about…no…well, let's see…"

She looked him straight in the eye. "Oh, yeah, now I remember. *There's not enough money in the world.*"

His brows dived together. His hand tightened on her

shoulder and pulled her in, and his other arm started to come up. She didn't stop to find out what he had in mind. She swung out with the camera as hard as she could.

He was so close she couldn't get much leverage. Still, the camera connected with his cheek and made a nice little thump, followed by a grunt of shocked outrage.

"Shit," he said, recoiling. "What the hell's the matter with you?"

She didn't bother to answer. He was holding his cheek, looking at her as if she'd broken his jaw, which she definitely had not. She knew what that sounded like. She'd broken a bone once, the left radius of a university teaching assistant who'd thought he could teach her something more than algebra and had to be set straight the hard way.

This guy wasn't hurt. He was just a big baby.

She reached out, lifted his hand from the cheek and eyed it calmly, pleased to see she'd drawn at least a little blood. He'd have a nice colorful bruise there tomorrow.

She felt like blowing smoke from the tip of her camera, gunslinger style. But that would have been gloating.

Still, she was pleased to discover that, even after ten years of learning to play nice and conform, she hadn't lost her touch entirely.

It wasn't until she was halfway home in the cab that she realized what she *had* lost.

She leaned her head against the cracked vinyl seat and let out a groan.

Blast it. She'd lost four-and-a-half thousand dollars.

DEBRA PAWLEY DECIDED to go over to the Millner-Frome mansion a couple of hours early so that she could make sure everything was spiffed up and gleaming for the open house at noon.

She was by God going to sell this house *today*.

Tuxedo Lake was one of the most desirable communities in this part of upstate New York. It was about thirty minutes northeast of Albany, just close enough to be considered a bedroom community…if you didn't plan to sleep late.

The lake itself was big and elegant, with sandy shores you could get away with calling a beach in your brochures. A picturesque ring of low granite cliffs nearly circled the lake, and if a sailboat drifted by at the right moment, your brochure illustration looked dynamite.

The mansion itself was gorgeous. A 6,462-square-foot French château jewel, complete with marble vestibule, formal library, swimming pool with central fountain and Jacuzzi. Nanny quarters over the four-car garage.

Debra didn't often let herself envy the houses she listed. But she envied this one.

When she sold it, she'd make a bundle in commission.

If she sold it. The house might be perfect, but the house's history was a mess. Justine Frome had mysteriously disappeared two years ago and had never been heard from since. The police suspected foul play, and so did her parents. Justine's father had dragged the lake and jackhammered up the swimming pool looking for her, but no body had ever been found.

That was the problem in a nutshell. Debra didn't mean to be insensitive, but who wanted to pay a couple of mil for a beautiful lakefront home if they were always going to be wondering when a body might bob out of the lake, or start stinking up the basement?

She left her car out on the street, planted her Open House sign in the most visible spot and then hiked up the long, showy entry to the mansion. She liked to let the buyers drive into the main portico. It tempted them. They loved the look of their own cars under that elegant, shady arch.

Please, God, let there be buyers today. Her last open house had brought in half a dozen gawkers and only two legitimate lookers who had scurried out of the house like cartoon mice when they heard the *Where's Justine?* story. Legally, she had to tell it.

Debra propped her bag of cleaning and cooking supplies against her shin while she fumbled with the front door keys. Off to the right, she heard the growl of Richie Graham's hedge clippers. He was probably shaping the boxwood hedge, which surrounded a glorious garden of White Persian Lilacs. They probably would be in full bloom thanks to all the rain.

Richie…well, that was a good news–bad news situation. Richie had been the gardener for this house, and many of the Tuxedo Lake mansions, for about ten years now, and he created some spectacular lawns. He'd lived in the nanny quarters, serving as caretaker for the mansion ever since Justine's father, Alton Millner, had moved out a few months ago.

He was as scruffy, rugged and sexy as Lady Chatterley's lover, which was the good news. Debra had watched the female prospective buyers watching Richie, and several times she'd been tempted to hand them one of the Chinese lacquer bowls to catch the drool.

The bad news was that he was terrible about tracking mud all over the marble floors, especially when the weather was as soupy as it had been lately.

The hedge clippers stopped just as she got the dead bolt to turn. In a matter of minutes, as she was arranging her supplies on the kitchen's granite counter, she felt a shadow fall into the room, and she knew Richie had arrived.

"Hey, there, gorgeous," he said in his husky voice that always seemed to be laced with amusement.

He might well be amused by that comment. Debra knew she wasn't gorgeous. She wasn't even really pretty. She was, as her mom put it, "acceptable."

It had been a hard lesson to learn, but she'd learned it. She'd even learned to compensate for it, though good makeup and a flattering haircut could go only so far.

"Hi, Richie," she said, twisting her head to smile at him.

Now *he* was gorgeous. He was wearing his regular uniform, a pair of white jeans that somehow managed to cup his butt and practically fall off his bony hips at the same time. Work boots. And nothing else.

She wondered if he picked white because he knew that, on him, smudges of earth were paradoxically sexy, making you think he might grab you and make painful, thorny, but ecstatic and perfumed love to you in the rose garden.

Or did he just know that the white set off his tanned torso to perfection? Once, hiding here in the kitchen and looking out the window, she'd watched him hose off his dirty chest, the clear water finding that fault line down the center, the one that bisected the pectorals and ended at the navel....

She wiped her flushed brow with the back of her hand and wished that she weren't always, always attracted to bad boys.

"You showing the place today?"

She nodded, pulling herself together. She already had one bad boy lover. She didn't need two, not even in her fantasies.

"Yes. It starts at noon. I hope you haven't tracked mud all over the foyer."

"I might have." He rubbed his chest lazily, still grinning. "It's rained every day for two weeks. It's like a swamp out there."

She sighed, reached over and grabbed a damp sponge.

"Here," she said, tossing it to him. "You can clean it up, then."

He caught the sponge with one hand. He looked at it a minute, then squeezed it hard, until water oozed between his fingers. He rubbed it slowly over his face, and then, when it was gray with dirt, he tossed it back to her.

"Can't," he said. "The boxwood is only half-done. Gotta get back to it. I'll help you with that gingerbread when you're done. Just leave it in the stove."

She made a face, but she wasn't really mad. She didn't mind if he wanted the gingerbread. She made it only to fill the air with the comforting scents of cinnamon and nutmeg during the open house.

And she didn't even mind that he wouldn't clean up his own muddy footprints.

That was her problem. She simply didn't know how to get mad at a sexy rascal like that, even when he deserved it. It was, as her mother was fond of pointing out, her Achilles' heel.

Turned out Richie had been pulling her chain anyhow. The house was spotless, and the little touch-cleaning she did was largely unnecessary. She opened a couple of windows to let the fresh spring air in. Then she dusted a couple of picture frames. Finally, she vacuumed the library's Persian rug and the plush wall-to-wall in the master bedroom.

Done. And still an hour to go before anyone showed up. She was going to sell this house, she told herself again. Her mom had called last week and offered to let her come home to live if things got too tough up here in New York.

No way in hell was she going back home. She'd sell this house *today*.

Still in the master bedroom, she gazed through the lake window that led onto a small, circular overlook. From up here you could see the entire lawn. Richie was still taming the boxwood, his muscular arms hoisting the heavy clippers as if they were made of feathers.

On the other side, the west side of the house, she could just glimpse Phil and Judy Stott's yard. They didn't use Richie, and it showed. They were out there now, fertilizing a bulb garden that was just about played out for the season. Debra and Judy were friends, but she was glad you couldn't see much of their yard from the ground. It wouldn't be a selling point.

The glistening blue lake was, though, especially on a clear morning like this, when half a dozen sailboats floated out there, as white as scraps of fallen clouds.

Thank God the torrential rains had ended. Debra had been here in bad weather, and it gave the lake an eerie silvery-green cast. On stormy days, you could imagine poor Justine lying there on the mucky bottom, small fish camouflaging themselves in the waving strands of her faded hair.

What *had* happened to her?

This tiny balcony, for instance… The wrought-iron railing was too low. If she'd been standing here, and someone had come up behind her, it wouldn't have taken much. One push, and she could easily have lost her balance.

But who would have pushed her? The most obvious answer, of course, would be her husband, Mike Frome. And Debra knew that wasn't possible.

Her boyfriend, Rutledge, worked for Mike. Mike was one of the good guys.

At least she had always thought he was….

She moved away from the window. None of that. She needed to fill this house with good vibes, with optimism and promise. She spied an empty cachepot beside the bed. Yes, that's what it needed. Flowers. Nothing said "home" like flowers fresh from your own garden.

She grabbed a basket and a pair of gardening shears from the mudroom just beyond the kitchen, and then she wandered out into the yard. Richie hadn't been kidding. It really was swampy. But it was as if the rain had intoxicated the flowers, eliminating their inhibitions, making them dress in gaudier colors, spread their lush, ripe petals wider than was prudent.

The larkspurs were the most spectacular. They dominated a multicolored patch of blooms down near the cliff edge, flanking the small stairway that led to the beach. Debra decided she had time to go that far and still wash her shoes when she got back to the house. So she settled the basket over her arm and made her way down the sloping lawn, enjoying the way the sun warmed her hair and painted lime-gold patches on the grass.

Once she stood among the larkspurs, the muddy ground giving underfoot, the lake was so close its sunny sparkles almost blinded her. When a motorboat went puttering by, someone called and waved, though she couldn't identify the shadowy figure. Was everyone around here that friendly? She didn't live on this lake. She couldn't begin to afford such a snazzy address.

She squinted into the sun, wondering if it might be Rutledge, who was supposed to be doing some bookwork at Mike's office today but who always preferred to be out on the water if he had a choice. She sure hoped he hadn't ditched work again. There were limits even to nice Mike Frome's patience.

When the boat curved and turned away, for several minutes she could still hear the lake lapping against the shore in nervous eddies.

She went back to cutting flowers, long purple-blue stalks that were going to look gorgeous in the white bedroom. She filled her basket to overflowing, and then stepped carefully through the mud to the other side of the stairs. She didn't want to leave the garden lopsided.

Over here the rain had really pummeled things. The mud had run down, out of the bed, onto the grass beyond. She wasn't sure she could find many stalks that weren't bruised and spattered with dirt.

She bent, searching, sifting with her fingers….

Suddenly she straightened and backed up a step, her blood running cold, shrinking in her veins.

What the *hell* was that?

She made herself look again. She made herself stand there, her feet sinking into the cool mud. She reached out numbly and parted the tall stalks of larkspurs. She must have been mistaken.

But she wasn't wrong. There, half-exposed by the spring glut of muddy rain, were the elegant and bony fingers of a human hand.

"SO…YOU FEEL LIKE maybe taking the boat out this afternoon?" Mike looked at Gavin, who was slumped on the passenger seat, fiddling with the strap of his backpack. "Ledge is minding the office, so I could get free if you're in the mood."

Gavin shrugged. He had hardly spoken ten words since Mike had picked him up from a birthday-party sleepover at Hugh's house.

Well, okay. He didn't have to talk. It was okay if he wanted to just stare out the window, watching the roadside flowers rush by in a smear of color.

Mike wasn't usually the hovering type. He allowed his kid the right to a few grumps and sulks, and he didn't try to jolly him out of them. Sometimes life just sucked, and he wanted Gavin to learn to fight his own way clear of a crummy mood.

Gavin had been blessed with a cheerful nature, and so he usually did just fine.

But this felt different. The air in the truck was dark, though it was a bright spring Sunday. And Gavin's face, caught in a stream of light from the window, looked oddly pale. Mike had even felt his forehead, a real no-no since Gavin had been about six.

But no fever.

Then he'd probed gently into the usual suspects… teachers, tests, girls, playground scuffles.

But no hits.

He wondered whether Gavin might have wet the bed at Hugh's, which would naturally have been mortifying. Why would Gavin have reverted to that, though? He'd wet the bed for about six months after Justine's disappearance, but not lately.

Still…something about this mood reminded Mike of that terrible time.

Shit. His hands tightened on the steering wheel, his heart aching.

He'd thought Gavin was doing so well. But maybe that had been naive. It had been two years, a long time in a ten-year-old child's life, but maybe not long enough. Gavin seemed fine most of the time, but their psychiatrist had warned Mike that losing Justine this way might function like post-traumatic stress disorder. Despair and grief could strike without warning, with the slightest of triggers.

Especially since there had never really been any closure. Mike knew why Gavin was always jumping up to answer the phone, or the door. He knew why, when Gavin saw a blue Mercedes like Justine's, he went rigid and followed it with his eyes until it disappeared.

He thought every car might be the car that brought his mother back to him.

Mike didn't. In his heart, Mike knew Justine had to be dead. She'd been a bitch on wheels, and he wasn't going to sugarcoat it—he'd hated her. But she had loved Gavin in her way. If she'd been alive, she would have been in touch with her son.

Mike parked the truck in front of the boathouse office and killed the engine. Gavin started to open his door.

"Gavin, wait."

Mike fought the urge to put his hand on that silky gold head. "Buddy, I'm sorry, but you're making me nervous. Please give me a hint what's going on here."

Gavin might look like his mother, but he had a much softer heart. He obviously heard the anxiety in his dad's voice. He frowned, took a deep breath, then let it out heavily.

"It's nothing, really, Dad. It's just—"

Mike forced himself not to push. If Gavin only knew how many demons could run through his dad's mind during even a three-second pause. What? Had someone told Gavin that his mom ran away because she didn't love him? Had they told him that Mike himself must have killed her? Had they invented ghoulish fictions about what happened, just to see if they could make him cry?

If the little bastards had done any of that, Mike would go over there and shake them until their pea-brains rattled.

"We're having this thing at school," Gavin said finally. "Lunch With Mom Day, they call it. It's super dumb, really. But it's this Tuesday, and…"

Mike's first thought was, *thank God*. That was all? Just Lunch With Mom Day?

But then he saw the tears shining in Gavin's blue eyes, and he realized how dense that was. Lunch With Mom Day mattered. The tough stuff, the nasty, bullying stuff, Gavin could probably handle. He could punch out a bully. He could fight back.

But how did you fight back against Lunch With Mom Day? How did you fight back against the thousands of little losses, the subtle moments in every day when you were simply different? When you were somehow…less?

Mike felt himself getting mad all over again. What insensitive Volunteer Mommy had thought up this stupid idea? In any elementary school classroom, there would be kids whose moms had jobs they couldn't leave. Moms who had divorced daddy, or even moms who were dead.

But in this particular elementary school, everyone knew there was at least one child whose mom was cruelly missing.

By lifting his chin and breathing deeply, Gavin had managed to keep his tears from falling. Damn, Mike thought. He loved this tough little kid, and he'd do anything to keep him from hurting.

But there was nothing he could do. The world didn't revolve around them. They couldn't deny the other families the fun of Lunch With Mom Day just because it made Gavin feel bad.

"They said we could bring some other woman, if our moms couldn't make it. But the only lady I could think of was Miss Pawley, and everybody knows she's Ledge's girlfriend, not yours."

Mike nodded. "Yeah, I see the problem."

But darn it, was there no way to get this mess right? After Justine's disappearance, he hadn't even considered dating. He didn't want to confuse Gavin, and he certainly didn't want to give the police or Justine's dad any more ammunition against him. They already thought that, jealous of her new lover, he'd strangled Justine and dumped her in the lake.

Millner had even paid teams to drag the lake. Mike had taken Gavin away while they did it, up to Firefly Glen, where Mike's parents fussed over him and kept him distracted.

And besides, who would want to date Mike anyhow? A black cloud of suspicion followed him everywhere he went. No woman in her right mind would voluntarily join him under there in the shadows.

"Still, you could ask Debra," Mike suggested. "She's fun. She's pretty."

Gavin looked at him. "Not as pretty as mom."

"I know. But—"

Mike stopped there. What else was there to say? Gavin wasn't ready yet to learn that beauty wasn't everything. Hell, it wasn't *anything*.

"I know," he said again, lamely.

Gavin smiled a little. "But maybe I'll ask her anyhow. She knows how to make a spitball, and Hugh will think that's cool."

Mike rolled his eyes. "Gavin…"

"I'm just kidding." Gavin gathered up his portable video game and once again put his hand on the door handle. "Come on, let's go. You've gotta tell Ledge we're taking the boat out."

But when they entered the cool front office, Rutledge was nowhere to be seen. Damn it, Mike thought, trying to keep his face expressionless. Had the son of a bitch gone missing again? He wanted to help an old buddy, but not if it was going to cost him his business.

"Maybe he's in the back," Gavin said as he moved toward Mike's office, where there was an armchair he liked to plop on and play his video game.

Mike heard a strange noise. A thumping noise.

Gavin looked up from his game. "What's that? Is he busting up boxes or something?"

"I don't know." Mike listened a minute. Then he narrowed his eyes. That noise sounded disturbingly rhythmic. Disturbingly familiar.

He turned to Gavin. "Wait for me in my office, okay?"

Gavin's brows tightened, and he started to move

back toward Mike. "Why? Is it something bad? Is it a burglar?"

Mike smiled and shook his head. Gavin had never been fearful before Justine's disappearance. Once, when he was only five, he'd caught a large, hairy spider under a glass and sat guard over it until morning because he didn't want to bother Mike and Justine, who were sleeping.

Now the slightest noise in broad daylight had him as tense as a guy wire.

"No, it's nothing. It's just Rutledge, being a dork. I'll take care of it."

"Okay." Gavin headed into Mike's office, the little dinging and chiming sounds of his video game already audible.

Mike headed back to the receiving area, where the thumping noises had just reached a crescendo and died away. He rapped roughly on the door, though he felt like busting in and letting the damn fool get caught with his pants down.

This wasn't the first time he'd heard those thumping noses. Not the first time Rutledge Coffee had used Mike's business as a by-the-hour motel room.

It was beginning to piss him off.

Worst of all, Mike knew that the thumpee wasn't Rutledge's girlfriend, Debra Pawley. Debra was handling an open house at Justine's mansion this afternoon. Ledge must have found some other poor fool to join him in a little afternoon delight.

Mike's knock had brought thirty seconds of scurrying and scrabbling noises. When they stopped, he opened the door. Sure enough, there between the cabinets that held pens and pencils and spare paper was Rutledge.

He grinned at Mike, though he was flushed and disheveled. He sucked in his belly, which had just a hint of beer bloat, while he put the finishing touches on his belt buckle.

Standing behind him was a curvy redhead who looked familiar. Mike noticed the smell of melted cheese, and then he remembered. Bonnie, the girl who delivered their pizzas when they had to work late.

"Hi, Bonnie," he said.

"Hi, Mr. Frome," she responded shyly. She swiped at her hair, which was decorated with tiny Styrofoam packing peanuts. They must have been using the mail table. "I'm sorry… I mean I brought Mr. Coffee a pizza and—"

Rutledge gave her a look. "And you were just leaving." He shook his own hair with his fingers. "Right?"

"Right." Bonnie slipped by Mike carefully, as if it would be rude to touch him. "Goodbye, Mr. Frome."

When she was gone, Mike turned to Rutledge. "You stupid son of a bitch."

Rutledge had decided to brazen it out. "Why? She's got great tits, and we got the pizza for free." He held up a slice and bit into it. "Want some?"

"No. My kid's out there, Ledge. What I want is for you to stop treating my business like a brothel."

Rutledge chewed a minute before responding. "A *brothel*?" He grimaced. "You sound like my Victorian uncle. You know, I think you may be hungrier than you think. What's it been, two years? You're starving, my friend, and you just don't know it."

For a minute Mike wanted to punch him. What the hell did he know about the two years Mike had just been through? What did Rutledge Lebron Coffee III, who had spent his life taking, whether from the pizza girls or from his parents, know about real loss? He thought that because he'd run through his inheritance and had to work for a living, he had really suffered.

And on top of that he was idiot enough to cheat on Debra. Sure, they'd both done crap like this in high school, but they were grown men now, supposedly. And Debra just might be the best thing that had ever happened to a jerk like Rutledge.

"Get out," Mike said. "Go home and don't come back until you're ready to work for your paycheck, not sit around eating pizza and screwing the delivery girl."

Rutledge frowned. "Come on, Mike. You know I was kidding. I—"

But just then Mike's cell phone rang. He tugged it out of his pocket roughly and answered without looking at the caller ID.

"Yes," he said tightly. "What is it?"

"Mike? It's Debra."

Debra? She sounded stuffy and wet, as if she'd been crying. Had she somehow found out about Rutledge and the pizza girl already? Mike tightened his grip on the phone.

"Hey," he said. "What's wrong?"

"I—" She began to cry in earnest. "Oh, Mike—"

"Honey, calm down. What's wrong?"

"I found her," she said. "In the garden, in the larkspurs. I saw something and—" She couldn't go on. She was crying so hard she was hiccuping.

Saw something? That wasn't much to go on, but Mike's blood was already running cold. He knew he still held the phone, because he could hear Debra crying, but he couldn't feel his fingers. Rutledge had gone very quiet, too, and was watching him carefully.

"What? Debra, try to tell me. What did you see?"

"B-bones," she spluttered out. "A hand. A human hand."

"Oh, my God," he said in a stranger's voice. He felt dizzy. It was as if he'd been holding his breath for two years, waiting for this call.

For a minute, he saw the slim white bones against the black mud, in the blue shadows of the larkspurs.

But then a more terrible image took over his mind's eye. He saw Gavin, sitting innocently in his office, playing video games, never guessing that the blue spring sky had exploded and was already falling around them.

"Mike? Did you hear me? It's— It's—"

"I know who it is," he said. And then, in his head, he heard the cruelest words in the English language.

It's my son's dead mother.

CHAPTER THREE

JUSTINE'S MANSION WAS every bit as overblown and pretentious as Suzie remembered from her visits here four years ago. Suzie stood in the center of the great room and shook her head. All this sprawling marble, frou-frou Louis-something furniture and cherubs grinning down from celestial ceilings.

Ridiculous. Marie Antoinette might have been comfortable here, but Suzie darn sure wasn't.

But Mayor Millner had asked her to come. And considering that his daughter's dead body had been found buried in the yard just two weeks ago, she hadn't been able to say no.

She picked up a millefleur glass bowl, which was the only truly pretty thing in the room, lots of red and blue and yellow and green coils of glass captured inside it like a field of wildflowers. It must have been a wedding present. Justine would never have picked out anything so sweet.

Deep in the recesses of the house, a thump sounded. Then a whispering shuffle, as if someone dragged something heavy over the marble.

Suzie set the bowl back down carefully, replacing it in its same circle of dust. She looked over her shoulder toward the circular staircase. A shadow lay on the checkerboard marble floor, and it had a watery quality, as if something or someone just out of sight was stealthily moving.

"Mayor Millner?" Suzie walked to the edge of the room and looked out.

There was no answer. The shadow was perfectly still now, bisecting one white and one black square. She scanned the hall and realized that it came from a door, which was propped half open and cut off the light from the etched-glass front entry.

"Dork," she told herself, and went back into the room.

She twisted her watch on her wrist and looked at the face. Where the heck was Millner? She didn't like being down here all alone.

At least she hoped she was all alone. A half-naked gardener, who clearly believed he had come into the world gift wrapped and labeled To Women, From God, had opened the front door. He had licked her all over with his eyes, and then, when she'd given him her best no-way-in-hell look, he'd deposited her in this room and ambled out the back door.

He'd told her he needed to put out some poison for the rabid raccoons, which she had to admit was pretty funny as a response to her rejection. She did have on a lot of eye shadow today.

But who knew what he was really doing? Any dude who liked to strut his six-pack and his five-o'clock shadow at nine in the morning simply couldn't be trusted.

He was probably the murderer himself.

She shivered. That didn't come out as funny as she'd meant it to.

She looked out the big bay window toward the lake, which shimmered so violently under the bright morning sun that it seemed to be on fire.

And then, for the very first time, she realized that this wasn't a scary story; it wasn't a dream. And it wasn't a joke.

Justine was really dead. Her body had been found right out there, between the marble house and the fiery lake.

There really was a murderer.

Suzie's stomach tightened, which made her mad at herself. When did she get to be such a bundle of nerves? No one was after *her*. At any given moment, there were probably a hundred people in Justine's life who might have been driven to murder. Ten years ago, Suzie could have been one of them. It wouldn't necessarily follow that those people would ever kill anyone else.

Justine had always been a law of her own.

Suzie sat on the piano bench, her legs oddly weak. Back in Albany, when she'd heard about Justine's body being found, she'd thought, *oh, poor Mike*. And then, *poor Gavin*. And then, though she wasn't proud of this, *good riddance*.

But never once had she truly assimilated the reality. A real, breathing woman, a woman with laughter and dreams and passions and fears, was dead. All her possibilities for good or bad were extinguished.

And a son was motherless.

Much as she'd disliked Justine, Suzie wished that the beautiful blonde would saunter into the room, tossing her wavy hair and laughing through her full red lips at what a gullible dork Suzie Strickland was, falling for yet another of Justine's mean practical jokes.

But it would never happen.

Suzie flipped open the sheet music and hit a few

keys, thinking the noise might chase away the image of Justine's red lips rotting in the garden just a hundred yards away.

The piano was so out of tune it made her ears hurt. She wondered whether Justine had been tone-deaf. Mike had been musical, she remembered that. Probably, after Mike moved out, no one had touched the piano at all.

"Suzie?"

She looked up at the sound of Mayor Millner's voice. He stood in the entryway, and for a minute they just stared at each other, as if neither one could believe their eyes.

"Suzie Strickland?" He squinted. "Is that really you?"

She stood, smoothing her long hair, her blue cotton skirt falling around her shins. She was used to this stunned double take when she saw people who'd known her back in Firefly Glen. Sometimes it annoyed her. Had people really been so blinded by her purple hair and black glasses that they didn't recognize her without them?

But it didn't annoy her today. She was too shocked herself. The last time she saw him, Mayor Millner had been black haired, bold and big chested, in his prime and enjoying it. Exuding importance.

The man she saw now looked fifty years older, not ten. His hair was thin, unkempt and the color of un-polished silver. His shoulders were rounded, sloping in, like a person carrying a boulder on his back.

She flushed with instinctive shame, remembering her callous "good riddance" when she'd heard of Jus-tine's death. How could she have been such a bitch? To Suzie, Justine was little more than a bitter memory, a cartoon caricature of aggressive breasts and predatory lips.

To this man Justine had been life itself.

"Hello, Mayor," Suzie said, about ten times as gently as she'd intended to. Mayor Millner had treated Suzie like dirt in the old days, and she'd been looking forward to a little payback. But that was unthinkable now.

He came into the room. His left arm seemed to be trembling, and he held it close to his side.

"Thank you for coming," he said. "I wouldn't have recognized you. You look lovely."

She ignored the barb. Though she knew it hadn't been intentional, it was true. She hadn't been exactly "lovely" back in her high school days. She'd gone out of her way to avoid it. She'd been making a statement, or so she'd thought.

Mostly, she knew now, she'd just been hiding behind it.

"I know this must be a terrible time for your family," she said. "I'm so sorry."

"Thank you." His eyes, watery from the beginning, glistened in the light from the bay window. "It's been a two-year nightmare, but in my heart I've always known she was dead. She would never have put her mother through this."

Suzie nodded, though she wasn't quite as certain about that. In the past, Justine had rarely seemed to concern herself with the fallout from her outrageous behavior. But she had to allow that perhaps Justine's parents knew her better than Suzie did.

"Why did you want to see me, Mayor?"

She couldn't imagine calling him anything else, though he wasn't the mayor of Firefly Glen anymore, she'd heard. When Justine disappeared, he had resigned that job and come to live alone here, in this house, for eighteen months, looking for his daughter and waiting for her to come home.

She wondered if that haunted him now, knowing that, every time he walked down to the lake, he had passed within feet of Justine's dead body.

If Suzie had ever needed proof that there was no such thing as ghosts, this would be it. Surely Justine's ghost would have called out to her father as he tromped by, supervising the divers who dragged Tuxedo Lake.

"I need you to help me," Mayor Millner said with more force than Suzie had seen yet. "I want justice for my daughter."

Something invisible skittered down Suzie's spine on tiny cold feet. What was he talking about? Did he think *she* had done something to Justine? Exactly how crazy had grief left this guy?

"Justice?"

"Yes. I want that bastard Mike Frome arrested, but the police say they don't have enough evidence."

Suzie frowned. "Mike? You think *Mike* killed Justine?"

"I don't think he did. I know he did. And I'm going to make him pay for it, if it's the last thing I do. I need you to help me."

"Mayor Millner, I don't think—"

"He did it, damn it. He never loved her. He just used her, and then, when he got caught, he had to marry her. He never gave a damn about her except as a plaything."

The tears she'd seen in his eyes a minute ago had been replaced by a fanatical gleam. She had a cowardly urge to just turn and get the heck out of here, but she forced herself to remain calm. Maybe she could make him see reason.

Mike hadn't loved Justine when he married her, that much was definitely true. Suzie had been with Mike the night he found out Gavin was his son, and that he would have to marry Justine. A sheltered Firefly Glen teenager, Mike Frome had been faced with the first problem so big his rich, loving family couldn't fix it, and it had damn near broken his heart. He'd sat on the floor of her kitchen and cried like a child.

She had thought back on that night often, and wished she had been more sympathetic. But her own heart had been a little cracked, and at the time she hadn't been very good at tenderness or compassion.

Still…Mike Frome, a cold-blooded murderer? Not until penguins ice-skated in hell.

"But why would he kill her? Even if he didn't love her, they were already divorced."

"That's what the police said. But that doesn't matter. He killed her. She had a new lover, did you know that? She was going to spend a month with him in Europe. Mike couldn't stand that, so he killed her."

"But…" She tried again to be logical. "If he hadn't ever loved her, why would a new lover bother him?"

Millner shook his head roughly. "It's not like that for a man. It's not about love. It's about…territory. Men get crazy when other men try to take away what belongs to them."

Okaaaay…so logic was out. This guy had crawled out of the Dark Ages. He thought women were chattel, and he assumed all other men agreed.

"Well, assuming for a moment that you're right, that he did kill her, how could I help you? I haven't seen him in ten years."

Millner's eyes began to glow again, sensing hope. "But you saw her. You saw Justine, back when you painted Gavin's picture. She told me about that. You must have heard something. Seen something. Maybe you heard them fighting."

"No. I didn't."

"Not even on the phone?"

"No."

"What about bruises? Was there ever any sign that he'd hit her, or pushed her around?"

Suzie scowled. "*No*," she said firmly. "Mayor Millner, I'm sorry, but—"

He frowned, but he didn't look defeated. "I thought for sure—well, no matter. You can always say you saw things."

Good grief. She was through being gentle and logical.

"Are you out of your mind? You want me to lie?"

Millner didn't seem to understand why she was so upset. "Not lie. You know what he was like. He toyed with you, too, didn't he? Everyone says he broke your heart. Surely you'd like to see him pay for all the people he's hurt."

"Actually, you're wrong on so many counts I can't cover them all. I would *not* like to see him go to jail for a murder he didn't commit. For God's sake, Mayor. Would you pin a murder rap on an innocent man?"

His face was turning red. "An innocent man? You think Mike Frome is an innocent man? He didn't love her. He used her. He broke her heart."

"But that's very different from—"

He looked at her through wet, bulging eyes. She wanted to look away, but the intensity of the gaze was mesmerizing.

"Did you know he left her alone that day, that last day? He pushed her out of his car and left her alone in the dark, all alone on the side of the road. If he didn't kill her with his bare hands, at the very least he delivered her, helpless, to the man who did."

Suzie stared at him. He was so red he was almost purple. She wondered if he had heart trouble. She thought of that trembling arm, and she wondered how long he had to live.

"I'm sorry," she said softly. "I can't help you."

He began to cry openly. They were harsh tears, torn out of him. Tears of frustrated fury, not simple grief. It was a horrible sound.

"You could help me," he said raggedly. "You just won't. And I know why. You still hate Justine. You hate my poor baby girl because she has everything you wish you had. You're willing to let a man get away with murder because you won't let go of your petty high school jealousies."

She couldn't even find the heart to refute it. How could she tell this man that high school jealousies died as soon as you hit the real world and discovered how big and rich and exciting it was—and that it definitely did have a place for you, after all?

Envy Justine? How could she tell him that she wouldn't live in this expensive marble mausoleum for anything on earth? That she would rather paint than get a manicure, that she'd rather read a book than go to a party? That she'd rather have a child when she was old enough, when she was ready. That she'd rather have no husband than one who hated her?

Or the most unspeakable truth of all. That she'd rather be alive than dead.

"I'm sorry," she said again. She meant it. "I'm sorry

you're so unhappy. I hope you'll come to terms with that before you destroy an innocent man."

He didn't answer. He sank onto the Louis XIV chair beside the piano and put his face in his hands. The morning sunlight found a few black strands remaining in his silver hair, but it was like the echo of something sad. You knew it was already dying away even as you listened.

She let herself out the front door, her heart heavy.

When she heard footsteps, at first she thought it might be the gardener, and she took a deep breath, ready to breathe fire if he dared to get smarmy.

But, as she rounded the pillar to the portico, she saw a woman walking toward her. About forty, maybe. Pretty in a completely unglamorous way, but a nice face.

"Hi," the woman said. "Is Mr. Millner in there?"

"He's in there, but he seems a little distraught at the moment."

"Oh." The woman looked toward the house, looking concerned. "He asked me to come see him at noon, but I can't. I wondered if he could maybe make it earlier."

Suzie hesitated. She should leave, but…

"Do you know why he wants to see you?"

The woman shook her head. "Not exactly." She held out her hand. "I'm Judy Stott. My husband and I live next door. I got the impression Mr. Millner wanted…well, that he was wondering if we might have…seen anything. You know, the night his daughter disappeared."

Suzie's jaw felt tight. "Did you?"

Judy Stott looked a little wary. After all, she didn't know who Suzie was, and she probably wondered how much she should say.

"Never mind," Suzie said. She beeped open the

door to her Honda, and said a prayer that it would start. She couldn't wait to get out of this place.

"Just promise me you won't lie for him."

Judy Stott smiled uncertainly. "Lie for him? I can't imagine he'd ask me to."

Suzie climbed in her car. She rolled down the window and poked out her head.

"Still. Promise me," she said. "He's not right in the head. Two wrongs don't make a right, you know. And they damn sure won't bring Justine back."

Judy Stott backed away, clearly uncomfortable.

Hell, Suzie thought. She was acting as crazy as Millner. Besides, nothing was going to stop him. Even if this Judy Stott person had enough character to tell him no, he'd just move on to the next person.

What about that trashy gardener? He looked as if he'd tell a few lies for the right number of zeroes.

She turned the key to her car, which started up with a nice thrum, as if it understood that they were now on a mission.

She knew exactly where she had to go next.

MIKE AND GAVIN were playing paintball in the big empty Tuxedo Lake lot that he'd bought four years ago, intending someday to build a house. With one thing and another, someday had never come. He and Gavin were still living in the boathouse.

But the wooded lot made a great paintball field.

Today was the first time in two weeks that Gavin had expressed any interest in playing paintball—or anything else, either. When Justine's body had been found, Gavin had simply shut down. He must have known Justine was dead. God knows Mike had talked to him about it often enough.

But "knowing" it and *knowing* it were two different things.

So when Gavin had suggested they play a little paintball, no matter how odd the choice sounded, Mike had said yes with enthusiasm. Maybe they could both work off some of this pain and anger.

Mike stood sideways behind a fifty-year-old hemlock and tried to peek around the trunk without getting nailed by a yellow paintball. Gavin's aim was lethal. He'd hit Mike in the kneecap ten minutes ago, and those suckers hurt.

His mask didn't fit quite right, and he considered taking it off, but he darn sure didn't want a paintball in the eye. He could never be a bank robber. He didn't like being all bundled up. He liked the sun on his skin and the wind in his face.

Maybe he'd ask Gavin if he wanted to move to Malibu and they'd become a couple of beach bums. As soon as the police would let him move anywhere, that is. Murder suspects weren't allowed much mobility, as he'd learned over the past two years.

"I see you!"

He heard Gavin's footsteps running toward him. He lunged out from behind the hemlock and, dropping to a squat to provide a smaller target, he pointed his gun in the direction of the sounds.

But the body he pointed at didn't belong to his son. It belonged to Mrs. Cready, his ninety-year-old neighbor who had put her house up for sale the day they found Justine's body. She told everyone who'd listen that she had no intention of living next door to a murderer.

Mike had considered warning her that comments like that wouldn't exactly help her find a buyer, but then he thought, to hell with it. She'd treated him like a leper ever since Justine disappeared. If she liked the adrenaline rush of believing the guy next door was a murderer, who was he to spoil her fun?

She must be loving this, standing here at gunpoint. She let out a shrill "eeek" and threw her hands into the air, a move she learned on television, no doubt.

He lifted his mask and propped it on his forehead.

"Hello, Mrs. Cready," he said. "You can put your hands down. I'm not worried that you might go for your six-guns."

She frowned. "You're the one with the gun. *I* don't have any guns."

He smiled wryly. "I think that's my point."

Slowly she lowered her hands, but she still looked terrified.

He wiggled his gun. "It's not real, Mrs. Cready. It's a toy. Gavin and I are playing paintball."

She drew herself up, and her scowl deepened, as if the fact that it wasn't real was somehow an insult. "A fine thing to be teaching your son." She ended with a sniff.

He sighed. Was there some law that said a man's next-door neighbor had to be an old bat?

"Well, anyway," she said haughtily, "I wouldn't have come down here at all, except that you have a visitor. A woman. She's trying to find your house and got confused. Perhaps because *you don't have one.*"

Yeah, that had always ticked Mrs. Cready off, too. Clearly, she thought, only a hopeless degenerate would live in a boathouse. She didn't seem to think it mattered that, at 2,100 square feet, the boathouse was as big as most regular houses.

Not the Tuxedo Lake houses, of course. And that's

what snobs like Mrs. Cready considered the standard of respectability.

"Okay, thanks, just send her on down." Mike would have asked who it was, but he didn't really care. It was probably a reporter, or maybe a lawyer looking for business, or maybe even a plainclothes police officer.

Mrs. Cready sniffed again and walked away, her back as erect as a pylon. Mike called Gavin and explained that the game was over. They began pulling off equipment.

When he again heard footsteps and looked up, he saw a young brunette walking toward him. An eye-catching woman, who moved with a natural, unaffected grace. She wore a simple blue skirt and brown hemp sandals. Her glossy brown hair bounced on her shoulders.

Not a policewoman. Way too feminine, in spite of her thin, boyish figure. Her body language too open and free to be a cop. Too casually dressed for a lawyer, too outdoorsy for a reporter.

Still…he had a fleeting sense that he knew this woman, but before he could catch it the wispy image was gone.

He stared at her as she picked her way across tree roots and fallen branches. He realized suddenly that the perfect paintball field might actually look kind of scruffy as a lawn.

But she didn't seem to mind. She didn't tiptoe in exaggerated horror and scrunch up her nose, as Justine would have done.

Who *was* it? Even when she got close enough to see her features, he had no idea. Whoever she was, he decided he liked her. She had great cheekbones, a jaw that said she didn't take any shit, and a mouth that knew how to laugh.

Finally, when she got close enough for him to see her eyes, he knew.

It was impossible. This graceful, good-looking woman was…

Mike's heart began to race, and then it skidded in his chest, as if he were trying to throw on the brakes. He didn't want this pretty woman to be Suzie. He wanted Suzie to stay geeky and smart-mouthed and purple…and permanently pissed at the world.

He needed her to stay the same. Something in this godforsaken world ought to.

Gavin didn't have any such ambivalence. He threw down his paintball gun and began to run toward the woman, laughing.

"Suzie," he said. "It's me, Gavin. Do you remember me?"

Mike watched as the woman bent over and hugged his son. He waited until she lifted her gaze over Gavin's head and met his eyes.

"Hi, Suzie. It's me, Mike." He tilted his head. "Remember me?"

"Yeah, I think I do," she said, laughing, and when her eyes crinkled like that his heart stopped thumping quite so hard. It was still Suzie. In spite of the long, glossy hair, the contact lenses and the mind-boggling sexiness, the old Suzie, the real Suzie, was still in there.

She'd been a good friend to him once. Maybe she still could be.

He smiled. "How can you be so sure it's me? You've changed. Haven't I?"

"Not a bit," she said. "You're still the only dork dumb enough to be roaming around at a time like this holding a goddamn *gun*."

She whisked her hands up over Gavin's ears. "Ooops. Sorry."

Mike laughed out loud.

"Don't be," he said. "I'm not. Come on, let's go inside. I think I'm about ten years overdue for a good Suzie Strickland thrashing."

CHAPTER FOUR

SHE KNEW IT WAS CONSIDERED bad form to speak ill of the dead, but Suzie had always thought Justine Millner was trash, and she hadn't ever disliked her as much as she did right now.

Look what Justine had done to Mike. Suzie didn't know whether it was marrying Justine or losing Justine that had done it, but Mike Frome was a different man.

Ten years ago, he'd been one of the most infuriatingly smug boys in their high school. He'd also been one of the most attractive. Just being around him had been like chugging caffeine. He gave off this exciting *zing* of vitality that was addictive, even for Suzie, who ordinarily avoided the preppy crowd like poison.

The zing was gone.

Of course, he was still too handsome for his own good, she thought as he politely led her on a tour of his boathouse. On the outside, it was charming, white trim over dark wood, with dormers that overlooked the lake. Inside, it was large and surprisingly homey for a bachelor pad.

Following behind him, she realized that he still had the sexiest back she'd ever seen, though now she looked at it purely with an artist's eye. If she were to paint it, she'd start with a long triangle—she always reduced a face or body to its underlying geometric

basics first. Then she'd add finely cut, fluid muscula-
ture, no artificial steroid bulk here, just a genetically
blessed body that worked for a living.

"That's about it. The bedrooms are on the second
floor, well, third floor if you count the boat slips
beneath, but they're both too disgusting to show
anyone right now." Mike lifted one eyebrow. "I think
we're going to have to fire the upstairs maid."

He winked at his son, who grimaced back. Must be
a running joke.

They had made it to the kitchen, an efficient space,
not too big, but somehow airy and comfortable. Suzie
caught Mike looking at her speculatively as she admired
the cabinets. Under his polite exterior, he must be wondering what the heck she was doing here, after all these
years.

She smiled back and cut a subtle glance toward
Gavin. She couldn't explain herself until they were
alone.

She didn't know whether he actually got the
message, or if it was just a coincidence, but Mike immediately turned to his son.

"I'm going to show Suzie the porch. Any chance
you could toss in a load of towels and fold the ones in
the dryer? We're just about out."

Gavin looked as if he'd like to complain, but he
didn't. "Okay," he said. He turned to Suzie. "You
won't leave right away?"

"I'll be here a few more minutes," she said. "If you're
not back when I've got to go, I'll come say goodbye."

Gavin grinned, and for the first time Suzie could see
Mike in the boy. "Well, better not actually come into
the laundry room," he said. "Our downstairs maid isn't
all that great, either."

Mike dismissed Gavin with a shooing motion. He grabbed a plastic container of store-bought cookies from the counter, and then he led Suzie through a pair of large, glass-paned French doors.

As she stepped out onto the porch, she caught her breath. It was absolutely gorgeous, a wraparound deal with an amazing view. Out here, with water on three sides, you were intensely aware that this house was actually built right on the lake.

Mike held out one of two white wicker armchairs, and she took it, appreciating its soft old cushions, and the companionable creak when she leaned back.

Mike sat, too, and for a minute they were silent, just watching the afternoon sunlight play on the water. It bounced off and danced against the walls of the porch, too. It would be a challenge, she thought, to capture this living light on a canvas.

It probably had been a happy place, once. Mike and Gavin had probably spent hours out here, watching the breeze ripple the blue lake. But it was clear that they had pretty much forgotten what happiness tasted like.

God only knew what they saw when they looked out at the water now. Somewhere on the other side of that lake was Justine's mansion. And the muddy spot where her body had been buried.

She glanced at Mike, and she realized he was smiling at her, a hint of that old smile. She couldn't quite meet it. It was still strong stuff, and even after all this time she wasn't completely immune.

"God, Suzie-freaka, it's good to see you. It's been a long, long time."

His voice, and his smile, were strangely unsettling, like haunted echoes from the past, from way back when she hated herself almost as much as she hated him. Suddenly the air felt tight, even though the breeze was cool and fresh, fingering her hair and ruffling the sleeves of her dress.

She was irked with herself for reacting like this. The past wasn't the issue, damn it. She wasn't here to reminisce about the bad old days. She was only here out of common humanity. She was here to give an old friend—no, an old *acquaintance*—a heads-up.

Mike held out the cookies. "So, want to tell me what's happening?" He pulled in one corner of his mouth, creating that annoyingly attractive dimple. "Somehow I don't think you just woke up this morning and said, 'hey, I wonder how that obnoxious boy I hated in high school is doing?'"

The boy she hated in high school… He must have read her mind. But was that all he was? Maybe. She had definitely hated him. Even when she…didn't.

"No," she said, waving away the cookies, which were hard and sandy, typical grocery store pseudo food. "It's something more serious, I'm afraid. It's about Justine. Well, about Justine's father, anyhow."

Mike set the container down slowly. "What about him?"

"He asked me to visit him this morning, at Justine's house."

She watched Mike's face, wondering how he could stay so impassive. Where had all those quicksilver emotions gone? The easy laughter, the twitching frown, the worried squint, the sarcastic eyebrow? The restless, young-animal body.

The *zing*.

He was so still now. So controlled. It was like looking at a picture of Mike instead of the real thing.

"Oh, yeah?" Mike flipped a cookie between his fingers, keeping his eyes on the water. "What did he want?"

She took a breath. This was it.

"He wants me to help him pin Justine's murder on you."

That got his attention. But it didn't completely surprise him. As he slowly faced Suzie, she saw anger but not shock behind his dark brown eyes.

"*Pin it*…how would you be able to do that?"

"He hoped I might have seen something while I was painting Gavin's portrait. Something between you and Justine. An argument, maybe."

"But you couldn't have. I was never at the house when you were there."

"I know." She chewed on her lower lip, wishing she could stop herself from asking the next question but knowing she probably couldn't. She'd never had very good impulse control. "I always thought I might run into you, but I never did. Was that deliberate? Were you avoiding me on purpose?"

"Yes."

She frowned. "Well, that's a hell of a note," she said. "Just 'yes'?"

"Well, what do you want me to say? Yes, it was deliberate. Yes, I was avoiding you on purpose."

"Why?"

He shrugged, and it, too, held the echo of the old days. He always did have a large, infuriating repertoire of smug-jock mannerisms. "I thought you'd prefer it that way."

"You thought I…" She frowned for a few seconds, feeling herself heating up, though she wasn't sure why. Mike Frome had always been able to confuse her in world-record time, which inevitably ticked her off. "Why?"

"I thought seeing me might make you…" He seemed to search for a word. "Uncomfortable."

Uncomfortable? Her temperature rose even higher. What the heck was that a euphemism for? Did he think she was still a geeky, untouched virgin who would blush at the memory of the night he'd copped a feel?

"Know what, Frome? That's BS, and you know it. I haven't got anything to be *uncomfortable* about where you're concerned. Sixteen seconds of touchy-feely ten years ago doesn't exactly require me to wear the scarlet letter for the rest of my life."

He shook his head. "I didn't mean that. I meant that seeing me might make you unhappy. You know, you might—"

Unhappy? Oh, this was even worse. Did he think she'd actually spent the past ten years carrying a torch for Mr. Most-Likely-To-Succeed? *Oh, brother*.

"Might what? Might turn to stone just from looking at your irresistible bod? Sorry, but that's baloney, too. You may have been the king of the sandbox in Firefly Glen, but it's a pretty small sandbox. Out in the *real* world, where I've been living for the past ten years—"

To her surprise, Mike began to laugh. He reached out and grabbed her hand. "Easy, Fang. You're getting it all wrong."

She forced herself to take a deep breath. Man, was she regressing. She didn't do this anymore, didn't fly off the handle, didn't read insults into perfectly innocent comments. Her tendency toward irrational ferocity had disappeared the minute she left Firefly Glen, which in her opinion proved that Mike Frome must have been the problem all along.

However, there was such a thing as protesting too much. She inhaled one more time, just for good measure.

"Or maybe," he said, "I'm *putting* it all wrong."

"Probably both," she said tightly. "We never did really communicate all that well. But, look, we're getting off topic. This is serious. I'm trying to tell you that your ex-father-in-law wants to see you spend the rest of your life in jail."

"Okay." He gazed at her, the poker face returning. "So what did you tell him?"

"I told him I hadn't laid eyes on you in ten years. That frustrated him, but it didn't really slow him down much. He made it clear that if I'd just *say* I saw you shove Justine around or something he'd make it worth my while."

The smile remained on Mike's lips, but it was as if he'd simply forgotten to put it away. He still had hold of her hand, so she knew how tight his fingers were.

"And what did you say to his offer?"

She pulled her hand away. "What do you *think* I said?"

"I don't know." He shook his head slowly. "I think you said no. I hope you said no."

"But you're not sure?"

He stared at her a moment, and then, his body stiff, he rose from his wicker chair. He leaned against the railing, his back to the sunshine, which threw his face into shadow.

"How can I be sure? The Suzie I used to know— she would have told Alton to take his money and stuff it up his hairy ass. But I haven't seen you in ten years. I don't know you anymore. Not really."

"You think ten years is enough to turn me into a liar?"

He hesitated again. "Ten years can do a lot of rotten

things to people, Suzie. If you don't know that yet, I'm happy for you."

She stood up. "Let me get this straight. You think it could turn me into a woman who would send a man to the gas chamber for something he didn't do?"

"Perhaps not." He lifted one hand. The effort to look suave, indifferent, world-weary failed miserably. He was just plain tired. "But am I sure? No. To tell you the truth, I'm not sure of anything anymore."

Her annoyance faded slightly in the face of his exhaustion.

"Well, you can be sure of this. Millner is going to try to frame you for this, Mike. He's going to do any dirty thing he can to see that you pay for what happened to Justine."

"I know." He glanced toward the French doors, obviously wondering if Gavin was within earshot. "But frankly, Suzie, Alton Millner isn't the only vulture out to get me. He isn't even the most dangerous one. The D.A. has a bead on me, too. I guess it's pretty standard for the cops, even if it feels outrageous to me. They always look at the husband first."

She felt an upwelling of incredulous indignation. Was everyone around here insane? Mike Frome couldn't kill anyone. Heck, Suzie herself was a more likely candidate. She'd hated Justine, and she was, after all, the one they called "Fang."

But neither of them had done it. They just weren't that kind of people.

"That's the dumbest thing I ever heard," she said. "Jeez. Shouldn't you be a better judge of people than that if you're going to be the D.A.?"

Mike almost smiled. "You're so sure he's wrong, then?"

Suzie rolled her eyes. "I've known you since you were about six, Frome. You can be a horse's ass, and you do have an irritating tendency to think you're God's gift. But kill somebody? No way. Kill your own child's mother? Not in a bazillion, trillion years."

"Damn." His half smile turned into a grin. "Why couldn't *you* have been the D.A.?"

She shrugged, but she felt herself smiling, too. "Couldn't have handled law school. Problems with authority, you know."

"Yeah," he said. "I know."

Man, this was getting weird. A minute ago she'd wanted to punch him out, and now she had this stupid impulse to go over and hug him. She felt a disgustingly maternal urge—perhaps the first in her whole life— to help him hang on to that smile.

But she forced herself to stay where she was. "Well," she began. "That's all I had to say, so I guess I should—"

"Suzie."

She frowned, just on principle. "What?"

"Thanks for coming by to warn me. It was very— very sweet."

"Wow." She found herself smiling again, and she made a few adjustments to make sure it was a sarcastic smile. Behind her, she heard footsteps approaching. Gavin must be coming back. "You've used a lot of words to describe me through the years, but I don't think you ever used that one."

Mike was still looking at her in that soft way that made her feel like squirming.

"No, I didn't," he said. "Just one of my many mistakes."

SOMETIMES MIKE BELIEVED that if he hadn't let Justine talk him into leaving Firefly Glen, everything would have been fine.

There was magic here. The Sunday after Suzie's visit and her disturbing news, he went home for Spencer Fairmont's sixteenth birthday party. And as he watched his son playing touch football on the front lawn of Summer House, he felt his whole body relaxing.

Though there were about two dozen Glenner children out there, Mike couldn't take his eyes off Gavin. Look at that smile. He hadn't smiled like that since his mother's body had been discovered, almost a month ago.

Magic wasn't an exaggeration.

And it wasn't just the magic of "home." Mike knew that, when faced with your first mortgage payment, your first endless, numbing workweek, or your first real personal crisis, it was easy to get all misty about the innocence of youth.

But Firefly Glen was more than that, and he'd always sensed it, even as a child. Firefly Glen was special. Nestled in a small Adirondack valley, the town was ringed by wooded mountains and spangled with flowers, waterfalls, rivers and birds. It was peopled by gentle eccentrics who argued constantly, and yet stuck together with a loyalty that seemed to belong to another century…or a fairy tale.

Many of those quirky townsfolk were Mike's own kin. He was a fourth-generation Glenner, and his parents and grandparents still lived here. His cousin, Natalie Granville Quinn, had once owned Summer House, though the crazy old villa was now open to the public as a historic site—and rented out for parties, like this one.

"Can you believe how grown-up he is?"

Mike looked up and saw Natalie standing over him with a cup of punch in each hand. He wasn't sure which kid she meant. Birthday boy Spencer had come to Firefly Glen as a scared little boy of six. And of course Gavin had left here, ten years ago, as an infant. Three of Natalie's own four boys were out there, too—the fourth was still in diapers, too young to romp about with the big kids.

Mike took the punch. Natalie gathered her full yellow skirt under her knees and sat down on the step beside him. "Aren't you glad someone else is mowing this monstrosity now?"

He glanced around at the smooth carpet of grass, which was glowing with gold highlights as the afternoon sun began to drop in the west. "You bet I am. Aren't you glad someone else is in charge of the repairs?"

Natalie made a swooning sound and leaned her elbows back against the marble gracefully. "Giving this place up was the best decision I ever made."

Just then Matthew walked by, their youngest son in his arms, and ruffled her hair. Both males made loud, wet kissing noises. Natalie kissed back, then grinned at Mike. "Make that second-best."

Frankly, it was hard to believe that this happily sex-crazed blonde was now a thirty-eight-year-old mother of four. She hardly looked a day older than she had at Mike's wedding ten years ago, while he felt about a hundred.

Guess true love really was the fountain of youth, he thought, trying not to be bitter.

"You make marriage look easy," he said. He glanced around. Now that twilight had settled in, the band up on the balcony had begun to play slow songs. Couples were swaying together in little love pods all along the front courtyard. Spencer had a new girlfriend, and they looked so sweet, foreheads touching, hands folded between their bodies as if the dance were a prayer. Ward Winters, who was nearly ninety, was in a lip-lock with Madeline Alexander. Griffin and Heather Cahill were nuzzling like newlyweds. It just went on from there.

He turned back to Natalie. "You *all* make it look easy."

Natalie's brown eyes were gentle. "It is easy," she said. "If you're married to the right person. You can't judge from your experience, honey. That was…well, it was like getting caught in a freak storm at sea."

He noticed she didn't say Justine's name. As if there were a conspiracy to shelter him, whenever Mike entered the town limits, the problems of his "real" world dropped away. They had welcomed Justine back while the marriage lasted, and after the divorce no one ever said a word against her, especially not to Gavin. In fact, they rarely mentioned her.

Sure, occasionally crusty Theo Burke would begin to make some snarky comment, or maybe Ward Winters would start to grouch about Mayor Millner, but someone would always poke them hard, or stomp on their feet, and they'd swallow the words with a gruff apology, and the comforting cocoon would remain unbroken.

"Hurricane Justine wasn't completely unexpected," Mike corrected. "Plenty of people warned me. I just wasn't listening."

Natalie patted his shoulder. "That's not entirely your fault, either. You just had a really bad case of TB."

He gave her a curious look. Natalie had always been eccentric. All Granvilles were. You rarely had any idea what she'd say next. He was actually kind of glad that he was only one-sixth Granville. He had troubles enough.

"TB?"

She nodded. "Testosterone Blindness. It afflicts young men from the ages of twelve to about twenty. Its symptoms include bad judgment, night sweats, following some gorgeous girl around with their tongue hanging out, and—"

"Are you guys talking about Granville?" Parker Tremaine, the Glen's favorite local lawyer, plopped down on the other side of Mike. "Because, much as I like your grandfather, Mike, I honestly think he's too old to be having quite so much fun dancing with Suzie Strickland."

Natalie made an excited sound and immediately began scanning the dance floor for her irrepressible great-uncle. "That old devil," she said, chuckling. "I didn't even know Suzie was coming. Is he really making a pass at her?"

"I might not go that far, but he certainly is enjoying himself." Parker raised one eyebrow. "Can't say I blame him. It's been a couple of years since I've seen her. She looks *amazing*."

Natalie glanced back at Parker irritably. "But of course she looks amazing, dummy. Didn't you know she always was a beauty under all that goop?"

"No," he said flatly. "I didn't. I knew she was cuter than she wanted to let on, and of course she was always a work in progress. But this—"

"There they are! Hmm…oh, dear. This may be the beginnings of a Granville moment." Natalie scrambled to her feet, dusting off her yellow skirt. "I'd better go throw some cold water over him. Later, boys. Be good."

Mike had located his grandfather and Suzie, too. He watched her smiling up into the old man's face, accepting his ridiculous flirtation with sardonic good humor. She was wearing red jeans and a halter top that had a surprisingly sexy updated-Grecian look, with ribbons crisscrossing her breasts, then falling with a seductive flare around her hips.

She still looked different from everyone else, but she didn't look wrong anymore. She just looked special.

As the music swelled, Granville dipped her, in old-style ballroom elegance. He bent over her arched body, nearly putting his nose in her cleavage. Mike felt annoyance squeeze his gut briefly...*Granddad, you dirty old bastard.*

But when Suzie straightened up her eyes were sparkling with laughter, and her cheeks were almost as red as her clothes. She put her hand on Granville's chest and pushed, removing him to a respectable distance. But she didn't look mad. She looked...

Amazing might be an understatement.

Parker was watching, too. He looked over at Mike. "Did you know? Have you seen her lately?"

Mike nodded. "Actually, I saw her a few days ago, for the first time since I—left town. I was shocked. I'm like you. I knew she had something, but at the same time I didn't know...this."

Parker smiled. "Obviously she didn't want anyone to know. I guess she wanted us to appreciate her deeper qualities."

Mike laughed. "Like her sweet personality?"

"Well, no." Parker laughed, too, and the two of them had a moment of silence, remembering just how little sugar Suzie had bothered to apply to life. "Like her brains, I mean. Her talent. And her spunk. I never knew anyone with more spunk."

Both men watched as Natalie grabbed Suzie and spun her into a bear hug. The two women had always been great friends.

When Parker spoke again, Mike observed that the older man's voice was carefully casual. "So you saw Suzie again for the first time just recently? That's quite a coincidence."

That's exactly what Mike had been thinking. He'd been home to Firefly Glen frequently during his decade of exile. He'd brought Gavin here as often as possible, so that at least some of the magic would rub off. But he had never run into Suzie. Her parents still lived here, and he heard she was in town fairly frequently. Though they didn't exactly run in the same circles, it was hard to believe they hadn't ever bumped into each other—unless she planned it that way.

She might have needed to ask him whether he'd avoided her deliberately while she painted Gavin, but he didn't need to ask her about this. Ten years of dodging him in Firefly Glen could not have been a coincidence.

And, hell, he didn't blame her.

So why, all of a sudden, would she abandon that plan and show up at this party? She had to know he'd be here.

Somehow he dragged his gaze away from the dance floor. He couldn't let himself get distracted by Suzie. He had something important he needed to say to Parker.

It wasn't going to be easy. He liked the protective oasis the Glenners had offered him. It had always been such a relief to be able to pretend, even temporarily, that there was no Justine.

But, deep inside, he'd always known the oasis was a mirage. Now he had to give it up. He'd finally met a battle so big, so uniquely his, that no one else could fight it for him. Not even the entire town of Firefly Glen.

"Parker, I need your help," he said. "I think I may be in some trouble."

Parker was about fifteen years older than Mike, and had always been like an uncle to him. He had called Mike immediately after Justine's body was found and offered to recommend a criminal attorney, just for safety's sake. Mike had been naive enough to say thanks but no thanks.

Parker looked concerned now, but not shocked. "It's Justine, I suppose. You've been questioned, I'm sure. Did it go badly?"

"I didn't think so. But they've been back twice, asking the same things over and over. They asked if they could look at my car. The one I was driving the day she disappeared."

"Did you let them?"

"Of course I did. I don't have anything to hide."

"Did you retain counsel?"

Mike shook his head. He had trusted that innocence was everything. He had believed in the system. He still believed in it, at heart, but...

"I didn't think I needed one. I thought it would look bad if I got a lawyer."

Parker sighed. "So many people make that mistake.

But everyone needs representation. Even innocent people need help handling the system."

He reached into his pocket. "Here—this is Harry Rouge's card. I brought it today because I had a feeling you might need it. I knew Harry in D.C. He's good, and he's got some experience with murder trials."

Mike felt the hair on the back of his neck stand up. "Surely you don't think this is going to get that far? To a murder trial?"

"Of course it will, with any kind of luck. She was murdered—there's no getting around that." Parker smiled grimly. "But Harry will make sure it doesn't go to trial with you as the defendant."

Mike took the card. It all felt like a bad dream. Even the card felt unreal. Or maybe it was just that his fingers were numb.

"Thank you," he said. "I appreciate it."

"You're welcome. Now you do me a favor, okay?" Parker pointed to the back of the courtyard. "See my poor beautiful wife over there being bored to death by Bourke Waitely?"

Mike looked. Sure enough, Sarah was sitting next to Bourke, a polite smile plastered to her face like a bumper sticker. She looked desperate.

"Yes," Mike said. "I do."

"Well, go save her, would you? Ask her to dance. I'm going to see if I can pry the amazing Miss Strickland from your grandfather's clutches."

Mike stood, then held out a hand to help Parker to his feet, too. He looked over at Suzie, but he'd barely begun to formulate his idea even in his own mind before Parker began shaking his head.

"Bad idea," Parker said softly. "The last thing in the

world you need right now is to appear interested in another woman."

Mike frowned. "For God's sake, Parker, I'm not— I mean Suzie's not 'another woman.' I've known her forever. She's just a friend. She's just…Suzie."

"Wrong," Parker said flatly. "She used to be *just Suzie*. Things are different now. Look at her, Mike. Now she's a motive."

CHAPTER FIVE

"OKAY, NOW…MAKE SURE you're balanced, and that your legs are touching the wall, right?" Suzie, who was standing on her head, took a quick look over at Gavin, who had just arranged himself, also upside down, next to her along the wall of Summer House's back porch. "You comfortable enough?"

Gavin wobbled, but steadied himself. "I guess so. This marble is pretty hard on my head."

"Yeah, it helps if you have grass, or a pillow or something. But we'll just have to make do. Now, the whole point is to stare at something interesting."

She used one hand to fold up the loose part of her shirt, which was dangling down over her face, and tuck it under her chin. Good thing she'd worn jeans to this party instead of that skirt she'd been considering.

"How about the stairs that lead to the grotto?" She pointed. "Right over there, with the statues on each side."

Gavin moved his hands for better purchase. "Yeah, the statues look goofy upside down. And look—there's Cordelia, way out there. Hey, weird. I didn't know she looks like her mom, but when you see her like this, upside down, you can tell. And she's really got crazy hair."

Suzie smiled, which was actually easier while you

stood on your head. Gravity worked with you for a change.

She hoped it was making Gavin smile, too, or at least distracting him a little. When she'd run into him a few minutes ago, here in this secluded corner of the back patio where she'd come to hide from Granville, he had seemed upset. He hadn't wanted to talk about it. He'd been willing to say only that one of the boys at the party had been a jerk.

But he had appeared on the edge of tears, so she'd pulled this old game out of her hat. It was the kind of crazy thing sensible people rarely did, so she hoped it would shock him out of his distress.

Her gaze caught on something nearer, something red and pointy. It was her fancy shoes, which she'd taken off before she'd stood on her head.

"Hey, look at my shoes. Man. I had no idea they were so plug-ugly."

"Yeah!" Apparently Gavin was too young to know he was supposed to disagree. He laughed, which made his legs wobble again. "Those spiky heels look like knives, like weapons or something."

Well, he was right. They did.

"I need new shoes, that's for sure." She brushed them aside. "But that's the point, see? Sometimes, when things start to get you down, you need to step back and view the world from a new perspective."

"Hey! There's Dad! It's like one of those movie tricks, where he seems to be walking upside down."

Suzie watched Mike coming toward them, climbing the stairs with the physical grace that marked every-thing he did. Viewed this way, it was even more apparent. His body seemed to belong to him in a way hers had never belonged to her. She was always tripping on her own feet and flinging her elbows into things. He was a thoroughbred racehorse, and she was a just-hatched duck-billed platypus.

He was squinting, as though he couldn't quite understand what he was seeing, and she saw his smile dawn as he finally comprehended. She briefly considered scrambling to her feet, but realized that would just look even dumber.

Better to brazen it out, even though she could tell that his gaze was locked on her bare stomach. Damn it, the blood had been flowing to her head for five minutes now, but he'd probably think she was blushing because of him.

"Hi, Dad," Gavin said. "We're getting a new perspective."

"It's a game we used to play in art school," Suzie put in, trying to sound rational in spite of her bare feet and her hair pooled all over the marble. Also, with her lungs pressing into her throat like this, she sounded like Daffy Duck.

"Yeah?" Mike was still smiling.

"Yes. It helps you to start seeing what's really there," she explained, "instead of what you're expecting to see."

"Okay. So, what do you think, Gavin? Does the world look better from that angle?"

That was all it took. Gavin, who obviously had remembered his earlier distress, did a kind of backward somersault—just as gracefully as his father might have—and leaped to his feet.

"Dad, where've you been? I was looking for you. I want to go home."

Oh, well. It had been worth a try. Suzie dropped her feet and stood up, too, though it involved a lot more undignified wriggling. She tugged at her shirt, trying to make it settle around her hips again, but one of the ribbons was stuck inside her bra. She had to drag it out like a long strand of red linguini.

"Can we, Dad? Can we go home right now?"

"We really ought to stay for the cake." Mike hesitated. "Why would you want to go so soon?"

"It's Spencer's friend Joe. I don't like him. He said—"

The boy cast a quick glance at Suzie. But then he decided that either she could be trusted, or his frustration was too intense to leave room for discretion.

"He said some really bad things about you, Dad. There's a cop out at the edge of the driveway, and Joe said that's because you're here. He said the cop is following you to make sure you don't—"

Mike's face was suddenly dark, his jaw clenched. "Make sure I don't what?"

Gavin stared at floor, but his jaw looked exactly like his dad's.

"Don't *kill* anybody."

Oh, boy. Suzie thought about the crowd of kids they'd left behind on the front lawn. Which one was Joe? He must be a visitor. Apparently someone forgot to hand him the official Firefly Glen credo, *thou shalt not poison paradise*, as he passed through Vanity Gap.

And what about the even more universal law? *Don't be cruel.*

Suddenly Matthew Quinn appeared, loping up the stairs toward them, looking worried and annoyed. This Joe kid must not be a very smart bully, Suzie decided. Obviously he'd let his comments be overheard by one of Gavin's guardian angels.

"I'm sorry, Mike," Matthew said. "Joe Streaker's a

brat. Parker's over there scaring the crap out of him right now."

The tension in Mike's face remained. "Is it true?"

"What? That there's a cop in the driveway?" Matthew kept his voice low. Suzie had to strain to be sure she heard every word. But she wasn't the type to be a demure little female and pretend not to listen. "Yeah. An open tail, obviously. They're sending you a message. They want you to know they're watching."

Mike peered across the grounds, though of course he couldn't see all the way to the drive. Then he put his arm around Gavin. "You okay?"

Gavin, who clearly had worked himself back into an emotional stew, swallowed twice, as if his throat were too tight. Once again his eyes were shining with unshed tears. Tears of fury, no doubt.

Suzie had fought back about a million of those in her day. Matthew Quinn, who was watching Gavin with sympathetic eyes, probably had, too. He'd once spent three years in prison for a crime he didn't commit. That was probably why he was such an expert on things like "open tails."

"Of course Gavin's okay," she answered for him, to give him time to get his throat under control. "He's just ticked off. Frankly, I think he deserves a medal for not handing Joe Streaker his bloody nose on a platter."

Gavin looked up at her. "I was going to, I was going to kick his ass. I don't care if he is sixteen. But he ran away. He was *laughing*." His hands folded into white-knuckled fists. "He thinks it's funny that my mom is dead."

"Oh, yeah?" Suzie felt her own hands tightening. "Well, come on. Let's find this jerk. I'll hold him down for you."

"*Suzie,*" Mike and Matthew said at the same time, and both of them held out their hands, as if to restrain her from racing off in search of Joe the Jerk.

"Okay, okay," she said. She turned to Gavin. "Grown-ups are such buzz-kills, aren't they? It would have felt so good."

Gavin smiled. "Yeah. It would have felt great."

"Hey." Mike bent down and took Gavin's elbows. "What did I tell you about kicking people's asses?"

Gavin screwed up his mouth, as if he were trying to remember. *"Don't?"*

Chuckling, Suzie met Matthew's amused gaze over the heads of the other two. Gavin really was a chip off the old block, wasn't he? Served Mike right.

"Come on, Gav. What did I tell you?"

Gavin sighed. "You told me violence is for stupid people. You said smart people *think* their way out of trouble. But Dad, this guy is *soooo*—"

"Gavin, think it through. This guy believes we're the kind of people who would hurt other people. Want to make him right?"

"No, but—"

"Then let's go be civilized. Let's watch Spencer open his presents, and we can drive straight home after that, okay?"

Gavin scuffed the ground with one heel. "Okay," he said reluctantly.

Mike stood. He gave his son a forward nudge and Gavin started moving. Matthew went with the boy, his hand on his shoulder for moral support. Mike turned to Suzie. "Thanks," he said. "That was a very creative diversionary tactic."

"No problem," she said. "I've always been willing to make a fool of myself for a good cause."

He gave her a long look, taking her in from head to toe. She caught herself fiddling with the ribbons on her top, checking their status. Damn it, was she going to start blushing all over again?

"Oh, and by the way…" He paused.

"What?"

She wondered whether he might be going to ask her why she'd shown up at a Firefly Glen party, after all these years. She had her answer ready. Because she wanted to, that's why. Because, now that she'd seen him once, she'd decided it was stupid to go on avoiding him.

But he didn't ask. Three, four, five seconds ticked by.

She tilted her head. "By the way…what?"

He reached out and tugged lightly on the tip of a red ribbon.

He smiled. "Nice shirt."

As Marston County District Attorney Keith Quigley pulled his Audi up to the squad car parked in front of Summer House, he could see right away that the policeman behind the wheel was half-asleep.

He idled his engine for at least thirty seconds, waiting for the officer to notice him. Nothing. Fifty murderers could have danced across this road in top hats, and Officer—was it deLuca?—wouldn't have noticed a thing.

Finally he tapped lightly on his horn. DeLuca jerked to attention, bumping his elbow on the edge of the window.

"Sir!" The cop, who probably was no more than about twenty-five, squeezed his eyes, trying to make them track in the same direction. "I'm sorry, sir. I didn't see you there."

Keith smiled, but he kept it cool. "Good thing we don't believe Frome is a flight risk," he observed.

The officer flushed, opened his mouth as if to make a defensive comment, then closed it. DeLuca didn't report to Keith, not technically. But he reported to the sheriff, who knew better than to annoy the D.A. Keith didn't believe in keeping a "hands off" policy in his investigations—especially murders. He got involved as soon as he had a body, and he stayed involved until he got a conviction.

DeLuca flushed. "Yes, sir. I'm sorry, sir."

Was there a hint of sarcasm in the kid's voice? He was young, tall, good-looking—all things Keith would never be. But he was also a nobody, and that was another thing Keith would never be. Keith had climbed a steep ladder to get where he was, and he didn't plan to let failure ever force him back down those slippery rungs again.

"Frome is still at the party?" Keith glanced up at the beautiful villa, which was so extravagantly lit that it glowed like a giant topaz on the hillside above.

"Yes, sir."

God, all these *sirs* made him feel old. Maybe it was because he suspected they were being deliberately overdone. Or maybe he just *was* old—his sister had thrown him an "Over The Hill" party for his fortieth birthday last week. She was only thirty-two, so she thought the black balloons and joke gifts of canes and prune juice were a riot. She hadn't come as far as Keith had. She still thought small.

They didn't think small up there in the Summer House. You'd think they were holding an inaugural ball up there, not some kid's sixteenth birthday party. They must have a million lights blazing, and the cars that lined Blue Pine Trail were all glossy new superstatus machines.

Keith felt his mouth go sour. His own status machine was a lease car, and the lease was just about up. He'd either have to find thirty grand or give it back.

"You're sure he's in there?"

"Well, his car hasn't come out, sir, and this is the only exit from the property. But my instructions were not to maintain visual—"

"Yes." Keith nodded. "You're right. Well, carry on, then."

Keith chose not to explain what he himself was doing in Firefly Glen, though he knew that the young officer was curious. Let the kid think Keith had shown up just to monitor him. That would keep his nose clean for months.

As he drove away, though, in his rearview mirror he saw deLuca raise his left hand and thrust out the middle finger. Adrenaline surged through Keith's body, and he almost slammed on the brakes and backed up, right into the stupid bastard's patrol car.

He controlled himself with effort. He knew that most of the officers on the force hated him. He'd seen their vulgar cartoons, picturing Keith as a pop-eyed toad licking the ass of the Lady Mayor, who was drawn as a recoiling, horrified princess. The street cops were superficial people, and of course they would fixate on his looks.

As if IQ and determination didn't trump *pretty boys* every day of the week.

Also, it was a strike against him that he hadn't come from their ranks. Some district attorneys were former policemen who worked their way through law school—they got the best cooperation, of course.

But Keith had gone to law school first, and the people of Marston County had elected him district attorney two years ago, when he was only thirty-eight. He fully expected them to elect him again, in two years time.

Which was one reason he needed a conviction on the Justine Millner case, and soon.

This one had caught the public's imagination. Beautiful young mother disappears off the face of the earth. It was just the kind of thing they lapped up like kittens facedown in a saucer of milk.

They'd turned out to search the woods, back then, because it had been exciting. And they'd come to her memorial service for the same reason. They hadn't cared whether Justine was dead or alive, not really.

Not the way he did.

Which was why he'd come all this way tonight, following a lead that would probably turn out to be useless. He kept driving, leaving both Summer House and deLuca behind and clearing his mind for the meeting ahead.

It was a long drive. Summer House was not in the glen proper, but overlooked it from the mountainside. He followed Blue Pine Trail into the town, and when he finally arrived, the roads were nearly empty. Small towns were like that. He still had trouble believing that Justine had come from a place like this. She must have set the pavement on fire just by walking down these sleepy streets.

He knew where the cemetery was. Under the pretext of watching for any possible suspects, he had attended the funeral. He'd sent flowers, too, anonymously. His had been the most exotic offering of all, bigger even than the family's.

This time he parked under a hemlock with low, dense branches. The car was black, so from ten yards away you couldn't see it at all. The iron gates weren't locked, more small-town thinking. He shoved one side open a few inches and squeezed through.

Ignoring the paved path that wound through the gravestones, he cut across the grass, which was so thick from all the spring rain that his footsteps didn't make a sound. If the dead objected, they weren't able to say so.

The older half of the cemetery, with mossy head-stones tilting at quaint angles and scattered cherubs standing guard, was much more attractive than the new half, where Justine was buried. About fifty years ago, a bunch of anal-retentive councilmen had legis-lated grief moderation and had prohibited any markers except uniform granite rectangles sunk into the grass.

The result was that the crowded, eccentric land of the dead suddenly flattened and became the visual equivalent of a golf course.

He found Justine's marker somehow, and he stared at it a long time, his hands balled in his pockets, his shoes crushing the plush grass. In the moonlight, he could read the simple words, Justine Ariana Millner, and the dates.

It wasn't enough, wasn't nearly enough to capture her essence. It reduced Justine Ariana Millner to the same nonentity as Mary Jane Johannes, who stretched out above her head, or Susan Elaine Dalby, who slept at her feet.

You'd never know the truth—that Justine Ariana Millner had been magic. A witch with white-fire hair, and blue eyes that didn't care whether you looked like a toad, because she saw deeper. She saw inside you, where you were as brilliant and driven and full of imaginative passion as she was.

She saw your dark, rotten places, too, and didn't find them repulsive. Sometimes, when she made love to you, you could feel her touching them. The more dangerous those places were, the more they excited her.

Everything excited her, because she was in love with life.

One harsh sob escaped him, and he clamped his lips shut. The guilty, poisonous toad had no right to weep over the princess's grave. She must hate being here, hate the uniformity, the anonymity, the obscurity. He was surprised her bones didn't reject it, didn't come bursting out, fleshless joints clicking, white and furious, and clutch him by the throat.

He heard a noise behind him. He took a moment to compose his face before he turned around.

"Is that you, Mayor Millner?"

The form that stepped out from the shadow of a newly planted elm was, in silhouette, not unlike Keith's own—short and pudgy, the kind of man who made cartoonists dream of toads. Justine's father had obviously contributed nothing to his amazing daughter.

She'd never mentioned her father, and yet Keith knew she had hated him. Fiercely. Every time she humiliated Keith, or any other of the older men she collected, he knew that she was really punishing her father.

But for what? Neglect? Abuse? Just being disappointingly human? He'd never been able to discover.

"You said you have something for me," Keith said. He was suddenly impatient with Millner's broken posture, his crumpled face. Millner didn't have the right to cry here, either.

"Yes." The older man moved forward ponderously, as if he were confused, as if he'd just awakened from a long nap and found himself in a strange place. The choice of locations had been Keith's. He wanted an excuse to visit Justine one more time, and he didn't care squat about Millner's feelings, if he had them.

"Well?" Keith held out his hand.

Millner reached into the breast pocket of his jacket. He extracted a lumpy, two-inch stack of papers. "There are only about eight. A couple of them are from his neighbors. One is from—some other man. Only five are from Mike."

Keith took the letters. He didn't flip through them. There wasn't enough moonlight, and besides, he wanted to be alone when he read them.

"Remember, you can't use them, not officially." Millner's voice was plaintive. "I promised my wife I wouldn't stir up trouble. She doesn't believe that Mike—" He swallowed. "She's weak. She always had a soft spot for him, just because he's good-looking, and he's a Frome."

He'd promised his wife? Keith wondered if Millner had always been this spineless. "Yes, of course. They're just for background. I won't use anything unless I can confirm it independently."

Millner nodded. He looked vaguely around the cemetery, as if he were trying to orient himself. The wind had picked up, and it blew limp, greasy strands of his hair across his sweaty brow.

"How can this, this *place*, be where my baby is? My little girl."

She wasn't a little girl, you fool, you toad. Keith

wanted to scream it across this cursed lawn, scream it until the cherubs on the old tombstones covered their ears in fear. *She was a beautiful, passionate woman.*

"You'll get him, won't you?" Millner's eyes bulged strangely, as if grief were a tumor, swelling up from the inside, stretching him beyond endurance. "You were her friend, I remember that. She said she liked you."

"I liked her, too."

"Then promise me. You won't let anything stop you? You won't let any other case come first? Promise me you'll get him."

If only he knew. Keith's reasons for wanting to get Mike Frome were more powerful than Alton Millner, with his popping red eyes and his pathetic memories of a little girl who hadn't existed for more than a decade, could ever imagine.

"I'll get him," he said.

And for a minute, in the wind, he thought he heard Justine laugh.

CHAPTER SIX

DEBRA HAD BEEN WANDERING the aisles of the jewelry store for twenty minutes, waiting for her friend Judy Stott, who was arranging to have her new eternity ring resized.

Judy was frustrated about having put on a few pounds, but since she'd been happily married to Phil Stott for ten secure years, Debra figured Judy could be excused. The eternity band had been her surprise anniversary present. Paul obviously still saw his wife as a svelte eighteen…hence the too-small ring.

Lucky Judy. As the debate continued over whether to go slightly tight, in case Judy lost weight, or slightly loose, in case she didn't, Debra found herself idling past the glittering displays of diamond solitaires.

The very sight of all these gorgeous chips of rainbowed ice lying here, untouched, made her ache. Though she knew it was stupid, she couldn't help herself. She wanted one so bad. She ran her fingers along the glass countertop, trailing a haze of embarrassed longing.

Finally she heard the chatter of a receipt printing. Judy signed a piece of paper, then came Debra's way.

"All done." Tucking her receipt in her purse, Judy glanced at the diamonds. "Are you shopping? Or just dreaming?"

Debra flushed. She knew Judy didn't mean to be unkind, but the comment stung. Judy had always said any woman would be crazy to pin her hopes on Rutledge Coffee. She had a point. How far could a relationship go when the man had already announced that marriage is the ultimate trap, and all women are just waiting to clamp their lethal teeth around his helpless heart?

Of course, he'd been drunk at the time.

"Neither. Just enjoying," Debra said, turning away from the case. "They're pretty."

Judy looked sympathetic, but skeptical. Debra felt a flash of annoyance. Honestly, sometimes married people could be so smug. But it quickly turned into a wave of self-disgust. What kind of sap was she becoming, falling for the whole lace and flowers and happily-ever-after package?

"Truly," she said, taking Judy's arm. "I was just admiring the view. I know Ledge isn't ready for marriage. He starts twitching if he even hears the word on TV."

"And you wouldn't say yes even if he did ask, right?" Judy had said this about a million times. "You know he's definitely not good husband material, right?"

Debra sighed. "Of course I do. But who is? Frankly, you and Phil have the only happy marriage I've ever seen."

It was true. Her own parents had a sick servant-master arrangement. And though many of Debra's college friends had married in the past few years, some with diamond solitaires so big they could blind you, look at them now! The lucky ones had already escaped in divorce. The others just seemed to be settling in for lifelong misery.

So why did Debra persist in thinking of herself as somehow inferior? *Unwanted.*

"Anyhow, that eternity ring is fantastic." She shook off the self-pitying mood and grinned. "Did I ever tell you about the time I found a jewelry box in Rutledge's sock drawer?"

"I don't think so. When?"

"Two years ago. I was putting away laundry, and—"

She caught Judy's wry expression. "I wasn't prying. It was early in the relationship—things hadn't deteriorated to the prying point yet."

They both laughed. Debra didn't have many secrets from Judy these days. Everyone needed a confidante, and over the past few months Judy had become hers.

"Anyhow, it was only a couple of days from the anniversary of our first date. Not that I'd expected Rutledge to remember that. So how could I have resisted looking?"

"You couldn't have," Judy agreed immediately. "And…"

"And inside was the tackiest ankle bracelet I've ever seen. It had a nice chain, I guess, but dangling from the chain was this charm shaped like a huge, revolting pair of puckered lips."

Judy stopped in her tracks. "*What*?"

"I'm serious. It was the ugliest thing I ever saw in my life."

"What did you do?"

"Well, what could I do? I wouldn't have been caught dead in it, so I slipped it back under the socks. Then I made a couple of strategic comments about how I preferred understated jewelry. Ledge isn't the most subtle guy in the world, but I guess he got it. The jewelry box disappeared."

"He never gave it to you?"

"Nope. I guess he took it back, but he must have been offended, because he sure didn't exchange it for anything. The anniversary came and went. *Nothing.*"

Judy looked even more appalled. Though Debra nudged her arm, she didn't start walking again. They were just frozen there on the sidewalk in front of the jewelry store.

Debra scanned her friend's face, beginning to wish she hadn't shared this particular Rutledge story. Judy was a great friend, but she was a little bit of a prude, and she already hated Rutledge enough. Perversely, Debra felt herself getting defensive for him.

"Hey, it's not like a mortal sin, you know. Most guys have rotten taste in jewelry. You're lucky Phil is so—"

"No." Judy's eyes were stretched so wide they quivered slightly from the strain. "That's not what— *Oh, Deb*…Deb, look. Across the street."

Debra turned curiously. They were in the middle of downtown Albany, thirty miles from home in Tuxedo Lake. She wasn't even sure what else was around here. A sandwich shop, a bookstore. A small hotel.

"What?"

But then she saw it.

Saw *him.*

Rutledge stood on the opposite sidewalk, looking extremely happy and handsome, his white shirt crisp and clean, his blond hair shining in the sunlight. He obviously hadn't been working on anybody's boathouse today.

She thought at first he was alone. She was just about to raise her hand and call to him when he suddenly let out a happy laugh, the way he sometimes did when he played basketball at their apartment complex and sank an impossible shot.

He turned and grabbed the woman walking next to him, an incredibly beautiful brunette. Like a fool, until that very moment, Debra had thought she was just a stranger coincidentally strolling nearby.

Don't, don't, don't….

Debra's mind was empty of anything that could be called thoughts. Just the one word, cycling over and over, as if she were trying to communicate to him telepathically. *Don't…don't break my heart.*

But of course, nothing went through. Rutledge was an action man, not an empathizer. He never noticed nuance. He could see her crying over her checkbook and still ask to borrow money. He would pronounce their lovemaking "the best ever" when she'd felt nothing at all.

So why would he hear her silently begging now?

He didn't. He wrapped his muscular arms around the woman, who was laughing, and twirled her around triumphantly. And then he kissed her, so long and hard and sexy that people passing by started to stare and grin.

Finally, Debra's mind formed a real thought.

But wasn't it just so typical? Out of the hundreds of outraged, furious, scathing things she could have, *should have*, thought, she chose this pathetic doormat's lament.

You'll never get that diamond ring now.

"OH, SUZIE, I LOVE IT." Isabel, who had been Suzie's best friend, roommate and biggest fan during the years they attended art classes together, turned around with tears in her eyes. "It's…it's poetry."

Well, that was an exaggeration, but Suzie had to admit the portrait had come out okay. She'd painted Isabel lying on Suzie's sofa, with the light from the window pouring over her. Isabel's infant daughter, Phoebe, was stretched across her stomach, sleeping.

Painting babies was tricky. It could go wrong in so many ways…they could be blobby, or way too cute, or just generic.

But she'd nailed this one. It was all about the light, about the halftones that made mother and infant seem to be separate, and yet not separate. Two bodies, but still, for a little while, at least, one spirit.

"You always were the best," Isabel said without any apparent resentment. "Guess that's why you can make a living at it, and I can't."

Suzie laughed. Isabel's postmodern cubist canvases hadn't yet caught on, but they were beautiful, like the inside of a kaleidoscope.

"No, I can make a living at it because I've sold out. I paint what people want. You've stuck to your own vision. And besides—" She extended a finger and let Phoebe grab it. "You've been busy creating some other cool stuff."

In the month since Suzie had last seen Phoebe, the baby had changed so much. She seemed to be growing every minute, features sharpening, consciousness dawning. Someday, Suzie realized, Isabel would be awfully glad to have this painting, which had captured a sacred but painfully ephemeral moment.

That was the real reason people spent thousands getting their children's portraits painted. They weren't driven by vanity, as she'd originally thought, but by a wistful awareness that this child, this day, would never exist again.

The phone rang. Since she didn't have any commissions right now—and this picture of Isabel and Phoebe had been a gift—Suzie couldn't afford not to answer it. Nor could she afford to open with one of the grouchy joke greetings she used to employ back when she was a teenager working at the sheriff's department in Firefly Glen.

Snaking her finger free from Phoebe's little fist, she clicked the "talk" button of the cordless phone and said, "Strickland Studios!" in her most welcoming, professional voice.

The pause on the other end had a distinctly nervous quality.

"Umm." The voice was male, and quite young. "This is Gavin Frome. Is this Suzie?"

Well, that was a surprise. "Hey, Gavin," she said, putting a genuine smile in her voice. "How are things?"

"Pretty good," he said. "I'm sorry to bother you at work. I found your number in the phone book."

"It's okay." She tossed an apologetic smile to Isabel, who waved it away and began prowling through the studio, checking out the stacks of paintings and sketches tilted against every wall. "I've got a few free minutes. What's up?"

"I just—I wanted to ask if you would do me a favor."

"Sure, if I can."

"Um, I don't know where you live, really. Is it very far away from here? From the boathouse?"

"About half an hour. It's not a big deal, as long as my car is actually running." She and Isabel exchanged a grin. Isabel knew all about Flattery. It used to let them down on the way to class all the time. "Do you need me to come over there?"

"Well, maybe. If you can. My dad, his birthday is pretty soon, and I want to buy him a picture. I was hoping you'd help me pick it out. I don't have any lessons or anything after school tomorrow. If you're not too busy, that is."

Suzie hesitated. She knew a fork in the road when she saw one. She could let Gavin down easily, pleading too much work, too little time. He'd be hurt, but he'd get over it, and he'd probably never call her studio again. It might well be the last time she ever saw him.

Or she could say *yes, I'll be there, just tell me what time*. She could commit to being his friend.

The only problem was, Gavin was the ten-year-old center of his father's universe. She couldn't very well agree to be his friend without agreeing to be Mike's friend, too.

Once, ten years ago, Mike's life had been falling apart, and he had asked for her friendship. She'd said no. Did she really want to get involved now, when his life was falling apart all over again?

She looked at Isabel, who represented everything that had happened to Suzie since she marched out of the oppressive Sugar Plum Fairyland of Firefly Glen, with a scholarship in her hand and an eat-my-dust skip in her step.

Ten years of education, experience, independence, risks, lovers, clients, friends, self-discipline, maturity... even a home and a business of her own.

Isabel had never heard of Mike Frome—that's how far Suzie had come. Right now Isabel was looking at a pencil sketch of him, and she had no idea who it was.

That particular sketch was one of Suzie's favorites. It had captured the rare flash of sweetness that sometimes played over Mike's rugged, rich-boy features.

Suzie must have drawn it on one of her softhearted days. Or was it soft*headed?* She had quite a few less flattering Mike pictures buried in that stack somewhere, too.

Isabel held out the sketch, smiling with lifted brows and shaking her fingers in the universal *hot-hot-hot* sign.

Suzie stared at the sketch, though she knew Gavin was waiting for an answer. It might be nice to find out which was the real Mike. Once and for all.

"Okay," she heard herself saying, planting her foot squarely onto the path less traveled. "Tomorrow it is."

FOR A TEN-YEAR-OLD, the kid had pretty good taste.

After only about half an hour of prowling through Tuxedo Lake's artsy district, Suzie and Gavin had narrowed the choice down to two pictures.

They were both prints, of course. Gavin had saved up a hundred and twenty-two dollars and ninety-three cents by working on weekends with his dad, a sum that impressed the heck out of Suzie, who at that age had never met a nickel she wasn't dying to spend. But he was determined to buy a framed picture, and frames cost a lot.

The whole expedition had almost ended right at the first gallery, where the owners specialized in flowers and cottages and still-life fruits. Gavin had glared at the walls with an expression so horrified Suzie had nearly laughed out loud.

"Maybe we'd better think of something else to give him," he'd whispered to her, edging toward the door. But she'd assured him that not all pictures were dumb and mushy, and they had finally found this little framing shop, which had some wonderful nautical things, rugged seascapes, and lighthouses, and boats with strong masts. All that subliminal manly stuff.

Gavin had relaxed. Now they were debating the relative merits of two different sailboat prints. One was very Impressionistic, a boat racing at high noon, with a lot of fractured light and color. The other was nearly monochromatic, representational to the point of being photographic, just a lone gray boat on a moonlit blue lake.

They were both good, though Suzie thought the gray boat might have the edge artistically. But she wanted Gavin to be happy, so she just watched while he tried to figure it out.

"I don't really know anything about paintings," he said finally, looking at Suzie as if to see whether that disappointed her. "I think they're both pretty, but maybe they're not."

She did laugh out loud this time. "Hey, that the great thing about art. Nobody can tell you what you like. If you think it's pretty, it *is* pretty."

Gavin chewed on the edge of his thumb. He obviously felt awkward even here in this studio, which was more like a boathouse than an art gallery. It was too fussy, too crowded. Though he had Justine's fine blond hair and elegant features, he also had Mike's rough-and-tumble masculinity, and he couldn't hold still for long.

"Yeah, but the picture isn't for me, that's the hard thing." He squinted at the two boats, which Suzie had propped side by side where the light from the window would strike them. "I like the blue and gray one best, I think, because it feels nice, kind of peaceful. But what if it makes Dad feel sad?"

He tilted his head, as if a different angle would

make it all come clear. "It might be kind of sad, don't you think? The boat looks all alone in the dark."

Immediately Suzie was glad she hadn't indicated her preference for that one. Looked at in the only light that mattered, the light of Mike and Gavin's personal tragedy, the picture did project isolation and gloom.

"I think you're right," she said. "The other one is really happy. And, if I remember correctly, some of these tints—" she pointed to the sunlight on the water "—match the beige in your sofa, right?"

Gavin nodded excitedly. Here, at least, was something he could be sure of. "Yes, they match exactly. That's great!" He smiled at Suzie as if she'd just decoded the Rosetta stone. "I knew you would be better at this than Debra."

Debra. That was the name of the woman who had been at the boathouse with Gavin when Suzie arrived to pick him up. Suzie, who had been expecting to have to deal with Mike, had been surprised, but Debra had explained that she was a friend of the family, and she often watched Gavin on Thursdays, if Mike had to work late.

Friend of the family. *Hmmm…*

Debra had been stylish but basically kind of a plain Jane. She didn't really look like Mike's type—but then maybe Mike's type had changed, after ten years. After Justine. Maybe Mike was over the busty, bitchy bimbo type for good.

Still, it was intriguing. It might not be any of Suzie's business how Debra fit into the picture, but she sure would like to know. She had decided not to pump Gavin for information, though. He was smart. She'd been a smart kid, too, and she knew what it felt like to have some grown-up assume that, just because you were little, you were too stupid to see through a bunch of patronizing baloney.

"I'm sure she would have done fine," Suzie said. "She seemed nice."

"Yeah, she's really nice, but she didn't want to come with me anyhow. Ledge was coming over."

"Ledge?"

"Yeah, Rutledge—Mr. Coffee. He's my dad's friend, and he's Debra's boyfriend. I thought you must know him, he's from Firefly Glen, too."

Oh, yeah, she knew Rutledge Coffee.

Yuck.

Double yuck.

Poor Debra.

"So she wanted to stay at the boathouse anyhow. They've been having a fight, and she says she's going to make him crawl till his knees bleed."

"Good grief," Suzie said, trying to hold back her delight at the mental image of Rutledge on all fours. "She sounds pretty mad."

"Yeah, but she'll end up giggling and letting him kiss her and everything. She's always mad at him, and it always ends up like that."

Come on, Debra. Suzie sent righteous sisterhood vibes out to the other woman. *Hold out a little longer, and make the sucker pay. It's high time someone did.*

They bought the picture, and Gavin even had enough money to pay for gift wrapping and still have about fifteen dollars left over. He insisted on buying Suzie an ice cream with it—a well-bred gesture of thanks that made her wonder whether Mike had known about this outing and had given his son instructions.

As they walked back to her car after the ice cream,

they passed a Grand Opening sign swaying between two balloon-covered goalposts in front of a new electronics store. Gavin's wide-eyed, curious dawdling was too obvious to miss.

"Want to go in? We've still got time, if you'd like to look around."

He nodded. "That would be awesome."

She had to agree. It *was* an awesome store, and immediately she could see how much more at home the little boy was in a place like this. Equidistant from the front and side entrances, the owners had set up a "Welcome" table. It was loaded with coffee, soft drinks and doughnuts, and decorated with more balloons.

Smiling employees sat behind the table urging customers to enter contests to win the plasma TV, satellite radio or "gaming system of your choice."

While he gobbled down a doughnut, Gavin filled out three separate forms in a shaky cursive, then dropped them eagerly into the boxes.

"I have one," he explained as he entered the gaming system contest. "But Dad doesn't. He's always using mine."

Suzie smiled. "Bummer," she said. "He should definitely get his own."

She pointed to the gaming area, where several pods had been set up to let customers sample various popular video games. "Hey, that looks like fun."

"Oh, man, yeah!" Gavin was off in a flash. Suzie followed and took up a position right next to him. Within minutes they were both twirling joysticks and blasting evil aliens off the surface of the planet Nuperdorf.

After a few rounds, Gavin glanced at her totals. "Hey," he said. "You're good."

She grinned. "I know. I used to date the guy who designed this program."

Gavin frowned thoughtfully, as if he were going to have to rearrange his mental image of her. "That's awesome. Are you still dating him?

"Nope," she said without taking her eyes off the screen. "He was a dork. I was, too. But when he started talking to me in Nuperdorfian, he outdorked even me, you know?"

Gavin laughed. "I don't think you're a dork."

She killed another Dorfblat. "You should have seen me in art school."

Five minutes later, Gavin moved to another machine, but Suzie was on a roll. Another five minutes after that, she realized she wasn't quite sure where he was.

She took her hands off the joystick and gazed around the game area. She heard the Dorfblat attack her character and begin to chew its bones. Then she heard the little descending cascade of notes that meant her character was dead.

But she didn't even look at the screen. She'd started to feel tight around the chest. Where the heck was Gavin?

The store was busy, filled with at least a dozen kids who might be Gavin…but weren't. She asked two other boys hanging around the area, but they just shrugged. A third thought he'd seen Gavin playing the last video game toward the back, just a minute ago, but there had been a guy with him, an older guy….

She felt her breath coming faster. She might not be a dork, but she was a fool. A dangerously shortsighted fool. She shouldn't be trusted with a kid. She had no experience. She was still a kid at heart herself and had no common sense to boot.

"Gavin!" She called out loudly, not caring how many heads turned in her direction. "Gavin!"

She thought she might have heard someone call her name…but over the pinging and blasting of the video games, the swelling of a U2 song as someone tried out the car stereo speakers and the constant yammering of the customers, how could she be sure?

She began to run. And as she reached the Welcome table, she saw him.

A man was with him. She'd never seen the man before. He had his arm around Gavin's shoulders, and he was pushing him forward. Gavin wasn't refusing, exactly, but he was resisting, as if he weren't sure, as if he were confused, or frightened….

They were only a few feet from the side door. She knew she'd never reach them in time.

"Gavin!" she cried again.

Gavin tried to turn, but the older man wouldn't let him. They were going to get away.

Think quickly….

She turned to the refreshments table. All the utensils were plastic. All the plates were paper.

But the coffeemaker was real.

She reached over and lifted it up. She heard the shocked protest of the employee behind the table, and she heard the *pop* as the cord jerked free of the outlet.

"Gavin, duck," she screamed.

His reflexes were fantastic. He would make a good football player someday, she thought as everything went into slow motion. Gavin ducked and swiveled, pulling free of the arm that held him captive. The coffeemaker sailed neatly through the air toward the stranger.

Damn it, she was going to miss. She had a pretty

good aim, but her arm wasn't quite strong enough. The coffeemaker fell with an insane bang and splatter, just behind his feet.

People jumped away in all directions, yelling.

Coffee went everywhere—but a gratifying amount of it splashed forward, onto the man. He made a strangled sound, clutched at his back and stumbled. But somehow he didn't lose his head. He righted himself and began to run.

And before anyone could quite figure out what the hell had happened, he had disappeared through the side door and into the street.

CHAPTER SEVEN

THE AFTERMATH WAS HIDEOUS.

Everyone in the entire town of Tuxedo Lake was annoyed with Suzie, it seemed, from the customers who had coffee stains on their pant legs and the store manager whose grand opening had turned into a circus, to the police, who seemed unable to accept the fact that she couldn't identify a man when all she'd seen was the back of his head.

And she couldn't even bear to remember the look on Mike's face when he showed up at the store. He'd played it cool, of course. That was the official Frome way. He'd entered with a mild frown, and he'd chucked Gavin on the shoulder, saying, "Hey, goof, what did I tell you about talking to strangers?"

But then he'd knelt and wrapped Gavin in his arms, and Suzie had seen his face over the little boy's shoulder. He looked as if someone had just given him a private glimpse of the end of the world.

Of course, no one was as annoyed with Suzie as she was with herself. She hadn't felt this wretched, scared and guilty in…in her whole life.

Add four hours at the police station, the three of them going over and over the same info in separate cubicles, and you ended up with a pretty hairy day.

But when District Attorney Keith Quigley entered

Suzie's interview room and shut the door behind him, she knew things had just gone from bad to worse. The minute he introduced himself, she remembered what Mike had told her about Quigley: the D.A. was out to get him.

Quigley held out a sheaf of papers. "I've been looking over your statement," he said, chewing on his lower lip. Suzie knew it was an affectation, designed to imply that something troubled him.

It didn't work with her, because her statement had been honest and straightforward, and she had nothing to hide anyhow.

So Quigley could just chew away.

Which he did. She found herself fixated on his lips. Fat, pouty and unpleasantly wet. She would never accept a commission to paint this guy. Portrait painting was always a tightrope walk between reality and flattery, and there would be no way to flatter Keith Quigley.

He had a round face and hypothyroid eyes that looked weirdly wet, too. He was not exactly fat, but he gave the impression that he should have been a taller man, as if some computer photo program had been used to compress his image.

He looked smart, though, and the overall effect was of some abnormally evolved reptile. But he was clearly too smug, too sure of his power and his intellectual superiority, to invite any real sympathy, so she didn't bother trying to find any.

He must have noticed that she wasn't intimidated, because he quickly changed tactics. When he sat, he ignored the power chair behind the desk, and pulled out the one beside her.

Suzie wanted to roll her eyes. He thought he could

play Harmless Uncle Keith with her, did he? That offended her even more than the monotonous repetition of questions from the earlier detective.

Suzie watched as Quigley settled back and got comfortable. Two friendly people, his posture said, just talking things over. She sighed audibly, so that in case they were recording this somewhere, the machine would register that she wasn't buying it.

"I'd like to talk to you a little about how you came to be with Gavin today."

"It's on my statement," she said. "About ten times. I don't have anything new to add. I'm sorry, but… shouldn't you be out looking for the bad guy?"

Quigley smiled. Not an improvement. When he stretched his lips, it exposed little pink pockets of wetness at the corners.

"I'm the D.A., Miss Strickland. I'm not on the 'looking for bad guys' team."

No, she thought. *You're on the "harassing the good guys" team.* But she kept her mouth shut somehow and waited for him to continue.

"So, let's see. You said that Gavin called you yesterday and asked you to come over and help him secretly pick out a painting to give his father as a birthday present. Is that accurate?"

"Yes."

"You said that his father knew nothing about it."

"If he did, it wouldn't be a secret, would it?"

"Would it surprise you, Miss Strickland, to learn that Mike Frome knew all about your assignation with his son?"

"Yes," she said irritably. She knew how these people worked. Well, okay, she didn't know, but she'd seen it on TV often enough. They'd offer up one of their speculations as fact, hoping that you'd confirm it. "It darn sure would. Gavin was really happy about pulling it off. He talked about how surprised his dad would be."

She shifted, trying to release some of her annoyed tension. "And it wasn't an assignation. What an absurd word."

Quigley didn't seem phased by her criticism.

"I know that's your story," he said, flipping through the pages he held. "But unfortunately, Mike has given a statement, too. And in his he admits suggesting your name to Gavin. Apparently the whole outing was his idea."

Suzie found herself without a good response. She was shocked. It could be true…. Heck, it probably *was* true. What a dummy she was—why hadn't she found it suspicious for Gavin to call her out of the blue like that?

She realized that she'd still been operating under the Old Suzie rules. A kid could relate to the Old Suzie, with her funky hair and adolescent *who-cares* attitude. The Old Suzie had never attracted much male-female interest, not from handsome, self-possessed guys like Mike, anyhow.

But she wasn't the Old Suzie anymore, at least not on the outside. And apparently she didn't understand the New Suzie rules quite as well as she'd thought she did.

"Okay, so it was Mike's idea. Is that so weird? I hope, Mr. Quigley, that you don't think Mike used me as a pawn in a conspiracy to kidnap his own son. His son, as you may have noticed, is already in his custody anyway."

She wondered why Quigley annoyed her so much. She didn't usually react this way to a person's appearance—in fact, she ordinarily far preferred the homely to the beautiful.

And, in the end, she had only Mike's word for it that Quigley was unfairly persecuting him over Justine's murder.

"Point taken," Quigley went on, seeming satisfied to have unsettled her, and not requiring a response. "But I've just learned something else that interests me. I've learned that, ten years ago, you and Mike Frome had a relationship."

That jerked her out of her musings. The detective who had interviewed her earlier had taken great pains to feel out this possibility and had gone away empty-handed.

"A relationship? That's nuts. The relationship of salt to pepper, maybe. Oil to water."

Quigley gazed at her calmly. "It's well-known," he said, "that opposites attract."

She felt her hackles rising. "It's also well-known that people who gossip frequently get it wrong. Who laid this particular rotten egg for you? Alton Millner?"

"No. I heard this one from an informant a little closer to the source."

"Well, it's absurd, and frankly, unless you can show me the connection between my high school love life and what happened to Gavin today, I don't care to discuss it with you."

"Don't you want to know where I heard it?" He was watching her carefully, as if he had a nice big bomb to drop and he was enjoying toying with the trigger.

But he was out of ammunition. She was on to him.

"Not really," she said. "It's pretty clear you heard it from Mike."

He was good, she had to admit. His eyes flickered

for a millisecond—just enough to let her know he was surprised—and then he covered it.

"You think I don't know what you're doing?" She leaned forward. "You aren't really investigating what happened to Gavin today, are you? You're investigating Justine's murder."

He didn't deny it. He raised his eyebrows. "What if they're connected?"

"They may be." The idea had, belatedly, occurred to her, too. "But not this way, Mr. Quigley. If you think that Mike Frome killed his ex-wife because he was pining for a girl he left behind in high school, you're barking up the wrong tree. In fact, if you think Mike Frome killed his wife *period*, you're not quite as smart as you look."

Quigley laughed. He put his palm on the table and hoisted himself to a standing position. "I hear you, Miss Strickland, and I appreciate your…intensity." He folded her statement and slipped it into his breast pocket. "Actually, I'm glad to know there's one thing I obviously wasn't wrong about."

She stood, too. "And that is?"

He smiled enigmatically.

"You."

ORDINARILY MIKE KNEW that Gavin would wheedle for an extra hour, half hour, ten minutes, whatever he could get, at bedtime. But the day had been so stressful the poor kid fell asleep the minute they got home from the police station, though it wasn't even dark yet.

Mike tucked him in and then sat on the chair beside his bed, waiting for the world to stop spinning. He stared out the window at the lake, which was as bright as gold leaf in the approaching sunset, and wondered how it could all look exactly the same as it had yesterday.

Gavin whimpered in his sleep. Mike touched the top of his head, the way he'd done back when Gavin was a baby. Gavin settled down quickly with a sigh.

The turmoil inside Mike couldn't be as easily soothed.

For the first time in his life, he actually felt that he could do violence. If the man who had tried to grab Gavin were here right now, what couldn't Mike do to him? He felt out of his control whenever he even thought about it.

It was terrifying, like having swallowed a tiger.

And always the question, roiling around inside him. *Why?*

Why would anyone try to kidnap Gavin?

He heard a small sound, and he bolted from the chair so roughly it banged against the wall. Sheepishly, he glanced at Gavin, who frowned in his sleep, and then turned over.

Mike heard the sound again. It was a soft tapping. It came from downstairs.

He had bought a gun right after they realized Justine was missing. He wasn't sure why, except that finding himself mentioned over and over in newspaper articles next to the phrase "police suspect foul play" had undermined his sense that the world was benign—or even sane.

They clearly weren't in Firefly Glen anymore, Toto, and it was time to play tough.

He went and got the gun now. He shut the door to Gavin's room, then made his way quietly down the stairs.

The tapping was louder down here, and it was coming from the front door. Probably no need for the gun, then. He would assume that kidnappers didn't usually ask permission to enter. But he tucked it into the back waistband of his jeans, just in case.

He hadn't installed a peephole when he built the boathouse. At the time, his imagination hadn't stretched to kidnapping and murder and cold gun barrels crammed down his pants. He put his right hand behind his back, resting on the butt of the gun, and opened the door with his left.

It was Suzie.

He realized with a streak of relief that she was probably the only person in the world he would actually enjoy talking to right now. She had more common sense than anyone he'd ever met, and enough butt-kicking candor to tell him the truth when she thought he needed to hear it.

"So…" She scrunched her mouth up to one side self-consciously. "Are you still speaking to me?"

"Of course I am," he said, moving aside to let her in. He was glad that Debra had cleaned up this afternoon. He'd left in a hurry this morning, and the sink had been full of breakfast bowls that probably would smell pretty rank by now. "Why wouldn't I be?"

"Because everything that happened today was my fault. I came to say I'm sorry, Mike. I never should have agreed to take Gavin out. I don't know squat about taking care of kids. I should have watched him like a hawk. He just seems so mature, and it never occurred to me—"

"Hey." He touched her shoulder, trying to calm her the way he'd calmed Gavin. "It's not your fault. Do you have any idea how many times I've done exactly the same thing? It wouldn't have occurred to me, either."

She looked at him suspiciously, a frown between her eyes. "Are you just feeding me a bunch of baloney to be nice?"

"Cross my heart," he said. "I've let him wander around the video arcade by himself a hundred times. I won't do it anymore, that's for sure."

He moved toward the sofa, bending down to sweep away the controls for Gavin's video game and a couple of candy wrappers. Debra hadn't exactly gone for the Good Housekeeping award. Ledge had probably shown up and distracted her.

"Have a seat. I don't think anything will actually bite you."

Suzie dropped her purse and fell onto the cushions with a sigh. "Well, even if you're being nice, I'll take it. The guilt is killing me." Leaning her head back against the cushion, she looked at him through heavy-lidded eyes. "How's he doing? Is he totally fritzed?"

"He was exhausted. He went straight to bed."

"Good," she said. "Because I think you and I need to talk."

"I know," he said. He mentally inventoried his cabinets and fridge. "Want something to drink? I think I've got a Dr Pepper and a beer."

She wrinkled her nose. "Well, not together, I hope."

He should have gone grocery shopping. But Thursday was pizza night at the Frome boathouse, and they always let the delivery guy bring a couple of two-liter bottles of cola on the side. It was one of Gavin's favorite traditions. He'd been big on traditions, ever since his mother disappeared.

"We could split the beer," Mike offered with a

smile. "We probably both need it. I could get two straws."

"Make that two plastic cups, and you've got a deal."

He went into the kitchen, thanking his lucky stars that Suzie Strickland was such a down-to-earth woman. Justine would have been in such a sanctimonious snit by now. She would already have uttered the words "my son" and "live like this" about ten times each.

It was one of the reasons he'd never let her set foot inside the boathouse.

He rooted around in the pantry and was rewarded by the sight of an unopened, and therefore unstale, box of wheat crackers. He tried the refrigerator's cold tray, and his luck held. A block of nice yellow-and-beige cheese sat there, with only one corner missing.

He sniffed it just to be sure.

"I don't have much experience with drugs, but I don't think you can actually snort Muenster cheese," Suzie observed politely.

He looked around the refrigerator door. She had followed him into the kitchen, and was leaning against the doorjamb, grinning.

"What? Suzie-freaka of the purple hair and raccoon eyes doesn't have much experience with drugs?" He tilted his head. "You're smashing all my stereotypes."

She rolled her eyes and pushed the refrigerator shut. She pulled out a couple of drawers, found the silverware and extracted a knife.

"My superfreak image was mostly just costuming, I'm afraid," she said as she sliced cheese expertly. "Underneath that grungy black flour sack was a normal teenage girl who really just wanted to be like everyone else."

"Just like everyone else?" He handed her one of the half-full beer steins. He took a sip, then watched her drink. "I'm sorry that didn't work out."

She might be absurdly beautiful, but she was still Suzie. Still too honest to pretend she didn't know what he was talking about. Still too insecure to be certain he wasn't handing her a bucket of BS.

"Thanks," she said, flushing. "I think."

"You're welcome," he said. "Definitely."

If this had been a normal date, he would have taken the cheese and crackers out to the porch, and they would have sat together watching the river and listening to the crickets. And he would have told her more about how different she was from other women.

But it wasn't a normal date.

It wasn't a date, for starters. And for the past two years not a damn thing in his life had been normal.

So they camped out at the small kitchen table, where he and Gavin had breakfast every morning. It was near the foot of the stairs, so that he could hear Gavin if he called. He left the gun in his waistband. He heard a small inhale when Suzie first noticed it, as they set the table, but she didn't make any comment.

"So let me go first," she said, taking a cracker and putting it on her paper plate. "If I don't tell someone how much I hate District Attorney Quigley, I'll pop."

"Go for it," Mike said. "I'm the perfect audience for that story."

He let her spill it all without interruption. Very little of what she said surprised him. He'd known for weeks now that Quigley's dearest dream was to put him behind bars. Quigley had always had a hopeless crush on Justine. She had crooned over him at parties, just for the fun of making him drool. But when she and

Mike came home, she had mocked the man mercilessly.

Too bad Mike hadn't taped her. He wondered if Quigley's thirst to avenge her death might be slaked by hearing that brittle, elegant voice saying, "I'll probably break out in warts where he touched me. The man is absolutely a toad."

"My interview wasn't much different," Mike said when Suzie was finished. "I'm not sure where he's going with this, but I agree that he's trying to tie the kidnapping to Justine's murder."

"But how?" Suzie popped a small slice of cheese into her mouth. She had propped her foot up on the chair and was hugging her knee. "What could Gavin possibly have to do with his mother's death? Could he have…seen anything?"

The idea had been slinking around the back of Mike's mind all day, and he'd been trying to ignore it. The idea of Gavin seeing anything as terrible as his own mother's murder was impossible to accept. The coroner's report said that Justine had been killed from blunt trauma to the head.

He closed his eyes now, instinctively rejecting it. "God, no," he said. "No."

Suzie took a deep breath. "I know, but we have to face this if we're going to stop Quigley, don't we? Where was Gavin the night Justine disappeared?"

It was disturbing how much he liked hearing her say "we." "We're" going to stop Quigley. It would feel bloody fantastic to have a partner in all this. But of course that was a fantasy and would have to stay that way.

He had a good lawyer finally, the one Parker recommended. That would have to be *partner* enough.

The only problem was, the lawyer had made it clear he didn't want Mike to tell him too much, for fear he might someday have to put him on the stand. Mike was no fool—he knew what that meant. It meant, for fear Mike was guilty.

Suzie Strickland didn't seem to consider that possibility for a minute. She didn't seem to feel one bit nervous, sitting alone here on a darkened lake with a suspected murderer who had a gun tucked into his jeans.

For that comforting blind faith, he would never be able to repay her.

"Gavin was at home that night," he said. "After the school play, he went to Hugh's house for a party. But they all went back to Justine's afterward, for a slumber party. Even though she wasn't going to be there, they all liked Justine's house best. The house was so big, with a whole video game room and the pool. Anyhow, the plan was for me to pick him up the next morning and bring him here. You knew Justine was going on a trip to Europe?"

Suzie nodded. "I read all about it, back when they first realized she'd disappeared. She was supposed to be gone a whole month, right? That's why it took them so long to know anything was wrong. I heard that her Swedish boyfriend finally called Mayor Millner and—"

She broke off, looking uncomfortable.

"That's right," Mike said. If she only knew how little he minded Justine's other love interests. "Her boyfriend called, because she hadn't ever shown up to meet him. He didn't worry at first, because Justine was so unpredictable. But eventually, when he couldn't reach her on her cell, or at home, he—"

Suzie leaned forward. "Did the cops look at him? I mean, is it possible he—"

"No." Mike shook his head. They all would have liked to think that the handsome Swede might have been the bad guy. But it would have been too easy. "When they checked, they discovered that Justine had never used her airline ticket. She never reached Europe."

"But what if the boyfriend came over—"

"No." Mike found Suzie's eagerness touching, but it was pointless. "Passports leave a pretty clear trail. He never set foot in New York."

She subsided with a sigh. "Okay. So who stayed with the kids at the mansion that night? I know it wasn't you. After you dropped Justine off on the road, you just came here, right?"

"Right. I was at the end of a project and had a ton of work to do. But when the boys got to the house for the slumber party, they said everything looked perfectly normal. Everyone assumed Justine had walked home, called a cab, as planned, and gone straight to the airport, as planned."

"So who did babysit the slumber party?"

"Debra," Mike said. "Debra Pawley. She's a Realtor. She was just starting out then, not making a whole lot, and she needed the extra money. So Justine used her as a babysitter sometimes. She's a nice woman. She's dating Rutledge. You remember Rutledge?"

Suzie laughed. "Oh, yeah. Some things you just never forget."

"I'll bet." Mike remembered, too, how shitty Rutledge had always been to Suzie. Once, when Ledge had been particularly obscene, Mike had knocked him off their motorboat into Llewellyn Lake.

"Anyhow, Debra said everything was fine. The boys were good, nothing out of the ordinary happened all night. So what could Gavin have seen?"

Suzie shook her head. "I don't know. It doesn't make sense. But that must be what Quigley is thinking. And we don't really know when Justine—" She swallowed. "God, it's awful to have to talk about things like this, but—"

"It's okay," he said. "You're right. We can't just pretend they didn't happen. They did."

"Well, we don't really know when Justine's body was buried out there, do we? I mean, she could have been killed somewhere else, and—"

"Yes. In fact, it would have been much easier to do it later, because for the next several weeks there was no one at the house at all, except the gardener, who lives in the guest quarters. If you needed to hide what you were doing, it would have been much better to wait."

"Which brings us back full circle." Suzie raked her hands through her hair. "There probably wasn't anything Gavin *could* have seen that night. So why would anyone want to hurt him?"

Mike shook his head. "I don't know."

They sat in silence for a few minutes.

Suzie shifted in her chair, getting comfortable. "Who do you think it was, Mike?"

He took a deep breath. "I just don't know," he said. "I've thought about it a million times. When I left her on the road, there was a car right behind us. I've tried and tried to remember what the car looked like, but I just can't. I was angry. I wasn't paying attention."

"It doesn't have to have been that car," she said. It was sweet how eager she was to take the weight from his shoulders. "As Justine was walking, anyone could have come by. They could have offered her a ride, and—"

He nodded. He'd imagined it that way, too. Justine had been out there alone on Woodcliff Road, walking home after their spat. She would have been angry, offended. If someone offered her a ride, she would have been so relieved. He could just see her smiling, climbing into the car with…

With whom? Quigley? Certainly the D.A. would have seemed respectable enough to be completely safe. Richie Graham, the gardener who had always acted way too familiar? She obviously hadn't disliked Richie as much as Mike had. She'd kept him on, whereas Mike would have fired him so fast he wouldn't have had time to wash his hands.

What about Phil Stott? Phil was happily married, but still, he'd always watched Justine with that same hungry expression Mike had seen on a hundred men's faces. Or even Rutledge, who liked to play rough and had always envied Mike's conquest of Justine?

And what about all the lovers? He didn't know who they were, but the field was wide open. The fathers of Gavin's classmates, the husbands of her own friends, Mike's clients, her aerobics instructor, the postman, the priest? Justine had the power to hurt any man enough to make him want to hurt her back.

God knows he would have preferred a total stranger. It would be so nice to believe it was a drifter, an anonymous evil who just happened by at the wrong moment.

And yet, even as he wished it, he knew it couldn't be true. A stranger would have disposed of Justine's body out in the woods, or in a ditch, even in some deserted train yard near Albany or Niagara Falls or Troy.

Not in her own backyard.

Mike heard a small noise upstairs. He pushed back his chair.

"I should check on him," he said.

"Go ahead." Suzie smiled. "I'll put away the left-overs."

Gavin was fine, just restless, and he'd knocked his alarm clock off the nightstand with his pillow. Mike got everything sorted out, gave Gavin a kiss on the forehead, which made him roll over again, and then went back downstairs.

The breakfast table was clear, and the French doors were standing open. Suzie must have walked out to look at the lake.

He stood in the open doorway, one ear listening for Gavin, but his eyes locked on Suzie, who leaned over the railing. Her long, shining hair blew in the wind, which was unusually strong tonight. And the lake smells were more intense, too. That usually meant there would be a storm by morning.

He was acutely aware of every tiny motion of the boat below them, as it thudded softly against its slip, adjusting to the edgy water. Maybe it was symbolic. He'd tried to build a stable world for his son, but he'd built on flowing water, not solid ground. If he wasn't careful right now, everything could come tumbling down.

After a couple of minutes, Suzie seemed to sense his presence. She straightened up and turned around.

"Everything okay?"

He nodded. "He's asleep."

She dragged her tousled hair out of her face. "I've

made a decision," she said. "This is going to sound crazy, but I'm not leaving. I'm not going back to Albany. Not until this whole thing is cleared up."

He wasn't ordinarily a slow thinker, but this caught him so completely by surprise he could hardly find words. "What do you mean, you're not leaving?"

She smiled grimly. "Well, I don't mean I'm going to squat on your living room sofa and refuse to budge, if that's what you're afraid of. I just mean I'm not leaving Tuxedo Lake. I can get a motel room nearby. But I think we need to work together to figure this whole mess out."

"No, Suzie," he said. "This isn't your problem. It isn't your mess."

"It is now. I've got some anonymous son of a bitch trying to kidnap Gavin on my watch. I've got a D.A. breathing down my neck, implying that maybe I helped you kill your ex-wife so that we could—"

She paused, then waved her hand irritably. "Well, that whole line of logic is so convoluted I'm not sure *what* the heck he thinks we wanted to do. I mean, we were both free and, since your divorce, single. If we'd wanted to have sex 24-7, there wasn't anyone who could stop us."

Mike felt a painful lurch in his groin. *Yes*, his body was saying, *yes we could have. We still could.*

But his mind was throwing on the brakes. What the hell was he thinking? She said they *were* free, but he wasn't now. Not really. At any minute, his son might wake up and come downstairs in terror.

Even more deadly, at any minute the doorbell might ring, and a cop would be standing there, holding a warrant for his arrest.

And besides, Suzie hadn't said she *wanted* to have

sex with him, just that there would have been no obstacles preventing it if they had wished to.

In fact, the one time he had asked her to have sex with him she'd said *hell, no* so fast it still made his head spin to remember it.

She was offering friendship, that was all. She couldn't know that he was so damn lonely, and had done without the comforting release of sex so damn long he'd gone half-mad and was thinking all kinds of impossible things.

"So, what do you think?"

He organized his mind with effort. "I think it's crazy. I think you should go home and forget about all this. Quigley isn't really after you, Suzie. He's after me. You're just the tool that's closest to hand right now. If you go away, he'll find some other tool."

"Yeah, well, I'm not going away, so he'll just have to get used to that."

"Suzie, this is a very generous gesture, but I really think—"

"Hey. You're just a dumb jock, remember, Frome?" Her voice was saturated with the saucy, bossy tone he remembered so well. "So you'd better let me do the thinking. After all, I'm the geeky freak who got blessed with a big brain instead of a big bra."

He smiled and somehow kept his gaze from dropping to the curve of her firm, high breasts. He didn't know a single sane man who would say she wasn't designed just exactly right.

"Suzie, I can't let you—"

"*Let* me?" She frowned. "Have you forgotten who you're dealing with, Frome? Last time I checked, you weren't the boss of me. So stop being noble, and help me. We'll make better progress if we put our heads together."

"You think so?" He couldn't help smiling. God, he had missed that determined line that showed up between her eyebrows when she got fussy. "Even if one of the heads belongs to a dumb jock?"

The furrow smoothed out, and she chuckled. "Well, that may have been a slight exaggeration."

She moved past him, on a breath of wind that smelled like the past, like the freshly mowed lawn of Summer House and the earthy moisture of Natalie Granville's greenhouse. It made him ache for all the things he'd lost, because he had been the biggest fool God ever created.

Just inside the door, she turned.

"I've always been sorry I said no when you asked for my friendship the last time, Mike. I was—very selfish. Maybe I can make it up to you now." She held out her hand. "Friends?"

He took her hand. It was warm, and even stronger than it used to be.

"Yes," he said. "Friends."

CHAPTER EIGHT

IN SPITE OF EVERYTHING, Suzie felt almost lighthearted as she drove through the rain to Mike's office the next morning.

For one thing, she'd just had one of the best night's sleep she could remember in years. Mike hadn't wanted her to go out hunting for a hotel room by herself, given how late it was when they finished talking. He couldn't go with her, because of Gavin. So they'd compromised by throwing sheets and a blanket over the sofa. Mike had offered to take it himself, but Suzie had pointed out how disturbed Gavin would be if he woke in the night, came searching for his dad and found a strange woman in the bed.

"How do you know he'd find that disturbing?" Mike had given her a playful grin. "How do you know it doesn't happen all the time around here?"

"Puh-lease," was all she'd said. And that had settled that. She'd wrapped herself up and fallen asleep instantly, lulled by the sounds of the water, and the rocking of the moonlight on the walls.

By the time she woke, Gavin and Mike were already in the kitchen, cracking eggs for breakfast. Gavin accepted her presence without surprise, and Suzie wondered what Mike had told him.

They were full of news. Mike had made a decision

in the night. He was going to drive Gavin up for a visit with his grandparents in Firefly Glen.

Gavin wasn't thrilled. While they ate their surprisingly good omelets, Gavin had argued against it. He didn't want to be away from his dad. He didn't want to miss school. He was learning to play Hugh's drum set, and they'd been planning to practice this weekend.

Mike had handled it well. From the beginning, it had been clear who was boss. But Mike brought the boy around, until, by the time they were washing dishes, Gavin seemed to be looking forward to the trip.

That's when Mike asked Suzie for a favor. He wanted to stay at the boathouse to help Gavin pack, but he needed some blueprints from his office. He asked if Suzie would mind driving over there, only a couple of miles, to pick them up. The office was closed, but he could give her a key and specific directions for how to find the blueprints.

She'd agreed without hesitation, glad to be put to use. Plus, Gavin seemed to take it for granted that Suzie would come along on the Firefly Glen trip, which meant Mike couldn't try to leave her behind.

All around, a very good morning so far. She hummed as she ducked through the rain and let herself into the small, attractive gray-shingled building whose plaque pronounced it the offices of Sheltering Shores Inc. Docks, Slips And Boathouses By Design.

It was modest but tasteful, exactly what she expected from Mike Frome, the professional. His father was a doctor back in Firefly Glen, and his offices were much like this. They'd probably hired the same quietly elegant decorator.

Mike's office was at the front, the big office with

the wide bay window. His desk was covered with books, papers, blueprints and models of boathouses they either had built or were hoping to build.

The papers were right where he'd said they'd be. It was organized chaos, a lot like her desk at home. It was the desk of a man who loved his job.

A photo of a grinning Gavin, taken back when his front teeth were still missing, dominated the credenza behind the desk. Suzie smiled back at it—she'd be willing to bet everyone smiled back at that goofy kid.

It wasn't until she was leaving the room that she noticed something lying on the seat of the guest chair.

It was a gun.

She started, taking a step back, and then she bent over to get a closer view. It didn't look like any gun she'd ever seen before—although, since she hated guns with a passion, that wasn't saying much. It was black. Large and clumsy-looking, with a canister on the underside.

She knew she was getting paranoid when her first thought was…*someone planted this here.*

Someone is trying to frame Mike for Justine's death.

But that wasn't only paranoid—it was illogical. Justine hadn't been shot, she'd been bludgeoned.

So what the heck was this thing doing here? She took one edge of her skirt—once again, she'd seen enough episodes of crime TV in which the innocent moron incriminates himself by picking up the gun that just shot his wife and leaving fingerprints everywhere. She wrapped the fabric around the gun, lifted it and held it toward the window.

She laughed out loud. With better light, she could finally see what was inside that odd canister. And it wasn't bullets.

It was paint. About two dozen little green and yellow balls of paint. She'd seen Mike and Gavin playing this game in the empty yard behind the boathouse. They'd seemed to be having a blast.

She dropped her skirt and held the gun normally. She put her finger on the trigger, testing it.

Nope. She still hated guns. Even this kind.

She was deciding whether to leave it here or bring it to the boathouse when she heard a door open in the back of the building, followed by the sound of voices.

Two people, a man and a woman. They were arguing. Or at least the man was. The woman's voice was so tearful it was hard to tell what she said.

"Just listen to me, listen to me," the man ordered harshly. "Come here, damn it. If you're going to keep me on a short leash, don't you think you owe me—"

Suzie heard a whimper, followed by scuffling noises. Something that must have been made of glass fell with a loud, shattering crash.

"Oh, yes, you will," the man said, and then Suzie recognized the voice. It was Rutledge Coffee.

She picked up the paintball gun and headed to the back of the building.

The people were so noisy she had no trouble finding the right room. The woman was still crying and scuffling. Rutledge had stopped talking, which wasn't a good sign.

Suzie flung open the door.

"Get away from her," she said, pointing the gun at Rutledge. She tried not to let her face show how ridiculous she felt. It was a fairly Rambo moment, the kind of thing she seemed to be doing far too often these days.

Apparently she'd arrived just in time. Rutledge,

who was wearing only a pair of hideous Hawaiian print swim trunks, had the woman up against the wall. Her red face was streaked with tears, and her shirt was torn on one side, exposing a white lace bra. His left forearm was jammed up against her throat, and his right hand was digging around in his trunks.

Disgusting bastard. He was probably so lathered up right now he hadn't even heard her. So she raised her voice.

"I said, get away from her."

"What the—?" He whipped around. His arm fell from the woman's neck, and she bent her head forward, gasping for air. "Who the hell are you and what the hell do you think you're doing?"

"Gosh, Rutledge, I'm hurt that you don't remember me. I'm Suzie Strickland." She aimed the gun at his crotch. His penis had almost escaped, and was peeking pinkly over the waistband of the trunks. "And I think I'm doing my good deed for the day."

"Shit, put that gun down, are you crazy?" He crossed his legs and began shoving his personal parts back where they belonged. She didn't shoot, but she squinted one eye shut, to assure him that, when she did pull the trigger, she had no intention of missing.

"I might be," she said. "But then, I'm not the one slapping people around and trying to rape them, so maybe not."

He tried to laugh, but his voice was wobbly, and Suzie realized he was probably drunk. At noon? God, Rutledge Coffee was grosser than ever.

"Rape? You're still clueless, aren't you, Suzie-freaka? Deb here is my girlfriend. We live together. What kind of games we play is no one's business but ours."

Games? *Like hell.* She glanced at Debra, who still hung her head and wouldn't meet Suzie's eyes. She might be afraid to contradict Rutledge, or she might simply be embarrassed.

"Fine," Suzie said coldly. "You run on home, then, and if Debra wants to *play* any more, she can meet you there."

He was recovering. He obviously had figured out that she held only a paint gun, which couldn't really hurt him. And Debra wasn't disputing his claim that what Suzie saw as a struggle had actually been consensual sex.

So if Rutledge decided to claim that she'd assaulted him, Suzie didn't have much of a defense. She could tell he was growing more confident by the second, sure she wouldn't shoot.

But she had embarrassed him. Like all bullies, he couldn't let that pass.

He smiled, a tipsy attempt to be sexy that failed completely. "Mike told me you'd turned into a looker. Nice legs, he said."

He scanned her body while rubbing at his chest with such drunken self-satisfaction that her finger trembled on the trigger.

"Not bad," he said, returning his gaze to her face. "Kind of flat chested for my taste, but what you do have looks nice and tight. Maybe we could think of a game all three of us could play. Would you like that?"

"Sorry," she said. "Can't. Haven't had my shots."

He flushed. "Suit yourself." He reached out and threaded his arm around Debra's waist. "If you'd rather watch, I'm cool with that."

Suzie cast one last look at Debra. *Come on*, she thought. *Time to get a spine.*

Debra's cheeks were still wet with tears, but finally she met Suzie's gaze.

"Are you any good with that?" She nodded at the paint gun. "Can you hit a very, *very* small target?"

Suzie smiled. *Atta girl.*

"I can try," she said, and pulled the trigger.

MIKE AND SUZIE ENDED UP staying in Firefly Glen much longer than they'd intended, though not, as Suzie had feared, because Gavin got clingy and wouldn't let his father leave.

Gavin clearly loved the Glen. Why not? Mike's parents doted on their only grandchild. The little boy had a tree house, a bicycle, a skateboard and a fort, all on the Frome estate. He also had his own room, complete with TV and video games and about a million books and CDs.

Plus, he had friends all over town. The Fromes had already invited the cousins over, three of the four little Quinn boys, all of whom hero-worshipped Gavin and let him order them around mercilessly. Cordelia Tremaine, Parker and Sarah's daughter, had shown up, too, but she was just about Gavin's age and insisted on being treated as an equal.

Gavin was up in the tree house now, plotting something with Cordelia, while the Quinn rascals climbed up and down the ladder, bringing them soft drinks and popcorn. He didn't even seem aware that his dad was still there.

No, Mike and Suzie hadn't stayed to comfort Gavin. They stayed for the same reason a man lost in the desert might linger at an oasis. They stayed because they felt safe here.

They had all eaten an early dinner on the back lawn, and Mike had gone off with his father to discuss the arrangements one last time. Suzie found herself sitting with Ellen Frome while she graded the music theory workbooks turned in by her piano students.

The room was comfortable, with the sound of the children seeping in through the open window alongside the warm, slanting rays of the approaching sunset.

Maybe too comfortable. Suzie was getting sleepy. Rubbing her eyes, she stood and walked over to where the fresh air could touch her face. The fat summer trees were like black balloons silhouetted against the golden sky.

"I'm glad you're here for Mike right now," Ellen said suddenly. "He needs a loyal friend."

Suzie looked back at the older woman, wondering what to say. She'd always liked Mike's mother. Back in the old days, when Ellen used to chaperone field trips and dances at the high school, she'd been one of the few adults to treat Suzie like a real person. Suzie had always assumed it was because Ellen, too, was a little different. As the wife of a very successful doctor, she didn't need to work, but she always did anyway. "I'd go crazy if I had to lunch for a living," Suzie had once heard her say.

Suzie decided to be honest.

"I'm not sure how much help I'm really going to be," Suzie said. "At first, I was just mad, and I got this fever to set things straight. But deep inside I actually do realize it's not going to be that easy."

Ellen laid down her red pencil and smiled. "You don't have to *do* anything in order to help him. You really believe he's innocent. That's the gift you bring."

"Oh, that." Suzie laughed. "You say it as if believing in him is a choice. But it's not. He *is* innocent. Anyone who knows him knows it. It's just a fact."

Ellen shrugged. "You'd be surprised," she said softly.

Her gentle face, with its dark eyes so like Mike's, looked sad. Suzie wondered if she'd heard something. It made Suzie angry to think it possible. Hadn't this family—one of the most decent in the Glen—been through enough?

"You know," Ellen said, her eyes running thoughtfully over Suzie's face. "Once, a long time ago, David and I thought that maybe you and Mike…"

Suzie held her breath. Again, she wasn't sure what to say. Sometimes all that seemed so long ago—and so little had ever been spoken, really.

When Mike found out that Justine's baby was his, he had come to Suzie's house so emotionally wrecked that she couldn't tell whether her heart was breaking over her own pain or his.

He had tried to tell her something, something about his feelings, but, in her tormented disappointment, she had refused to let him speak. He was going to marry Justine, so *goodbye* and *good luck*. He was going to create a family with that screaming baby and that conniving bitch, and that was the end of it.

Suzie had hated him so much at that moment she had hardly been able to keep from crying.

But Ellen didn't seem to be waiting for an answer. She even seemed to have forgotten what she'd said. She seemed mesmerized by the sight of the children pouring down out of the tree house, laughing and stumbling like puppies.

"But we have Gavin," she went on finally, as if she spoke only to herself. "We have Gavin, so how can we regret any of it?"

She turned to Suzie with bleak eyes. "How can we even regret Justine?"

MIKE HAD ALWAYS THOUGHT that the road away from Firefly Glen seemed shorter than the road leading to it. It was all attitude, of course. He had always longed to reach the Glen, which made it seem to recede like a mirage. And he'd always dreaded returning to Tuxedo Lake, which made it seem to come zooming at him like a bullet.

Tonight, though, he didn't care how long or short the road was. He was simply enjoying the ride.

He and Suzie had talked about all kinds of things. They'd rehashed the scene with Rutledge and Debra—the story still made him laugh, picturing Ledge with a green crotch, although he was disgusted to learn that his friend had sunk so low. They talked about Debra, who they'd left at the boathouse, waiting for her sister to come and pick her up. Debra had refused to file any charges against Ledge, which mystified Suzie, who obviously would have liked to hang the jerk by the thumbs—or whatever—from the nearest roof beam.

Suzie had told him all about her portrait business, which was an amazing success story that didn't, in the end, surprise him. He'd always known she had grit enough to accomplish whatever she dreamed.

But they'd talked about inconsequential things, too, like whether spaniels or terriers were better dogs. He was surprised to learn that after her adored retrievers had died a year or so ago, she hadn't bought another dog. She said it wasn't fair to ask an animal to live in a town house with a little yard. But picturing Suzie without a dog was like picturing Justine without jewelry.

After about an hour, though, Suzie dozed off. At first, she tilted toward her window, but later she shifted, and her head dropped onto his shoulder. Since then, he'd been careful not to move much—he didn't want to make her turn away again.

It had been a long time since anyone but Gavin had leaned against him like this. People really were pack animals, he thought. Just like dogs. The instinct to be close to someone, to share warmth, was born in you and couldn't be wished away.

He drove on, the broken yellow line sliding endlessly under his tires. He reached out carefully and put on a classical station, very low. He felt all his sharp edges softening. He might be leaving Firefly Glen behind, but he had created another little refuge here in this car.

She murmured in her sleep. As if that startled her, she woke up. She lifted her head with a jerk.

"I'm sorry," she said. She wiped at her mouth, as if she feared she might have drooled, though he wouldn't have cared. She blinked a couple of times, and shook her head softly. "I don't know why I'm so tired."

"You probably tossed and turned all night on that lumpy sofa."

"Oh, that's not it. It was comfortable, honestly."

He smiled. He'd slept on that sofa once or twice, and he knew better.

"I should build a real house," he said. "Gavin and I can't stay there forever. It's nice for a boathouse, but he deserves a real home. Something that feels more...permanent."

She had moved to her side of the car, but she looked at him in the darkness. "Why haven't you built one already? You bought that big lot intending to put up a house, didn't you?"

"I guess so," he said. "I bought it right after the divorce. All I was thinking was that I needed to be near

Gavin. I did the boathouse first, because it was cheaper. But somehow I never could make up my mind to start the main house. I can't picture myself living on that lake for the rest of my life."

"Because of what happened to Justine there?"

He thought for a minute. "That was the final straw, I guess. But I've never liked the neighborhood. It's so pretentious. All those cookie-cutter Tudor mansions that were all built the day before yesterday."

"Snob," she said, chuckling. But he thought perhaps she understood. "So then why—"

"Nobody asked me. Tuxedo Lake was Justine's choice, and the house was bought with Alton's money. I was only eighteen. I couldn't possibly supply the splendid setting she thought she deserved."

Suzie made a skeptical raspberry. "All those Frome millions—"

"Belong to my parents. I don't take money from them. That really annoyed Justine. She thought I was punishing her for 'making' me marry her. I think, deep inside, she felt cheated that I wasn't willing to play glamorous-young-jet-setters with her. She knew that, if she hadn't insisted on leaving, I'd still be in Firefly Glen."

"Would you really?" Suzie sounded surprised. "I guess it was different for you. I was more like Justine. I couldn't wait to get away."

He squeezed the steering wheel. "You are *nothing* like Justine. You wanted to leave because you needed freedom to reinvent yourself. You needed scope to realize your talent. She just wanted a snazzy house and new men to cast her spell on."

Suzie was silent for a minute. "Maybe," she said finally. "But she needed some reinventing, too. Maybe she wanted to go someplace where people didn't see her as a fallen star, an ex–beauty queen who got herself in trouble. I certainly wanted to go somewhere people didn't expect me to have purple hair and fangs."

He chuckled. She was wrong, but he didn't argue. Under that feisty temper, Suzie had a big heart and an even bigger conscience. She'd always hated Justine instinctively, but she blamed herself and wasted time trying to dissect and understand her enemy.

The truth was she never could. The two women were from different planets.

"Fang," she said with a sleepy laugh. "God, I hated that."

She shut her eyes again. He drove on in silence, and before he knew it, they were back in Tuxedo Lake.

But what—what were those lights?

All escape from real life was an illusion, and this one was about to come to an end with a bang.

The area around his boathouse was bright with lights, lights that shouldn't have been there. He had a tight budget. He never wasted that kind of electricity when he wasn't home.

His heart thudded hard. Maybe, when Debra's sister had finally come, she'd been careless. Maybe she'd left everything burning.

But of course he knew it couldn't be that simple.

When he tried to turn into his driveway, he couldn't. The entrance was blocked by a trio of black-and-white police vehicles.

An officer pacing the lawn squinted toward Mike's car. It took him less than two seconds to identify it. Immediately he grabbed his walkie-talkie and began muttering into it. Then he loped over and motioned Mike to lower his window.

"Michael Frome?"

Beside Mike, Suzie opened her eyes. She leaned toward him, peering out his window.

"Yes," Mike said. "I'm Mike Frome."

Suzie quietly touched his fingers.

The cop rested his hand at his waist, near the butt of his gun. "I'm going to have to ask you to step out of the vehicle, sir."

Two other men had joined the officer and spread out around the car, as if they thought Mike might suddenly gun the gas and make a run for the Canadian border. He might have smiled at that, if he'd been able to smile at anything.

Run?

Without Gavin?

Hell, no.

Not with Gavin, either. Fromes didn't dodge trouble. He hadn't done anything wrong. Whatever these officers wanted, he would handle it. Somehow, he'd face it down.

He unbuckled his seat belt and turned to Suzie. He didn't know exactly what those officers wanted, but he knew that this might be their last chance to speak privately for a long time.

"Look, I know you've never asked me. And I appreciate that. But I'm going to say it anyhow. *I didn't kill her.*"

She gazed at him a minute, then gave him one of her classic eye-rolls. "Well, duh. But don't waste time telling me, Frome. Get out there and tell *them.*"

CHAPTER NINE

EVEN WHEN THE BANGING and thumping got so loud it made you sick to picture what a mess the policemen must be making, Suzie couldn't help feeling relieved.

A search warrant was a thousand times better than an arrest warrant.

When the cop had handed Mike the folded sheaf of papers, she'd thought her heart might pound its way right out of her chest. She'd been so bloody mad at their dangerous, narrow-minded, half-blind *stupidity* that she'd been afraid she might pounce on the officer like a crazed chimpanzee and try to beat some sense into his thick head.

Mike, on the other hand, had been impossibly calm and dignified. Guess that was what a zillion generations of good breeding could produce. Suzie, who was a scrapper with no pedigree at all, could only force herself to take deep breaths and try to imitate him.

It got easier when she found out the papers were only a search warrant. That was no problem. They could search this boathouse until every policeman on the premises was a hundred years old, and they'd never find anything. There wasn't anything to find.

The officer had escorted Mike and Suzie to the wicker chairs on the porch and left them there with a policeman watching over them. The spot clearly had been strategically chosen, because there were only two ways off this balcony. You could go in through the French doors, which were guarded by a cop with biceps as big as tree trunks, or you could jump off and swim.

Good thing the chairs were comfortable. The search had already taken about four hours.

Mike's lawyer, a sixty-something guy named Rouge who had a white bottlebrush mustache and smart eyes, had arrived within ten minutes of Mike's call, and he'd read the search warrant so thoroughly it had begun to annoy the cop. Afterward, Rouge had taken Mike aside, and they'd murmured privately for several minutes. When Mike returned to sit beside Suzie, his face had been set in tight lines.

He hadn't been willing to discuss it, not with the guard cop standing only five feet away. Suzie had been frustrated, but knew she'd have to wait. You couldn't fight four hundred years of tight-lipped Mayflower genes.

Behind them, the French doors opened. Both she and Mike turned their heads instantly, so she knew that, in spite of his preternatural calm, he was just as tightly wired as she was.

She heard herself growl under her breath. It was Keith Quigley.

Rouge was right behind him, giving Mike a look. He must be a Mayflower stoic, too, because Suzie, who made a living reading faces, had no idea what he was thinking. But her instincts warned her that the presence of the D.A. could not be a good sign. Quigley obviously wasn't there to congratulate Mike on passing the search test with flying colors.

The D.A.'s face was easier to read. He looked smug as hell.

"We're finished," he said. He held out the search warrant. "Here's your copy of the paperwork. We've attached a detailed list of everything we're taking away."

Mike stood and accepted the warrant. He flipped to the list and began to read. Suzie couldn't see the words, but she was shocked by how long the list was.

"The headboard of my bed?" Mike looked up, clearly stunned. "Why?"

"We found smears of blood there."

"The *hell* you did."

"You can't spot them with the naked eye," Quigley explained politely. "But when we sprayed with luminal, the area clearly fluoresced. Your attorney was present."

Mike looked over at Rouge, who nodded, again without expression. "A small spot," he said. "It could be anything."

Suzie saw Mike inhale carefully, then return to the list.

He looked up again almost immediately. "Master bathroom sink trap?" His voice was as cold as the plumbing at the North Pole.

"That's correct," Quigley said.

Suzie practically had to clamp her hand over her mouth to keep from jumping in. So they must have found a spot of blood in the sink trap. So what? Mike did hard, physical work for a living, and he had a rambunctious ten-year-old son. They probably cleaned more cuts and scrapes in this house than in a hospital.

Besides, if it were Justine's blood, it would have been sitting in that sink trap for more than two years. Was that possible? With water going through it several times every day? Unfortunately, she had to admit she had no idea what the life span of a blood spatter actually was.

Mike kept reading. His body was so tense that Suzie could feel heat and vibrations humming off him, the way you could tell from a distance that a piece of electrical equipment was plugged in and running.

Without warning, Mike let the paper fall and lurched forward. "You son of a bitch! You took my son's baseball bat? You think I killed my son's mother with his *own* baseball bat?"

Rouge stepped between the two men. "Settle down, Mike. He's just doing his job."

Mike had locked eyes with Quigley, and Suzie felt sorry for the pudgy little man, who had to tilt his neck to maintain the contact.

"This isn't a job, Rouge." Mike didn't look at his attorney. He enunciated slowly and clearly right into Quigley's face. "This is a vendetta."

"Oh, really?" Quigley narrowed his eyes. "Tell me, Frome. Do you still maintain that your ex-wife has never been inside this boathouse?"

"Don't answer that, Mike." Rouge held up a hand, but it was too late. Mike was blind to anyone except Quigley.

"Of course I do," he said. "Justine never set foot in this house."

Quigley smiled, and Suzie's heart skipped a beat. It was a terrible, knowing smile.

"Your neighbor Mrs. Cready says otherwise. She says she saw you bring Justine here on three separate occasions."

Mike shook his head. "That's bullshit, and you know it. Mrs. Cready is ninety years old. She can't see past her own nose."

"Mike," Rouge warned, obviously disturbed by the level of his client's hostility. "Be smart."

"I *am* being smart," Mike said. "I'm smart enough to know what this is really all about."

"Three times," Quigley repeated. "If she was here three times, she will have left something behind. We vacuumed all over your bedroom. We'll find a hair, a fingernail—"

Mike pushed forward again, as if Rouge's body, firmly planted between them, wasn't even there. He thrust out his index finger and shoved it into the D.A.'s shoulder.

"I'm on to you, Quigley. This isn't about how many times Justine was in my bed," he said. "It's about how many times she was in *yours*."

The little man puffed up, and his resemblance to a bullfrog grew so strong Suzie was sure his next sound would be a croak.

"Why, you slanderous bastard." Quigley's eyes bulged, and his face reddened. "Your wife was never in my bed. *Never*."

"I know." Mike stepped back with a cruel smile. "And *that* is what this is all about."

THAT NIGHT, the dream changed.

The dreamer tossed, trying to wake up. *Oh, God…* He was frightened.

This wasn't right. This wasn't the way it had really happened.

This time, when he heard the girl whimpering, he began to sweat under his mask. He rocked in place, terrified. His bowels began to liquefy, because he felt himself about to be brave, and he didn't want to be brave.

This wasn't the place for courage.

This was the place for weakness and cruelty, for deviance and pain. That's why each of them had come, because down here they could admit that they had needs, needs that shamed them above ground, in the light.

The rules required silence. This was not his time to speak or touch. He was a watcher only. And yet a protest, which had built unseen somewhere deep inside him, began welling up in his throat like vomit. He tried to choke it back, swallowing spastically, but it continued to rise.

Inside the box, the girl began to weep.

"No!" he cried. "Let her go!"

The other black masks turned toward him. He couldn't see their faces, not even the color of their eyes.

But he felt their hatred.

"I'm sorry," he said, but it was too late. They had already decided. They dragged him toward the box. They tore off his robe, and made him stand naked in front of them. They saw him, saw his ordinary face that had no beauty, his flaccid body that had no power, his withered heart that had no love.

They knew him. They knew why he was here.

"Please, no," he said, just as the girl had said before him. But they took his arms and legs. They opened the box and put him in.

It was all darkness and the smell of fear. He felt the walls. He tried to pray.

He couldn't find the girl, though the box was not large. She should have been manacled, hand and foot, to the floor. It frightened him that she seemed to be gone. This wasn't right. This wasn't how it had really happened.

He touched the steel cuffs that had been drilled into the floor, and, in the way that impossible things often happen in dreams, suddenly the cuffs were around his wrists. He was spread-eagled where the girl should have been.

He heard a hissing sound, and she slowly materialized out of the shadows. He writhed on the cold stone floor, sickened by the sight.

God, what had they done to her? Her eyes were red, and her mouth was bloody. Her body was tattooed with bruises. There was a large hole on the side of her head.

That's when he knew it was Justine, and she was dead.

She came toward him, though he begged her to stop, to get away, please, please….

She was deaf to him. She knelt between his legs. When she smiled, blood dripped onto his thighs.

"The rules require silence," she said.

CHAPTER TEN

MIKE WASN'T HUNGRY. He wasn't sleepy. He didn't want to talk. He damn sure didn't want to clean up the mess the cops had made of his bedroom.

So he'd decided to do the only thing he could. He was a physical man, so he got physical. He went running.

Suzie insisted on coming along, saying she needed to let off some steam, too. He believed her. She'd sat beside him through the search, and, though she hadn't spoken up, she'd crackled and popped with anger the whole time.

He gave her a pair of Gavin's sneakers, which were a little too big, but nothing a double pair of socks wouldn't cure. Locking the house behind them, they climbed down the jagged cedar staircase to the lake and began to run.

It was one in the morning, so they were the only ones out here. He rarely ran at night anymore, because of Gavin. He used to do it, back in Firefly Glen, and he remembered now how much he'd loved the feeling of being alone in a silent and mysterious world.

It was a warm night with a breeze that had picked up pine scents as it came down over the wooded cliff edge. The lake was like a black mirror under the nearly full moon.

He usually ran once around the lake, a loop of about four miles. He wasn't sure Suzie could keep up—she'd never been much into athletics, as he remembered—but those long, boyish legs surprised him. She kept pace with him, and though her breath came fast and hard by the halfway mark, it was no more labored than his.

They stopped there for a breather. It was near his old house, which was so dark it looked exactly like the ghost house it was. He paused, his hands on his knees, and stared at it. Even the gardener's wing, which was connected to the main house by a porte cochere, looked abandoned, though he knew Alton had kept Richie Graham on as caretaker and gardener.

Suzie pulled up beside him. She wore no makeup or jewelry. She'd scooped her hair back into a rubber band, and the contours of her naked face were exposed. So that's what natural beauty was, he thought. Her high, jutting cheekbones had the graceful strength of a water-smoothed rock. Her eyes had the liquid soul of the lake.

She was looking at the house, too, as she swabbed a sheen of perspiration from her neck. After a minute she grunted softly and bent to retie her sneaker.

"Well, I hate to be the one to tell you," she said, "but that house is just plain creepy."

"Yep," he said. "That's what I always thought."

Suddenly she straightened, frowning. "What was that?"

He looked around. "I don't see anything," he said, though a frisson of discomfort skimmed across his spine.

Some of the cliff faces had large stromatolites, a kind of fossil that created pale designs in the rock, domes and arches and stripes that seemed to glow if the moonlight struck them just right. Add to that the constant winking of the granite, and the cliffs could seem half-alive at night.

"No…it's voices." She squinted, as if that could make her ears sharper. "Who lives in that house, that smaller one on the left?"

"The Stotts," he said. "Phil and Judy. She's the principal at Gavin's school. They're a very nice—"

And then he heard them, too. Phil and Judy were outside, near the edge of their property where it sloped down to the lake, though the angle of the bluff rendered them invisible from the beach.

The breeze blew the voices toward the lake, or Mike and Suzie would never have heard them. As it was, only the occasional word came through—and the unmistakable tone of hurt and anger.

"Hate you" and *"be ashamed,"* both in Judy's tones. And then, in Phil's voice, *"…love to a fish."*

Suzie wrinkled her nose. "Did you say *'very nice'*?"

Mike shook his head. He'd never heard the Stotts argue before. But then, it had been four years since he'd lived here. Even a good marriage could go bad in that amount of time.

"You even care?" floated toward them on an undercurrent of tears. And then *"my heart."*

Suzie made a disgusted sound, though she kept it low. "And *that,* my friend, is why I don't intend to get married. Ever." She tilted her head in the direction of the voices. "You might as well just hire someone to come in daily and beat you with a stick."

"Not all marriages are like that."

"Some of them are worse." She gave him a look, daring him to deny it.

He couldn't, of course.

"Okay. You're right. Some marriages are hell. Mine certainly was. And it looks as if there's trouble in the Stott paradise, too. But what about my folks? Or yours? What about Natalie and Matthew, for Pete's sake? They've been married ten years now, and I'll bet they still have sex on the roof."

Suzie grinned. "Yeah, but they're going to have to cut it out. The last time, a helicopter flew over, and the pilot really got an eyeful. Apparently he darn near crashed into a tree."

"It's disgusting…" Judy Stott's voice was reaching high C.

Mike grimaced and decided to abandon the argument. What a joke for him to be standing here defending marriage, anyhow. Suzie was right. The institution was as appealing as life in a maximum security penitentiary.

"Let's get going," he said, "before things really get ugly."

Suzie nodded and began to run. He deliberately lagged behind for a few yards, enjoying the view. Sometimes he still found it hard to believe this was Suzie.

What had become of that gangly string bean he used to know? Nothing made him more aware of the lost years than looking at this graceful woman in front of him. They really had been just kids, hadn't they, back in Firefly Glen? She had been a puppy, cute and clumsy and falling over her own feet. Now she was a greyhound, long and lean and unconsciously elegant—

And then, without warning, she fell to the ground in a heap. She let loose a small cry, followed by a string of curses. So much for the purebred greyhound.

He hurried up to her. "Are you okay?"

"Damn it to hell," she said, rubbing at her ankle and glaring up at him. "I can*not* tell you how much I did *not* want to do that."

"Hey, it's okay—"

"It is *not*. Now I'm all muddy, and it's all your fault. I could tell you were watching me, and it made me nervous. Plus, there was this rock in the sand. And these shoes don't really fit—"

"Wow." He laughed. "That's an impressive list of excuses for one little stumble."

Ignoring him, she sat cross-legged on the sand for a minute, and then suddenly, she began untying her shoes. She took them off and set them side by side on the ground. She peeled off her socks, too, and stuffed them inside. He thought she'd decided to run barefoot, but when she stood, she gave him a grin and then turned and made a beeline for the lake.

"Hey," he called softly. "What are you doing?"

She was thigh deep already. She splashed water out toward him with her palms. "What does it look like I'm doing, genius? Playing checkers?"

He shook his head. She really was a loose cannon. "Is it cold?"

"Not once you—" She shuddered as the water rose up around her hips. "Once you get used to it."

While he watched, she lowered her body, inch by inch, grinning at him the whole time, until she was completely submerged. She stayed under for nearly a minute, and then she popped up about six yards to the right with a splashing whoop of excitement.

"It's wonderful! Come on in! It's the perfect cure for what ails you."

He hesitated. It was doubtful that a midnight swim

could solve even one of his many problems, but on the other hand, could it hurt? He kicked off his sneakers, yanked off his socks and splashed in to join her.

For the next fifteen minutes they were kids again. They splashed each other sophomorically and grabbed each other's ankles underwater, creating hilarities of happy panic that were quickly smothered so that they didn't wake the neighbors. They jumped and dived like dolphins in the moonlight, and then competed for the breath-holding award.

Finally, they tired themselves out. They floated on their backs, counting stars.

He found Orion. She found a cluster of stars that looked like Elvis's ear.

Mike turned his head and found her profile, outlined in moonlight. "Hey," he said. "Want to hear about my other house?"

She twisted her whole body toward him, which of course made her feet fall down. She got a mouthful of water, spit it out and grimaced. "What house?"

"The house I used to think I'd live in when I grew up."

"In Firefly Glen?"

He shrugged. "Maybe. It could be anywhere. I was going to build it myself. Do you want to hear about it or not?"

"You bet I do," she said. She situated herself back into the perfect floating position and shut her eyes. "Okay, I'm ready. Don't do that guy thing and say, 'well, it's big and it's blue' and think that tells me anything. I need lots of details if my mental picture is going to be accurate."

He smiled. She had floated into him, and her shoulder was touching his. "I wouldn't dream of short-changing your mental picture. But I can't start if you won't shut up."

She made a zipping motion across her mouth.

"Okay. When I was sixteen," he said, "I decided I wanted to be an architect. So I sat down and drew myself the perfect house."

The water ebbed and flowed gently against his body. Her fingers drifted against his, then slipped away. He blinked water from his eyes and fixed his gaze on Orion. "It was just a kid's fantasy, really. I knew exactly zilch about houses. It was kind of a mishmash of movies I'd seen and books I'd read."

"Like The Great Gatsby's house," she said.

"No, not like that. Hush up and listen. It had three stories. It was covered in gray shingles, with dark green shutters and two brick chimneys puffing out marshmallow-colored smoke. It was big, but not too big—just big enough that, when the whole family was home, every room would be filled with laughter. It had an old-fashioned blue kitchen, a large, sunny family room where everyone would always want to gather, and bedrooms for at least four kids."

"Four kids!" Suzie twitched, sending ripples of lake water over him. She immediately grew contrite and zipped her lips shut again.

"Sorry," she mumbled through clenched teeth. "Go on."

"At the top I put a light-filled attic room. That was where I would design my skyscrapers, I thought, when I became an architect. And there were windows every-where, big windows that always glistened—"

"Hope there's a maid in this picture. Do you know what it takes to keep a million windows glist—"

"Suzie."

"Sorry."

"Windows that always glistened, and porches with views of the mountains. A green lawn that stretched out for acres and wild climbing roses that went up trellises and tried to grow right in through the open windows."

"What color are the roses?"

He turned his head. "Are you making fun of my house?"

She scowled indignantly and fanned her feet to keep them up. "No. It's just that I think in color. I have to know what the roses look like, or I'll have this big canvas-colored spot in the picture."

He thought for a minute. He'd never seen the roses as any particular color. He knew what they smelled like, though. They smelled like the sweet spot under his imaginary wife's ear, and the powder beside Gavin's crib.

They smelled like love. What color was that?

"White," he said. That had been the color of Gavin's crib. "The roses are white."

She was silent, finally, and he wondered if she could see it. He had, once. He'd seen it so clearly he hadn't even considered the possibility that the dream might not come true. Of course, back then he'd assumed he was eternally golden, the beloved son of the influential Frome family. He had assumed that life would just hand him whatever he wanted, gift wrapped.

He felt the swish of cool currents as she let her feet drop. She stood quite still, just inches away, and looked at him.

"Why didn't you ever build it, Mike? What happened to that lovely dream?"

He let his feet fall, too. They touched the muddy

lake bottom, and he knew that, once again, the respite was over. He wasn't golden anymore. He didn't always get what he wanted.

What he wanted right now was to kiss Suzie Strickland, who looked like a water fairy, with her long dark hair pouring down her back and her dark eyes reflecting silver shards of moonlight.

But he wasn't going to get that, either.

"You know what happened," he said. "Justine happened."

DEBRA LET HERSELF into the apartment quietly. She'd seen Ledge's car in the parking lot, so she knew he must be here clearing out his things.

They hadn't spoken since the paintball episode at the office. She'd left with Suzie, and her last words had been, "Be out of the apartment by Friday."

She'd stayed the past two nights with her sister in Albany, after making her sister promise not to tell their mother. She neither knew nor cared where Ledge had stayed.

Her sister, Lizzie, who had six kids and called her husband *pookie*, nonetheless always turned into a raging man-hater where Rutledge was concerned. When Lizzie heard the paintball story, she'd toasted Super Suzie with a baby bottle, and then spent twenty minutes waxing creative about where Ledge's various body parts should be placed.

When Debra announced that she was going back to Tuxedo Lake, Lizzie had shaken her head, murmured the words *hopeless case*, and offered Debra her choice of a can of pepper spray or a shotgun.

Debra had taken the pepper spray. But she was starting to think she should have chosen the gun. She'd just received a cell phone call from a reporter at the Albany newspaper. Because Debra had found the body, the reporter hoped she could confirm a rumor going around about something the police had found on Justine Millner's body.

Debra didn't think so…she hadn't seen very much… she'd been in shock…what had they supposedly found?

A gold ankle bracelet, with a charm in the shape of a pair of large lips.

The words were still ringing in Debra's ears as she entered the apartment.

Everything was quiet. Ledge must be in the bedroom. The living room was empty.

She slipped the pepper spray into her pocket. Her fingers weren't quite steady, and she wondered if she was making the right decision. Her sister, Lizzie, her best friend, Judy Stott, and even the nice reporter from Albany, all would have told her to go straight to the police.

But how could she do that?

She had been in love with Rutledge for three years. She'd lived with him, shared his bed. She'd loaned him money when he was overdrawn and held his head when he puked up the one six-pack too many.

They'd made each other laugh, and they'd made each other crazy.

So didn't he deserve a chance to explain himself? Even if he had given Justine that awful anklet, it didn't mean he had killed her.

She took off her shoes so that she'd make as little noise as possible walking down the hall. She wanted to know what he was really doing in there. If there was a woman with him, she'd drown them both in pepper spray and then she'd head straight for the cops. She wouldn't even stop at red lights.

But when she opened the door, there was no woman.

The room was filled with dozens and dozens of red roses. In vases, wrapped in paper, in boxes and scattered across the furniture. Rutledge himself was curled up in the only clear space on the bed, sound asleep.

The sight brought stupid tears to her eyes. She was such a sucker for a good-looking bad boy, and this one really was something special. His blond hair needed a cut, and his bare, bronze chest was so sexy....

She knelt beside the bed. She picked up one of the roses and held it to her nose. A needle-sharp thorn pricked her finger.

"Ledge," she whispered. "Ledge, wake up."

He stretched, but didn't wake. He murmured something. It sounded like "baby," which was his generic endearment, sprinkled thoughtlessly over every female from eight to eighty. She couldn't quite convince herself that he was necessarily dreaming of her.

"Ledge, wake up. I have something important to ask you."

He sighed and rolled away from her, scratching his chest. Then her words seemed to sink in. He rolled back with a jerk. "Deb?"

"Hi," she said. She gave him a minute to fully wake up.

"I missed you," he said. He smiled, which morphed into a yawn. "Do you like the roses? I wanted to do something to show you how sorry I am."

"They're pretty," she said. She didn't ask him how he'd paid for them. If he'd used her credit card, she didn't want to know that right now. "Ledge, sit up. I have to ask you something."

He yawned, but he did what she asked. A suddenly objective part of her noted that he was always easy to get along with after a fight. Until the next fight.

"What's up?" He picked up a rose and tickled her upper arm with it suggestively. "Besides me, that is."

Could she really be getting over him? Once, that would have sent sexy shivers through her torso. Now it just felt annoying. She moved it away with her hand.

"This is serious, Ledge. I'm going to ask you something, and I don't want you to give me a snow job. I need a straight answer, okay?"

He frowned. He obviously knew that if the rules excluded snow jobs, he was at a disadvantage. "Okay," he said. "But why are you acting all Gestapo all of a sudden? It's going to kill the mood, and these roses weren't cheap."

Kill the mood? If he only knew what kind of mood she was really in. He'd be lucky if she didn't kill *him*.

"Okay, listen, Ledge, because this is important. Two years ago, I saw something in your sock drawer."

He laughed. "Sounds like the opening line of a *Monty Python* episode."

She didn't even smile. "It was an ankle bracelet, Ledge. It had a charm shaped like a pair of big lips."

His smile dropped, and her heart sank along with it. She knew him the way a mother knows her little boy, and this subject made him nervous.

He reared back in a huffy indignation that wasn't at all convincing—especially coming a beat too late. "You were snooping around in my private things?"

"Yes," she said. It was easier than arguing the point. Did washing a man's laundry and putting it away constitute snooping? Or was it just typical doormat behavior?

"I need to know what happened to that ankle bracelet, Ledge. You didn't give it to me."

"No, I didn't," he said stiffly.

"What did you do with it?"

"What do you care? You wouldn't have liked it. You would have thought it was vulgar."

"It was vulgar. But what did you do with it? Where is that anklet now?"

"I—" He glowered at her for a long moment. Then, with a low curse, he stood. He had unbuttoned his jeans, and they sagged around his hips as he walked out of the bedroom, deliberately stepping on roses whenever he could.

She followed him, her hand in her pocket. He stalked into the laundry room and yanked his toolbox down from the plastic shelf over the dryer. It hit the metal lid with a violent clatter.

He threw open the box and began to dig around. She had no idea what he was doing, but if his hand came out holding a nail gun, or a hammer, or even a screwdriver that was a little too big, he was getting a faceful of pepper spray.

He didn't pull out any of those things.

He pulled out a little gold ankle bracelet, with a charm shaped like a pair of very big lips.

CHAPTER ELEVEN

SUZIE WOKE WITH HER HEART in her throat, sitting bolt upright on the sofa. The telephone was ringing.

Ordinarily she loved the sound of a phone. She supposed it meant that deep inside she was an optimist. She always secretly believed any call might be more business, a new commission, a million-dollar sweep-stakes win.

But here in the living room of Mike's boathouse, which was still upended from the clumsy hands of the police, it sounded like a scream ripping the air.

Who was it? His lawyer? D.A. Quigley? Gavin?

What was wrong now?

Mike must have answered it upstairs, because after the first ring it fell silent. She sat on the sofa, holding the blanket in one fist, waiting for her heart to settle back into her chest. How had Mike had survived two years of this kind of uncertainty and dread? After only about a week, all it took to send her into cardiac arrest was one ringing phone.

When he didn't come down to fill her in, she decided to go up and ask. She might have closet optimism tendencies, but she was not hiding any secret talent for patience.

Because her clothes had still been wet from their swim, she'd worn one of his old T-shirts to bed. She checked her pale reflection in the glass of the French doors just to be sure she didn't look as if she were staging a trashy come-on, but no way. The shirt had long sleeves, no shape, and it was so long it skimmed the tops of her knees.

Besides, washed-out, past-its-prime gray was not her color.

She went up, but at the top of the stairs she hesitated. Both doors were shut. Which one was Mike's room?

She knocked on the one that overlooked the lake. She leaned her head in toward the door and whispered, "Mike?"

Behind her, the other door opened. Feeling like a fool, she twirled around and smiled sheepishly.

"Morning," she said. "I was just wondering who was on the phone."

He was tucking in his shirt. "It was my dad," he said.

Why was he getting dressed? It couldn't be more than nine, and they'd had only about four hours sleep. "Is anything wrong? Is Gavin okay?"

"He's fine," he said. "But I have to drive up to Firefly Glen. Apparently he had a disturbing nightmare last night. He told my dad he's had it before, ever since Justine disappeared. It's all about being in a tunnel and meeting a scary man."

Suzie felt her pulse accelerate. "A man? What man?"

"He says he hasn't ever seen the man in real life. He thinks he's just a nightmare. And maybe it is. But—"

"But of course we have to check it out! I think my clothes are almost dry. I'll hurry."

"No, I really think you—"

She set her jaw. "Damn it, Mike. This isn't fair. I'm involved here. I *care*. Don't try to shut me out now."

He shook his head, and she thought she heard him chuckle.

"It sure doesn't take much to detonate that temper of yours, does it? I was *going* to say I think you need some fresh things. I was going to suggest we run by your apartment first and pick up a suitcase."

"Oh." She tugged at his T-shirt and looked down the hall, toward nothing. "Oh, well, then, never mind. I'll just go back downstairs and…" She grimaced. "And hit my head against the wall for a while."

"Okay," he said, turning back into his room. "But remember, this is only a boathouse, so go easy. That's a mighty hard head you've got there."

"I HONESTLY DON'T KNOW who he is. It's not a real person, Dad. It's just a nightmare. Granddad was over-reacting. It's scary, but it's no big deal."

Gavin sat on the picnic table just behind the Fromes' house, in the shade of a hundred-year-old maple tree. He had his portable video game on the bench seat next to him, and a plate of tuna-salad sand-wiches—his favorite—in front of him.

Childhood in Firefly Glen. Mike remembered it well.

But, even so, Gavin looked miserable. Mike's chest tightened. The hardest thing in life was watching your kid hurt and not being able to stop it.

"How often have you had this dream? When did it start?"

Gavin shrugged. "I don't know. Not all that often, just when I'm worried about something. Or missing

Mom real bad." He toyed with his sandwich and blinked hard. "I guess it began right after Mom left, but I can't really remember. I'm sorry."

Mike touched the boy's shoulder. "You don't need to be sorry. It's just that—look, Gav, you understand that we don't know yet who hurt Mom, right?"

"*Hurt* her?" Gavin frowned. "Somebody *killed* her, Dad. I'm not a little kid. You can say the real word to me."

This wasn't a little kid? Mike looked at his son with an aching heart. That unflawed skin, those blue eyes as clear and shiny as new marbles. Those hairless, bony arms and legs that seemed to be stretching even as you looked at them. Hell, yes, this was a little kid.

"I'm sorry," Mike said. "I didn't mean to be patronizing. It's just that it's very important for us to find out who did it."

He saw the flicker in Gavin's eyes. *Did it?* Another euphemism, but he couldn't help it—he wouldn't just toss the word around. *Murder. Kidnap. Kill.* Those were not normal words. They weren't words a ten-year-old should have to be blasé about.

Even adults should think those words were evil.

Gavin was watching him carefully. "But aren't the police supposed to find out who did it?"

"Of course. They're looking, too. But they have a lot of crimes to investigate, so I want to help them if I can. And sometimes dreams—"

Suzie, who had been in the house with Mike's parents, appeared at the back door. She had her arms full of...

From this distance, Mike couldn't quite make out what it was. But he figured he was going to find out. She gave them a wave, and began strolling toward them. She was wearing another of those long, soft dresses that seemed to be her new uniform, replacing the baggy black sweatshirt and black leggings of high school.

She looked great.

Gavin tapped his arm. "Dreams are what?"

Mike refocused. "Dreams can be completely imaginary, or they can be all mixed up with bits and pieces from our real lives."

Gavin's eyes darkened. "You think the guy in my nightmare might be *real*?"

Suzie had reached the picnic table. She exchanged a quick glance with Mike, then smiled at Gavin.

"Hey, there," she said, her tone matter-of-fact in that special Suzie way. She plopped a bunch of colored pencils and paper on the table. "I need your help with something."

"Yeah?" Gavin looked interested. "What?"

"A picture," she said. "Here's the deal. Just in case the rat fink in your dream is a real-life rat fink and not just a nightmare bogeyman, I want you to describe him for me. I'll draw what you say, and maybe we can get a picture of this guy for our own personal 'wanted' poster."

She held up a piece of paper. "Sound good?"

Gavin nodded. "You mean like when I was at the police station, and I described the man at the video store, and the artist did a picture on the computer?"

"Yeah, only without the computer." She picked up a black pencil. "Now, if I get it wrong, you've got to say so right away. Don't worry about hurting my feelings. I know I am good at drawing, so if I don't get it right, that probably means you didn't describe it right. I need a lot of detail." She winked at him. "Boys aren't very good with detail, I'm afraid."

Gavin laughed. He knew he was being goaded, but his budding male ego still couldn't let it pass. "I'm *great* with detail. I can always remember every single thing about my video game characters, and their weapons, and their skills—"

"Good, then. Let's get started."

Mike took a backseat from then on. He was fascinated by this experiment, and by the way Suzie had managed to make it sound fun instead of scary. She hadn't said anything very different from what Mike had said. So it must have been accomplished with body language and tone. She simply projected sassy, bogeymen-can-kiss-my-backside confidence. She always had.

He lounged backward on the bench, leaning on his elbows on the picnic table to help communicate his ease and relaxation. As often as he could, he tilted his head and stole a glimpse of the sketch over his shoulder.

There were plenty of do-overs and giggle fits, but never once did Suzie lose patience, and never once did Gavin lose his nerve.

Watching her nimble fingers making the pencil fly across the paper, and her mobile mouth pursing with concentration, then twisting with amusement, Mike realized there might be a lot Suzie-freaka could teach him about life. He knew plenty about how to maximize the good times. But face it, he stunk at handling setbacks.

When things started to quiet down, he realized they must be getting close.

"What do you think?" Chewing her lower lip, Suzie angled the paper toward Gavin. "Mouth like that?"

A shimmer of anxiety had returned to Gavin's face.

He hesitated, swallowing several times in quick succession. "I don't know. It's almost right, but not. It's hard to be sure, because in my dream I'm really scared. He's always smiling, so maybe if you could make that mouth smile."

"Smiling..." Suzie erased the mouth quickly and began again. "Ugly smile? Mean smile? Twisted smile? Wide smile? One-sided? Dimples? I need details here, buddy. Come on, you promised me details."

Gavin began jerking his leg, pumping his heel nervously on the ground. "I don't know. No dimples. And it's mean, but not *obvious* mean, you know? It's not twisted, but it's really long, side to side. It's kind of gross...." He closed his eyes and scrunched them tightly, as if he were forcing himself to remember.

Suzie's hand kept moving.

"I know!" Gavin's eyes shot open, and he jumped on the seat. "Wet! That's what his smile is! It's wet!"

Suzie's hand froze.

Giving up the pretense of nonchalance, Mike turned all the way around. He couldn't see the paper well enough from this angle, so he stood and walked to their side of the table.

He met Suzie's gaze. Then she turned back to the table, picked up a silver pencil and began adding tiny highlights at the edges of the long, reptilian mouth. It looked exactly like light bouncing off saliva, and something turned over in his stomach.

"Like that?" Suzie's voice was utterly neutral.

Gavin looked at the picture for a long, silent moment. He seemed to be holding back, too, as if he needed to keep his fear under control.

Then, finally, he turned to Mike.

"That's him, Dad," he said. "That's exactly what the guy in my dream looks like." He sneaked his hand into Mike's. "See why it's so scary?"

Mike did, indeed.

The man in the picture was District Attorney Keith Quigley.

SUZIE SPENT THE NIGHT at the boathouse again. Mike had to do some work on a dock project the next day, and she'd offered to help clear up some of the mess the cops had left behind.

She began as soon as he left for work, and it didn't take as long as she'd thought. Most of the chaos was superficial, just books tossed out of cases and boxes of old checks and carefully folded blueprints dislodged from the backs of closets.

She tried not to pry, but she couldn't help learning things as she worked. Mike apparently liked classic detective novels, biographies and books about the sea. He had an old copy of *Treasure Island* that he'd put his name in twenty years ago. The cute, looping handwriting showed he'd just learned cursive. The "Frome" sloped steeply up, until it almost went right off the page.

Best of all, the book had a marker at chapter twelve. She'd bet anything he was reading this to Gavin right now.

Frankly, the sheer volume of books surprised her. Once upon a time, she would have bet big money that Mike the Dumb Jock didn't know how to read.

By midafternoon things were in pretty good shape. She'd rehung the pictures and refolded the clothes in the drawers. She'd even arranged Gavin's impressive display of action figures on the windowsill. She didn't

know how he usually staged them, so she improvised
an intergalactic battle. She actually enjoyed that part.
However, when she found herself making vibro-flash
star-blaster noises, she decided she should call it a
day.

She forced herself to call her mother, though she
didn't enjoy the grilling she always got. Her mother
was clearly torn between the thrill that Suzie was
hanging out with one of the prestigious Fromes, and
the anxiety that she might be hanging out with a
murderer. She was glad when at about two o'clock, the
doorbell rang and she had to hang up.

But…should she answer it? She hesitated, unsure
what Mike would want her to do. If she went all the
way to the door so that she could look out the side-
lights, she could be seen, too. The last thing she
wanted, until she and Mike decided what to do with
the information Gavin had provided, was to get into a
tangle with Quigley.

She and Mike had accepted that, if they took the
sketch to the police, they'd be laughed right out of the
station.

The police would undoubtedly contend that she'd
led Gavin to the identification. Could she deny it?
When Gavin talked, maybe Suzie's inner eye had
conjured up Quigley because she hated him. Hundreds
of other men looked like that. Her sketch wasn't
evidence of anything except her antipathy.

In the end, she decided to answer the door, and to
her relief, it wasn't Quigley. It was a woman—and she
looked strangely familiar. More importantly, she didn't
really look as if she might be one of Mike's girlfriends.
She was in her midthirties, maybe, and had a distinctly
matronly look.

Suzie opened the door and smiled. "Hi," she said. "Mike's not here right now. I'm Suzie. Can I help you?"

The woman was attractive, in a favorite-aunt sort of way. She wore a very professional gray suit and sensible heels, but the suit was too expensive for a door-to-door salesman, or a religious pamphlet peddler.

She held out her hand. "I'm Judy Stott."

Judy Stott? Suzie tried to remember where she'd heard that name.

"I came by to update Mike about Gavin's incident on the playground last month."

Oh, yeah. Judy Stott. The next-door neighbor, the lady who had been arriving to see Mayor Millner just as Suzie was leaving that first day. Judy Stott was the principal at Gavin's school. She was also the one Suzie had heard arguing at the lake last night.

Right now, the woman sounded one hundred percent professional and composed—nothing like the angry, tearful voice that had floated toward them from the bluff.

"Oh," Suzie said, pretending as if she knew all about Gavin's "incident," though she'd never heard of it. "Come on in. Mike's out on a job right now. Would you like to tell me, and I can pass it along?"

The woman looked dubious. She obviously took herself very seriously. "I suppose I could. It isn't anything confidential, after all."

She held out a sealed envelope. "This is just a copy of the official incident report. As you know Gavin was seen talking to a young man near the fence of the playground about three weeks ago. We looked into it at the time, and determined it was nothing alarming, but this morning Mike called and asked for more details. I fully understand that he's overly anxious right now, with the untimely discovery of Justine's body and—"

"Yes," Suzie said, already bored with this woman and her orgy of unnecessary syllables, but still interested in anything related to Gavin. She was also curious about this woman's personality. Was she likely to have agreed to participate in Mayor Millner's "Frame Mike Frome" campaign?

"Don't you want to come in?"

Judy Stott hesitated, but then she stepped over the threshold as carefully as she might have stepped over a snake. What was the deal with this woman? It was as if she didn't move or speak or even breathe without sorting through the possible legal consequences of her actions.

"At any rate, it's all here," she said, putting the envelope on the coffee table. "As I said, I understand his concern, and I want him to rest assured I've interviewed everyone involved, from Gavin's teachers to his classmates. I'm satisfied that the young man who approached Gavin that day is not a stranger at all. He's a college student who lives near the school. We know his family well. He was looking for his lost dog."

The woman paused. Suzie frowned. Mike hadn't mentioned this. She wondered how many lines of investigation he'd already cast into the water without mentioning it to her.

"Of course, if Mike is still concerned that it might have any bearing on the recent situation, he can feel free to call the school. Naturally, my secretary has instructions to put him through whenever he calls."

"Thanks," Suzie said politely. She was definitely sensing that this woman was nervous about something—probably just fearful that Mike might somehow try to tie the school to Justine's unsavory death. That made her curious. How on earth would he do that? "Would you like a cup of coffee?"

"No, I really should be going. Please tell Mike I'm sorry I missed him." She held out her hand. "It was very nice to have met you, Miss—"

Suzie laughed. Jeez, what a priss. "Please. Call me Suzie."

The other woman's smile looked pained, as if she found that unthinkable.

Suzie wasn't sorry to see the woman go. Pompous people always rubbed her fur the wrong way. But, if you thought about it, Judy Stott's ramrod-stiff personality could be a good thing. Any elementary school principal who took herself that seriously was unlikely to participate in Millner's frame.

Suzie wondered who Millner had turned to, after both she and Judy Stott told him to get lost. Quigley? That would be a risk.

The gardener, maybe? That scruffy stud hadn't exactly looked as if his scruples were screwed on tight enough to chafe.

Maybe she'd go have a little chat with the guy. He had a weakness that should be easy to exploit.

And it wasn't just women. His major weakness was that he liked himself way too much.

She could exploit both. She didn't look half bad in this T-shirt. If she purred like a bimbo and admired his big, strong shovel, he'd probably tell her anything.

She thought about calling Mike, but decided just to leave him a note.

He'd called Judy Stott without telling her. If he could do a little investigative moonlighting, so could she.

CHAPTER TWELVE

DEBRA HADN'T HAD A SALE in three weeks. She didn't even have a serious buyer to trot around. She still led the occasional gawker through the Millner-Frome mansion, but that was a waste of time. No one would buy it now.

Not since the spring rains had unearthed the body.

Sometimes she wished she could simply have kicked the dirt back over Justine's ghastly hand and continued with her open house. Would that have been so terrible? Was one grave so different from another? It's not as if anything could bring Justine back to life now.

Debra sometimes wondered whether, if Richie Graham hadn't been on the property and likely to witness it, she might have done exactly that.

She put her head in her hands and fought back self-pitying tears. She wasn't a bad person. But how much could she take before she snapped?

If something didn't happen, she was going to have to go home to her mother.

Judy, who had recommended Debra to Millner, was apologizing for sticking her with the doomed listing. But Judy had meant well. If Debra had been able to sell it before the body surfaced, she would have been financially set for months.

As it stood, she was much too dependent on Rutledge. They were trying to resolve their problems, but something had shifted inside Debra's heart. When he reached out to touch her, some internal flinch made her pull away. He was taking it well, so far, but every night she wondered…was this the night he'd lose control?

Even more pathetic, while her heart might have shifted, her finances hadn't. Quite simply, without Rutledge, she wouldn't be able to pay the rent.

She could feel her mother waiting, standing in the big Kansas kitchen, wearing her Donna Reed apron and just itching to say "I told you so."

Her mother had always thought Rutledge was bad news.

Everyone did.

Debra stared at the computer screen, where she'd been researching the multiple listings, but all she saw was Rutledge, handing her that awful gold anklet. Surely that proved he hadn't been involved with Justine, right? It wasn't as if he was a murderer, right? So why was Debra still unwilling to let him touch her?

What doubt lingered in her psyche, poisoning her against him?

Without any specific plan in mind—at least consciously—she rolled her cursor up to the top of the screen and typed in the name of a search engine. In the empty bar, she typed *anklet* and *gold*. She got about eight hundred thousand responses.

Well, that was useless. She narrowed the search. *Anklets. Gold. Charm.*

Four hundred thousand.

Anklets. Gold. Charm. Lips.

That was a little more manageable…but still rather

daunting. She ignored the smutty sites—apparently just the word *lips* was enough to bring up some pretty weird stuff. If she hadn't been used to doing Internet searches, she never would have stuck it out.

It took her half an hour to find the right place. Then she had to hunt some more to find the manufacturer. Finally, she had the 800 number. She called them and asked for the names of all shops within a thirty-mile radius of Tuxedo Lake that had ever carried that particular anklet.

She scribbled down the names as they read them. At the sixth name, she dropped her pencil.

That was it.

It was the Albany jeweler with the beautiful cases of solitaire diamond engagement rings. The jeweler who, even now, was resizing Judy's eternity ring.

The jeweler across from Rutledge's favorite love-in-the-afternoon hotel.

Before her hurt and anger could take over, reducing her to a puddle of self-pity, she stood, grabbed her purse and rushed out the door. It was crazy, but she couldn't get rid of this last niggling doubt. She had to know.

She was there within thirty minutes. The same woman stood behind the counter, an elegantly groomed brunette whose multiple face-lifts made it impossible to tell whether she was fifty or seventy.

She seemed to recognize Debra and welcomed her warmly. She probably hoped Debra was ready to pick out one of those six-figure solitaires she'd been drooling over last time.

"I have a strange request," Debra began. She'd thought this through on the way over. She had to make it sound innocent. "My boyfriend bought me an anklet here a couple of years ago. I lost it the other day, and I don't want to tell him. You know how it is. I was hoping I could buy another one, so that he'll never find out."

The saleslady's face had been nipped and tucked to the point that it wasn't extremely mobile, but Debra thought she looked sympathetic. The woman moved toward one of the cases, her lovely, long-fingered hand extended.

"Of course. But we do have an extensive selection. Do you think you'd recognize the pattern of the chain? As you see, we have rope, Byzantine, anchor—"

Debra gave the display only a cursory look. "You couldn't forget this one. It was very unusual. It had this charm hanging from it." She held up her fingers to indicate the size. "A big pair of gold lips."

The woman laughed softly. "Oh, yes, of course, I remember those! A real novelty. But I'm afraid I haven't any more. I ordered only two—they weren't really for everyone, you know. And one gentleman bought them both."

Debra kept the smile on her lips, though inside everything was falling apart. "Both?"

The woman nodded. She smoothed her stiff hair with her hand, as if she remembered this particular customer quite fondly. "Yes, he bought one for his girlfriend a couple of years ago." She smiled. "That would be you."

"Yes," Debra said numbly. "That would be me."

"And, just when I thought I might never sell the other one, he came back and bought it for his best friend. It was actually rather sweet. You see, his friend has a bad habit of forgetting his wife's anniversary. He wanted to help his friend out so that this year wouldn't be a repeat of the same."

Debra put her hand on the counter for balance. Surely she'd misheard. "*This* year?"

"Yes," the woman said sadly. "You just missed your chance. He bought the second anklet less than a week ago."

SUZIE WAS FUMING.

Darn it, she was not a wimp. She was not a scaredy-cat. She was not the kind of girlie girl who got spooked every time a boy blew in her ear and said "boo."

But, though she'd sat out here in front of the Justine's house for at least ten minutes now, long enough for the sunny afternoon to turn gray and rainy, she could not work up the nerve to get out of the car.

She drummed her hands on the steering wheel and watched the drops pelt the windshield. What the devil was the matter with her? So the house was creepy, with all those big, shadowy rooms sitting empty, listening for the sound of Justine's footsteps. So the gardener was creepy, with dirty hands and his eyes that slithered all over your body until you felt dirty, too.

So what? "Creepy" was a mind-set, not a threat.

She needed to help Mike. She had to start somewhere.

But apparently she wasn't quite ready to start with the gardener.

Maybe, she decided, she could just check things out, look around a little. If she went down to the lake, she could probably walk up the dock stairs unnoticed and get a glimpse of the property.

And she wouldn't have to get quite as close to the house—or to that creepy gardener.

She drove about three houses down, to the open

green space between estates that provided the legally required public lake access.

The rain had begun in earnest, so she rummaged in the backseat and found a jacket, pocketed her keys and headed down the wooden stairs that led to the beach, whistling to buck up her courage.

The path cut through the cliff was beautiful, lined with tall, green pines whose needles sparkled in the rain. The staircase provided a great view of the lake, a cool, dark gray under the heavy clouds.

She wondered how she'd mix that color, if she wanted to paint this scene. She'd need raw umber, ultramarine and white...but where would she get the shimmer of silver and green?

Focus, Suzie, she reminded herself. But thinking in terms of paints had become second nature. And she couldn't really take herself seriously as Miss Marple, anyhow. She wanted to help Mike, but she had no idea how to go about it. Maybe Mrs. Frome had been right. Maybe the only thing Suzie had to offer was moral support.

Oh, well, she was here now. She might as well look.

When she reached the lake, she jogged through the rain until she drew even with the Frome mansion, which dwarfed the houses on either side.

Rats. She couldn't see much from the lake, as she'd feared. Well, at least she'd confirmed that one piece of the puzzle. People out here couldn't have witnessed the gruesome burial, but at the same time, no one up there could ever see what was happening directly under the cliff edge.

She was going to have to get closer if she wanted to look at the grounds. For a moment, as she stepped onto the stairs that led steeply to the Frome property, her angle changed, and the house almost disappeared behind the cliff. As she rose, so did the house. It loomed ever larger…its bulk dominating the sky.

No nerves, she instructed herself. The house was just a pile of bricks and stone. She eyed it analytically, as if she were preparing to paint it, reducing it to its component parts. Shadow and color, angle and geometric masses. The familiar exercise comforted her. It gave her control.

But then she saw the dying larkspurs.

Clearly no one had tended this garden at the cliff edge since Justine's body had been found. Maybe the police had prevented it, at first. And then…

Then no one had cared—or dared. The grasses and weeds had slithered in, seizing the chance, and had begun to strangle the flowers, which were beautiful, but weak. Those that survived were in their death throes, leggy and pale. The rest lay in wilted stalks that even the rain couldn't revive.

She dragged her gaze away.

Who had a view of this backyard? The gardener's suite over the garage definitely did. The Stotts' house, on the other hand, was blocked by hedges, unless you were standing fairly far out toward the lake. From that point on, their view of the Frome estate was unbroken. The neighbors on the other side—she made a note to find out who they were—had much the same setup.

About two dozen windows of the main Frome house, all dark and hooded now, overlooked the backyard, as well. Anyone who'd been in the house could have seen what happened.

Suzie's gaze kept being drawn to the second floor, as if something were out of place. In the center of the house, a small, circular balcony extended out from one of the windows. For her painting, Suzie had trained her eye to analyze and understand proportion, and she realized that something was wrong with that balcony.

The wrought-iron balustrade that formed the barrier was too low. Most railings came to just above waist level, so that no one could ever get dizzy and, in a nanosecond of bad balance, simply pitch over and fall.

This one was almost a foot lower than that. It would have hit a woman of normal height somewhere on the thigh. Suzie had a sudden mental picture of Justine tumbling, her golden hair flying out like ribbons as she slammed to the ground—and a shadowy figure retreating silently into the darkness of the room.

She shook her head to dislodge the vision. That was absurd. It couldn't have happened that way.

Discouraged, she turned back toward the stairs to the lake. This had been just as pointless as she'd feared. The police had undoubtedly already done this, and had questioned both the Stotts and the gardener. If they'd seen Mike doing anything suspicious out here, he'd already be in custody. If they'd seen anyone else digging in the larkspurs, Mike would be off the hook.

She cast one last look back, and caught a glimpse of motion. Something had moved in one of the windows in the east wing. The gardener's wing.

She descended the rest of the stairs so quickly she slipped twice on the wet wood. She skinned her knee, but once she was back on the sandy beach, with open sky around her, she pulled herself together and ordered her heart to behave.

She pulled her hood over her hair and made her way calmly along the beach. Remember how she wasn't a wimp?

But then…

The drumming of the rain on her hood drowned out most other noises, so she wasn't sure why she suddenly looked behind her.

Had there been a noise? Her peripheral vision caught the tail end of something moving near the cliff, though by the time she really looked, nothing was there. Just more proof, as if she needed it, that she was thoroughly spooked.

Above her on the wooded cliffs, branches swayed. Wet leaves shifted and glimmered in the wind. The lake itself was twitching and heaving. It was hard, in the middle of so much motion, to believe she was entirely alone.

"Hello?" Her heart beat faster, which was stupid. Whatever bird or squirrel had just darted by searching for shelter probably thought she was crazy.

No one answered, of course. No one would be fool enough to hike out here in this weather. No one but Suzie.

The minute she said that, a figure came jogging toward her, wearing a jacket much like her own. The hood was tightened, protecting the runner from the rain, and also rendering him or her completely anonymous. Her heart sped up, but the person jogged casually by, raising a palm in friendly salute.

She breathed normally again and continued on. She'd almost made it to the stairs when the sky opened up, and the rain fell in a deluge. She didn't want to risk the steep steps in this kind of weather, so she darted for an outcropping, over which a hemlock grew, providing a natural umbrella.

She wedged herself as close to the granite as she could. To her surprise, her hand slid around a curve in the stone, and she realized that there was an opening.

This rock wasn't solid, as it appeared. There was something like a cave back there.

Curious, she felt her way in. The air was dank and at least ten degrees cooler than the outside, but it was blissfully dry. She let her hood fall back.

It was pitch-dark. She tried to get her bearings with her hands, but the walls were slimy, so she jerked away her fingers with a muffled "yuck!"

Luckily her key chain had a tiny, bright flashlight on the ring, a gift from her overprotective dad. She found it and thumbed the button.

Amazing. The space she'd entered was so small the tiny flashlight illuminated every inch. It wasn't really a cave—more like a nook, about four by four, and definitely empty, just damp granite walls and a rocky floor.

In theory, it made a wonderful refuge from the rain. Very Tom Sawyer-ish and cozy. But in only a few minutes she began to feel edgy. Nervous. It was so small. She didn't have claustrophobia, but…

What if that movement hadn't been a squirrel? What if it had been the creepy gardener? He could have seen her duck in here. If he followed her, there would be no escape. He might not be a murderer, but he was definitely an oversexed sleazeball.

The hair on the back of her neck prickled. Time to get out. She turned abruptly, but something—or someone—blocked her way.

She jerked her flashlight, its bright beam darting across jagged granite walls and finding the entrance, where a man stood.

It was Mike.

He was holding a gun.

Her thumb slipped on the flashlight, and the cave plunged back into its natural, eternal night.

CHAPTER THIRTEEN

HE COULD SEE that she was afraid of him.

And why shouldn't she be? The minute he saw that terrified look on her face, he realized that he had been waiting for it, subconsciously, ever since she first walked back into his life.

It had been inevitable. He was surprised it had taken so long, given how the evidence was stacking against him.

Still, he was glad he'd been prepared.

Otherwise, it might have hurt.

"Mike," she said in a tight voice. She had turned her pocket light back on, and was obviously trying not to stare at the gun. "You startled me. What are you doing here?"

He saw that the area behind her was empty. No one had found her. He took a deep breath of relief.

"I think the better question is what are *you* doing here?" He tried not to sound as tense and angry as he felt. "I saw your note, but when I got here all I could find was your car. You scared the hell out of me."

She scowled. "Well, *ditto*. And at least I'm not pointing a loaded weapon at you."

"Sorry." He tucked the gun behind his back. "I wasn't sure it was you. I was just following a couple of people in hooded jackets. I didn't know exactly what—or who—I'd find in here."

Her scowl deepened. She looked almost demonic, with the pocket light illuminating her from under her chin. He wondered if he looked equally weird.

"A *couple* of people? How could that be? I'm the only one out here."

He shook his head. "No, you aren't. Didn't you see that jogger pass you a few minutes ago?"

"Oh, yeah." She nodded warily. "So?"

"Not long after he went past you he turned around and jogged behind you the rest of the way. I followed, but I was too far back. You both disappeared around an outcropping, and I couldn't tell who went where."

Her already-pale face blanched further. "He followed me?"

"Yes."

"Who was it? Did you see his face? Are you sure it was a man?"

"No. All I can tell you is the person was about your height. Until I found you just now, I wasn't sure which of them was you. Heck, I wasn't sure *either* of them was you. I was just hoping."

She seemed to be sorting it all out in her mind. Finally, she shrugged. "You know, it's quite possible we're both making a mountain out of a molehill. I've been spooked and paranoid all day. The runner may have been perfectly innocent. He may have decided it was just too wet to keep going and turned around to go home."

"Maybe," Mike said, but he was unconvinced. He had seen the smooth wheel-around the jogger had done, and the purposeful way he kept his stride a safe distance behind Suzie, one black form shadowing the other. Every instinct Mike possessed had gone on alert.

"Anyhow, thanks for coming to check on me," she said. She scuffed the ground, looking a little like Gavin when he'd been caught doing something dumb. "I have to admit this may not have been one of my best ideas."

"No kidding." He couldn't help letting one side of his mouth go up. "This isn't a game, you know, Suzie. You can't go tearing around trying to find a killer the way you might look for a polka-dot tie in a scavenger hunt."

"I know," she said defensively. "But I was annoyed that you hadn't told me about Judy Stott."

"What about her?"

"She came by the boathouse today, to report about some guy Gavin talked to on the playground. Apparently it's nothing to worry about."

He looked relieved. "Good. But why did that annoy you?"

"Because I didn't know anything about it. I know you don't have to— But, look, obviously I didn't expect to really find a murderer out here. But if I had, I know better than to jump up and point my finger and scream '*murderer!*' I would play it very cool, I promise you."

He laughed softly. The sound echoed in their tiny granite chamber. "Suzie Strickland playing it cool. That would be a first."

She smiled, too.

"I just want to say—" She looked uncomfortable. "That is, when you first showed up in the entryway, I—I was just startled, you know. I wasn't actually afraid. I mean, I was afraid, of course, but not of you."

"Yes, you were," he said. "It's okay. I understand. You've been great, Suzie, but you're human. There's always going to be that little kernel of doubt, lying there at the bottom. But if you're even seventy-five percent sure I'm innocent, that's more than most—"

"I'm *one hundred percent* sure, damn it. There is no kernel. There is no doubt."

"That's not possi—"

He never got the word out. She leaned over and kissed him hard.

Oh, man…

It had been ten years since he'd kissed her, and yet he would have known her mouth anywhere. She had generous lips, soft, strong and full of warmth. She tasted today just as she had then, spicy-sweet and intensely female. That had surprised him ten years ago. It didn't surprise him now.

The only difference was that she was more accomplished now, more confident. She extended the kiss with easy sensuality. She nipped at his lower lip, then teased the tip of her tongue along the inner rim, so lightly he wasn't sure he hadn't imagined it.

But his body knew it was real. Every inch of him responded in a flash, generating its own answering heat. He wasn't sure how he held back.

After a minute she pulled away and looked at him with a smile. "Hey. Didn't you used to be better at this?"

"Maybe. I never used to let anything like common sense get in my way."

"You know, I'm sure there's a time and place for common sense, but right now, don't you think you could—"

"I know what you're trying to tell me, Suzie." He met her gaze honestly. "That attraction—whatever it was—that *spark* we used to feel. It's still there."

"Yes," she said, dropping her gaze to his mouth. "In

fact, it seems to have survived a rather long dormant period quite well."

"But a spark isn't enough," he said. "It's just chemistry. It doesn't mean anything. It doesn't *prove* anything about how you really feel."

"Yeah." She touched the edge of his lips with a fingertip. "It does."

He pulled her finger down. He hoped he wasn't too rough. His body was furious with him for resisting, and it was stepping up the pressure.

"You're wrong. It's quite possible to be attracted to someone you don't trust. Believe me, it's even possible to be attracted to someone you don't *like*."

"Guess that's where you and I are different," she said, sighing. "And frankly, Frome, this seems like a dumb time to get into a philosophical discussion about the cosmic meaning of sparks." She grinned. "I'm not sure whether you're trying to tell me you don't like me, or that you're not attracted to me."

He didn't even bother to answer that. She was just hoping to drive him crazy. A lot of things might change, but her sense of humor wouldn't.

Thank God for small blessings.

"I guess I'm trying to tell you that there's no way you could really trust me. There's so much you don't know. Things about Justine and me. Things you should know, if you're really going to be involved in all this."

She sighed. "I already am involved. I already know everything that matters. I know you did a superdumb thing when you were in high school, and you've paid for it big-time. If you want to talk just to get it off your chest, that's okay. But don't tell me anything because you're afraid I think you're a murderer. If I did, I would have used that kiss to snatch your gun."

He wondered whether she'd always been this perceptive. If so, she must have seen very early what a fool he was, and how far in over his head he had been with Justine.

If he'd listened to her, could she have saved him in time?

At any rate, she was right. He did want to get all the secrets off his chest. They'd been crushing him for years. He hadn't told his parents, because he hadn't wanted to transfer the weight of the misery to them. He hadn't told his best friend, or his minister, or even a psychiatrist.

He hadn't told a soul. And not to protect Justine. There had been a time when he'd hated her enough to print her dirty secrets in the newspaper and laugh to see people avoid her on the street.

He'd kept Justine's secrets only to protect Gavin. He didn't want anyone to look at his little boy differently, thinking *that kid's mom is a freak.*

But somehow he knew that Suzie would never charge Justine's sins to Gavin's account. Suzie was the only person he'd ever met both strong enough and kind enough to trust with the truth.

"I do want to tell you," he said. "But I should warn you. It's not pretty."

She shrugged. "Very little connected to Justine ever was."

TWO HOURS LATER, showered and dressed in nice clothes, Suzie found herself at Chapman's, the most upscale restaurant in Tuxedo Lake. She'd ordered filet mignon and a carafe of pinot noir, and she planned to get crème brûlée, too. She had a feeling she might need it.

They'd decided on this restaurant because Suzie's theory was that ugly things should never be discussed in ugly places. It just made things look worse.

Plus, she was starving.

Mike was finishing his second glass of wine, and his tension seemed to have eased a little, so she figured he might be ready.

"Okay," she said. "Try to shock me. But remember, I'm an artist, and I move in very avant-garde circles. It may not be as easy as you think."

That was a lie, of course. Her friends were mostly art teachers and secretaries, maybe a journalist here and there. Most of the "real" artists she knew were a little strange, and besides, they thought she was a sellout, painting pictures of rich peoples' brats.

But she needed to get Mike talking. Obviously the story of his past stood like a boulder in his emotional road. He wasn't going anywhere until someone shoved it out of the way.

After that kiss in the cave, which had been remarkably sizzly for a one-sided affair, she knew she needed to roll up her sleeves and start clearing that path. Just imagine what the next kiss might be like, if he decided to help.

"Okay," he said. He put his knife and fork in the traditional take-this-away position on his place and leaned back, his wineglass in hand.

"You know the first part," he said. "She didn't tell me Gavin was mine for a year. Everyone thought he was—well, the speculation went all over the place."

Suzie remembered that, all right. In fact, she'd always felt a little guilty because she was the one who had forced Justine to cough up the truth. And yet, even in the heart of the pain, she'd known it was cruel to make that baby grow up without a father.

"Anyhow," he said. "By the time I found out he was mine, I was over Justine. Really over. She had nothing but contempt for me, either. It was a terrible way to start a marriage. My parents told me I didn't have to do it, that arrangements could be made so that I could be Gavin's father legally. But once I really knew Gavin, I…"

He didn't seem to have the words to express the enormity of fatherhood, but he didn't have to. Suzie knew. Gavin had trumped everything.

She toyed with her potatoes, wondering if it had been hard for Justine to see Mike look at her with empty eyes, then watch him turn a dazed adoration toward his son.

It had been hard for Suzie, too. When she saw him hold Gavin as if every dream he'd ever dreamed was wrapped up in that tiny body—she knew it meant there was no hope. Mike Frome's only remaining chance for happiness was inextricably tangled up with his son.

That was the day Suzie decided she'd never mention Mike Frome's name out loud again. For ten years, she hadn't.

"I honestly thought I could make it work," he said. "That's how young and stupid I was. I thought that, because of Gavin, we'd both try hard, and everything would somehow magically come right."

She lifted one shoulder. "Believing that a baby will save a bad marriage—I'm pretty sure that's common enough to be a cliché."

"I guess so. But it didn't save mine. Justine couldn't be happy with a quiet life, and that's all I was good for. I had planned to be an architect, but she threw a fit. She wanted to be important right away, not just some student's wife. That was too common. If you wanted to make her really mad, all you had to do was call her ordinary. She needed life to sparkle. She wanted everything to be big."

"She thought you were a pretty big fish when she first reeled you in."

"Maybe in high school, maybe in Firefly Glen. But, as you once pointed out, that's a small pond. Justine was ready to swim in the ocean, and I think she felt gypped to discover that I'm just a small-town boy at heart."

"I'm sure you tried."

"I damn sure did. I gave up the idea of being an architect and took a much shorter course in basic construction. I bought the boathouse-building business from a guy who was retiring. He stayed on part-time until I knew what I was doing. After that I let Justine's father buy us that monstrosity by the lake. I played golf with the men she told me to play with. I went to her parties and flirted with the wives she told me to flirt with. I just kept thinking, maybe if I do this, or this, she'll be content and we'll finally have a normal family."

"I assume it didn't work."

"Of course it didn't. *Content* wasn't in Justine's vocabulary. All I accomplished was to make myself a doormat. She probably despised me. I certainly despised myself. After a couple of years, I couldn't stand it anymore, not even for Gavin's sake. I told her I was through. I was leaving."

"After two years? But you were married—"

"Six years. I know. She seemed genuinely shocked that I planned to walk out. She begged me to stay, and, for a while, things seemed to get better. She'd been cold as ice, during those first two years, but suddenly she was on fire. She wanted to make love every day, every night. Sometimes several times a night."

Suzie felt her cheeks flaming. She poked at her steak and tried not to hate Justine too much. "Well, that must have been a dream come true."

He shook his head. "Not really. It took me a while to catch on, but underneath all the theatrics, she was still as cold as ice. It was the weirdest thing. She acted insatiable, but she actually wasn't enjoying it at all."

Now that was hard to believe. Suzie frowned. "Give me a break."

"I'm serious. It was all make-believe. In the first five years of our marriage, I'm not sure Justine had one single truly satisfying sexual experience."

Suzie tapped her fingers on the table. "Okay, here's where I may be stepping over the line, but…" She wrinkled her nose. "Are you that bad?"

He chuckled. "She said I was wonderful. She said the earth moved. But it didn't."

"Well, umm. Not to be indelicate, but were you really giving it the old college try? I mean, you do know how it works for women, and—"

He blinked innocently. "I think I do. I did look it up in a book once. Maybe you could tell me."

She smiled. What a damaged lady Justine must have been. Suzie had a sneaking suspicion that she might be able to have a "satisfying sexual experience" here at this fancy table, if Mike looked at her just the right way.

"Maybe someday I'll show you," she said. She made her voice tart to keep her emotions under control. "But you were in the middle of your story. Carry on."

"After a couple of years of that, she got tired of pretending, for obvious reasons. I think that's when the other men really came into the picture, but I didn't care. I was tired of the charade, too. Unfortunately, that respite lasted only about a year."

What an emotional seesaw the whole marriage must have been. Suzie wondered whether that had been part of the fun for Justine, bouncing Mike's emotions up and down like a rubber ball.

"About six years into the marriage, she came back to my bedroom. That's where the story gets ugly. Because that's when I found out what really worked for her sexually. That's when I found out what she really wanted."

Darn it. Suzie set her jaw, getting ready for the hard part. "And that was?"

"Pain."

She let her fork fall with a clatter. "What?"

His face was set in tight lines. He clearly did not like reliving this.

"Pain."

"Yours or hers?"

"Hers. Justine wanted me to hurt her. It was the only way she could—find any release."

Suzie swallowed. She wasn't sure what she'd been expecting, but it wasn't this. She'd thought maybe stories of other lovers, arguments in the night, letters intercepted….

Apparently her imagination simply wasn't creative enough. "When you say pain, do you mean—"

"I mean *pain*. I don't mean tussling on the bed, or love nips, or even sex so vigorous you ache in the morning. I mean pain. I mean welts. I mean blood."

Suzie looked at her filet in its pool of red juice and felt her stomach turn sideways. "Oh, my God," she said.

"I tried to help her. I begged her to see a psychiatrist. I even tried, a few times, to meet her halfway. I agreed to little things." He closed his eyes. "But hurting someone is…for me, it's simply not compatible with lovemaking. I found that I could do one or the other…but not both."

Oh, my God.

"We limped along like that for a while, but eventually I could barely stand to touch her. It was too sick. The last night we ever tried to make love, she wanted me to bite her breasts. She was furious when I said no. She wanted me to draw blood. When I refused, she tried to bite me."

Suzie put out her hand. "Mike—"

"I held her away—she wasn't any stronger than a child, really. She was so frustrated that, in the end, she bit the inside of her own forearm. She bit until she bled, and then she spit the blood in my face."

"Oh, *Justine*." Suzie closed her eyes. "And then?"

"Then I left. I never touched her again."

ON THE WAY BACK to the boathouse, they were both unusually subdued. Mike turned on a Chopin CD, which Suzie thought was a good choice. Chopin was very tender, and they needed to remember that tenderness still existed in this crazy world.

They didn't touch—who could think of kissing, or even holding hands, after a story like that? But she hadn't ever felt closer to him. She hadn't ever admired him more. He had been through hell to make a good life for Gavin. And he hadn't tried to turn Gavin against his mother. That alone practically qualified him for sainthood.

She shut her eyes, letting the sweetness of Chopin wash over her. She remembered how passionately she had envied Justine, once. That seemed so long ago now.

It was hard to imagine any of the things Mike had described. She couldn't imagine that gorgeous face twisted, begging for Mike to hurt her. She couldn't picture that pampered mouth smeared with her own blood. Her breasts…

Suzie instinctively put her hand up, as if to protect her own breasts. And as she did, the gesture reminded her of something. Some other time she'd reacted with a wincing horror to a similar story.

Yes, she'd heard another story like this, some-where….

Biting…sexual sadism…

But where? For all her big talk, Suzie's own life had been pathetically tame. She had a friend who had a friend whose sister reported using handcuffs in bed, but that was as close as Suzie had ever come to stuff like this.

Suddenly, she remembered. About two years ago… there had been a torrid news article about a fifteen-year-old Albany girl who had run away from home. When she returned, she brought back a bizarre story. She said she'd been drugged and taken to an under-ground cave where she'd been raped and sexually tortured. Suzie couldn't remember the details, but she did remember that the girl said the man had bitten her, especially on the breasts.

The TV stations had exploited the drama for a few days, but the police hadn't believed the girl's story. She'd been a runaway before, and she had a history of telling horrific tales that turned out to be pure fantasy.

The girl had died shortly afterward, of a drug overdose. If she hadn't done it in a public place, that part wouldn't have made the news at all.

No one thought there was a word of truth in it.

Still…was it possible the girl hadn't been lying? What if there was a sexual sadist with a fetish for biting women's breasts….

What if Justine had run into him?

Suzie looked at Mike. She glanced at the gas gauge, to see how much gas they had.

"Hey," she said softly.

He glanced over at her. "I thought you were sleeping."

"Nope. Just thinking."

He adjusted his hands on the wheel and smiled. "Sounds dangerous."

"So, I was thinking…want to go to Albany?"

"Now? Why? Did you forget your favorite baggy black sweatshirt? I've been wondering where that old standby had disappeared to."

She rolled her eyes. "Get over it. I burned that thing years ago. This is something else."

She told him what she remembered.

It did sound pretty far-fetched, when she said it out loud. For a minute she thought he was going to tell her she was nuts.

But he didn't. He tapped his finger thoughtfully on the steering wheel, and then, finally, he shrugged.

"Why not? We can go in the morning. I've got no objection to taking a long shot. Especially if it's the only shot we've got."

CHAPTER FOURTEEN

SUZIE USED TO HAVE A SAYING: Whenever Luck seems to be going your way, brace yourself. It's about to take a big U-turn.

When she and Mike went home after dinner that night, Luck definitely seemed to be on their side. They looked up the old news reports on the Internet, just to be sure Suzie had remembered the story correctly. She had.

Because the girl had been a minor when she first came forward claiming abduction and rape, most papers hadn't published her name. But after her death, her mother, Arlene Cesswood, had given quite a few interviews and openly discussed her daughter Loretta's ordeal.

Then they used the online white pages to locate Arlene Cesswood's address. Bingo on the first try.

With everything ready, they went to bed by eleven, planning to get an early start the next morning.

That's when Luck put on its blinker for the U-turn.

They had just finished up a quick breakfast when they heard a knock on the boathouse door. Mike got up to answer it. Her heart thudding, Suzie leaned all the way over the table so that she could see who it was.

It was Harry Rouge, Mike's lawyer. The minute Suzie spotted the bottlebrush mustache, she plopped back onto her chair and crossed her fingers under her thigh. *Please*, she prayed, *don't let it be really bad news.*

Mike let the lawyer in. *Oops*...Suzie remembered that her blanket and sheets were still on the sofa. She rushed over and, with a murmured apology, snatched them out of the way so the older man could sit.

As he settled himself, she tried to read his expression. She didn't know him well, but she'd guess he was very worried about something. Every line in his face angled down, from his eyebrows to the corners of his mouth.

He was not the bearer of good tidings.

As she stood there hugging the linens, Harry shot her a stern look from under his shaggy white eyebrows. "You slept here last night?"

"Yes," she said, wishing she didn't sound so defensive. But darn it. She'd spent every single night on this sofa, though she would have far preferred to be upstairs with Mike. If she was going to suffer through a stint as a vestal virgin, she at least wanted credit for it.

"Suzie's just a friend, Harry." Mike took a seat on the armchair nearest the sofa. "I haven't had a lover since Justine disappeared, if that's what you're asking. I've always understood that, until she was found alive, or her death was explained, I was standing on very thin ice."

"Good. I'd say that's a fair evaluation." Harry again looked at Suzie, and again she smiled, trying to look perfectly platonic.

He turned back to Mike. "However, right now I'm not sure that's your biggest problem."

Mike sat very still. "Okay," he said calmly. "What is?"

Harry cleared his throat. "Would you rather talk privately?"

"I don't have any secrets from Suzie. I've known her since we were kids. She's trying to help. Whatever it is, I want her to hear it."

The lawyer lifted one hand, as if to say, *if his client's bullheaded, what can a lawyer do*?

"All right," he said. "I had a call from the D.A.'s office this morning. They have a preliminary match on several hairs they found when they vacuumed your bedroom. Unfortunately, at least at this stage, they seem to be Justine's."

Suzie knew her mouth fell open. She was well aware of how many times Mike had insisted Justine had never been inside this boathouse.

"It has to be a mistake," Mike said, but Suzie could tell he was shaken, too. "Or else it's a lie. She was never—"

"Never in this house. I know, I know. They're running the DNA tests now, and if they do turn out to be hers, they'll have to be accounted for. I have already pointed out some of the possibilities to Quigley, which I think may be why he isn't preparing an arrest warrant as we speak."

"Possibilities?" Mike's voice was rough. "What do you mean, possibilities? I'm telling you, she wasn't ever—"

"I wonder if you might want to soften that statement a little. If those hairs are hers, we have several options. They might have come in on Gavin's clothes, after one of his visits with her. The tricky part for that line of thinking is that these are pubic hairs."

Suzie's knees felt a little weak, so she sat down on the sofa next to Harry. Mike looked as if this news had paralyzed him.

Harry continued, as mild-mannered as ever, as if he hadn't just dropped a nuclear bomb into the room.

"However, that's still a feasible explanation. With clothes tumbling together in the laundry, hairs can be transferred. Jurors won't like that, though. It sounds desperate. More plausible, however, would be that someone else, not you, let her into this house when you weren't home. Gavin, perhaps?"

"No."

Harry sighed. "Categorical statements, particularly at this stage, may work against us. We have to think strategically. We'll have to talk to Gavin. He may not have wanted to admit letting Justine in, given that you had told him not to."

Mike's hands tightened on the arms of the chair. "Your *strategy* is to call my son a liar?"

Harry cast a look at Suzie, as if he wondered whether she might be objective enough to think more clearly. She was. She saw what Harry meant. But she also saw why it was unacceptable to Mike.

"I think it's just hard," she said carefully, giving Harry a look that said *be patient*, "for anyone to believe that strategy is required to keep an innocent man out of prison."

"The sooner you let go of that fallacy the better. This is a very serious matter. Who else could have let her in, Mike? Do you have a housekeeper?"

"A friend sometimes cleans for me, while she watches Gavin. Debra Pawley."

"Does she have a key?"

"No."

"Does anyone have a key?"

Mike shook his head. "I wouldn't risk it. Not with Gavin here."

"Do you have a spare key hidden on the grounds that someone might have been aware of?"

Mike shook his head. "Gavin has one, and I have one. That's it."

Harry steepled his fingers at the mound of his belly and stared across them. "Okay, we'll work with what we've got. I think I can handle the hairs, one way or another. The evidence I'm really worried about is the blood. The type matches. If the DNA results go against us, that will be much harder to explain."

"That's bullshit," Mike said. He leaned forward. "Whatever they took from the headboard of my bed, it was not Justine's blood."

"It was definitely human blood. And it wasn't yours, or your son's. You both have type A, and this is type O. Justine was type O."

Suzie put her hand on Harry's arm. "Something's not right here. Can't you see that? Someone must be setting him up."

"I was there," the lawyer said gently, "when they used the luminal. It was old blood. Someone had tried to wash it off." He turned to Mike. "That bed wasn't ever in your other house, was it? The house you shared together?"

Yes, Suzie thought, hope rising. Yes, that would account for it. Justine liked to have rough sex. There would have been blood—she'd begged for blood. Mike could have brought it here on the bed unaware.

But Mike was shaking his head. "I didn't take anything from that house. I started over completely."

The lawyer sighed again, and this time Suzie thought he sounded more weary than exasperated. The thought frightened her.

"Well, we'll cross that bridge if we come to it. " He stood. "I'm sorry to bring bad news, Mike, but I wanted you to start thinking about some of these questions. Because it looks as if we're going to need some really good answers."

ARLENE CESSWOOD'S HOME in Middleton Heights was a brick town house, one of about thirty identical attached buildings lined up in an attractive row.

Middleton Heights was one of the newest "reclaimed" neighborhoods on the fringes of downtown Albany. Mike knew the type. Five years ago it would have been deteriorating and unloved. Today it was overpriced and highly sought after by young professionals who hated long commutes.

Loretta Cesswood had run away from this house four times in three years, according to the newspaper reports. Mike wasn't sure why. It looked nice enough, with geraniums in a tub on the front porch, and an "Ode to Joy" doorbell.

Even Loretta's mother, Arlene, an attractive blonde in her mid to late thirties, seemed like a decent person who had honestly loved her troubled daughter.

"Loretta used to be the happiest, prettiest little girl you've ever seen," she said as she showed them into the living room, which was air-conditioned, tidy and very green, with everything upholstered in lime silk.

She pointed to a photograph on the wall that showed a blond child of about six, wearing a cowgirl uniform.

"See? She used to say she wanted to be a cowboy when she grew up." Arlene Cesswood laughed at the little joke, which she'd probably told a million times. But she ended it by putting a tissue to her nose and sniffing back tears. They must never have been far from the surface.

Mike wondered if it ever went away, that eggshell vulnerability. He let his mind edge just close enough to picturing what he'd be like if he lost Gavin. But looking into that abyss was dizzying in its horror, so he pulled back. No, he concluded. It probably never went away.

As Arlene led them to the green sofa, he wondered why she'd let them in. She hadn't asked for identification, or probed into their motives. They had offered a simple opening statement, that they'd like to talk to her about Loretta, assuming they'd have to elaborate from there. But she'd opened the door and ushered them in. Either she was very naive, or she'd welcome the devil himself if he offered a chance to take out the old memories again.

The TV was on in the living room. Arlene muted it without turning it off, as if it were some kind of eternal flame that must never be allowed to go out. That made sense, too. They knew that Arlene had been a single mother, and Loretta her only child. The connection to the world through the TV was probably how she kept from going mad.

"Would you like something to drink? A snack, maybe? I've just made some fruit squares, which came out quite well."

Mike had a *no* on his lips, and a *God, no!* in his mind, when Suzie jumped in and said, "Sure. Thanks, that would be great."

When Arlene left to bustle around in the kitchen, Mike saw that Suzie had a method to her madness. It gave them time to look around the room and figure out a little about Loretta on their own.

Other than the television, the entire room was like a shrine to the girl. Dozens of framed photographs crowded every flat surface. Swimming medals and horseback riding trophies paraded across the windowsills and wall shelves. The refrigerator, which was visible through the kitchen pass-through, was covered in crayon artwork that said, Happy Mother's Day, I love you! and My Pet Dog Bill.

But everything, he noticed, was a memento of Loretta the child. From birth up to about eleven or twelve. She'd died at fifteen. Three missing years. It was as if, from the moment Loretta hit her teens, she hadn't done a single thing her mother wanted to commemorate.

In a few minutes Arlene returned with a tray of gooey things. They looked like a cross between the slices of Christmas fruitcake his aunt Birdie used to send and the mud pies his girl cousins used to concoct in the backyard. Mike shot Suzie a glance, but she picked one up and bit right in. He felt his mouth pursing, just imagining it.

"Fantastic," she said happily, and took another bite.

He turned to Arlene. "I guess you're wondering why we're here," he said. "We're hoping you might be able to tell us more about what happened to Loretta two years ago, when she was abducted."

The woman looked surprised. Maybe she was used to hearing people add the skeptical qualifier, "when she *said* she was abducted."

"Why do you want to know?" In her lap she held a small photo of baby Loretta, which she'd had to move to make room for the tray. She fingered the frame nervously. "Are you reporters? No one has wanted to write about Loretta's story for a long time now. They thought she was making it up."

"No," he said. "We're not reporters. That's what I wanted to tell you. I live in Tuxedo Lake. That's about twenty miles from here. Two years ago my wife disappeared. We didn't know what happened to her, but then, a few weeks ago her body was found. She'd been murdered."

Arlene put out her hand, the instinctive recognition that they belonged to the same club, the club of lives that had been suddenly, senselessly, broken. She couldn't know how ambivalent his feelings had been for Justine, but that didn't seem to matter.

"I'm so sorry," Arlene said. "But how can Loretta's story help you? She wasn't murdered, you know. She took her own life. Or it may have been an accident." She looked down at the picture. "That's what I tell myself, anyhow."

"I know the situations seem very different," he said. "And you may be right. It may not be connected at all. But there were some similarities, at least from what we read in the papers. I need to find out who killed my wife. I have to look at anything—everything—that might provide even the smallest clue."

Suzie sat very still, saying nothing. Mike knew she didn't dare upset this delicate moment. When Arlene looked over at her, as if she had started to wonder how Suzie fit in, Suzie smiled and indicated with a gesture that, if Arlene didn't mind, she'd like to have another fruit square.

Arlene nodded and patted her hand, obviously pleased.

Then she turned back to Mike. "Do you think the person who abducted Loretta might be the same man who killed your wife? Is that what you're hoping?"

Smart woman. He couldn't have put it more succinctly himself. "Yes," he said. "I think it's possible.

It would be nice, wouldn't it, to be able to solve two crimes at once?"

She frowned. "It would be nice to prove Loretta wasn't lying."

"Yes," he said. "It must have been very hard when the police wouldn't believe her." He understood that, too.

"You can't really blame them," Arlene said. "I didn't believe her, either, at first. She'd told crazy stories before. She was always getting into trouble, and then inventing dramas to try to get out of it. She had a no-good boyfriend. He used to knock her around. I don't know why she put up with that. Her dad was a rough one, too. I threw him out ten years ago."

"Good for you," Suzie put in. "That took guts."

"Yes, it did," Arlene agreed, and Mike could feel her pride. "I didn't even have a job. He'd always wanted me to stay home with Loretta. But I got one, didn't I? I'm making more money now than he ever did."

"Wow," Suzie said with a smile. "Take that, tough guy!"

Arlene nodded firmly, and ran her hand along the expensive green silk. "Anyway, Loretta took up with this boy, Sean, and he was cute, all right, but he was a bad one. She'd come home black-and-blue, swearing they'd had a car accident or a fall or whatever, but I knew better. I told her she couldn't see him anymore. When she came home that last time, and she'd been all bruised up, and…the rest…I thought it was Sean, naturally. I thought she'd dreamed the whole story up so I wouldn't know she'd been seeing him."

Mike was momentarily, selfishly, glad he had a son. Daughters were so vulnerable. He looked at the picture right behind Arlene's head. It was a Halloween photo of Loretta at about five, dressed up like Sleeping Beauty. When Arlene had shot this picture, could she ever have guessed that, less than ten years later, her beautiful daughter would be angry, deceitful, tormented, in a destructive relationship with a violent man?

"You've changed your mind, though, haven't you?" He eyed her carefully. "You don't think she was lying anymore."

Arlene shook her head slowly. "No. At first I wouldn't even take her to the police. But then, a week or so later, I saw the—I saw what they did to her. Sean was a devil when he drank, but that…he didn't do that."

She was crying, her nose running, her face red. "They bit her, all over. If I'd taken her to the police right away, they said they might have been able to prove who did it, from the tooth marks. But they didn't really care anyhow, because they thought it was Sean. They thought she'd wanted him to play rough, and then, when they'd quarreled, she'd made up a story to get him in trouble." She let the photo slide to the carpet and put her face in her hands. "It's my fault they didn't believe her. I waited too long."

Mike wasn't sure what to do. This was the crucial part. But was it inhuman to push her for details?

"Arlene," he said softly. "I'm sorry, but I need to know more. Did Loretta say anything else, anything that might help us track down this bastard?"

She shook her head without taking her hands away. She kept shaking it, as if she didn't know how to stop.

Mike looked at Suzie. Her face was pale, her eyes shining.

"All right," he said. "I understand. Thanks for—"

"No, wait!" Arlene lifted her face. She swallowed hard. "I don't know if there's anything you can use, but...would it help if you looked at her diary?"

CHAPTER FIFTEEN

IT WAS, SUZIE THOUGHT, as if they could hear Loretta's voice speaking to them from the pages of her little blue journal.

Mike and Suzie both spent at least an hour in the girl's bedroom, which obviously hadn't been changed since the day she died. It was one of the longest hours of Suzie's life.

On the surface, it was the room of a typical teenage punker, with black-on-gray paisley sheets, posters of rock stars with metal-studded dog collars, and a fake bumper sticker that said, If You Can Read This, Get The Hell Out Of My Room.

But though Loretta was clearly trying, she hadn't completely shed the sweet little girl of her mother's living room photographs. The black sheets were topped with a yellow Care Bear. The DVD cabinet still had *National Velvet* and *The Last Unicorn* on the same shelf with *Velvet Goldmine* and *The Rocky Horror Picture Show*.

And on the computer desk, right next to a photo of a snarling sexpot who must have been Sean, a pink ceramic horse pranced, its tail and mane sparkling with cheap glitter.

For Suzie, the reality of Loretta was much stronger here than it had been downstairs. And, because she felt real, the fact of her death seemed more terrible. This hadn't been a paint-by-numbers Mommy's Princess, the kind you might find on the pages of a Sears catalogue. This had been a complicated, intelligent, foolish girl who had jumped into the deep end of adulthood without first making sure she knew how to swim.

When Arlene showed them to the room, she had held on to the diary for a long minute, as if she weren't sure she could bear to let them look.

Finally she handed the diary to Suzie. "I think Loretta would mind less," Arlene said, "if another woman reads it."

She turned to Mike. "I'm sorry."

He'd been quick to assure her he understood. He asked if he could look at Loretta's computer instead. He'd like to see what sites she'd visited, in case some clue might have survived.

Arlene nodded, as if she didn't trust herself to speak, and then she left them alone. She obviously didn't want to watch.

While Mike turned on the hard drive and began checking the temporary Internet files, Suzie sat on the edge of the bed and read.

It wasn't like any diary she'd ever seen before—certainly not like her own teenage journal, which had been full of long, self-indulgent rants against the Perilous Ps, as she'd called them: Parents, Popular People and Pimples.

Loretta's personality was so vivid mere words couldn't contain it. She didn't write every day, only when something important had happened—and her entries could be anything.

For January 3, for instance, the entry was just six huge exclamation points, each one a different color and shape. August 25 was a movie ticket stub taped to the page, next to the word *Awesome* underlined in red. Sometimes she doodled or sketched. Sometimes she put down a quote she'd found. May 9 said, "To create something, you must be something." Next to that she'd written, "yeah, but *what?*"

Sean's name showed up a lot. Loretta either believed her diary to be secure, or didn't care how much her mother knew, because she wrote in great detail about their sex life. Sometimes she sounded moved to the point of poetry. Other times she sounded angry. Once or twice she was actually pretty funny about the whole thing.

Her longest entries were in the few days after her abduction. Suzie wondered if the police had ever read this. If they had, how could they ever have doubted the truth of her story? These were the words of a girl who had been traumatized beyond endurance.

She didn't remember much, unfortunately—or perhaps fortunately, at least for her. She'd been angry with Sean, and to punish him she'd gone to a bar in downtown Albany, one where she knew they didn't look too carefully at IDs. She'd made herself up to look as old as she possibly could, and she knew she'd done well, because the minute she sat down guys began hitting on her.

One of them was really sexy. He was old, maybe thirty, but had a young personality. He had sexy eyes and he was fun to talk to. He had a lot of dark hair, which made her a little nervous. Her father had a lot of hair, and she associated that with a macho bullying streak.

But this guy hadn't acted rough. He'd made her laugh. They went to a table at the back, and he'd done all the trudging back and forth from the bar, getting their drinks.

Here, Loretta switched to a red pen and began to berate herself for being so stupid. She knew that was dangerous. Everyone knew the new "roofie" rules: You didn't let a guy bring you a drink from the bar. If you had to go to the restroom, you never finished your drink after you got back. If you accidentally turned your back on your drink even for a minute, you threw it away and got a new one.

So why hadn't she followed her own rules? The red pen laid it down, three times. *You asked for it. You asked for it. You asked for it.*

After that, she remembered very little. She knew he'd taken her to his car, and it seemed as if they had driven a long time. She thought she smelled the water, but she might have been mistaken. He had been carrying her at one point, she was sure of that. She was in his arms, and she looked up, and she saw an angel floating over her. One of the angel's wings was much bigger than the other.

She wondered if she was dead. That made her begin to cry.

She drew a clumsy sketch of the angel's wings. They looked like deformed silvery-gray butterfly wings. Each one had asymmetrical whorls inside it, like the rings of a tree trunk.

The place where they took her felt like a cave, she said. She couldn't be sure, of course. It could have been a basement. She knew only that, when her fingers grazed the wall, it was hard, like stone. Everything was gray and dark and wet-smelling. And cold.

The rest, she said, was just pain. It was like you'd been given anesthetic for surgery, but inside your head you were still awake. She couldn't see, she couldn't move. All she could do was feel.

The next couple of sentences had been scratched out with a black Magic Marker. "No melodrama," she'd scrawled next to the blot. Below that, she'd made a completely dispassionate, nearly clinical, list of her injuries.

It was a list that brought tears to Suzie's eyes. Eight items, each more horrifying than the last. The inventory of a debased body, and a dismantled mind.

She must have made a sound, because Mike turned around.

"What is it? Are you all right?"

She closed the book. "I'm finished," she said. To her surprise there hadn't been any more entries after the list. No discussion of taking drugs to escape the memories, of going to the police, of telling her mother, of suicide.

It was as if Loretta's life had ended with the last entry on that list.

Rape.

She felt sick, but she tried to pull herself together. She felt Mike watching her, and she knew what he wanted to know. Were there any clues? The computer search had just been busywork, so that he didn't go crazy waiting to see what she found.

As quickly as she could, she gave him the basic facts. His face was grim.

"There's a bar downtown we could try to find," she said. "Apparently she met the guy there, and she believes he put something in her drink."

She read him the passage that described the bar. They both knew there wasn't enough to go on.

"Nothing else?"

She stared down at the page with the angel's wings. "Just one thing," she said. "I don't know what it means, really. Maybe nothing. But there's something about it…"

"What?"

She felt silly. How could she say that those blobs reminded her of something? That she felt as if she'd seen them before.

She held out the book. "Loretta said she saw something like this as she was being taken to the cave. She said it glowed, and seemed to float above her like angel's wings."

He didn't touch it, but he leaned forward, studying the sketch. "I don't know," he said. "If she was drugged, there's no telling what she really saw. This could be a distortion of something as simple as an overhead light."

"I know," she said. "But there's something…." She turned the book around to get a different perspective. "I'm used to thinking in shapes, because that's how I paint. I'm more likely to see two vertical lines than I am to see two trees. Instead of a house and garage, I see two interlocking cubes. It's a habit. And I could swear I've seen these shapes before. Two similar winglike shapes, but one much smaller. The interior whorls. I can't help thinking I've seen these."

He tilted his head, playing with the angle.

Suddenly his eyes widened.

"You're right," he said. He kept his voice low, but excitement ran through it like electricity. "I've seen them, too."

"Where?" She held the book against her chest. "Where?"

"They're called stromatolites. They can be very

pale, and they can really stand out in a darker stone. They don't really glow, but when the moonlight hits them, they can seem to."

"But where?" She took a breath. "Where have you seen *this* one? One that looks like angel's wings?"

"At the lake," he said. "In the bluffs below Justine's house."

SUZIE WOULD HAVE RACED out there in the pitch black, but somehow Mike persuaded her to wait until sunup. It was too risky in the middle of the night. They couldn't even know for sure that the cave was empty. Did she want to end up like Loretta Cesswood?

Besides, he knew where the angel-wing formation was. They didn't need moonlight to find it, not that there was much tonight, anyhow. The rain had never quite moved on. Clouds still hung over Tuxedo Lake like a heavy woolen blanket.

She was rotten at waiting. He could almost see the adrenaline coursing through her. She fidgeted constantly, like a racehorse confined too long in the stall before the starting gate opens.

For a while, in the last hour before dawn, he thought she just might go without him. She was getting cranky. She'd slept a little, curled up on the wicker porch chair, but mostly they'd both been up all night, talking things over and watching the sky for a glimmer of sun.

"It's going to take us twenty minutes to get around to the right spot," she grumbled. It wasn't the first time she'd made the observation. "If we start right now, it will be light by the time we find it."

"No," he said. "Suzie, listen. If there is a cave, it's been there thousands of years. It's not going to wash away in the next hour."

She drummed her fingers on the railing. "You're a real pain in the ass, Frome," she said. It wasn't the first time she'd mentioned that, either.

"I know," he murmured. He dropped his head back against the chair and shut his eyes. He was so damn tired. He should have gone to bed, at least for a while, but he hadn't wanted to leave her. Being around her made him feel better, cleaner. It was kind of like the way he felt around Gavin.

She met her problems with so much energy and bulldog determination, as if it hadn't occurred to her there were any enemies out there she couldn't vanquish, if Mike would just let her off the leash.

He even liked her cranky complaining. It was honest. It was alive.

It was like breathing clean air after a decade of sucking in noxious fumes.

He must have dozed off, because the next thing he knew she was leaning over him, her hands on his knees, trying to jiggle him awake.

"Light!" She pointed to the east, where you could finally see the outline of the tall, black pines against silver sky. "You can't deny it. Right over there!"

"Okay, Fang, okay." He stood, cracked his neck a couple of times to get rid of the kinks, and smiled. He'd actually been dreaming about her, and when she put her hands on his knees, his dream had jumped to conclusions. "Let's go cave hunting."

Yesterday's bad weather must have thwarted all the health nuts of Tuxedo Lake, leaving a pent-up need to jog. Even as early as this, they encountered at least half a dozen runners before they reached the other side of the lake.

Once there, he took a couple of minutes to find the

formation, which gave Suzie a chance to make a few snide comments about big talkers. But then he took her by the shoulders, positioned her in the perfect spot and pointed.

She finally saw it. The snarky attitude dropped away.

"Oh, my God," she said. "That's it."

He felt a ripple of excitement—or nerves—run through her. He tightened his hands to settle her down. "It certainly looks like what she described, doesn't it? But we still could be wrong. If you put your mind to it, you could probably think of a hundred things it could have been."

Suzie shook her head. "No, this is it. I can feel it. The proportions are perfect, and—"

She covered his hands with hers. "We're going to find something, Mike. I just know it."

He should have moved his hands right away, the minute she touched him. He knew that he was weak, and it wouldn't take much to send him over the edge. These days, he constantly fantasized about making love to her. It was almost like being eighteen again, so obsessed with getting your girlfriend naked that you couldn't think straight.

Only problem was, he wasn't eighteen. He was a grown man who knew that getting naked had consequences.

He was a father.

He was a murder suspect.

He was a fool.

Still holding her shoulders, he lowered his head to the side of her neck. She had a beautiful neck, long and pale beneath her dark hair. Her veins were like tiny blue fairy webs.

He pressed his lips against the throbbing ivory spot beneath her ear. She went very still. She stopped breathing. Her throat moved in a sudden, vulnerable swallow.

He could have kept going. He could have moved down to her shoulders, so fragile under her cotton T-shirt, and all the way to her breasts, which had been driving him crazy for days.

But he didn't. He straightened and let his hands fall to the side.

She didn't turn around. "Mike," she began.

"It's okay," he said. "I just wanted to say thanks."

She opened her mouth and awkwardly drew in a lot of air. "For what?"

"I'm not sure." He wanted to touch her ponytail, from which her long, shiny hair was pulling free in all directions, the result of their sleepless night. "I guess for never changing. For still being you."

She swiveled her head and gave him an odd look. Then she smiled. "I've tried, you know. I just haven't had much luck."

He didn't let himself answer that. He would have said either too much or too little. The middle ground was hard to find.

So he turned toward the cliff face. "Okay, let's get serious. Let's start here, right under the stromatolite, and move out in opposite directions. We know more or less what we're looking for. The cave you found yesterday was small, but it probably was similar."

She nodded. "If it's like the one yesterday, we'll have to be careful, or we'll miss it. From a distance, the opening just looks like a fold in the rock."

They started shoulder to shoulder, under the angel's wings. He moved left, she moved right. After only about two minutes, she called out in excitement.

"Mike! Mike, come over here!"

He joined her in time to see her disappear behind a jutting rock. He followed, but bumped into her almost immediately. They were just inside the opening, in what he knew was called the dark zone.

It was like being closed off from the entire world. They couldn't even hear the lake lapping against the shore.

"It's so dark," she said, as if to explain why she hadn't made it any farther. She shook her flashlight irritably. "And I don't know how this dumb thing works."

He'd given her one of his. It had the usual kind of switch, so if she couldn't find it, that told him how nervous she must be. He flicked on his own and raised it over her shoulder. A large, circular area in front of her immediately turned an unnatural yellowy white.

"Here," he said. "Let's switch."

She took his, he got hers lit, and together they walked slowly through the narrow entryway. After a few feet it widened into a large opening. He ran his flashlight along the walls, surprised at how far back the place seemed to go.

It took a while, because he was traveling slowly, but finally he completed the circumference. The cave wasn't quite round—there were some odd pockets and angles, which perhaps led to further passages—but it must have been at least eighteen feet in diameter.

"Amazing," Suzie whispered, as if someone could hear them. The sibilant sound seemed to bounce oddly, coming back at them from other places. She ran her fingers along the wall, which resembled a sheet of rippled gray ice.

"It's damp," she said. "And very cold."

Toward the back, a small stalactite hung from the ceiling, and Mike's flashlight caught hints of yellow and green in it.

He was getting oriented now, and he realized that, at evenly spaced intervals high along the jagged walls, cone-shaped smudges of black soot appeared.

That was odd. He brought his flashlight closer to one of them.

"Look," he said. "Someone has drilled holes into the limestone here. And here."

Suzie came over and peered at the wall. "Yeah," she said. She touched her finger to the drill hole. "That couldn't possibly be natural."

She ran to the next black smudge and found a similar pair of drill marks. Stepping back, she surveyed the room with a narrowed gaze, as if she were trying to picture what the various shapes and intervals added up to.

"These smudges—could they be from fire? Could someone have put sconces up along the walls to hold torches?"

There were six places with the same markings. In Mike's imagination, the room suddenly blazed with torchlight, which would have played on these rippling walls with a weird, dancing motion, finding every mineral deposit that had left strange colors in the rock.

"Yes," he said. "That must be it. They needed light."

They looked at each other in the gloom, both obviously processing this piece of information and coming up with the same answer. Whatever had happened to Loretta here had not been an isolated event—and it hadn't been an act of savage impulse.

It had been planned. Someone had prepared this room for her—and for God only knows how many others like her.

The room was empty now, though. Whatever had once decorated this secret place was gone. He wondered why the "owners" had moved out? Was it because, one night about two years ago, things had escalated out of control? Because someone had died?

For the next few minutes, he poked around in the nooks and passages. Nothing seemed to go very far back, and there was no sense of incoming air, except from the opening to the lake. Probably this was a self-contained room, with no other exit. That would make sense. They wouldn't have wanted Loretta to be able to escape.

But in one of the larger nooks at the back, an eighteen-inch-wide area about five feet high and eight feet long, he found something. Several very large pieces of plywood had been stuffed into the opening vertically, as if it were a slot at the lumber section of any home store.

"What do you suppose this is?"

Suzie joined him. She pulled one of the plywood pieces forward—it was too heavy to pick up—and ran her light over it, from corner to corner. "I have no idea," she said.

But he'd seen something, or thought he had. He pulled the wood out the rest of the way and set it on the ground. Kneeling beside it, he used his light to study the surface.

There it was. Irregular smears along one side of the wood, as if something had been dragged across it, leaving a stain behind. It was dry now, and clearly old—the stain was an indeterminate shade of reddish brown.

He started to feel it, and then pulled his hand back. He didn't know what the stain was, but he knew he didn't want to touch it. He knew he didn't want his fingerprints on it. He wished, now, that he'd worn gloves.

How stupid could he be? How naive? But the truth was, he hadn't really believed they'd find anything out here. He'd just come looking because there was nothing else to do. He couldn't just wait for someone to come arrest him.

He slid the plywood back into its slot. What had the wood been used for? The dank air must be getting to him. He was starting to feel uncomfortably cold.

"Mike…look. What do you think went here?"

Suzie knelt in the center of the room, pointing her flashlight onto another drill hole in the rocky floor. "There are eight of them," she said. "Four sets of two."

She slid the beam across the ground, lingering at the four separate spots. He tried to imagine what had been bolted to the floor here. The four places described a rectangle about five feet long.

The pieces of wood were longer than that, so it wasn't where they had stood.

He had a disturbing thought.

"Hold this," he said. He knelt down, and prepared to lie on the floor. But then he changed his mind. "No," he said. "I'm too tall. You do it. Lie in the center of those four spots."

She looked uncomfortable, but she did as he asked without question. She handed him both flashlights, then carefully arranged herself on the floor.

"It's cold," she said. "What do you think…"

He put the flashlights down to free his hands, and their abandoned beams threw everything into bizarre combinations of sharp shadows and bright light.

He knelt beside her.

"I'm just going to move your arms," he said. He

pulled the one nearest out and up, so that it stretched to about a forty-five degree angle from her head. Then he leaned over her and did the same with the other arm.

Oh, God. Each wrist lined up squarely in the middle of two drilled holes.

"Move your legs," he said. "Spread them apart."

"I—" She began. But then she stopped. She did as he asked.

He looked. It didn't quite line up. "Can you make your legs go any farther?"

She frowned. "Not without a lot of pain," she said.

There was a moment of silence.

"But yes," she said finally. "They could go farther."

She widened her legs another few inches. It still wasn't quite far enough, but it was close.

He picked up one of the flashlights and let it play over all four points. Her hands, her feet.

"They did it here," he said. His voice sounded odd in this echoing place. "Manacles, probably. Some kind of restraint, anyhow."

He put his index finger into the smooth, drilled hole in the limestone floor. He noticed his finger was shaking. "The bastards must have nearly torn her apart."

Suzie didn't answer him. She lay there, frozen, for another minute. And then, slowly, as if her limbs were half paralyzed with horror, she closed her legs. She slid her arms back to her body.

And then she rolled over on her side, curled her feet up, and softly began to cry.

CHAPTER SIXTEEN

SHE COULD HAVE SPIT, she was so mad at herself.

Once, ten years ago, she'd cried in front of Mike Frome, over a stupid encounter with a puppy. She'd been seventeen at the time, and she'd sworn she would never show him her weak side again.

But now look at her. Right when he most needed her to be strong, she started blubbering like a baby. If anyone had the right to cry over what they'd found in the cave, it was Mike, not Suzie. After all, it was his wife who might have died, spread-eagled and in pain, in this place.

Though Suzie's mind flinched from the idea of *anyone* being hurt here, at least Justine had admitted a preference for masochism. It was Loretta who broke Suzie's heart. Loretta who wanted to be a cowboy and slept with a Care Bear, and knew she should "be something," but couldn't figure out what.

Suzie had always thought of herself as a pretty tough cookie. And, to be brutally honest, back in the old days she'd sometimes thought Mike was just a pampered little playboy.

Guess she'd been wrong on both counts.

Look at the two of them now. When things got unendurable, she was just lying here on the cold stone floor, useless and crying. But he was strong. He came to her. He wrapped his arms around her, under her back and below her knees. He picked her up as if she were no more than a doll and carried her out of there.

She'd forgotten it was daylight outside. She'd forgotten there was such a thing as sunlight. When the brightness hit her eyes, she turned her head and hid her face in his chest.

He held her until her breathing evened out. And then, carefully, he shifted her balance and allowed her feet to drop to the sand.

He dug in his back pocket and handed her his handkerchief. She took it, thanked him, wiped her eyes and then blew her nose openly—what was the use of pretending she didn't need to?

"I'm sorry," he said. "That was unforgivable. I was so focused on trying to figure it out…." He shook his head. "I can't believe I asked you to do that."

Hoping she didn't look as swollen and blotched as she felt, she looked him straight in the eye.

"It doesn't matter. We had to know. And I'm not as fragile as I look. When I cry, it's usually because I'm so angry I can't deal with it. I'm angry now. What kind of sick son—"

"Don't think about it," he said. "Not yet. Not while it's so fresh."

She drew a bracing breath. "You're right. But I have to say one thing. You do know we can't tell the police about this place, right? Not yet."

"We have to, Suzie. The police won't even try to find Loretta's abductors unless they see the cave. They don't believe it ever happened."

"We *can't*. We don't know what's in there, Mike. They went through your boathouse, and they found a two-year-old hair. Just a hair. Who knows what they'll find in that cave?"

He had to know what she meant. If he alerted the police to the cave, they would wonder how he'd found something so well hidden. What had his connection to the cave really been?

And now his fingerprints would be in there. If they found Loretta's blood or hair or DNA in there, too, that was bad enough.

But if they found Justine's...

"We were foolish not to call them first," she said. She knew it was dumb to say that now, when it was too late. *Hindsight is whine sight*, her father used to say. *Deal with things as they are, not as they should have been.*

"We should have let them go in and check it out. They couldn't have tied you to it then, even if they'd wanted to. Now—"

"Now they can." He didn't seem shocked. He must have thought of this already, but he still looked stoic. That scared her. She didn't want him being a martyr now.

"Mike," she began.

"Suzie, I want you to think about this."

"I am thinking! That's how I know we can't tell them."

"No." He took her by the shoulders. "You're feeling, not thinking. Two women are dead. If what we believe is true, terrible things happened to them in that cave. Whoever did that is still out there. He could do it again. Could you live with that?"

Damn it, he was going to make her cry all over again. She scowled to hold the weakness at bay. "I can't live with you getting arrested, that's what I can't live with."

"Suzie."

His hands massaged the tension in her shoulders. She wished he'd stop. Didn't he understand that the tension was what held her together when she felt like falling apart? If he was too gentle with her, she'd collapse again.

"It's going to be okay," he said. "I'm not guilty. In the end, that will have to count for something."

"Not if D.A. Quigley has anything to say about it."

He smiled. Even he had to know that was true.

"And what about Gavin, Mike? Surely there's some way we can find Justine's killer without bringing all this out into the open. Do you want him to know that his mother—"

"Please," he said, and his voice sounded exhausted. "Let's wait. I can't think straight about it just yet, not with those pictures in my head."

She nodded. "I'm sorry," she said.

"Look, we're hungry, and we haven't slept in forty-eight hours. Let's eat our way through a stack of blueberry pancakes, grab a nap and we'll argue some more when we feel a little more human."

He reached down and took her hand. She thought about pulling it away, just in case he was implying she was too weak to walk by herself. She wasn't weak, by God, in spite of that momentary crying fit. She could argue this police issue with him until they were blue in the face. He'd better get used to losing.

But his palm was warm, and his fingers wrapped around hers with just the right amount of pressure. She decided she liked it too much to relinquish it just for the sake of looking tough.

They didn't talk much on the way back around the lake. It seemed like a great effort just to wade through the sand, which was soggy from all the rain.

By the time they climbed the steps to his boathouse, she was so tired she wasn't sure she could even stay awake for the pancakes.

She was the first to see the blond-haired man standing just inside the boat slip. She didn't recognize him right away—she was busy confirming that he wasn't Quigley, or any uniformed officer with a warrant.

But then she recognized Rutledge Coffee, and, without warning, her infamous temper erupted.

"Oh, my God, look! I can't believe that jerk would come here. Debra probably finally kicked him out, and not a minute too soon. But if he thinks he's going to just come camp out at your house, he—"

She put her hand over her mouth. She glanced over at Mike. "I'm sorry. Argghh. I'm sorry. I have no business saying stuff like that. He's your friend. Besides, I'm just *camping out* here myself, and—"

Mike squeezed her hand to interrupt the flow of embarrassed guilt. "Hey," he said. "It's okay. I'm mad at him, too. But, you know, he just *might* be here to talk about work. Back before all this happened, I did used to have a business."

"I know," she said, still flushing. "I know. God, will I ever learn to shut up?"

"I hope not," Mike said. He gave her hand one last squeeze, then let go so that he could wave hello to Rutledge. They were almost at the slip now, and Suzie took one deep breath after another, trying to calm down. The guy made her skin crawl, but he was Mike's friend, and she had to try to behave.

When they reached the boathouse, Rutledge didn't look any happier to see her than she'd been to see him.

"I have to talk to you, Mike," he said, rudely turning away from Suzie without even so much as a hello.

God, she wished she had a paint gun handy.

"It's not a good time," Mike responded calmly. "We were up practically all night, and we're tired. Can't it wait?"

Suzie lifted her chin and stared at Rutledge, mentally defying him to react sarcastically to the news that she and Mike had kept each other awake all night. *Just do it, moron*, she telegraphed. *Say something. Anything. After the morning I've had, I'm so ready for you.*

To her surprise, though, he didn't even seem to hear that part. "No," he said, his voice tense. "No, it can't wait. I'm sorry. It's really important."

"Ledge, look—" Mike's tone was stiff, and his body language couldn't have been less inviting, but Rutledge seemed blind to all that.

"I'm sorry," Rutledge said again. "I have to talk to you right now. It's about—" Finally he seemed to remember Suzie. He glanced at her, and she gave him a flat gaze that simply said, *yes, I'm here, deal with it.*

"About what?" Mike sounded so tired. What was wrong with this guy, that he couldn't take a hint?

But then she looked more closely and saw that Rutledge's eyes were red and bloodshot. He looked even more tired than they were.

No, not just tired. This guy looked wiped out.

"Ledge." Mike got harsh. *"About what?"*

The other man ran his hand through his hair. His fingers were shaking.

"About Justine."

CHAPTER SEVENTEEN

"FOR GOD'S SAKE, LEDGE. Quit pacing and start talking."

Mike hadn't invited Rutledge up to the living quarters, and the other man hadn't seemed to expect it. Instead, the three of them had moved into the boat slip to get out of the stiff breeze and randomly found places to sit.

At least Mike and Suzie had. Mike took the stool next to his workbench, on which several marine charts were spread out and held down by a bright yellow measuring tape. Suzie, who hadn't ever been down here before, grabbed a folding chair toward the back, next to a stack of water skis. Rutledge prowled restlessly from one spot to another, touching things, pretending to check them out.

The large, cluttered area had two boat slips. One slip was empty. The other held a sleek white daysailer, maybe thirty feet long. The mast was lowered, the sails wrapped neatly around it. The boat bobbed lightly as the brackish lake water pulsed in and out, driven by the easterly wind.

Rutledge knelt on one knee by the sailboat, and fiddled with a little metal thingy affixed to the dock.

"This cleat is loose." He frowned at it, as if it were the most important thing in the world.

"I don't care," Mike said.

Rutledge looked over his shoulder, as though Mike's tone surprised him. He gave the cleat one last jiggle and stood up.

"Give me a break, man," he said. "I'm trying…this isn't easy for me."

"I don't really care about that, either."

Rutledge nodded slowly. "Fair enough."

He moved away from the slip and went to the far wall, where a slew of life jackets—one of them so small Suzie knew it must be from when Gavin was very young—hung on bronze hooks.

He put himself between Suzie and Mike—naturally. He leaned one shoulder against the old, weather-beaten tongue-and-groove pine and took a breath.

"Okay," he said. "I can't sugarcoat it, and I can't defend it. So I'll just say it. If those hairs they found upstairs belong to Justine, it's my fault."

Oh, good grief. Suzie glanced at Mike, but she couldn't tell anything from his face.

"I think you're going to have to elaborate," Mike said. "How, exactly, could it be your fault?"

"Your neighbor wasn't lying. She did see Justine come here. But she wasn't with you. She was with me."

Ledge wasn't even meeting Mike's gaze, the weasel. He had begun picking at a thick rope coiled up on the wall. It looked, at least to Suzie, like a perfectly good hanging rope.

"I brought her here three times. I didn't want to, Mike. But she was obsessed with it. She said that, if I wasn't willing to sneak her into the boathouse, she wouldn't meet me at all."

Suzie rolled her eyes. "Would that have been such a tragedy?"

Rutledge ignored her. For the first time, he lifted his head and directed his gaze straight to Mike.

"I'm so damn sorry," he said. "But you remember how it was, don't you? To be so hot for her you'd do anything, no matter how dumb? You used to feel that way about her, once."

"Yeah," Suzie interjected. "When he was a *kid*. Some men, when they grow up, learn to keep their pants on."

Rutledge shot her a glance full of poison. "God, you're as big a bitch as ever, aren't you? Guess cleaning up the outside doesn't guarantee—"

"Shut up, Ledge," Mike said coldly.

"Why don't you tell *her* to shut up?"

"Because she's making sense. And you're not. How could you have brought Justine here? You don't have a key. Are you saying you broke in?"

Rutledge's tanned cheeks flushed a color as muddy as the wind-stirred lake water. "I had a key. I took yours from the office and made a copy."

Mike made a noise. "Shit."

"I know. It was wrong. I wouldn't ever have done such a thing, except…" He leaned his head back and groaned. "Mike, she did something to me. She made me crazy. It was like being under a spell. I couldn't eat. I couldn't sleep."

Suzie thought she might puke. But she held her tongue. No point making Rutledge even madder. Mike would just have to referee again, and then this would take forever.

Mike frowned. "Are you telling me you'd fallen in love with Justine?"

"Not in love. Just… Hell, I don't know what it was. I'm telling you, it was like I was crazy. If she'd told

me to tie concrete blocks to my feet and jump off a
bridge, I would have done it."

Too bad she didn't, then. Suzie was proud of herself
for not speaking the words out loud. But she was
feeling more generous suddenly, because she had just
realized that, however gross this confession might be,
Rutledge was actually revealing very good news.

If he'd brought Justine here, that meant the D.A.
had no case at all. The upstairs bedroom could be
carpeted with Justine's hair—a horrible thought—and
it wouldn't implicate Mike in any way.

"Why?" Mike sounded truly puzzled. "Why did
she want to come here?"

"I don't know. I guess it grated on her that you
wouldn't let her in. You know she couldn't stand the
word *no*. And, in a weird way, I always thought maybe
she was hoping you'd find out and be angry. Be hurt. Especially because she absolutely insisted that we use—"

He paused, as if realizing his confession might be
going too far.

"Use what?"

"Use your bedroom. That's where she wanted to do
it. In your bed."

It was Suzie's turn to groan. "Un-be-*lievable*," she
said. "And you call yourself his friend?"

Rutledge whipped around, and the look on his face
was so furious she reared back instinctively. "Yes, I do.
And what exactly do *you* call yourself, Suzie-freaka?
His slut?"

She sensed Mike standing up, too, but she was
closer. She didn't even remember making a fist, but
suddenly she was pulling her arm back like the trigger
on a pinball machine, and then shooting it forward,
landing one right in Rutledge's gut.

He doubled over, coughing, still hanging on to the rope, which slithered down to the wooden floor. Her hand hurt like hell, all the way up to her elbow, but she didn't care. She'd do it again in a heartbeat. In fact—

"Hey, Fang." Mike moved behind her and held on to her punching arm gently. "Leave the guy at least one kidney, okay?"

Her breath was still coming too fast. She hoped she wouldn't hyperventilate. That would be just too humiliating.

"Damn it, Mike," Rutledge said hoarsely, still bending at an odd angle, nursing his stomach. "I didn't have to come here. I didn't have to tell you all this. It's going to get me in big trouble, you know. They're probably going to think I killed her."

"They found blood on the headboard, Ledge. Is that your fault, too?"

For a minute Suzie thought Rutledge might deny it. Hair was one thing. Blood from a woman who just turned up dead was quite another.

But he surprised her. "Yes," he said dully. "She liked her sex rough." He took a shaky breath. "Once, when we were there, I actually drew blood. I was only doing what she asked me to do, Mike, I swear to—"

"I know," Mike said. "I know what she asked you to do."

"Well, I did it. I told you, I would do anything she wanted me to. Anyhow, I know there was blood on her breasts. Not a lot, but, when we changed positions, and she was up against the headboard—"

"Okay," Suzie said, "I am *definitely* going to puke."

Mike squeezed her arm.

"I think we get the picture, Ledge. Look, I appreciate that you were willing to tell the truth. I'm pretty goddamn pissed that you did it in the first place, but coming out with the truth took guts."

Rutledge grimaced. "Don't be too forgiving, Mike. It's not all courage and brotherhood. I have to admit there were some other reasons I decided to come clean. Debra's one. See, she found out that I gave Justine some jewelry."

"Ledge, you are so many kinds of fool, I just can't—"

"I know. Anyhow, this one thing I gave her, apparently she was wearing it the day she died. It was an ankle bracelet. Kind of unique, you might say. It had this big pair of lips, and—"

"You gave her that?" Mike shook his head. "That was the tackiest piece of crap I ever saw."

"Yeah, well, it wasn't supposed to be elegant. I didn't even think she'd really wear it. It was supposed to be like this inside joke, you know? Big lips because she liked, you know, the biting thing."

"Look." Suzie raised one hand weakly. "Just bring me a bucket, okay?"

To her delight, Mike smiled. "Suzie," he said. "You really are obnoxious."

Rutledge nodded. "That's what *I've* been saying."

"No, I'm not." She looked up at Mike. "Let's be honest here. You didn't love Justine. You hadn't loved her for a long, long time. You knew she slept with all kinds of snakes—I mean men—and you didn't care. So, while the idea that she and Rutledge played stupid sex games on your bed may be perfectly revolting, and will definitely require that you buy a new bed, it hardly breaks your heart. What it *does* do is keep you out of prison."

Mike gave her a long look. Behind his eyes, she

thought she saw another smile. It made her heart do a silly little hula jiggle.

He turned to Rutledge. "She's right, you know. I'm going to have to buy a new bed."

"I'm sorry," he said. He hung his head. "I really am sorry, I wish you knew. But you can't, because you've never been the guy nobody sees. You've never been second best in your life. I used to think I'd give my right arm if she'd just look at me one time, instead of you. And then, when she did—" He ran his hand through his hair. "I wish I'd never done it."

"Well, you did," Suzie said sternly, forgetting to stay out of it, "and you're going to have to tell the police, you know."

He glared at her. "I *know*."

Mike held up a hand between them, refereeing again. "Hey," he said. "There's something more important we need to discuss right now. Ledge, tell me something. How much did you know about Justine's other men?"

He shrugged. "More than I wanted to. There were plenty."

"Did you have any names?"

"No. Suspicions, but not names."

"Did she ever mention anyone who really gave her what she liked sexually? I know that comparing one lover to another was one of her favorite mind games. Did she ever try to make you do things by saying that, if you wouldn't, she knew someone else who would?"

Rutledge shook his head. "She didn't have to. I told you, I couldn't say no."

Mike set his jaw, obviously disappointed. "What about a cave? Did she ever say anything about meeting a man in a cave?"

For the first time Rutledge looked shocked. "No. I don't think so." He frowned. "Could that be where the Mulligan Club met?"

Mike's eyes narrowed. "What's the Mulligan Club?"

"You didn't know about it? It was a club, very specialized, if you know what I mean. I guess she must have joined it after you two..." Rutledge started digging in his back pocket for his wallet. "To be honest, I don't really know much about it, either. She had only just told me about it."

He was vain, so of course his jeans were a little too tight, and it took him a while to extricate the wallet. But finally he opened it and took out a small white business card. He handed it to Mike.

Suzie looked over his shoulder shamelessly. It was actually a pretty boring business card. It just said The Mulligan Club in large, handsome type, and then, below that, what was apparently the club's slogan, Where Nothing Counts Against You. And then a telephone number.

Mike turned it over, as if he thought there might be more on the back. But there wasn't.

"The Mulligan Club," he said quietly, as if to himself. He looked at Rutledge. "I take it you were supposed to call this number and get instructions for where to find the meeting."

"Right."

"Did you ever go to a meeting?"

"No, they only met once a month, and I'd just been invited. I was supposed to go to the September meeting, but Debra wouldn't let me out of her goddamn sight that night. By the next month, Justine was gone, and when I called the number, it was out of service."

"What was supposed to happen at this meeting? I assume it wasn't really golf."

Suzie held up her hands. "Golf? What the heck are you talking about? Why would it be golf?"

Rutledge gave her an infuriatingly condescending look. "I take it you don't even know what a mulligan is."

"No," she said. "The local deviants don't invite me to their monthly sex club meetings."

"I wonder why," he said, and if it hadn't been for Mike's light touch on her arm again, she might have wiped the smirk off his face.

"A mulligan is a golf term," Mike said calmly. "In friendly games, if the players all agree, they can let one person take an extra stroke, but they won't put it down on the official scorecard. It doesn't count against them. That stroke is called a mulligan."

She thought about it, and then applied it to Justine's sexual proclivities. "Okay, I get it. It was a club where you could do things, sexual things, but it would be kept secret. It wouldn't ever go down on your official score-card." She made a face. "*Mulligan.* Very cute. Do you suppose one of these good old boys might have chosen to use his mulligan for rape?"

"Rape?" Rutledge looked alarmed. "What do you mean, rape? Justine never said anything about—"

"Forget it," Mike said. "You know how she is."

Suzie realized Mike was just trying to keep Rutledge from asking more questions, so she let that pass. They both knew that the last meeting of the Mulligan Club, the one Rutledge missed, might well have been the one at which Justine ended up dead.

"Look, Ledge," Mike said. "I'm not sure I give a damn about your little sex club. My focus is saving my own neck. Suzie was right. You know you're going to have to go to the police and tell them how that blood got on my bed."

"I will," Rutledge said. He put his hand over his heart. "I swear I will. But—not right now, okay?"

"Hell, yes, right now," Suzie said.

"Hush." Mike pulled lightly on her ponytail. "Why not now?"

Rutledge wiped his hand over his brow, which had begun to perspire. "I need a little time. I want to talk to Debra, for one thing. And there's this—well, there are details I need to straighten out before—"

"Before they arrest you?"

He shook his head. "Come on, Mike. We go way back. I would only need a few hours. And you don't know how the police are going to react. I don't have a millionaire daddy up in Firefly Glen that they're afraid of. They might decide to arrest me on the spot. I should get some things in order."

"Mike." Suzie put her hands on his chest. "Do not let him do this. Don't you watch police shows on TV? This is classic dumb. Don't you know what will happen if you let him walk out the door?"

"No, what?"

"It will be one of three things." She ticked them off on her fingers. "One, he'll run away, and we'll have no corroboration for the story. Two, one of his 'details' will just happen to involve Justine's killer, and the killer will shoot him, and we'll have no corroboration for the story."

One corner of Mike's mouth was nudging upward. "And three?"

"Three, he'll decide in a fit of hari-kari nobility that he should shoot himself for dishonoring his family name, and we'll *still* have no corroboration for the story."

"She's nuts, you know," Rutledge said. He actually looked awestruck.

"Sometimes," Mike agreed. He touched her under the chin softly, and she knew she'd lost the argument. Oh, well. It was his friend, and his neck on the line. Contrary to what some people thought, she did know when to back down.

Mike turned to the other man. "Okay. You can wait until tomorrow morning, if you want to. I've known you a long time, Ledge, and I have to believe that you wouldn't leave me with a murder rap hanging over my head."

And ten minutes ago, Suzie thought, *you would have been sure he wouldn't break into your house and sleep with your ex-wife in your bed.*

But she didn't say anything. She watched Rutledge thank Mike with tears in his eyes. He almost hugged him, but obviously thought better of it, and settled for shaking hands on his promise to go to the police by ten tomorrow morning.

When he left the boathouse, she plopped back down on her folding chair. She picked up a small oar that had been left propped against the wall. She tapped her toe with it idly and sighed.

"Okay, you win," she said. "But what if you're wrong? What if you never see him again?"

Mike returned to the workbench and picked up a small, silver case. "Then I'll have to go to the police myself," he said. "And play them this tape."

THEIR NAP LASTED just three blissful hours.

Mike had clearly been ready to go up to his room, but Suzie had stopped him on the second stair.

"You aren't really going to sleep in that bed, are you?"

The question seemed to amuse him. "It's been two years," he said. "I don't think there are any cooties left up there, do you? I mean, I do wash my sheets."

He was right, of course, and she felt foolish. But she didn't want him to go, and she didn't know how to say so.

"I guess not. It's just that…well, it was such a bizarre morning, all around, and I thought…"

He eyed her for a long minute, as dispassionately as a doctor might, assessing her physical and emotional condition. He reached out and pulled the elastic band from her ponytail and let her hair fall freely over her shoulders. Half of it had already come free anyhow.

She reached up self-consciously. "I must be a mess."

"We're both a mess," he said. "You're right. It's been an exhausting morning, and a disturbing one. Would you rather not be alone right now?"

She squared her shoulders. "No, no, I'm fine. It's not that."

But he must have seen through her denial. He came back down the two steps and took her hand. "How about if we share the couch? It's big enough, I think, though it may be a tight fit."

She shrugged, attempting nonchalance. "I guess that would be fine, if it works for you."

There was room, but just barely. They had to spoon in order to make everything fit. Suzie positioned herself awkwardly at the very edge of the sofa, determined not to cling to him like a vine. She heard him chuckle, and then he put his arm around her waist and pulled her into him.

"Get comfortable," he said.

She forced herself to relax. It was nice. She was tall, but he was taller, and her body fit into the contours of his perfectly. He kept his arm around her, holding her so close that she could feel the slow thumping of his heart as he drifted off.

She liked it. She even liked the warmth of his knees thrust into the hollow behind her own. It was sexy in a completely nonthreatening way.

She thought she might be too aware of him to sleep. But within five minutes, she was out.

Though she'd been afraid she would, she didn't dream.

She awoke, three hours later, to a vibration against her hip, and the sense that he was trying to move without disturbing her. After a few seconds, the vibration switched to a low chime.

She raised up on one elbow and looked at him over her shoulder. "Is that your phone?"

He had just extricated it from his pocket. Nodding, he flipped it open and held it to his ear.

She was so close that she could hear almost everything said by the man on the other end, though it didn't quite make sense. Quigley had apparently just spent an hour with Richie, which struck the man on the phone as suspicious, given that it clearly wasn't an official visit. He thought Mike would like to know.

Mike agreed, thanked the man and clicked off.

She struggled to a sitting position and tried to make her hair lie flat. Hopeless, of course. "Who is Richie?"

"Richie Graham. He was Justine's gardener. Millner kept him on after Justine disappeared. I guess right now he's technically the caretaker at the house. He lives in the apartments above the garage."

"Oh, I know him—I just didn't know his name.

He's creepy." She yawned. "Why was Quigley over there? Is the gardener a suspect?"

"I think so."

She nodded. "Me, too. He's creepy." She smiled. "Did I say that already?"

Mike was still lying on the sofa, resting on one elbow with his head against his knuckles. He looked rumpled and relaxed and sexy as hell. She began fidgeting with her shirt, trying to look less disheveled.

"So who was that calling you? And how does he know what Quigley's up to?"

"It was one of my private investigators. The one who is keeping an eye on Graham for me."

Her mouth formed a big, round *what?* "*One* of your private investigators? How many do you have?"

"Two," he said. "Three, if the guy who's supposed to be following Rutledge got going soon enough."

"Are you kidding?" She folded her arms across her chest. "I had no idea. You never said one word to me. Just exactly how many things have you got going out there?"

"As many as I can think of."

She scowled. "Well, you could have told me."

He touched her shoulder. "Look, Suzie, you've been great. I can't tell you the difference it's made to have you on my side. But in the end this is my problem. If I can't solve this thing, I'm going to jail. Obviously I'm coming at it from every angle I can think of. I'm peppering the field. I'm spending money I don't have, checking on people who may be perfectly innocent."

"I know," she said, contrite. "I didn't mean to be bossy. You're under no obligation to update me on every one of your movements, obviously. I haven't got much money myself, but I have some credit cards that aren't completely tapped, so if you—"

"I'm fine," he said with a smile. "But thanks. If I really needed any, I'm sure my family would help out. Right now, I'm letting them pay for Gavin's bodyguards, and that's enough to ask."

She shook her head. "Gavin has *bodyguards*? Man, you don't tell me anything!"

His smile turned into a grin. "I thought I wasn't under any obligation to…"

"I didn't mean that, and you know it. I just said it because I ought to mean it."

He laughed.

"Come on, Mike. Please tell me. I'll pop if I don't know everything that's going on."

He widened his eyes. "You'll actually pop? Right here on my sofa? Cooties on my bed, popped female on my couch. Where will I sleep?"

"Darn it, you know what I mean. You know how I get. I'm emotional. I can't help it."

"I know you can't," he said. He swung his legs around and sat up, too. "That's why I know you're going to want to come with me when I ask Richie Graham a few questions."

She stood eagerly. She held out her hands to pull him up, too.

"Damn right I am," she said. "Let's go."

CHAPTER EIGHTEEN

RICHIE GRAHAM OPENED the door in nothing but a pair of white jeans and a smarmy smile, which he promptly dropped when he saw that Mike, not just Suzie, had come calling.

"Mr. Frome," he said without inflection. "Miss Strickland. This *is* an honor."

"I'm glad you think so," Mike responded, equally bland. "Because we've come to have a talk, and we're hoping you'll invite us in."

Richie leaned forward, and peered around the door, adding a glance down the street. "Is your friend still out there, watching?"

Mike was surprised that Richie knew about the tail, but he managed not to show it. "Of course," he said. "I always like to have witnesses. Saves a lot of trouble later."

Richie laughed. "Now isn't that funny? Myself, I'm not fond of them at all."

He opened the door, though, and let them in. Justine had hired Richie just after the divorce, so Mike hadn't seen the apartment since the gardener took occupancy. He scanned it quickly as he entered, a little taken aback by the expensive leather couch, the high-end electronics, the huge tropical fish tank set into the wall, the carved ebony bar.

How the hell much had Justine been paying this guy? And for what?

Richie gave him time to absorb it all—obviously aware of the impression it made. "Can I get you a drink?" He glanced at the ultramodern wall clock, which had probably cost as much as a normal gardener earned in a week. "It's not five yet, but my parole officer's not watching, so…what's your poison?"

"Nothing for me," Mike said. "He's joking about the parole officer, Suzie. He doesn't have a criminal record. If you want a beer, have one."

"No, thanks. I'm fine."

She seemed dramatically more subdued than she had this morning, when she had been feeding Ledge his ego on a plate. Mike wondered why. Was she just determined to control her temper, or did this guy scare her?

He could see why he would. Richie Graham was more disturbing than Ledge. Ledge was just a weak ex-jock who had managed to lose everything he had and couldn't stop feeling sorry for himself about it.

Richie, on the other hand, projected power, brains and a certain sociopathic detachment from other human beings. It was, potentially, a dangerous combination.

Which was why Mike didn't really mind letting the gardener know that someone else was aware of this visit and would bring in the cops if Mike and Suzie didn't walk out of here unharmed in a reasonable amount of time.

"So." Richie rubbed his hands together. "If you didn't come for a good lager, to what do I owe the honor? Have you finally decided to clean up that jungle behind your boathouse? I'd be glad to give you an estimate."

Mike picked up a black marble obelisk. "I'm not sure I could afford your rates."

Richie nodded, acknowledging the probable truth of that statement. He reached over and grabbed a white shirt that had been draped over a chair. He fed his arms into it, then let it hang, unbuttoned, showcasing his torso.

Mike noticed that his chest was clean, no body hair. Didn't quite jibe with the description Loretta Cesswood gave in her diary. But he did have lots of dark, curling hair on his head, and perhaps that was all Loretta had meant. Mike made a mental note to ask Suzie whether she'd specifically said "body hair."

Richie sauntered into the kitchen, opened the refrigerator and took out a bottle of beer. He opened it with his fingers. If he thought that would impress Mike, he was wrong. Mike worked with his hands, too, and knew that there was nothing mystical about a good, old-fashioned callus.

Richie took a swig of the beer. "So?"

"So…I'm hoping you can explain what Keith Quigley was doing here for more than an hour. I know it wasn't an official visit, so what was it?"

Richie smiled. "Maybe he's looking for a good gardener."

"I don't think so."

"No? Okay. Try this. Maybe he wanted to tell me why he hired a couple of stooges to try to kidnap your kid."

Mike felt the shock wash through him like white fire. He heard Suzie's intake of breath, and he knew that she, too, was struggling to assimilate Richie's bizarre statement. This wasn't even what they'd come here expecting to find. They'd been looking for evidence of a frame, or perhaps some clue that the gardener was implicated in Justine's death, or knew who was.

This was like lightning from the only part of the sky that had no clouds. Could Richie possibly be serious?

"Kidnapping? That's a slanderous accusation to make against the district attorney, isn't it?"

"Not if it's true. Truth is an absolute defense against slander." Richie propped one bare foot up on his coffee table, and leaned his elbow on his knee. "Besides, who's going to sue me? Quigley?" He chuckled. "Somehow I don't think so."

"And *is* it true?"

Richie shrugged. "It might be."

Mike narrowed his eyes. Clearly Richie loved a good cat-and-mouse game, and Mike had no choice but to give him one. "Okay. Let's say, hypothetically, it is true. Why would he have told you about it? That seems pretty dangerous."

"Maybe I already knew." Richie glanced at Suzie and winked roguishly. "Maybe I have, as the song says, friends in low places."

"Okay," Mike said again, drawing the other man's attention back from Suzie. "But why? What could Keith Quigley want with Gavin?"

"Still hypothetically?"

"Yeah. Hypothetically. What the hell would the D.A. want with my kid?"

"Maybe he wanted to know something, but he couldn't ask the kid himself. Let's say maybe the kid saw Quigley, saw him somewhere he shouldn't have been. Maybe Quigley wanted to know if the kid remembered that."

"Where?" Mike wanted to grab the other man by the throat and shake it out of him. This game of one crumb at a time was impossible to endure. He thought of Gavin's nightmare, and his blood ran cold. "Where did Gavin see him?"

Richie rubbed the beer bottle rhythmically across his knee. "You sound a little upset, Mr. Frome. Are you sure you wouldn't like a drink, to help calm you down?"

Suzie finally spoke up. "We don't need alcohol, Richie. We need information. If you've got it, you'd better give it to us now."

Richie laughed. "Oh, I've got it," he said. "But I don't give information, baby. I sell it."

"Are you out of your mind?" Suzie put her hands on her hips. "If you withhold information about a crime, then you've *committed* a crime."

"Ooooh," he said, shivering elaborately. He turned his amused gaze back to Mike. "Sexy little spitfire, isn't she? But I'm not sure she quite understands the rules of the game. She's a little…minor league. Which, don't get me wrong, definitely has its own appeal, es-pecially combined with those legs."

Mike took a step forward. "How much, Graham?"

Clearly enjoying the tension of the moment, the other man chose to stall. He leaned his head back and polished off the beer. Mike watched his throat move as he chugged. One correctly placed elbow to the Adam's apple, and Graham would be on the floor, wondering why he couldn't breathe.

But as satisfying as that might be, it wasn't an option. Mike needed this bastard alive and talking.

"How much?" he repeated.

"Depends." Richie put down the bottle and eyed

Mike speculatively. "How much information do you want? Or maybe a better question would be, how much information can you take?"

"Let me worry about that. Right now, I'm just looking for a number."

Richie glanced over at Suzie. "Actually, I'm not a big fan of group negotiations."

Suzie scowled. She took a deep breath, as if she might be winding up for something, but Mike quickly put his hand on her shoulder. "Maybe you'd be more comfortable waiting in the car."

"No, I wouldn't."

"Suzie."

"No." She had that look, and he knew it meant trouble. "I'm not leaving you alone up here, and that's all there is to it."

"Ahh. A guard dog. It's really sort of sweet." Richie waved toward the patio door. "Maybe you'd like to have a little fresh air? The storm's cleared off, and the view from up here is very nice."

She narrowed her eyes. "Is that so? What can you see? Can you see, for instance, the *larkspurs*?"

He moved to the patio door and held it open. "Maybe you'd like to look for yourself."

She gave Mike a glance, her eyebrows raised. He nodded.

Grace in defeat had never been Suzie's strong suit, but he thought she did okay. She gave Richie a dirty look, but she did manage to make it past him without sticking her fist in his gut.

Richie closed the door behind her and turned to Mike.

"I'd say you're a pretty lucky guy."

Mike laughed. "I was just thinking the same about

you. You should see what happened to the guy who pissed her off this morning."

"Oh, yeah? Well, she's a great-looking gal, and she's clearly crazy about you. Considering how your first swing at marriage went, it's nice that you're going to get a do-over. Guess that makes her your mulligan, huh?"

Mike met the man's sardonic gaze with a cold one of his own. "I wouldn't know," he said. "I don't play golf."

Richie laughed. "I know you don't. Believe me, we all know you don't."

Mike walked up very close to the other man. Richie widened his stance and locked his knees, signaling that he didn't intend to back up an inch.

"Look, Graham," Mike said. "I don't give a shit about your blackmailing sideline. If you want to ferret out every dirty secret in this state, and then get the poor suckers to pay you not to squeal, that's your business. What I do care about is some help getting this noose off my neck. If you're selling something that will do that, I'm buying."

"It won't be cheap," Richie said. "See, if I give you what you want, it just might dry up some nice little income streams that I've learned to appreciate."

"I'll pay what it's worth. But it has to be worth something. I'm not buying hot air and gossip."

"Come back tonight," Richie said. He glanced toward the patio, as if to be sure Suzie was still safely sequestered. "About midnight. And come alone. Call off the tail. And no friends, especially not the kind with badges."

"No problem." Mike laughed harshly. "I don't have any friends like that at the moment."

"And you can't bring *her*." Richie nodded toward the patio. "I know she's attached herself to you like a sucker fish, with all that adorable Girl Scout loyalty, but you've got to lose her tonight. We're going to have a lot to talk about. And I think we'll start by watching a movie."

Mike tilted his head. "A movie?"

"Yeah. A nice home movie. So ditch her. I guarantee it's not the kind of video that good little Girl Scouts are allowed to see."

ON THE WAY HOME, as she listened to Mike talking on the cell to his office, his private detectives, his parents and Gavin, she tried not to be mad that he had shut her out again.

But she couldn't help it.

It hurt.

And that made her mad, too. Because why should it hurt? Why should she care?

But she did. Which meant that the Emotional Moron prize went to Suzie Strickland, who had now been fool enough to fall in love with Mike Frome not just once, but twice.

When she'd stood there on Richie's balcony, trying to pay attention to angles and views and evidence, all she could think was, what if he hurt Mike? What if Richie was the murderer, and he thought Mike was a threat? What if he killed him?

It had practically stopped her heart. She'd found herself gripping the banister with white-knuckled hands, feeling the hole in her chest. It had been five whole minutes before she realized that, if he killed Mike, he'd probably saunter out to the balcony and kill her, too.

God*damn* it.

She stared out the window of Mike's car, her hands fisted in her lap. How could she be such a fool?

It was as if the past ten years had disappeared in a puff of smoke. Yesterday, she'd been a happy woman with a business, a home, a life she really liked. And plenty of men, if she wanted them.

Now, she was little Suzie-freaka again, wanting something she could never have.

Why the *hell* hadn't she seen this coming? She ought to walk right into that boathouse, pack her bags and say so long, good luck, hope they don't hang you on a Sunday.

But she knew she wouldn't do that.

He needed a friend. Even if he didn't deserve it.

And even if she wasn't just a friend.

Still, she didn't have to pretend she thought he was being fair, dealing her out like this. She strode up to the boathouse stairs ahead of him, still not speaking. He followed in a leisurely pace, entering some kind of text message into his telephone. She'd die before she'd ask him who he was writing to.

Once inside, she went straight for the refrigerator. Watching that disgusting Richie Graham swilling beer had made her thirsty. She yanked a couple of bottled waters from their plastic web and held one of them out toward him. "Thirsty?"

"Yeah." Mike took the bottle from her, twisted off the cap and drank about half of it in one go. "Thanks."

"It's your water," she said. "So technically I guess I should be thanking you."

He tucked his forefinger under her chin. "Suzie," he said softly.

She jerked her chin away. "What?"

He put the water down and put his hands on her shoulders. "Suzie, look at me."

She did, but she frowned, determined not to be won over. She didn't want to look at him. He was so handsome, damn him. The good fairies had hovered over his cradle and dusted him with a lethal combination of sex appeal and sweetness, courage and humor and just the right hint of sadness in his eyes.

It wasn't fair. How was she supposed to protect herself against that?

"Suzie," he said again. He moved her hair off her shoulders, then ran his hands down her neck, from her jaw to the edge of her shoulder where she had that bony tip because she was too skinny. It gave her goose bumps.

He dropped his hands to her waist and pulled her closer. "Don't be angry," he said. "I don't want to fight right now."

"Oh, yeah?" She refused to soften her spine, although his hands were so warm they almost decided the matter by melting her from the inside out. "What do you want to do?"

His eyes were dark. "I want to make love to you."

Oh, no.

But her body was already saying yes. She hadn't given her backbone permission to bend, but suddenly she was up against him.

"Why?" She concentrated on a spot on the wall behind his right ear. If she looked right at him, she'd be a goner.

He laughed, and bent down to kiss her neck.

"I mean why right now?" She tilted her head away. "I'm serious."

He looked at her with a half smile. He didn't look

cocky, exactly, but he didn't look terribly worried, either. He knew what he did to her, damn him. He'd always known.

"I'm not sure," he said, and to her surprise his voice was husky and gentle. "Maybe because we've been finding so much ugliness, and I need something beautiful. Or maybe I finally just ran out of willpower. I've been using it up pretty fast these past couple of weeks."

The honesty of his answer caught her off guard. She did feel herself melting a little, and then suddenly he was kissing her neck. Over and over. He slid behind her ear, behind her hair, then came back to the pulse under her jaw.

Shivers of delight ran down her body in overlapping waves.

She shut her eyes. Maybe if she pretended she was dreaming, she could let this wonderful thing happen. Maybe if she just didn't fight it…

But then he stopped. He took her face between his hands. "Open your eyes," he said.

When she did, she nearly drowned in the dark beauty of his gaze. She made a sound…she was helpless, damn him. She couldn't have moved away from him now, no matter what the cost.

He brushed her mouth with his thumbs. "Do you want this to happen?"

She closed her eyes and tried to catch his thumb between her lips. It was torture, this soft touch that was so disturbing, and yet so clearly not enough.

"Do you?"

She leaned toward him. Let her body say what needed to be said. This wasn't about words. It was about hands, and mouths, and bodies burning with need.

But he wouldn't let her get close enough. His hands stilled on her face

"Damn it, Suzie, look at me."

She opened her eyes one more time. "What do you want me to say? You know I want you, how could you not know that? Do I have to say it, too?"

"Yes," he said. "You have to say it, too."

She turned her face away. "It's hard for me, Mike. You know I'm not very good at—"

"At being vulnerable?"

She didn't answer.

"I love your strength, Suzie. I think you're funny, and wonderful, and goddamn amazing. But tonight…" He began to massage the small of her back lightly. "Tonight I need you to open up to me. Every time we've ever been together, there's been a wall. Even when I saw things that made me think you might care, the wall was always there."

"I know." She reached back and tried to stop his hand. If he kept this up, if he massaged the starch out of her, she might cry. "I can't help it. It's just who I am."

"No, it isn't," he said. He lowered his lips to her neck once more. "You're so much more than that. I want you to relax, sweetheart. Because you and I are going to tear that wall down tonight."

She felt herself shivering, as if he'd removed a layer of skin. "I don't know if I can."

"I'll help you." He kept kissing, leaving soft, melted places in his wake. "We'll do it together. There's nothing to be afraid of. "

But there was. There was. If she saved a part of herself, if she kept it private, behind the wall, then nothing he did could destroy her. Even if he took her, used her and then rejected her, it wouldn't matter. Because he would never really have *had* her.

His mouth was moving lower, down across her collarbone. Down toward her breasts, which were swelling and tightening, anticipating. She moaned and waited, her thoughts focused on the moment when his lips would reach the aching places and make them warm again.

He stopped just short.

"Tell me," he said. "Tell me that you want this."

She arched her back, showing him.

He licked once, and caught the fabric, moving it roughly against her tormented skin. "*Tell* me."

"I want you," she said hoarsely. "Please, Mike. I want you."

With one swift movement he reached his hands under her T-shirt, shoving it up. The air was cold, and then his mouth found her, covering her with wet heat and a perfect pressure. She trembled, driving her hands into his hair and holding him close, as if she feared he might not be real, as if she feared he might disappear.

But he didn't disappear. He seemed to grow more real, more physically real—less an idea, a memory, a dream, and more a flesh-and-blood man. She felt his need pressing against hers, and it made her feel strangely safe. She knew he ached, too. He was vulnerable, too.

"I've wanted this for so long," he said, lifting his face from her breasts to claim her mouth. His lips were hard, and his tongue was harder, and she opened her mouth to take whatever he had to give.

"Tell me, Suzie," he said, between kisses. "Tell me you've wanted it, too."

"You know I have. For so long."

"How long? When was the first time you knew it could be like this?"

"I don't know," she said. "Too long ago to remember."

"I knew that night in the greenhouse," he said. "I wanted you so bad I thought I'd die when you said no. I wanted to smash every piece of glass in the building."

"I knew before that," she said softly.

He looked at her, his eyes burning, but she couldn't go on.

He began to stroke her gently, as if he could coax the words out of her.

"Tell me," he said. "Tell me when you knew."

She had to breathe through her mouth now. Desire was this huge, coiling power inside her, and it took up all the room in her body.

"I was fifteen," she said. Even now, she couldn't believe she was telling him this. "I didn't even know what sex was, not really. But I dreamed about you, and you were touching me, and this amazing warmth was flooding through me—"

"Like now?" His fingers stopped, and it was like putting a stone in the ocean…waves of desire backed up and crashed and spilled all over each other. She needed him to start again, or she'd fall apart.

But he wouldn't start again, not until she put it into words.

"Yes," she said. "Like now. It was the first time I ever felt this. I thought it was the most beautiful feeling in the world, and somehow it got all tangled up with the idea of you."

He groaned. "If you knew how many dreams like that I had."

She laughed softly. "But you're a boy. You're supposed to have dreams like that. Girls aren't."

"Lies." He moved his hand again. He knew exactly where she needed the touch. "Girls are just like boys. They just pretend they don't think about sex all the time."

He stilled his hand, pressing gently against the perfect spot. Electricity streamed up into her body, as if he had opened a fiery circuit. "But you're not going to pretend anymore, are you? Not tonight."

"How can I?" She rocked against him. The geyser of sensation was almost too much. It had to stop, or it had to find its outlet. "Mike, I—if you don't stop, I—"

He took his hand away. She took a deep breath and squeezed her legs together, trying to calm the pulsing ache he left behind.

"Come," he said. "Let's go upstairs."

Upstairs… She hesitated. Just for a split second, but he saw it.

"Suzie, I—" He frowned, as if he were in pain. "God, Suzie…I don't think I'll make it all the way to a hotel."

"Let's just stay here," she said. "There's room. I don't need a pillow. I just need you."

He looked at the cold tiles, the hard cabinets. "Damn it, I didn't want it to be like this—"

And then, he smiled. "I know the perfect place." He took her hand. "Hurry. Come with me."

He pulled her behind him out into the night air, down the stairs, down into the boat slips, where they'd spent the morning wrangling with Rutledge. He flicked on the small lights hanging from the exposed roof beams.

She looked around, bemused. What was he

thinking? There wasn't even a sofa down here, not even a cot. But she wanted him so badly she didn't care. The bare floorboards would do....

He took her over to the boat. She looked at him. "Here?"

"You'll see," he said. "It's perfect. And it's all ours."

He climbed in first, and held out his hand to help her in after. He ducked gracefully around the mast and slid open the cabin door.

It was very dark inside. They went past a neat galley with table and chairs, all the way back to another door. This room, the berth, must be right under the pointed bow.

When he opened the door, and they took the few, narrow steps down to the cabin, it felt as if they were entering an unknown world. A secret world that no one even knew existed, except the two of them.

The bed took up almost the entire space, its blue spread shining in the watery light that seeped in through the bow windows. Teak cabinets and lofts rose above it, but there was no doubt—this room existed only for this bed.

"It's beautiful," she said, holding tightly to his hand. "I know it's foolish, feeling strange about your bedroom, but—"

"Shhh." He put his finger over her lips. He shook his head. "Nothing is foolish tonight. Tonight anything you feel is right."

"Yes," she said. She lifted his hand and pressed it against her heart. "But see how my heart is racing? Right now what I feel is afraid."

He grew still. "What are you afraid of?"

"I—I don't know."

But she was lying, and somehow he knew that.

"Suzie," he said. "We said no walls. Tell me what scares you. You know I would never hurt you, don't you? Nothing will happen unless you want it."

"Oh, no" she said. How terrible that he should think she doubted him. "I think—I'm just afraid that I won't please you. That somehow, I won't be enough."

He smiled. "Is that all?"

He lowered her onto the bed, and then he knelt in front of her. She could see his eyes gleaming in the lamplight. The boat undulated sensuously in its cradle of water.

Oh, yes, she thought. Her whole body began to pulse and flood again.

"Not enough for me?" He stroked her knees with his firm, hungry hands. "Lie back, sweetheart. I'm going to show you how very wrong you are."

CHAPTER NINETEEN

IT MUST BE ALMOST ELEVEN, Suzie figured. The storm
had completely passed. The full moon floated slowly
through the black sky over Tuxedo Lake as if it had
nowhere to go, and all the time in the world to get
there.

She stood at the edge of the swimming dock and
watched it, recognizing that fat, peaceful feeling. She
knew that, tomorrow, she'd be the same old tumultu-
ous, irritable Suzie, and the problems of the unhappy
world would once again clamor for attention.

But tonight she was just a big white moon floating
in an infinity of bliss.

She heard Mike walking slowly toward her on the
dock, and she closed her eyes. Even the sound of his
footsteps was sexy. In her mind she could see his long
legs, so strong and yet so graceful—that must be the
athlete in him. She wondered if he was smiling.

His arms closed around her easily, as if they
belonged there. Pulling her in, he lowered his lips to
her shoulder, and she reached back with one hand, to
welcome him. She let her head fall against his chest,
which was bare.

"Sorry I fell asleep," he said.

"I watched you for a long time." She tilted her head,
so that her ear touched him, and she could hear his

heart. "But I was afraid I wouldn't be able to keep my hands off you, so I came out here."

He chuckled. "Good decision," he said. "If you'd started me up again, I don't think I would have survived. You sure know how to wear a man out, lady."

She knew he was exaggerating. Nothing wore him out. Each time they'd made love, he'd outlasted her by a few critical seconds. Even that last time, when he'd collapsed beside her shimmering with sweat and trying to catch his breath, even then if she'd wanted more he would have given it to her.

But she hadn't needed anything. By the time he was through with her, she'd been drained and shaking, too, emptied of need or thought or fear or shame.

It had been amazing. Not since she was a child could she remember ever existing so completely in the moment.

The water lapped at the pilings, making soft, wet noises. She recognized the rhythm. It was the same gentle lift and drop they'd felt in the boat. The slight motion had given their lovemaking an exciting edge. You couldn't ever be lulled into complacency, thinking you could anticipate what was coming next. The pulse, the pressure, the angle…everything was always subtly changing.

"I don't know why everyone doesn't make love on boats," she said. "It's far superior to anything else."

He laughed. "Maybe we'll try it in a car next time."

"Or an airplane," she said. "Or a runaway train."

The rains must have raised the level of the lake, because little wavelets occasionally licked up between the boards of the dock. She suddenly found that unbearably sexy.

"Mike," she said, turning her head farther, so that

she could rub her cheek against his warm skin. "I was thinking—"

"Wait," he said. "Before you say anything, I need to ask a favor."

"Of course. Anything you want." She smiled. "Although I do hope it's that wonderful thing where we both…"

"Suzie." He tightened his arms, and she looked up, surprised by his tone. "This is serious. There's something I want you to do for me."

She tried to tilt her head so that she could see his eyes. She had learned to read so many things in his eyes. "What?"

He paused.

"I want you to go home."

THE DREAM CAME every night now, even though sometimes the dreamer didn't go to bed at all. He couldn't escape it. He could pray all night. He could sit up in a chair till dawn. He could leave lights burning everywhere.

Nothing protected him anymore.

He must have fallen asleep in the chair tonight, because in his dream he was back in the cave again, but this time he was sitting down. This wasn't right, he told himself, feeling that familiar crawl of fear when the dream decided to create its own reality.

The rest of the men were here, too, wearing their black robes and hoods. They were all in chairs.

Wrong. Wrong. He tried to reprogram the dream. The men always stood. There were no chairs down here….

But the dream didn't change, of course—it never did. It lived in his head, fed on his fears, but he had no power over it.

The men were absolutely motionless, and he wondered if they were strapped in place. He wondered, with a sudden jolt of panic, if he was strapped in place, too. But he couldn't tell. He found himself unable to bend his neck, unable to look down at his body. Something, whether it was leather straps or a terrible enchantment, held him immobile.

Justine was the only one standing. Her naked body was new again, as perfect and mesmerizing as it had ever been. He wanted to cry out, to scream, because it was wrong that she should be beautiful when she'd been dead so long, and buried with maggots and worms.

"I never broke my silence," he cried, but no sounds came out. His lips didn't even move.

He realized then that he could do nothing but wait.

And he wouldn't be put out of his misery quickly. She was dealing with the men one at a time.

He was the very last.

She stopped in front of the first man and smiled. She knelt before him, her full, wine-tipped breasts grazing his knees under his black robe. She stared into his black mask a long time, so long that the dreamer wondered how the man could bear it.

Finally, she put her hand into the robe's opening and the dreamer knew what she was doing. Her long, pale arm pumped slowly, like a machine, without mercy. The man had no hope. He jerked, and slumped, his hooded chin slack against his black-robed chest.

Justine shook her head, disappointed.

And then she killed him.

The dreamer writhed inside, but nothing moved.

Someone, please. Help me.

So this was how they were to be judged. Obedient

silence wouldn't save them anymore. They would be judged only by their animal desires. If, when she came to them, in her dead and impossible beauty, their bodies responded, if they rose up, disgusting and aroused, they would have to die.

He tried to bend his head. He was frantic, desperate to know whether he, too, was helplessly swelling. He wanted to ask the man beside him—*am I erect, am I guilty, oh, God, do I have to die?*

It wasn't fair, he screamed in his head. It wasn't fair that she could come to them, voluptuous, naked, tantalizingly evil, offering things no one else would ever give them, and then punish them for wanting her.

One by one, the men failed the test.

Until finally, she was upon him, and it was his turn to die.

"I'LL HAVE A DOUBLE cheeseburger, everything but onions and large fries."

Keith Quigley had been trying to stop eating so much crap, maybe take off a few pounds. But he'd had a really bad day, and a lettuce and tofu healthfest just wasn't going to cut it right now.

Did he say bad *day*? Make that bad week, bad month, bad year.

And if he didn't get what he needed from his anonymous tipster tonight, he was going to have a bad rest of his life.

He propped his elbow on the edge of the car window and tapped his fingers on the roof while he waited to give the drive-through kid his money. But the pimply kid seemed to be totaling up his drawer. For so-called "fast" food, every phase of this transaction was taking forever.

Finally the kid finished counting pennies and allowed Keith to trade him a fistful of money for a sackful of grease without ever once making eye contact.

"Have a nice day," he mumbled as Keith pulled away. In his rearview mirror, Keith saw that the moron was already picking at a sore on the side of his neck and getting ready to keep the next customer waiting.

Keith had an urge to get out of the car, go in and give the manager a few tips on how to run a goddamn business. But why bother? He didn't really give a flip how this greasatorium was organized. He was just in a hellish mood, and he wanted to take it out on someone.

Though he still had an hour to go, he decided to drive straight to the rendezvous point and eat his burger there. He didn't want to risk being late. This might be the most important appointment he'd ever kept.

He wished he knew more about the informant. Even knowing whether it was a man or a woman would help. Instead all he had was a letter that had come in Friday's mail.

It had been marked Personal. Inside, there was a generic sheet of white paper with two lines printed on it, no doubt by some generic, untraceable printer.

The letter had read:

I can help you prove Mike Frome killed his wife. Sunday, 11 p.m., the Cooney Street bridge. East end.

So here he was, on the wrong side of town, his mouth full of the worst hamburger he'd ever tasted, trying to believe in a miracle.

He had to get something new on Frome. The hairs the evidence guys had found were promising, and the results on them would be in soon. But that smooth-talking shyster Harry Rouge could argue it was purely an accident that the devil's DNA had ended up in hell, and the jury would believe him.

So far, Keith had nothing else.

The letters for which Millner had dragged him all the way to Firefly Glen had turned out to be useless. In one letter, Mike had come right out and said he couldn't stand to look at his wife, but that didn't prove anything. If every man whose wife made him sick got convicted of murder, they'd have to build a jail on every corner.

The most promising tidbit had been a line that said, "if you've got issues with the custody arrangement, call Parker." Keith had salivated over that one, until they sent a detective to talk to Parker Tremaine, who'd represented Mike in the divorce. Tremaine said his understanding was that Justine had planned to give Mike more time with Gavin, to free up some socializing time for herself. Unfortunately, Justine's lawyer had confirmed that, too.

Which left Keith with a big fat nothing.

And time was running out.

He'd made a promise to himself the day Justine's body was found. If he could find out who killed her—and prove it—within a month, he could keep the Mulligan Club a secret. If a month went by without an arrest, he was going to tell the truth.

He'd promised, and he'd meant it, at the time. He'd been overcome with emotion. He had always known Justine must be dead, of course, he wasn't a fool. But seeing her body—or what was left of it—had knocked a hole in his gut the size of a cannonball.

He had loved Justine. Even though she hadn't returned the feeling, wasn't capable of it, really, he had loved her with all his ugly, thwarted heart. He didn't mind that she was what others—like that stupid husband of hers—called "sick." He understood the sadomasochism that drove her. The same beast drove him, too, and he knew it couldn't be denied.

It was like being a fire-filled dragon. When everything inside you burned, a constant internal torture, sometimes you just had to open your mouth and roar out a little of the pain. It helped, like lancing a boil. For days, sometimes even weeks, afterward, he cherished the relief.

Maybe that made him a freak. But it didn't mean he couldn't love, just like everyone else.

He could. He had.

And loving Justine meant that, if it became necessary, he would give up his life for her. To find her killer and make him pay, he would expose the one secret that would ruin him.

The Mulligan Club.

The club must have led to Justine's death, one way or another. He'd been so sure, at first, that Mike must have found out about it and, in his injured male ego, or perhaps his puritanical disgust, he had lashed out, killing her.

But now Keith had to face the fact that he might have been wrong about Mike. If so, he would have to tell the truth, and it would be the end of his career. Perhaps, even, the end of his freedom. What they'd done to Loretta Cesswood was only one small moral step removed from murder.

Why not be completely honest? It wasn't what "they" had done to the girl. It was what "he" had done. He had been the chosen one that night. Loretta had been *his* mulligan.

He had seen how young she was. How scared. He knew she'd been drugged. It would be easy for people to say he should have stopped. But what did they know? They were not dragons. They were not tortured by fire every day of their lives.

When she'd begun to writhe under him, trying to escape, he'd known he had to have her. He had opened his mouth, and somehow her screams and her blood had saved him.

If he had to die for that, so be it. He would have died without it.

He felt himself near tears, and he jerked himself up roughly. He didn't have to start this kind of thinking yet. He still had hope. This anonymous letter writer… suppose he really had some evidence?

It was possible.

Someone might have seen something. A driver passing by, who had hoped he could stay out of it, but had finally come down with an attack of conscience. A boater on the lake, who had seen Mike Frome digging in the flowerbed late at night.

It was possible.

He let himself begin to hope. He would sacrifice his career, his pride, his life for Justine if he had to, but he was human, wasn't he? He couldn't help hoping he wouldn't have to.

He almost said a prayer, *please let the proof be good enough*, but he stopped himself. Unless he was bartering a deal with the Devil, there really wasn't much point.

Just after eleven, he heard a car pull up behind him under the concrete overpass. He couldn't tell what kind of car it was. In an old police trick, the driver left the high beams on, so that Keith was blinded and couldn't see anything except a shadow walking toward him.

A gloved hand reached down and opened the passenger door. Quigley jumped, spilling the bag of cold French fries in his lap, around his feet.

He held his breath.

Please, let the proof be good enough.

But then he saw the gun.

MIKE ARRIVED AT THE MANSION a few minutes before midnight. Suzie hadn't kept him long. When he'd asked her to leave, she had simply closed up like a flower in a sudden frost and departed without argument.

The "favor" he'd asked of her had been simple. He'd asked her to go back to Albany, to her town house, and spend the night there. He asked her to study the preliminary photographs she'd taken of Gavin before the portrait, looking for anything that might accidentally have been captured in the background.

She agreed, but he could tell by the look in her eyes that she wasn't sure whether to believe him. She had retreated behind that wall again—she wasn't giving a lot away.

If she didn't think his "errand" was genuine, she probably thought that he'd just lived down to every stereotype in the Dumb Jock book, using her to break his two-year sexual drought, and then shunting her out of the way when he was satisfied.

If she really believed that, she would not be back in the morning.

He hated to hurt her. But he couldn't say the words

that would set her mind at ease. At all costs he had to keep her from guessing the truth, which was that he was meeting Richie. Knowing Suzie, if she suspected anything, she might well pretend to leave, then double back and try to follow him.

His big mistake, of course, had been making love to her in the first place. He should have clung to his self-control a little longer and kept his hands to himself until the whole investigation was behind them.

But he wasn't that strong. When he and Richie met at midnight, the man planned to show Mike a video. Mike had no delusions about Richie's motives. If he wanted to show Mike a film, it was because he believed it would horrify or hurt him. Preferably both.

Mike wanted to go into this ordeal, whatever it was, with the taste of Suzie on his lips, with the memory of her on his skin.

So maybe the selfish-jock label fit after all. He had been using her to satisfy his own needs. The need to remember that, however dark it got, his world still held something wholesome and bright.

Tuxedo Lake communities were conservative, and very few cars were still on the roads this late, so he made good time. When he got to the house—he still thought of it as the Millner mansion, as if he hadn't lived here for nearly six years—he parked his car out on the street.

His spirits were leaden as he walked up the drive. Nothing new there. In all those years he couldn't remember a single happy memory of coming home to this place after his workday.

After his day building boathouses, coming home felt like reporting to prison after work-release. He loved building. Justine had been disgusted to find that her rich-boy husband actually loved hard, sweaty, absorbing labor, loved being on the water, in the sunlight.

Even Gavin's high, laughing voice, calling *Daddy, Daddy!* hadn't ever completely banished the heaviness that settled over him when he saw the blue tile roof appear through the trees.

Frankly, if it burned to the ground, he would consider the world a cleaner place.

The main wings were completely dark and silent, as he expected them to be. But when he reached the apartment above the garage, he was surprised to see the front door standing open a couple of inches.

Richie hadn't struck him as the type to take risks like that. Any experienced blackmailer had more than a few enemies, victims to whom an unlocked door would be an invitation to redress some grievances up close and personal.

He rapped his knuckles against it sharply. "Graham?"

Nothing.

"Graham, are you there?"

Still nothing. He pushed the door open, again using his knuckles, and scanned the interior without actually entering. He'd learned his lesson finally. He wasn't going to walk into any suspicious location, dropping DNA and fingerprints like a bread crumb trail for the cops to follow. It was bad enough that he'd been in there just that afternoon.

The room appeared to be both uninhabited and undisturbed. The electronics were powered on but silent, their blue control buttons casting a pale opalescence over the nearby furniture. The fish tank bubbled, though its light was off, which reduced the vivid yellow and blue fish to languid silver shadows.

In the shadows of the kitchen, just visible across the room, the refrigerator groaned, cycling through a new tray of ice cubes. The clatter as they fell into their bin was as startling as a gunshot.

Nothing was overtly wrong, and yet, Mike's instincts prickled.

Richie should be here.

He backed out quietly and stood for a minute on the catwalk, surveying the property below. Everything out here seemed normal, too. The grass was pearly gray, washed in the moonlight, which was so bright the trees threw elongated shadows on the lawn.

Could standing him up be merely another of Richie's mind games? Had he never intended to tell Mike anything? Maybe the bastard was at a bar somewhere, picking up an unsuspecting teenager.

Suddenly Mike heard a shout. It sounded a long way off, as if it had come from the water.

He took the stairs quickly, his footsteps echoing in the empty air, and then he hit the grass running. He knew he might be overreacting. He might have imagined the sound, or it might have been an animal, a neighbor, or even a late-night boater whooping it up with a keg of beer.

But he didn't think so.

Just as he reached the edge of the property, something heavy splashed into the lake. He pulled his gun from his jacket pocket and began descending the cliff steps, his feet flying dangerously in the dark.

As he reached the sand, he thought he saw something moving in the shadows of the cliff, and he turned in that direction instinctively. But then, out of the corner of his eye, he saw something else—a body, floating facedown in the water.

It had to be Richie. The body was large, and it was dressed in white pants and shirt, both of which billowed slightly, as if they hadn't yet become water-logged. The drifting hair was dark, and the out-stretched arms seemed to glow in the moonlight.

The body was only about twenty yards out, not far from the edge of the dock. Though Mike knew it could easily be too late, he had no choice but to try. When he got to the end of the dock, he took off his jacket, slipped his gun in the pocket, kicked off his shoes and dived into the lake.

He swam hard, his arms churning through the warm, thick water as fast as they could. The body kept receding, as if deliberately teasing him, though he knew it was just the eddies he himself was creating, pushing the body away as he approached.

The lake was deep out here, at least thirty feet, so there was nothing to brace himself on. Treading water, he grabbed the back of Richie's shirt and pulled as hard as he could.

But the body was a deadweight. Mike's forward momentum jerked to a halt, unbalancing him. He went under, and when he resurfaced, the body had floated a few feet farther out.

Damn it. He tried again. This time he grabbed Richie's left arm, which was utterly limp. He dragged Richie's arm over his shoulder, so that his weight slid forward, onto Mike's back.

The man weighed a ton, so Mike knew he couldn't raise him onto the dock. He'd have to swim all the way to shore. But for Richie to have any chance at all, he'd have to get him breathing soon.

And that was assuming he hadn't already been shot, or stabbed, or skull-crushed by a rock.

"Come on, come on," Mike said through gritted teeth. He spat out a mouthful of lake water, recentered Richie's deadweight and tried again.

He kept his eye on the shore, calculating his progress. When he was only about ten yards away, he thought he saw something move on the shadowy fringes of the moonlit beach. Something as stealthy as a cat…but bigger…

Where was he, exactly? Was he still in front of the mansion? Had he drifted from center? He scanned the cliffs, trying to place something he could recognize.

And then he saw the stromatolite angel, its misshapen wings hovering over the invisible entrance to the cave.

His skin broke out in gooseflesh as he hit a cold patch of water. A tendril of something that grew in the mud wrapped itself around his ankle.

But he ignored all that, keeping his eye on the angel as a point of reference. From here, it seemed tragic, trapped a few feet above the ground, as if its broken wings were unable to break free and fly.

Without warning, the body behind him jackknifed. Mike froze, an adrenaline surge paralyzing him as the hand in front of his face clenched, then grabbed him hard around the throat.

CHAPTER TWENTY

SOMEHOW, MIKE SNATCHED a mouthful of air before he went under. He fought against the heavy pressure of the other man's body, trying not to sink so deep that he couldn't fight his way back to the surface.

He opened his eyes, but it was like being blind. He saw nothing—only a thick, wavering blackness.

Had he been a fool? Was he going to die? Had this been Richie's plan all along?

But the body above him wasn't holding him down deliberately. The thrashing was too frantic, too unfocused. As the adrenaline receded, Mike's brain cleared. He knew that Richie had regained consciousness suddenly, and had lashed out in terror.

The man was mindless now. Clawing for purchase, trying to use Mike's body to hold him up.

He would drown them both, if Mike didn't stop him.

He had to escape Richie's panicked clutch. That meant he had to go deeper. It defied his every instinct for survival, but it would also defy Richie's instincts— and right now those instincts were killing them both.

He forced himself to kick out hard. He headed downward, where the water was cold. Vegetation skimmed across his face like unseen hands.

It worked. The other man's fingers clutched his

shirt so long it almost came off over his head, but finally he felt the pressure ease. Richie had let go.

Mike darted sideways. His lungs were bursting. But he kept kicking. Sweeping his arms. Kicking…

And finally found the air.

Miraculously, Richie was still above water, too. His eyes were wide and unfocused. He reached out weakly now, grasping, but finding only water. He was pale. A ghastly disembodied head bobbing on a nightmare lake.

Mike grabbed one of Richie's hands just as he began to sink. The man must have lost consciousness again, which was a good thing—as long as it didn't mean he was dead. Mike flipped him on his back and towed him the last few yards to shore.

Dragging his inert weight up the sand was harder. He had to settle for getting Richie's head and torso clear. He put the heels of his hands on the man's chest and pushed, then pushed again.

Richie groaned. A stream of liquid bubbled out of his mouth, oozing down his cheek and onto the sand. The chest under Mike's hands lifted, fell, and lifted again, all on its own.

After that, just finding his own breath had to take priority. He was going to pass out. He knelt on hands and knees, his hair dripping in his face. He coughed up lake water that tasted of dirt and dead things.

When he had emptied his lungs, they burned, but they seemed to be working, thank God. He turned his attention back to Richie, who hadn't moved an inch.

He put his hand on the man's chest. It was still moving. The heart under the wet shirt was beating, but weakly.

He felt behind Richie's head for a wound. He

checked his neck. Then he looked on the rest of the torso. And that's where he found the blood, about three inches below the heart.

Cursing, he pulled open the shirt. His stomach spasmed, forcing more dirty water into his mouth. Richie's abdomen had a hole in it, not big but deep and clearly dangerous.

A bullet hole, surely. It was too round and symmetrical to be a stab wound.

Mike looked up, his heart pounding. He scanned the cliff line one more time.

This shouldn't be a surprise. He'd always known that drowning wasn't Richie's biggest threat. Just the most immediate.

In the far, far back of his mind, he'd understood all along that Richie hadn't stumbled into the lake. He'd known that it would take more than a push to leave the tough guy unconscious. Someone had rendered Richie helpless first, tossed him in the lake and left him for dead.

The running shadow suddenly became much more important.

He mentally ran through his options. His cell phone and gun were at the end of the dock, about ten yards to his right and then forty feet out into the lake. There was no boathouse—Justine hadn't wanted one. Just the long, exposed stretch of dock.

If a killer really still waited, gun in hand, in the darkness at the edge of the cliff, Mike would make an unmissable target.

But if he stayed here, he'd still be a target. And Richie could easily die. The wound wasn't bleeding much anymore, and his pulse was weak.

He decided to risk it. He didn't know who Richie's

enemy was, or what that person was capable of. But whatever happened, he couldn't just kneel here in the sand and watch Richie fade away.

He had to call for help.

"Hang on, Graham," he said, though he had no idea whether the man could hear him. "I'll be right back. I'm going to call an ambulance."

He stood, found his balance and began to jog through the thick sand. He ran every day, so this should have been easy. But he felt uncoordinated, his clothes heavy and awkward. His esophagus still burned, as if the lake water he'd inhaled had been filled with acid.

Once he reached the dock, his feet sprayed clumps of sand as he pounded across the boards. He didn't look over his shoulder at the cliffs. If someone stood there, he didn't want to know. He had to stay focused on reaching the end of the dock and getting that phone.

His jacket still lay in a clump where he'd thrown it before diving in. He squatted and dug in the pockets, feeling first for his gun. Yes, it was there. He hung his head for a second, his neck muscles suddenly weak. He hadn't realized how much that untended gun had worried him until he felt the relief sweep through his veins.

His cell phone was in the jacket pocket, too. He found it, flipped it open with sandy fingers, and dialed 911.

He gave the dispatcher the information quickly but coherently. He knew he was safe now. If the killer had been waiting in the shadows, determined to finish the job of eliminating Richie and prepared to eliminate Mike, too, if necessary, the bullet would have reached him long before he picked up the telephone.

Once Mike actually placed the call, the window of opportunity had closed. The killer would have to run.

Taking a painful breath, Mike retrieved his shoes and jacket. He turned around slowly. He was suddenly exhausted, but he had to go back. He had to tell Richie that help was on its way. He had to encourage the man to hang on, to live.

Mike didn't have any particular love for this arrogant blackmailer—who might well have been the man who drugged Loretta Cesswood, too. In a place deep inside Mike, a hard place that he wasn't proud of, he believed it would be poetic justice if Richie Graham, who had clearly lived by the sword, died by it tonight.

But not before Mike found out the name of the person who had shot him.

One household, two murders—Mike didn't believe there could be two killers. It had to be the same person. He didn't believe in that level of coincidence.

Damn it. He *needed* that name.

But, to his shock, when he turned back the beach was no longer empty. From two different directions, two men were running toward Richie's body.

"Hey!" Mike began to run, too. He was closer, thank God. He pulled his gun out as he ran, and put his thumb on the hammer. "Hey, get away from him!"

Both men halted, their postures shocked, as if they regretted coming down to see what was going on.

One of them even raised his hands, dramatically surrendering to the lunatic running toward him with a gun. Mike was close enough now to recognize the horrified face. It was poor Phil Stott, who lived next door to Justine.

"Mike!" Phil's voice was as high as a girl's. He was wearing pajama bottoms and a T-shirt, and his hair was standing in all directions. "Mike, for God's sake, don't shoot. It's me!"

"Damn it, Phil." Mike transferred his gaze to the other man, who was also frozen in place. He had to work to keep his jaw from dropping. *"Rutledge?"*

"What's going on here, Mike?" Rutledge was dressed all in black, but his face was as pale as his hair. "What's wrong with Graham?"

"Somebody shot a hole in his stomach," Mike said, dispensing with the sugarcoating. He felt angry as hell. Why in God's name was Rutledge here? Phil Stott, yeah, that made sense. He had probably seen something from his backyard and come to investigate.

But Rutledge lived in an apartment on the other side of town.

It smelled bad.

"Phil! What are you doing? What's happening?" A woman's agitated voice carried toward them from the cliffs. Mike looked up in time to see Judy Stott barreling down the stairs that led from her property to the shore. She was in her nightclothes, too, something loose and shapeless that fluttered behind her as she ran.

"Oh, my God," she cried as she reached the sand and began trying to rush toward them. She wore fuzzy bedroom slippers and kept stumbling over them. "Oh, my God. What's happened?"

She stopped like a cartoon character when she saw the gun in Mike's hands. She opened her mouth, but nothing came out.

It was the first time Mike had ever seen Judy Stott in disarray. He suddenly understood why she always kept her hair and makeup and clothes so compulsively perfect. She was, under the surface, a sadly unattractive woman.

Of course, he would bet he didn't look like any young girl's dream right now himself.

"I don't know what's happened," he said. "I think he's been shot. I just pulled him out of the lake. The police will be here any minute."

Judy might look like a frumpy housewife, but apparently she still felt and acted like a tough school principal. She obviously had grasped the situation faster than either of the men. She brushed past her husband and knelt on the ground beside Richie.

"Don't touch him," Mike said.

She ignored him, bowing over Richie and placing her ear against his chest.

Mike fell to his knees. He put out a hand and pushed her shoulder, moving her away. The evidence was already compromised enough as it was. Footprints running back and forth across the sand, the wound washed in the lake, fibers and hairs and skin transferred from this gathering crowd...

"Don't touch him, I said."

In the background, they all heard the wail of sirens. Rutledge and Phil turned toward the sound.

But Mike wondered if Judy even heard it. She was still staring at Richie. She brushed a lock of wet hair from his sandy forehead so tenderly that, instead of swatting her hand away, Mike found himself glancing at Phil, to see if he'd noticed.

He hadn't. Phil stared vacantly up toward the noisy street, where now the trees reflected the flashing blue-and-white lights. He seemed paralyzed, a deer caught in headlights.

Mike looked back to Judy. Her hands rested on Richie's chest.

"Take your hands away," he said, though he knew it was too late.

She looked up at Mike. Her eyes were wet, shining in the moonlight.

"It doesn't matter anymore," she said. "He's dead."

SUZIE PAINTED until about three in the morning. It had always been her best therapy, and it didn't let her down tonight. This picture was going to be one of her best.

Then, when she needed a break, she went through the mail that had piled up while she was in Tuxedo Lake, living Mike's life instead of her own. She'd neglected everyone so long. One of her friends had been reduced to sending a card saying, "If you're dead, please be so kind as to let me know." Her water bill was two weeks overdue, and her ivy was living on borrowed time.

She dealt with most of that pretty quickly. Then she showered, brushed her teeth, put on her Snoopy T-shirt, pulled her hair back in a chenille-covered rubber band and climbed in bed.

She'd put all of the preliminary photographs for Gavin's portrait on the table in her third-floor studio. She had flipped through them once, but nothing had popped out at her. She decided to wait until she'd had some sleep, and look at them again in the morning with fresh eyes.

Problem was, she couldn't sleep.

She kept thinking about Mike, which infuriated her. She was not one of those pathetic women who let an unrequited love dominate her life. She didn't sit around thinking of ways to get him back, or to make him pay.

She rolled over and tried to find a cool spot on the sheets.

Nope, she wasn't that kind of woman at all.

Or was she?

The problem was, she didn't really have any scientific evidence about what she'd do now that she was cursed with an unrequited love.

Because she hadn't ever actually been in love before.

She punched her pillow irritably.

It was true. That thing she'd felt for Mike when they were in high school—that had been just a crush. A big, bad, hairy, steroid-enhanced crush, to be sure.

But not love.

This was love. This need to know, every single minute, if he was safe, if he was happy, if he was missing her.

This was love. This fury with anyone who hurt him. This longing to fill his life with white roses and blue kitchens, just because he had sounded so sad when he spoke of them.

This aching to fight with him, make love with him, face hell with him.

This sense that her beautifully constructed dream life had been built over a sinkhole, and the ground was starting to buckle, exposing the big empty place where her man should be.

Yeah, this was love. What a bummer.

Finally, she slept a little, restlessly. When her doorbell rang at about 5:00 a.m., she knew it was Mike.

She bounded out of bed, cast a longing look at her chest of drawers, where she had at least two perfectly gorgeous lacy nightgowns, but decided what the heck. If she played this right, she'd be out of this ugly Snoopy shirt in a very few minutes anyhow.

She flew down the stairs and twisted open the dead

bolt. Love apparently wasn't very good at playing hard to get, either. She practically threw herself into his arms and dragged him into her living room, kissing him all over his face.

He held her so tightly it hurt, but she didn't care. She wanted to be that close, because for the past six hours she'd felt so far away.

Finally, laughing, she put her hands on either side of his head and tilted his head back. She'd intended to say something sassy about how, if he ever sent her away again, she'd—

But then she got her first real look at his face.

She froze, unable to believe what she saw.

He looked exhausted beyond words. But the frightening thing was how beaten up he looked, like a prizefighter, like the survivor of a train wreck.

His eyebrow was split, held together with a butterfly bandage. His left eye was black, and his left cheek was scraped, as if he'd been given a rug burn.

And his neck was covered in bruises.

"Dear God." She dropped her hands. "What happened to you?"

He shook his head, as if that were an answer. "Richie Graham is dead."

She stopped breathing. She looked at his eyes. For the first time, they looked defeated, which frightened her.

"Did you kill him?"

"No. I tried to save him. I was too late."

"Do they *think* you killed him?"

He shook his head again. "No. He was shot, but the gun is a different caliber than mine. It was a .25. I have a .36." He laughed roughly. "Apparently the devil really is in the details. This time they're focusing on someone else."

She was trying to absorb it all, but she couldn't think clearly. Perhaps, she thought, human beings were like sponges. There seemed to be only so much horror she could accept before her mind simply began to reject it.

"Mike," she said. "You need to sit down. How about something to eat?"

He frowned, as if he couldn't remember when he last ate, so she didn't wait for an answer. She pulled him into the kitchen and turned on the light.

"You sit," she said, indicating the breakfast table, which right now held only her dying ivy. "I'll scramble eggs. Unfortunately, I didn't restock. I just bought some eggs and bread on the way home today."

He tilted his head back, as if it were too heavy to hold up anymore. Because his eyes were closed, she was able to study the bruises on his throat without being seen. They were dark and splotchy, with colors forming.

Someone had really tried to strangle him, and from the look of it, had almost succeeded. Her hand trembled as she whipped the eggs, spilling some all over the white countertop. She cleaned it up quickly and poured the eggs into the hot butter.

He didn't open his eyes until he could smell the eggs cooking.

"Thanks," he said. He gave her a smile. "I think I am hungry after all."

"Well, I guess so. Unless you had a big midnight snack, and I would presume you didn't, since you've clearly been out wrestling alligators, you haven't eaten all day."

He pulled his eyebrows together. "I haven't?"

"That's right. There wasn't time." She put the plate in front of him. "It's been the day from hell."

He reached out and grabbed her hand. "Not all of it."

She felt a trill of excitement, both an echo and a promise.

"No," she said, "I guess some of it was okay." She ruffled his hair, which felt very soft, as if he'd just showered and washed it. "Now eat."

She added a bottled water, toast and some old orange marmalade that she hoped wasn't too stale. He didn't seem to have any complaints.

She sat down at the other chair and picked at her ivy, refusing to talk until he'd eaten. By the time he was on his last piece of toast, some of his color had returned.

He finished off the bottled water as if he'd been living in the desert for the past several years. She got up and pulled another from the fridge.

"Thanks," he said. He looked up at her. "Do you want to hear about it?"

She nodded, and sat again. He told the story quickly, without a lot of frills, but she didn't press, as she usually did, for details. She had enough imagination to provide her own, and it was enough to send chills through her. She hugged herself and rubbed her arms, as if she had a fever.

When he stopped, she asked the question she should have asked half an hour ago.

"You said they are focusing on someone else this time. Who?"

"They're holding Rutledge," he said wearily. "He was there, almost immediately after the attack. He didn't have a good explanation, and when the police interrogated him, he admitted that Graham had been blackmailing him, threatening to expose that he'd been sleeping with Justine."

She frowned. "Did he ever tell them about the hair? And the blood?"

"Yes, he finally came clean about that tonight—" He looked at his watch. "I mean last night. I think that's when they decided to let me go."

He sighed, touching his bandaged eyebrow. "Or maybe they only let me go because Quigley wasn't there to insist on grilling me for the next twelve hours."

"He wasn't?" That surprised her. The D.A. had seemed to relish hassling Mike through every other step of the investigation. Why not this one, as well?

"No. Apparently they couldn't find him. A temporary reprieve, no doubt. When he turns up, he'll probably come after me waving a pair of handcuffs and an arrest warrant. I doubt that he'll let go of his favorite suspect that easily."

"Do *you* think Rutledge did it?"

He didn't answer quickly, and that was really all the answer she needed.

"Never mind," she said. "Time will tell."

He nodded. He toyed with the remnants of his eggs, pushing one little glob around on her plate, which was rimmed in blue flowers. Her table was blue, too. That wasn't quite a blue kitchen, but she hoped it was close enough.

"I didn't tell them about the room," he said, and his voice was somber. "I'm not sure why. I just—" He looked up. "I just couldn't."

"Well, I would *hope* you didn't," she said. "For God's sake. We don't know what's in that room. Maybe nothing. Maybe your fingerprints. Maybe Rutledge's. We can't just serve it up to them like a birthday present, not until we have some idea exactly where it fits in."

"I guess," he said. He touched his fingers to the inside corners of his eyes and pressed hard. "I'm tired, Suzie. I'm so tired of living this way. I don't know what was worse, those two years when I had no idea what had happened to her, or the past two months, when I seem to discover something new and terrible around every corner."

She had a couple of reassuring lines ready on her lips. But they seemed inadequate. This had simply been too much for anyone to bear. And yet he'd been so strong.

He leaned over and edged back the curtain of her breakfast nook window. She didn't have a lake outside, but she had a pretty garden with an apple tree that was not quite finished blooming. With the pink early-morning sky behind it, it looked nice. She hoped he found it soothing.

"Sometimes I just wish I could take Gavin and run away." He shook his head, still staring out the window, though she realized now he wasn't seeing the apple tree at all. "To some other place, some other country. Somewhere where we can forget."

She had to swallow back her response to that one, too. She wanted to say, *okay, but take me with you*. She couldn't ask that, of course. She had no right. They'd been temporary allies in this strange war, and they'd had one evening of fantastic sex. That didn't add up to forever, and she knew it.

He didn't mean what he'd said about running away, anyhow. He would never leave his family. The Fromes had been a closely knit Firefly Glen family for a hundred years. He'd rather see his parents and grandparents and cousins and nephews from behind bars on visitors' day than never see them at all.

Besides, his momma had raised him well. The Fromes knew all about honor, and held it above rubies and gold—even above happiness, if the choice became necessary.

When they encountered problems, they didn't look for easy outs.

Funny, how Suzie could see that now—now that she didn't have to hate them because she was so darn jealous. In Firefly Glen, they'd been the royalty, and she'd just been a peon. She had to get out in the world and find herself before she could discover how she really felt.

She had discovered that she liked and admired the Fromes. They were fighters, just as she was. They just had a different style.

Yes, they were fighters. And they were winners.

Mike was just exhausted right now. He'd remember who he really was when he woke up again.

"Come on," she said. She took his hand and tugged him to a standing position. "You need to sleep."

He tightened his grip. 'With you?"

"No," she said, surprising herself. She wouldn't have thought she had this much sainthood in her. "I have to paint. You sleep by yourself this time, and after that…we'll see."

CHAPTER TWENTY-ONE

DEBRA HAD JUST FINISHED putting the last of her clothes into the last of her suitcases when the doorbell rang. She assumed it must be Rutledge, finally back from the police station. He'd probably forgotten his key.

Or maybe he figured she had changed the locks. It wasn't a paranoid assumption. She would have done exactly that, if she'd been intending to stay.

She opened the door wearily, steeling herself for the inevitable scene, but to her surprise it was Judy.

"Hi," Debra said. She summoned up a smile. "Aren't you supposed to be at school?"

Judy looked…the word that came to mind was *downtrodden*. It gave Debra a shock. Though there were many differences between the two women, they were alike in one major way. Neither of them was a beauty, and they both compensated for it with meticulous grooming. This might be the first time she'd seen Judy without lipstick.

"I took a personal leave day," Judy said. "After last night, I just couldn't—"

Debra had forgotten that Judy had been on the scene when they found Richie's body. It must have been gruesome, to put her in such a state.

"Are you okay?" Debra held out her hand. "Come on in."

Judy looked around the living room as she entered. She took the nearest chair and sat with a heavy sigh. She didn't seem to notice that most of Debra's personal things were gone. "Rutledge isn't here, is he?"

"No, the police haven't released him." Debra pulled out the desk drawer and began going through the papers that had piled up in there, to see if there were any she wanted to take with her. "I'm not sure why. They can't really believe he had anything to do with Richie Graham's death."

Judy closed her eyes, and she seemed to shudder slightly. "Are you so sure?"

Debra frowned. "He hardly even knew Richie. Why on earth would he kill him? Rutledge is a bully and a tomcat and a heartless bastard. I've accepted that now. But he's not a murderer."

Judy's mouth worked, as if she were trying on words, checking them out to see if she could find some that were both honest and humane.

"Judy, what?" Debra was impatient. She had a lot more packing to do, and she was almost desperate to get out of this town. "Just tell me. I'm leaving him anyhow, so it doesn't matter."

"You are? You're really leaving him?"

"Yes. I've had enough. I'm going home."

Judy's eyebrows went up. "Home to *Kansas*?"

"Yes."

Debra didn't defend her decision against the shock she heard in Judy's voice. She didn't care whether it made sense to Judy. It made sense to *her*. Whether you were eight or twenty-eight, home was where you went if you had traveled as far down a lonely dead-end street as you could stand to go.

No matter how stupid it had been, Debra had loved

Rutledge. Now she was tired, and she was hurting. Her mother might say "I told you so," but then she'd roll up her sleeves and help Debra figure out how to start over.

Debra didn't hold Judy's lack of understanding against her. Judy had a beautiful home here in Tuxedo Lake, and a loving husband, and a career that was both prestigious and secure.

It had always flattered Debra that a well-educated professional like Judy would be interested in a struggling nobody like her. They'd met at a school function that Debra had attended with Gavin, as a favor to Mike, shortly after Justine had disappeared. Debra had been impressed with the special attention and gentle concern Judy had shown the little boy.

After that, Debra and Judy had become friends quickly. The relationship, in which Judy, though only about seven or eight years older, had definitely taken the maternal role, had been good for Debra. It had filled some of the lonely spaces.

But not enough of them. She realized sadly that Judy, Mike and Gavin were the only people she'd really miss when she was gone.

"Judy, please. Just tell me."

"Okay...it's just that...you know that we were all out on the beach when the police arrived." Judy hesitated again. "Deb, do you know why Rutledge happened to be at the house right then?"

"I assumed he was looking for Mike."

"No." Judy bit her lip, but then apparently decided to continue. "I heard him giving his statement to the police. He was there because Richie Graham was blackmailing him."

"*Blackmailing* him?" Debra's hands froze, an electricity bill in one hand, and an old Christmas card that had been kept for some unknown reason in the other. "Over what?"

"I don't know." Judy looked miserable. "He mentioned something about a videotape, but he didn't say what was on it. I guess he never mentioned anything like that to you?"

"No. Of course not." Debra let the papers fall back into the drawer. She fell, too, onto the desk chair. "It was something about Justine, no doubt."

Judy didn't look shocked. She was too smart, naturally, not to have considered that possibility.

"I had wondered about that," she admitted. "I had hoped not, for your sake, but… Were they having an affair?"

Debra nodded. The pain was a little less intense now than it had been when she first found out. She'd confronted Rutledge about the anklet yesterday morning, demanding to know if he'd been Justine Frome's lover. He'd caved immediately. He had wanted to rationalize, to offer all kinds of mitigating details, but she'd refused to listen.

She didn't care where, when, how often, or even why.

He'd lost her at "yes."

"Maybe Richie had seen them together," Judy said. "He must have taped them somehow. But why would a guy like Rutledge be so concerned about having an affair? I mean, he did it all the time, didn't he? What was one more?"

Her eyes widened, and she took a deep breath. "Oh, Deb. You don't think—you don't think Rutledge could have killed Justine, do you?"

Debra put her hands together tightly in her lap.

She couldn't answer. She didn't know. She simply didn't know.

But she did finally understand why, though she'd already known Rutledge wasn't faithful, this particular affair had made her open up her suitcase and book a plane for Kansas.

She wasn't sure anymore how far he'd go. And that mattered.

Because she didn't want to die.

She looked up and saw that Judy had come to stand beside her. The older woman held out her hand.

"Come on, Debra," she said. "I'll help you pack."

SUZIE HAD BEEN PAINTING with her back to the window, getting the best of the late-morning light. But the sun must have been too soothing. She didn't realize she'd dozed off until she woke suddenly when she heard a knock on her studio door.

Mike! She sat up, wide-awake.

He must have been knocking for quite a while, because he cracked the door and peeked in. "Suzie? Are you okay?"

She rose quickly, tossing her drop cloth over the painting. She wasn't ready to show this to him yet.

"You're awake!"

"Finally," he said, running his hand through his hair. "I called Gavin first, then came to find you. What is it, noon?"

"Almost. But you needed the sleep."

She crossed the room and checked his injuries. They didn't look as bad, now that the rest of him wasn't quite so drawn and pale. Heck, she'd seen him look worse than this after a football game with the Arborville Airedales.

She touched his cheek, which still looked pretty raw. "Does it hurt much?"

He smiled. "It hurts something terrible, ma'am." He reached up and caught her hand. "I need a whole lot of tender loving care."

She rolled her eyes. "Not a chance, you big faker. The photographs you asked about are on the table over there. I couldn't find anything, so now you have to look."

He gave her a crestfallen expression that was ridiculously sexy, but she remained firm. He turned over her hand and planted a quick kiss in her palm.

"Okay," he said. "Show me what you've got."

She led him to the table. As he passed her little blue-and-red waitress uniform, which hung on the wall, he raised his eyebrows. He reached out and flicked the ribbons on the cap, then gave her a quizzical look.

"Sailor Sam's Fish and Chips," she said, sighing. "It's complicated, so don't ask. Basically, I use it for inspiration."

He fingered the short-shorts. "Yes, I think I see. I'm fairly inspired right now. How about a fashion show?"

"Sure." She smiled. "I don't think they'll fit you, but hey…if you really want to…"

He slapped out at her backside, but she dodged neatly. "Look, Frome, stop being a dork. You have real work to do."

His eyes widened as he looked at the table. She knew he'd underestimated the job. She sometimes shot five or six rolls of film when she was preparing to paint a child's portrait.

The parents always had weird ideas, so first she needed to shoot those poses, just to prove her point that, in the end, the parents wouldn't really be happy with a painting of little Joey kissing his puppy on the lips.

Then she had to try out some ideas of her own. She showed them to the parents, and she always learned a lot from their reactions. If they said, "But you've made Janey look so fat," then she knew she'd have to shave off a few pounds in the portrait. Or if they said, "But Tommy's nose looks so crooked from that angle," she write that down in her book. *Nose job*, she'd say, and move on.

Best of all, the photo sessions were a great opportunity to bond with the child, which was important. The two of them would be spending a lot of time together before the portrait was finally finished.

Gavin had been so much fun. He'd been a natural subject, not too shy of the camera, but not too in love with it, either. The sessions had turned into playtimes. Sometimes Justine had seemed jealous. Suzie tried to get her involved, even hinting that it would be good for her relationship with Gavin. But Justine had always pulled back, too busy, or perhaps unwilling to get mussed.

Suzie had felt like a fool. Why should she give Justine tips on parenting, anyhow? Justine was the one who'd walked away from their embarrassing high school feud holding all the prizes.

The wedding ring, the husband, the adorable little boy.

But, much as Suzie might have liked for Justine to be miserable, she couldn't help wishing, for Gavin's sake, that the Snow Queen had somehow found the heart to be a better mom.

Oh, well. That was ancient history now.

Suzie sat back down at her easel while Mike pored over the photos. She tried to paint, but her gaze kept wandering to him. His profile was toward her. He had a great profile. No nose job required there.

And it was fun to watch him smile a little every time he ran across a particularly cute shot. After last night, it was great to know he still *could* smile.

He sure did love that kid.

Occasionally, he'd look up, too, and point that smile at her. It would go through her warm and deep, like an arrow-tipped sunbeam. She'd look back at her easel, but she knew she had a dumb grin on her face.

They'd found an oasis here, she thought. A safe bubble, a moment out of time. She wished she could stop time and make it last forever.

After a while, they got used to each other and settled into a comfortable rhythm. She began to paint in earnest. She mixed cerulean and cobalt, then added some white and held the palette up to the window to check the color in the light. It was important to get the perfect blue. The sound of Mike sifting through the photos settled into a pleasant background sound-track.

Suddenly, with an inarticulate noise, he jerked forward. A tremor of urgency splintered the peace of the room.

He bent low over one of the pictures. "Who is *that*?"

She dropped her palette and joined him at the table. The picture he held was one of Gavin climbing in the oak in Justine's backyard. Gavin had laughed, proud of his agility, one foot braced on each side of a big fork in the trunk.

"What?" She scanned the picture. "What do you see?"

Mike pointed to the top right corner, deep background. Two people stood there, completely out of focus. They were just two flesh-colored blurs.

But as she looked harder, she saw what Mike had seen. If you untangled the masses, you saw that one of the people was pulling away, and the other one was trying to hold on, grabbing a wrist.

"Wait," she said. She ran to her supply cabinet and pulled out the big square magnifying glass she used for the fine detail when she painted.

"Here." She handed it to Mike. "See if you can make out who it is."

He stood to get a better angle and moved the magnifying glass up and down, trying to find the perfect distance.

Finally, he stopped. He looked at it that way a long time.

Standing on tiptoe, Suzie peered over his shoulder. The figures were clearer, but hardly in focus. She recognized Justine, of course. She knew her well enough to identify the shape of her face, the contours of her hair. She even knew Justine's face well enough to realize that, at the moment this picture had been snapped, she was a very angry woman.

But she didn't recognize the man who held her arm.

"Who is it?" She touched Mike's back. "Do you know him?"

"Yes," he said. His voice was bewildered. Suzie knew that, whoever it was, it wasn't who he'd been expecting.

"Well, who is it? Is it Rutledge?"

"No. I just can't believe—" Mike shook his head and squinted. "But it *is*."

She was getting mad.

"Come on," she said. "Is it the gardener?"

"No," he said again. "Heaven help him, it's poor Phil Stott."

THE DREAM DIDN'T EVEN WAIT for sleep anymore. Now it came whenever it wanted—even when he was wide-awake, or working, or talking to his wife.

He finally recognized it for what it really was. Not merely a nightmare, not a flare-up of guilt, like a showy but essentially harmless St. Elmo's fire of the subconscious.

It was the beginning of true insanity.

He sat in his study and stared out at the lake, something he did more and more these days. He hardly ever went to work, though the money was drying up. He couldn't seem to make himself care, not even when his wife tried to prod him out of his lethargy with tears or insults or threats.

They all bounced off him, as if he were floating, fetal and inert, inside an invisible bubble. The walls of the bubble were thickening, the real world receding.

He wondered if, eventually, they'd have to put him away. Would they come in here one day and find him completely unreachable, standing at his window, staring at the green lake but seeing only the gray, torchlit cave, listening to Mozart, but hearing only the screams?

Or would his madness take a more active form? Would the bubble finally pop? Would the dream finally convince him—as it seemed to be trying to do—that everyone connected to the cave deserved to die?

Had it begun already?

He wished he could be certain where he'd been last night, when Richie Graham was killed. He believed he'd been in bed. But he'd come to consciousness standing at the door to his room, his heart pounding. And he'd felt a compulsion to run outside, as if he already knew something dreadful had occurred.

Perhaps this was the nature of madness: the person afflicted was always the last to know.

When the telephone at his elbow rang, he didn't even think to answer it. His wife did that these days, because he didn't want to talk to anyone. He couldn't be sure what would come out of his mouth if he dared to open it and speak.

The shrill sound screamed through the room, over and over. He felt his nerves burning, his chest tightening. *Shut up*, he thought. *Shut up.*

But he'd forgotten. His wife wasn't here. There was no one to make it shut up.

It stopped. And right away began again.

Maybe he should answer it. It might be important. It might be his wife. Or…it might be—though he had no idea what form this could take—salvation.

He forced himself to pick up the phone. He felt it vibrate in his hand, still ringing. Suddenly, illogically, he was terrified that the caller would give up, would disconnect before he could answer.

With clumsy fingers he pressed the button that said Talk.

"Hello," he said. His voice didn't sound right. He tried again. "Hello?"

"Phil, is that you? It's Mike Frome."

"Mike?" Phil felt a sudden onslaught of emotion. But he was so confused. He couldn't tell whether the emotion was relief or fear.

"Phil, I need to talk to you. Can I come over?"

"No," Phil said, though he knew that wasn't the

way normal, civilized people answered polite questions. He should have offered an excuse. "No. What do you want?"

"I want to talk to you. It's serious, Phil. Whatever appointments you have, they're not as important as this."

Appointments. He almost laughed. The only appointment he had was with the dream.

"What do you want to talk about?"

There was a silence. Phil gripped the phone, waiting for an answer. He stared at the sparkling green lake and saw smoky firelight.

"I want to talk about Justine," Mike said finally, in a voice so tired and sad that Phil wondered whether he, too, might have dreams. "I want to talk about the Mulligan Club."

Phil put the phone down for a second. He bent over and put his head down, riding through this sudden racing heartbeat as if it were a roller coaster. When it subsided enough for him to breathe, he picked up the phone again.

"All right," he said. "I'll tell you. I want to tell you."

He didn't know why he hadn't thought of this before. He'd been silent so long, thinking that would save him. But the dream had warned him. Silence was no protection anymore.

"Meet me in an hour, Mike. I'll tell you everything you want to know."

He heard Mike's exhale, and he knew the other man had been fighting a bucking heart, too.

"All right," Mike said. "Where?"

"I don't know…." He frowned, trying to think. "Not here. I don't—no… Yes. Meet me at Justine's house."

Phil felt something shatter inside him, and relief flooded through the spaces between the cracks.

"Yes," he said, nodding to himself. He looked out his window, and to his amazement he finally saw the lake again. He felt something warm on his face. When he put his fingers to his cheek, he realized it was tears. "That's where it all began. That's where it should end."

CHAPTER TWENTY-TWO

"So, NOT TO INSULT your nice neighbor or anything," Suzie said as they walked up to the mansion, "but you do have your gun with you, right?"

Mike nodded with a grim smile. "Phil's kind of a sad sack, and it would be hard to imagine him hurting anyone, but yeah, I've got it. Frankly, I don't trust anybody anymore."

She knew what he meant. It was particularly strange, she thought, that they couldn't even trust the police. In Firefly Glen, the sheriffs and deputies weren't your enemy. They were your neighbors, and they came over for macaroni dinner with your parents.

Out here it was different. They couldn't be sure what Keith Quigley's agenda was, or how far his power extended. They couldn't bring him speculation and half-baked theories. He was perfectly capable of using your information to weave the rope he'd hang you with.

By the time they reached the front door, Suzie felt as if she'd eaten a hive of bees. Her stomach was all wings and stingers. But she stayed as poker-faced as she could. You couldn't really insist on coming along and then start whining about how scary it was.

Phil answered right away. This was the first time Suzie had seen him, and the bees subsided a little. Mike's description of a "sad sack" was perfect. He wasn't ugly, but he looked weak and unhappy, with dark, drooping eyes, a long, fleshy nose and very little chin.

He wasn't at all threatening. He had no muscles beyond the ones required for walking and sleeping and lifting the remote control. He was half Mike's size. Except in diameter.

He looked out the door in both directions furtively, like someone in a cartoon. "No one saw you come, did they?"

Mike frowned. "Why would it matter if they had? You have every right to be here. Millner gave you and your wife a key, didn't he?

"Yes, but just for emergencies. And you—"

"My car's out on the street, Phil, for all the world to see. People are dying around here. I'm not making any secret rendezvous in dark alleyways with anyone, not even you."

Phil nodded, but his face was contorted with anxiety. "Yes, but they'll see you. They'll *see* you."

"Who?"

"I don't know," Phil said. "That's just it. They could be out there right now. They always wore hoods, so I never saw their faces."

Mike looked behind him, and Suzie did the same. Phil Stott's cringing fear was contagious. "Are you talking about the cops? Did they leave someone guarding Richie's apartment?"

"No." Phil cast a glance toward the driveway, where the yellow tape warned that this was a crime scene.

Obviously, Suzie deduced, the cops had already searched the apartment and, while they might not want anyone messing with the place, they didn't think it was important enough to station a guard.

Mike had told her that Rutledge was still in custody. Probably the cops thought they already had their man.

"They were here all day," Phil said. "But they're gone. Thank God."

Mike put his hand on the door. "You're getting yourself all wrought up. Let us in. You said you have information for us about the Mulligan Club."

"Yes." The man pulled his eyebrows together, as if he might be going to cry. "I'm sorry, Mike," he said. "I'm so sorry."

Suzie glanced up at Mike. She wasn't sure this Phil guy was coherent enough to be very helpful. She was starting to wonder whether he might be the murderer after all. What else could have him in such an agony of guilt and fear?

"The police know we're here," she said suddenly, though no one had spoken to her.

Mike looked at her. He knew it was a lie, but he didn't contradict her.

"Do they know why?" Phil's eyes were wide. "Do they know about the Mulligan Club?"

"Phil, you're supposed to be giving us information, not the other way around." Mike pushed open the door. "Let's get started."

"Yes." Phil moved away. Clearly he couldn't stand up to the slightest bit of pressure. Suzie's internal murderer-meter swung back to the "no" position. If Phil Stott had killed Justine, even by accident, they would have found him two days later, still standing over the body and wringing his hands.

Once in, Mike led the way. He headed toward the living room, and Suzie was reminded that this used to be his home. She tried to imagine him in these fussy marble-and-gilt rooms and just couldn't do it.

"Not in there," Phil said, holding out one hand. His fingers were very pale, and his nails were a half inch too long, as if he hadn't clipped them in quite a while. They didn't look quite clean, either.

"Too many windows," he said. "We should go to the library. I have to show you my tape. I don't know if we all got the same one. But it's the only way to prove—"

"What?" Mike turned, his face taking on that extra measure of calm that Suzie knew meant he was shocked. "You have a tape? Of the Mulligan Club?"

Phil frowned. "Don't you?"

"What makes you think I do?"

"I—" Phil looked confused. "I don't know. I guess I thought you must, because—because if you weren't one of us, how did you know about the club?"

"Someone told me about it."

Phil's mouth fell open. "Someone talked about the Mulligan Club? That's not possible. The rules require silence."

Suzie felt her flesh creep a fraction of an inch across her bones. She didn't like the way he said that last sentence. It had a really icky cult-programming sound.

"The person who told me wasn't exactly a member," Mike said. "The details will have to come from you. First tell me where you got this tape. Is that one of the perks of membership? You get to relive your fun on videotape?"

"Fun?" For the first time, Phil looked angry. "You think it was *fun*?"

Suzie was afraid that Mike might upset Phil so much he clammed up. This guy was on the edge, and he needed gentler handling. Mike must be incredibly tense, she thought, if *she* had become the subtle one.

"Look, Phil," she said. "You have to understand that we don't know very much about the club. We just know that you've got a lot on your conscience, and that you'll feel much better when you've shared it with someone. Why don't you begin by telling us where you got the videotape?"

Phil nodded. "He made one for each of us, just to prove he had it. He had to prove it, or we wouldn't have paid him, of course."

"Who?" Mike's voice was flat. "Who made the tapes?"

"Richie." Phil looked surprised that Mike had to ask. He had obviously lived with this situation so long he'd forgotten it was new to other people.

"Richie Graham? The Richie who just got shot here last night?"

"Yes, of course. That must be why someone shot him, don't you think? He was blackmailing us, *all* of us, or at least that's what he said. He must have hidden a camera in the cave. There were a million secret places in the walls, and he—"

Phil began to cry. "He gave us copies of the tape and said he'd send it to the police, and our families, our *wives*, if we didn't pay."

The police? Suzie's bad feeling got much worse. That one sentence told her that she and Mike probably hadn't been wrong about Loretta Cesswood. The Mulligan Club hadn't been just some overgrown former frat boys playing games with well-paid strippers and hookers and maybe a manacle or two just for kicks. If it had, why would the police have been interested in Richie's tapes?

But a fifteen-year-old girl, a drugged, unwilling participant in what amounted to torture, was another story altogether.

And so was a beautiful, foolish young mother who came for a sex game and ended up dead.

"I can't tell you all the things that happened," Phil said, lowering his voice. "I can't say those things out loud. You wouldn't believe me, anyhow, not if you weren't there. You'll have to look at the tape. The tape will show you. You'll see that I tried to stop them."

He moved toward the hall. Mike began to follow him, his face dark and rigid, but Suzie grabbed his elbow. "Wait. This is crazy. What's on that tape, Phil? You're not asking us to watch someone murdering Justine?"

Phil froze in his tracks. "Murdering Justine? What are you talking about?"

Man, this level of kookiness was really getting on her nerves. "Justine was murdered, remember? Is that what you were being blackmailed about? Did someone in the Mulligan Club kill her?"

To her surprise, Phil looked as if he might cry again. "I don't know who killed her," he said. "It's not on the tape, but of course it could have been one of us. She knew all our secrets. She mocked us, and we kept coming back anyway because she gave us what we wanted. But deep inside we hated her."

He looked at Mike. "I thought it might be the same for you."

"No," Mike said, and his voice was more kind than Suzie had expected. "I probably hated her as much as you did. But she didn't have anything I wanted."

Phil smiled sadly. "You are one of the lucky ones, then," he said. "If you don't have anything twisted inside, anything that the world doesn't understand, for her to exploit."

"God, Phil, what do you—" But Mike took a breath

and appeared to decide against finishing his question. "Maybe you'd better just show me the video," he said. "It might be easier than trying to explain."

Phil nodded. He looked at Suzie. "We should go alone," he said. "You don't want to see this."

"The hell I don't. And besides, everything that happens here today gets a witness. You're not taking him off into some room alone, and that's final."

Mike came up behind her and put his hand on her shoulder. "It probably will be pretty nasty. You know I can take care of myself."

"He won't have to." Phil smiled sadly. "I'm weak. But I'm not a killer."

"Great." Suzie squared her shoulders and moved toward the library. "I'm glad to hear it. Now why don't we get this over with?"

The library was just as pretentious as everything else about this house. It was a large room, self-consciously decorated with green leather furniture and lined with color-coordinated, leather-bound books. Suzie couldn't imagine that any of the paperback novels by Mike's bed at the boathouse would ever have been allowed on these shelves.

A huge television hung on the wall at one end of the room, with leather chairs arranged around it for elegant conversation. Phil stood close to the screen, operating the remote. Mike stood just behind him. Suzie hung back a little, closer to the door. Phil had drawn the curtains and turned off all the lights, so the place had a gloomy, claustrophobic feel and Suzie, for one, felt more comfortable the closer she was to the exit.

Phil slid the videotape into the slot below the television. Suzie couldn't help wondering how often he'd come over here, using his "just in case" key, and lounged in the library, a king in a borrowed castle.

She crossed her arms, lifted her chin and prepared to handle whatever this tape had to offer.

Like most dirty movies, this one didn't waste any time on the setup. It began with a shot of four men, at least she guessed they were men, standing in the cave. They looked ridiculous, and her first instinct was to laugh. They all wore identical black hoods that completely covered their faces, except for eye slits and mouth holes. They all wore the same black, flowing robes.

They looked like a bunch of jerks playing naughty monks at an Alpha Dorka Psicko fraternity costume party.

But she glanced at Phil, and she saw that he was mesmerized, staring at the television and kneading his hands around the remote. And she knew that it wasn't really a joke. These head-cases took their dress-up games very seriously.

The cave looked much as she and Mike had imagined. Torches hung in sconces on the walls, their blue-orange fire dancing along the walls and rising in gusts of black smoke toward the cave ceiling.

The camera must have been hidden somewhere toward the opening. It had been positioned high, so that it filmed down and caught almost the entire central portion of the cave.

The video itself was clear, although the lighting was low. And of course Justine's television was the best money could buy, so no detail was lost in translation.

The one surprise in the scene was a very large plywood box that stood in the center of the open area.

Unlike the monks, it didn't have any of the trappings of a Halloween party. It wasn't dressed up to look like a coffin, or a crypt. It was just a very large, very primitive box.

Suzie mentally redrew the cave as she'd seen it, and suddenly she felt something cold wash through her veins.

The box was directly over the place where they'd found the drilled holes. The manacles waited in there.

"That's me," Phil said, his voice cracking on the *e*. He paused the tape and went right up to the screen to touch one of the hooded figures. Suzie squinted, trying to figure out how he could even tell. The figure he pointed to might have been a little chubbier, a little shorter, than the others, but the robes rendered everyone anonymous.

He pointed to another short monk. "I'm pretty sure that's Quigley," he said thoughtfully.

Mike and Suzie exchanged stark glances. Then Mike turned to Phil. "Why would you think that?"

"I always thought so," he said, growing agitated as he stared at the video. "I always suspected. There was something…" He touched the monk's hood with his finger. "But then, when I heard his body had been found last night, I knew for sure."

"What?" Suzie couldn't help it. She wasn't a stoic Frome. When someone shocked the heck out of her, she squealed. "His *body?*"

Phil nodded. He didn't seem to be able to take his eyes off the screen. It was as if he was in this room, and in that cave, simultaneously.

"Quigley is dead," he said. "They killed him last night. Maybe before Richie, maybe after. The police don't seem to be sure."

He turned to face them. His eyes were glowing in the blue light from the television. "They're going to kill us all, you know. It used to be enough just to be silent. But we're going to be punished, because we were so weak."

"Who?" Even Mike sounded frustrated. Suzie wondered if they should believe any of this. Phil was a little unhinged. He might have dreamed the whole thing.

But the monks were clearly real. They stood at attention, waiting for the flick of Phil's finger to set their terrible video game in motion. It was a little like going through the looking glass, she thought. You didn't know what was real and what was just the contagious insanity playing with your mind.

"Who is going to kill you?" Mike's voice was tough. "Phil, if you know who is doing these things, let's don't waste time with the video. Just tell me and—"

"I don't know. That's the problem. I don't know. But sometimes I think it might be…"

Suzie wondered if Mike was holding his breath, too.

Phil lowered his voice. "Sometimes I think it might be Justine."

Suzie exhaled her disappointment. "Justine's dead, Phil," she said. "If anything she was the killer's first victim."

"I know," he said. "I'm not crazy. It's just that sometimes I see a woman in my dreams, and she—"

Mike cut him off. "Let's finish the video. Can you identify any of the other men in the robes?"

Phil shook his head. He pointed to a tall man. "I thought that might be you. She seemed to pay special attention to him."

"No," Mike said dryly. "Not me. Is one of them Richie Graham?"

"Yes, but you can't see him now. He's coming in just a minute. Watch the entrance to the cave."

He started the video rolling again, and almost immediately another hooded, robed man slid slowly through the cave's lakefront opening.

"That one. That's Richie." Phil pointed.

Suzie gasped. The man was half carrying, half dragging something. It was a young girl. Naked and limp with either fear or drugs, the girl was crying, whimpering for him to let her go.

It was Loretta Cesswood.

Mike made a sound. Suzie had to grab the back of the leather chair in front of her. Otherwise, her legs might have given out.

She'd imagined this, of course, back when she'd first read the diary. But words couldn't capture the infinitely pitiful quality of that pale, childish body drowning in the sea of black robes.

"They had never done that before," Phil said. "Never. You have to believe me. Before, the women had always been paid. They were professionals. They thought we were pathetic, of course, but they were glad to play the game if the price was right."

"Yuck," Suzie began. "What kind of—"

But Phil suddenly hissed at her.

"*Listen,*" he said. "You can hear me. You can hear that I tried to stop them."

Sure enough, the robed man he had identified as himself lurched forward, his hands extended. "No," the man called out. "You heard her! She said no!"

The men on either side of him put out their hands, too, and brought him back into his place in line. He continued to strain forward, but he didn't speak again.

Oh, yeah, Suzie thought. *You tried to stop them, all right. Big hero.*

The drama was continuing, of course, in spite of

Phil's halfhearted efforts. The man led the naked girl toward the box. She seemed to sense her danger, because she found spirit, just for a minute, and dug in her heels and screamed. But the man found her no more trouble than a kitten. He moved her forward, opened the front of the box, and placed her inside.

He stayed with her for a minute. Suzie imagined she heard the sounds of metal cuffs being locked down over fragile bones, but she couldn't have, not really. You couldn't hear any sound that small.

The man emerged again, alone, and took his place in the line.

From just out of camera range, a woman appeared. She wore robes, just like the men, but she wore no hood, as if she didn't care whether she could be identified. As if, Suzie thought, she was proud to be there.

It was Justine.

Oh, damn it. The Mulligan Club wasn't just a club Justine frequented when she got bored. It was *her* club. She had invented it, and she owned it. While they were here, she clearly owned these men, too.

Suzie tried to read Mike's face, but in the flickering light of the television it was just a jumble of meaningless shadows. His gaze was glued to the screen.

Justine paraded along the line of men, pausing for a second before each one individually, like a queen surveying her troops. Even in the video, Suzie could feel the tension, the anticipation, the tremor of sexual thrill.

Finally Justine stopped. She leaned in and kissed one of the men, the one Phil had identified as Keith Quigley. Her kiss was slow and deep. She salaciously tongued the hood's mouth hole, then nipped the fabric, and pulled it toward her slightly with her teeth.

The man stepped forward. Without haste, but with a rigidity that spoke of his excitement, he stripped off his robes. He left his hood in place. But under the robes he was naked. He was boldly aroused.

"He's been chosen," Phil said in a voice that was, even now, strangely awestruck.

Through her horror, Suzie analyzed the shape of the man's body. Phil wasn't crazy on this count, she realized. It *was* Quigley. She recognized that barrel chest, those just slightly bowed knees, that roll of the shoulders that gave him a toadlike hunch.

He entered the box.

The girl cried out in terror. There was a terrible silence, and then softly, she began to cry, and then to scream. She must have been struggling, because the box shifted on its base.

"Only one man a night is picked," Phil was explaining, as if he didn't even see the unspeakable crime being played out on the screen. "I guess that's why they brought a girl like this, a young one who would be afraid. I think Quigley likes pain. We all do, of course, either giving it or receiving it. But Quigley—it was different with him. He needed more."

"Turn it off," Mike said suddenly. He was looking at Suzie. She wondered if she had made a noise. Then she realized that she had almost sunk to her knees. She still clutched the edge of the chair.

"No, not yet. Here's where I try again—" Phil pointed excitedly at the television. His robed figure shook off the hands that held him in place and rushed forward. "Someone has to help her," the Phil on the screen cried.

But Justine stepped smoothly forward and blocked his way. He subsided instantly. With a smile on her face, she reached out and touched his cheek through his hood. She murmured something to him, something too soft to hear.

The two men moved forward, as well. They each grabbed one of Phil's arms. But Justine waved them away, and they stepped back obediently. She knew she didn't need them.

She reached down and found a slit in the front of Phil's robe. She slid her hand into it and began to move her hand in a gentle, unvarying rhythm.

Phil groaned, and then he let his head fall back as Justine worked on him.

Meanwhile, the girl in the box went on weeping, softer now. She called for her mother.

Suzie tasted bile in the back of her throat. She looked at Phil, and saw that he was sobbing, too, watching himself be humiliated, brought to climax in spite of his determination to resist. Even in spite of his fear.

"I'm sorry," he said. "I'm so sorry."

Mike took the remote control out of his hand and turned off the television.

The library fell into its silent gloom.

And a shot rang out in the darkness.

CHAPTER TWENTY-THREE

MIKE HAD HIS GUN OUT, and he'd already begun to move toward Suzie when he heard a firm voice speak into the darkness.

"Stay where you are, Mike. I've got her, and I'll shoot her if I have to."

His mind, already struggling to process the complex and chilling implications of the video, and then the horrifying sound of a gunshot, at first couldn't comprehend what he was hearing.

Could that really be Judy Stott? He knew that Phil, who had been standing by the television, had slumped to the floor. What the hell had happened here? Had Judy shot her own husband?

The dusky twilight in this shrouded room, especially after his eyes had become accustomed to staring at the television, had left him virtually blind for a few seconds.

But his vision was returning slowly, and he could see that there was a woman standing right behind Suzie.

It was Judy.

"Mike." Suzie's voice sounded angry, which he knew meant she was scared. She hated being scared and would do anything to hide it. "Mike, she's got a gun shoved in my back. At least it feels like a gun, and, by the way, Mrs. Stott, that hurts."

Mike's heart stumbled. "Suzie," he said as clearly and slowly as possible. "Do *not* do anything dumb. Do you hear me?"

She snorted. "I'll promise not to do anything dumb *on purpose*. But you know me."

At a different moment, he might have laughed. Yes, he did know her. He adored her. He had never believed he was capable of killing anyone, but if Judy Stott harmed a hair on Suzie's head, he thought he might tear her limb from limb.

"Mike," Judy said. "I want you to put your gun down slowly. I want you to kick it toward me."

He hesitated. Behind him, Phil's breath was coming raggedly.

"Right now, Mike. I will shoot her. Two bodies aren't any harder to explain than one."

He put his gun on the floor carefully, holding it by the barrel. Then he stood, and nudged it with his toe. It slid across the hardwood floor and came to rest right beside Judy's foot, like a successful toss in a deadly game of horseshoes.

She bent slightly—never taking the gun from Suzie's back—and lifted the gun. She slid it in the pocket of her jacket.

"Good decision," she said. "Now, I want you to check on Phil. I need to know whether he's dead."

"Why?" Suzie's voice was tart. "Do you hope he is or he isn't?"

Smart, smart lady, he thought, sending her a mental thank-you. He'd just been wondering which answer Judy was looking for.

"It doesn't matter to me," Judy said calmly. "If he's not dead yet, I have plenty of bullets."

Okay, then, the right answer was yes. Mike bent

down and felt Phil's pulse. He had been shot squarely in the back, and there was blood all over his shirt. His pulse was weak—so weak that Mike might be able to say yes truthfully very soon.

"I don't feel a pulse," he said. "I think he's gone." He stood. "What the hell is going on here, Judy?"

"I should have killed him two years ago," she said. "It would have saved me a lot of trouble." She looked at the lump on the floor, without the slightest evidence of pity. "He was such a weakling. He was the perfect prey for your predatory wife."

Mike knew what she meant. He'd thought the same thing himself, as they watched Justine subdue poor Phil with nothing but a cold smile and the promise of a hand job from the queen.

"I take it you saw the video, too. How long had you been standing there, watching?"

"Long enough," she said. "I didn't kill your wife deliberately, Mike. It was an accident. But I think if I had seen this video two years ago, I might have. God knows, the bitch deserved to die."

Mike felt a strange surge of an emotion so complex he couldn't put a name to it. Was it possible he was finally going to learn the truth? He'd lived so long with the questions, the doubts, the dread. Asking himself about every friend, every neighbor, every strange man on the street…*Did you kill my wife? Do you know where her body is?*

His mind had supplied so many nightmare scenarios. He'd learned to live with that. Oddly, he suddenly wasn't sure he could handle the finality of *knowing*.

And yet, of course, he had to know.

"How did it happen, Judy? Did you find her walking home that day? Did you give her a ride?"

"I tried to. But she was in a snit, because of some snafu at the play that day with Gavin."

Mike remembered. Justine had thought the other mothers, in collaboration with Judy, had conspired to steal Gavin's starring role. God, when Mike thought back on that day now, he couldn't believe how petty it all had been. The last day of her life, and she wasted it being upset over something so trivial.

"Anyhow," Judy went on. "She refused to get in the car. So I got out. I'd just found out that she'd brought Phil into her disgusting club, and I wanted to tell her I knew."

"You already knew about the Mulligan Club? How did you find out?"

"I'm not a fool. I know when my husband is lying. I followed him the first night. I saw enough."

Mike could only imagine how furious she'd been.

"So I told her she'd made a mistake. That my husband might be a fool, but I wasn't. I told her it was going to have to stop."

"What did she say?"

"She laughed. She really was the most arrogant woman I've ever met. She said she had no intention of closing her club, but that I could join, too, if I wanted. She said they really needed some women."

Oh, Justine. How insulted Judy must have been. Justine always went too far, way too far. When she was young, that had been one of her charms, that over-the-top, brazen sexuality and the certainty that the world was her plaything.

But in a grown woman, it was clearly a personality disorder. A sociopathic inability to recognize the humanity of others.

"She didn't mean it, Judy. She was just trying to embarrass you."

"I wasn't embarrassed," Judy said haughtily. "I don't embarrass that easily. I was *furious*. I slapped her. Hard. We were standing on the grass, near the tree line. I went to slap her again, and she couldn't take it. She darted away. She had on those stupid heels, and I think she must have tripped on something, because suddenly she was going down. She hit her head on a rock. She died instantly."

Mike saw it like another video in his head. Justine falling. Her blond hair matted with blood, her eyes open, staring, caught with a look of disbelief that her beautiful, intense flame could be extinguished so easily, just like any mortal.

"Why didn't you just call the police?" Suzie sounded skeptical. "If it really was an accident, why couldn't you report it?"

"With my handprint still on her face? Who would have believed my story? Do you understand how important your reputation is, in the kind of work I do? I would have lost everything."

"So in the end, you're not all that different from Justine, are you?" Suzie tilted her head to glare at Judy. "In the end, it's all about you."

"Suzie." Mike tried to send a warning in his voice. This woman had already shot one person. Now was not the time to let her temper have free rein.

"Let her rant, Mike," Judy said. "I've killed three men in the past twenty-four hours. Do you think I give a damn what this little twit thinks of me?"

"No." Mike had to be careful. He wanted to keep her talking, but he couldn't risk inflaming her temper. "No. I don't think you care. Why would you? You killed Richie, then?"

"Yes," she said. "He'd been blackmailing me for

two years. He saw me burying the body. He sent me a tape, too. It was dark, so you couldn't see much. But you could see enough."

"Oh, my God." Suzie sounded sick. "I knew that guy was a creep."

"So why now?" Mike tried to take the focus from Suzie, who was just too damn close to that gun. "Were you suddenly sick of paying?"

"Of course I was sick of paying. But that's not why I killed him. I killed him because I couldn't trust him anymore. Keith Quigley had been up there, and he was trying to cut a deal."

"So Quigley was being blackmailed, too?"

"Of course. But he was a fool, too. He actually believed he'd been in love with Justine, and he was getting ready to spill everything to the cops. The Mulligan Club, Phil, everything. Some romantic notion that he owed it to her memory to make sure her murderer was found."

"And he wanted Richie to corroborate?"

"I'm not sure what the details were. I think he was trying to get Richie to promise to keep his name out of it, in exchange for some kind of immunity. Richie said he'd think about it, then he made the mistake of trying to tease me with it, hinting about the deal. I knew what that meant. He was going to turn me in, to save his own hide. So I killed him. I killed them both."

"When you saw him dying on the beach, I thought—" He tried to summon up the expression he'd glimpsed on her face. "I thought you might have cared about him."

She laughed. "And men call women sentimental! I cared about him *dying*, that's all. I had been afraid that you might have spoiled everything, with your idiotic heroics. I was extremely relieved that you hadn't."

He wasn't sure he bought that entirely. He wondered whether, along the twisted way, Judy and Richie might have become lovers. Not real love—just sex. But Judy might have become a tiger in the hands of a man like Richie. It might have pleased her to punish her husband for being such a weakling by taking a strong man to her bed.

"What about Rutledge?" He was trying to find all the pieces, but he wasn't sure how much longer he could keep her talking. She was starting to look restless. And Suzie, of course, could only be kept quiescent for so long. "Was he being blackmailed, too?"

"Of course, but not because of the club. He never got into the club. I found his tape at his apartment, just now, when I was helping Debra pack. She was glad to get the help." She smiled unpleasantly. "I'm a very good friend."

"What had Rutledge done, then, to attract Richie's interest?"

"He'd been having some pretty violent sex with Justine. I suppose Richie convinced him that it looked suspicious to be roughing up a woman just days before she went missing." She made a disgusted sound. "Your wife was a nasty woman, Mike. I've always felt kind of sorry for you."

"Sorry enough," Suzie broke in wryly, "to let him walk out of here alive?"

Judy laughed. "No," she said. "Not that sorry, I'm afraid."

She looked at Mike. "Okay, enough chat. I want you to walk slowly over to that television and take out the videotape."

"And if I won't?"

"Then I shoot her. I'd rather do it later. I have a scenario in mind that will make a plausible cover story when I have to talk to the police. But I can do it here, if you make me."

Mike went over to the console and ejected the tape. "Now what?"

"Now go over to the window, slowly, and lift up the edge of the carpet. Suzie and I will be right behind you."

Mike did as he was told. He kept playing ideas through in his head, but none of them got him to the gun fast enough. If she intended to pull that trigger, it would take only one wrong move from him, and Suzie would be dead.

He kneeled down and lifted the edge of the carpet. To his surprise, he saw a small notch in the wood, and a metal trigger that seemed to operate a latch of some kind.

He looked up. "What is this?"

"You didn't know it was there, did you?" Judy shook her head. "You may have lived here, but your heart wasn't ever really in it. Maybe it's a kind of justice that you should take the blame for all this. Maybe it really is your fault. A woman can't live without any love at all."

Suzie groaned. "What a crock. Justine Millner loved herself so much she didn't need anyone else."

"What is this, Judy?" Mike touched the metal trigger. It was cold. "A trapdoor? Where does it lead? To the cave?"

"Yes," she said. "It's a part of the whole cave system, actually. The old owners had blocked it off. But Justine opened it up and put in the trapdoor. I suppose discovering the tunnel was what gave her the idea of the Mulligan Club."

"Hey." Suzie looked at Mike. "A tunnel? I wonder if Gavin stumbled onto it somehow? I wonder if that's where he saw Quigley? He may have been on his way to or from a Mulligan meeting."

Mike nodded. "Maybe." It made his blood run cold to think of his son brushing that close to something so sick and twisted.

"Open it, Mike," Judy said. "I want to get this over with."

He crooked the knuckle of his index finger into the latch and lifted. The hinges were rusty—they obviously hadn't been opened for more than two years—but not frozen. The trap came free neatly, exposing three downward steps and then a surprisingly wide tunnel that sloped gently toward the lake. It seemed to be tall enough for a man to stand in.

"Now what?" He looked at Judy, who had come closer, but not close enough.

"Now I want you to get in. Stay a few steps ahead of us. I'll have the gun against her head. If you so much as stumble, or look behind you, I'll shoot her. It's all the same to me, Mike. She can die now or she can die later."

"Umm, if I have a vote, I say later," Suzie said. She looked over at Mike and tried to smile.

He kept thinking through the options. Surely the tunnel would provide more possibilities. Down there, both he and Judy would be hampered, but at least it would force the pieces to move on the chessboard. If they were in motion, there was always the possibility Judy would make a mistake.

"All right," he said. "I'm not going to do anything funny, so relax. Are we going to the cave?"

"Yes."

"You know they'll find your husband's body," Suzie said. "Whatever sick scenario you've got in mind once we get down there, you'll still have to account for Phil lying up here in the library."

"Not a problem," Judy said in her businesswoman's voice. "Mike killed him here, to prevent exposure. Phil knew about the Mulligan Club, so of course Mike couldn't allow him to live. He'd already killed Keith and Richie to keep his secret, and Phil was just the next to go."

"Just out of curiosity," Mike said. "What exactly is my secret?"

"That you killed your wife, of course. You had found out about her dirty little sex club, and you killed her. Then, when you learned who the members were, and they threatened to reveal the secret, you had to eliminate them."

"Oh. And Suzie?"

"She found out about you, too. Everyone knows she's been your lapdog for weeks here. But when she found out you had actually killed Justine, she was going to leave you. You couldn't have that, so—"

"So I eliminated her. Yes, I see the pattern. But aren't you worried about your reputation anymore, Judy? You'll have to bring all this out in the open, in order to construct your alibi. Won't that put a pretty big dent in the reputation, too?"

She smiled. "I'll be the heroine of the piece. I'll be the brave woman who caught the serial killer that even the police couldn't find."

"Caught?" Suzie was frowning. "Caught, or *killed?*"

Judy didn't answer. "Move, Mike," she said. "We're wasting too much time."

He moved. Once he passed farther than the dim library light could reach, he was in total darkness. Luckily, there were no choices to make. Just a straight shot, touching the walls now and then to orient himself. They were just as cold and dank as the walls in the cave.

"You know, you're pretty arrogant yourself," Suzie said. Mike wondered if she was talking so that he'd always understand where everyone was in relation to everyone else. She was smart, so that was possible. Of course, she was also a smart-ass, so it was possible she just couldn't help herself.

"Is that so?" Judy sounded a little winded. Mike was glad to hear it. "How do you come to that conclusion?"

"Well, clearly you think you're smarter than the police. Do you know how hard it is to cover up three— no, five—no, *six*—murders? Don't you watch cop shows on TV? The killer always makes some little mistake, and they nail him with it. Nobody can think of everything."

"I don't have to think of everything. The police already suspect Mike. This will just confirm it. They won't look very hard for anything else."

"Typical dumb-criminal hubris," Suzie observed, unimpressed. "That's what they always say. They're still saying it on their way to the big house."

In spite of everything, Mike smiled in the darkness. God, he loved that woman. She was the bravest, most annoying female on the face of the earth, and when they got out of here he was going to tell her so.

Suddenly the tunnel took a turn, and he knew they were almost there. The air changed subtly, and he could smell the lake. He even sensed light coming in, but weakly.

"Turn left," Judy said. She sounded as if she were about ten feet behind him. She was smart, too. She always stayed just out of harm's reach.

He turned left. He squeezed through a relatively narrow passage, and suddenly there they were. The sunlight was stronger today, and it penetrated farther. Even without a flashlight, he could almost make out the soot marks on the walls.

Suzie emerged stiffly, followed by Judy, who had hold of Suzie's upper arm. The gun was at her head.

Suzie looked at Mike and rolled her eyes. "Sorry," she said. "I had planned to karate chop her, but I chickened out."

"That's okay," he said. "You're doing great."

She scowled. "Don't patronize me, Frome. I know I'm having a failure of imagination here. If you can do better, feel free to jump right in."

"Shut up," Judy said. "I'm sorry to have to do this, Suzie. If I had any choice, I wouldn't. You're a gutsy girl."

"I'm a bitch on wheels," Suzie said crossly. "If you do this, I guarantee you I'm going to haunt you for the rest of your natural life."

"I'm afraid I'm going to have to take that risk."

Mike knew he was out of time. Judy didn't seem to have any more urge to explain herself, even. She seemed to be starting to get anxious and want it to be over.

Still he had to try. "Won't they think it's strange that I shot everyone with *your* gun?"

"It's your gun, Mike. At least that's what I'll tell them. It's untraceable. You killed Richie with it, and you killed Phil…and finally I wrestled it away from you," Judy said. She looked at the gun. He wondered if she might be having a little trouble pulling off these last, cold-blooded murders. "I really am sorry, Mike, but—"

He couldn't wait. He lunged. He heard a shot. And then, just as he reached Judy, the tunnel entrance exploded, and a body came flying at her from behind.

Instinctively, she looked over her shoulder and saw her husband. As if he'd been a demon or a true ghost, she screamed. The gun went off again.

The sound was deafening in the stone enclosure. Mike saw Suzie yell, but he couldn't hear it. Everything was chaos and echoing thunder.

When the struggle ended, Judy's body was under him, and Phil Stott was lying beside her, gasping, his one courageous burst of energy spent. Mike had no idea who was alive or dead—but he didn't feel any movement from the woman under him.

He looked around, trying to find Suzie.

Please, he prayed. *Please*.

Finally he found her, just as the thunder subsided.

"She did it. That goddamn crazy woman really shot me."

Suzie sat on the floor, her back against one of the cave walls, staring at her shoulder, which was bleeding at an alarming rate. She used her good arm to dig her cell phone out of her pocket.

"I'm calling the cops," she said, as if she thought someone might try to argue her out of it. She angled her cell phone toward the entrance, searching for a signal. "And an ambulance. I'll be damned if I'm going to bleed to death in this stinking place."

Mike scanned the floor. He saw the gun. It had

fallen a foot or two from Judy Stott's outstretched hand. He reached over and picked it up. He grabbed his own gun out of her pocket. Then he slowly released the woman on the floor.

She didn't move.

She might be dead, and frankly he didn't give a damn. He was much more worried about Phil. But when he felt for a pulse, he realized the man still had one.

"I'm going to take your belt, Phil," he said gently. "You did great."

Phil nodded weakly. He struggled to a half-sitting position. "I'll be okay," he said. "Do what you have to do."

When Mike rolled Judy over to tie her up, he saw that she was breathing, too, though unconscious. She must have knocked her head on the stones as she went down. But, unlike Justine, her head had been hard enough to withstand the crack.

He used Phil's belt to tie her hands, and his own to tie her feet. Even if she came to, she wouldn't be able get herself to a standing position on her own. He had no intention of helping her. The police could do it when they got here.

He went over to Suzie. "Can you walk?" He looked at her face for signs of shock. "I want to get a look at that shoulder. Can you get outside, do you think?"

"Yes, I can walk," she said, snappishly. "She shot my shoulder, not my leg."

He tilted a smile at her, and she sighed. "Sorry," she said. She lifted her good arm to let him help her up. "That woman made me cranky."

Laughing, he put his arm around her. He didn't care

if she didn't like the implication that she was weak. He just wanted to touch her.

As they neared the exit, Judy seemed to regain consciousness. She struggled on the floor a few seconds, and then, realizing she was overcome, she began to cry.

"Oh, shut up," Suzie said. She looked at Mike. "I'm sorry, but she said that to me, you know. More than once."

"I know," he said. "Feel free."

He took her out into the sunlight. They both blinked owlishly. And then they looked at each other and smiled.

He checked her wound, which, thank God, seemed to be superficial. It had already stopped bleeding quite so much. Still, he'd be glad when the ambulance arrived. He couldn't risk losing her now.

"Suzie," he said. "I love you."

Amazingly, she blushed. He couldn't believe it. After all she'd just witnessed without flinching, this was what made her blush?

"I love you," he said again. "Get used to it. I'm going to be telling you that every day for the rest of your life."

"Oh, yeah?" She screwed up her mouth and glared at him. "Well, why exactly do you think I'm going to listen?"

"Because you love me, too." He brushed her tangled hair from her cheek. "And it might be nice if you told me at least once a day, as well. Starting today. Starting right now."

"Hrmph," she said, screwing up her mouth thoughtfully. "Maybe, but before I agreed to say anything of the sort, I'd need a promise from you."

Anything, he thought, his heart so full of relief and joy that he was afraid it might lift him off the ground.

A picnic on the moon, a basket full of stars. A diamond ring, a house full of children, a happily-ever-after that he hadn't used to think existed on this earth.

"What? Tell me what to promise, and I'll do it."

She put out one finger sternly. "Remember how you used to call me Suzie-freaka?"

He nodded.

"And Fang?"

He nodded.

"And weirdo?"

"Yes. I was a fool. I'm sorry. I'll never do it again."

"Damn right you won't," she said. "I've had a look at your friends and neighbors, buddy, and believe you me, *I* am not the freak."

"No, indeed you're not." He put his finger under her chin. "So it's a promise. And…"

Her eyes had begun to sparkle. "And what?"

"And you…"

"Oh, yeah." She smiled. "And I'm pretty sure I love you."

CHAPTER TWENTY-FOUR

SPRING IN FIREFLY GLEN was like getting a sneak preview of Heaven.

Everything was sweet green, with masses of flowers adding paintbrush touches of pink and white and yellow. The sky was Easter-egg blue, with cotton-tail clouds, and the sun poured like warm honey over the whole amazing thing.

Suzie wondered why she'd never appreciated this season before. She'd lived here for eighteen years. But maybe, she thought, you had to catch a little glimpse of Hell before you truly understood Heaven.

At any rate, she appreciated it now. Only two weeks after the showdown in the Mulligan Club, she'd returned to Firefly Glen for the June Spoon, an event that used to make her gag, but which was one more thing that suddenly made sense.

Firefly Glen was big on festivals. People as happy as the lucky two thousand or so Glenners apparently just had to celebrate everything.

In June they celebrated Love.

For one weekend, all the stores were decorated with hearts and flowers. The town square had cupids hanging from the gazebo, and pink-and-white barber-shop stripes on the frames of the swing sets. Starry-eyed couples from three counties chose that weekend to get married here, so the air was always ringing with church bells.

The Season Houses, the Glen's four premiere mansions, were all thrown open for tours. And at night, bands played love songs in the band shell, surrounded with fluffy spring trees sparkling with little pink lights. Everyone danced until their slippers—or their will-power—wore thin. Natalie and Matthew Quinn, who were infamous for being unable to keep their hands off each other, never lasted more than an hour or so.

And Saturday morning, Firefly Glen Elementary School always put on a play. This year the theme was "What's Love Got To Do With It?"

Apparently it was supposed to explore the great romances of all time, and how they had shaped history. Gavin had asked Suzie to come. The word was he was going to be King Arthur, which he thought was very cool. "I lose the girl to Lancelot, but that's okay, because he's a dork and he can't hit the broad side of a barn."

It had taken her a minute to figure that one out, and then she realized it meant the other kid was a crummy baseball player. Gavin was his father's son, all right, she thought, laughing to herself, and promised him she'd be there.

But now that she had arrived, she felt weirdly self-conscious. She hadn't seen Mike for two weeks. At first, after the police arrived, it had been all statements and paperwork, and interviews…and more hell.

After that, she knew he needed to get home to Gavin right away. She knew that, for a while, he'd have to concentrate on reassuring the little boy that every-thing would be fine from now on.

She told Mike to take all the time he needed. Then, when he was ready, he could call her, and they would talk.

Since then, she'd been painting furiously, trying to pass the time. She'd taken a commission to paint a group portrait of three pretty little sisters.

The portrait was a huge success. It almost made her mad to discover that she'd actually become a better artist during her crazy hiatus. This new portrait had more depth, more humanity, more…reality. The parents were thrilled, and said they couldn't wait to recommend her to their friends.

What had changed inside her? What had she brought to her work?

Was it the Hell—or the Heaven?

Or perhaps, the new awareness of both.

She drove up to the Frome house early Saturday morning and parked the car out front. She'd promised Gavin she'd come here first, and ride with them to the school.

But darn, it was awkward. Mike hadn't ever officially made that call, telling her it was time to discuss their future—if indeed they had one. She wondered whether this invitation from Gavin was really from the both of them. She hoped so, but she couldn't be sure.

She sat there a minute, trying to get up the nerve to go in.

And then there he was, standing next to her car window, smiling, looking so gorgeous she thought she might have fainted if she hadn't absolutely hated women who faint.

She rolled down the window and tried to look relaxed.

"Hi, there," he said. His smile caught the morning

sunlight and sparkled like a toothpaste commercial. The warm breeze ruffled his hair.

The tension was gone from his handsome face. This setting, this idyllic little mountain town, had always suited him. He glowed here.

"Hi, yourself," she said.

"It's good to see you."

This was dumb. She pulled on the handle and got out of the car.

"I came early," she said, "because I brought you a present."

"Oh, yeah?" He looked happy. He didn't look nervous about anything. "What?"

She opened the backseat. She'd put the painting there, wrapped in brown paper and tied with string. It was a little big, and the frame was heavy. Her right arm was still weak, so she tried to maneuver it out with only her left.

"Hey," he said. "Let me help."

She backed out and let him extricate it. He gave her a curious smile, and then laid the painting on the hood of the car. "Can I open it now?"

He looked like a little boy at Christmas. He looked like Gavin. She nodded, not trusting her voice.

He unknotted the string, then peeled open the paper carefully. She held her breath.

He didn't say anything for a long moment. She looked over his shoulder, terrified that she might have gotten something wrong.

It was his house, his dream house, the one he had described to her at the lake that night. She didn't usually do landscapes, but she had been so pleased with the way this had come out. She had been so sure she'd got the details right, down to the climbing, twining white roses.

The green, leafy hills around the house were clearly Firefly Glen.

That had been a risk. He'd never said that the house was in the Glen, but somehow she couldn't picture it anywhere else.

He belonged here.

"Damn it, say something," she said. "I told you I needed details. If I got anything wrong, it's probably because you didn't describe it right."

He turned and caught her in his arms. "It's perfect," he said. His voice was throaty, and not completely steady. She paused in her tirade, and looked into his eyes. They were shining.

"Oh," she said. "Well, good. I—" She swallowed. "I wanted you to like it."

"I love it," he said. "I knew you'd really seen it."

She nodded. "It's a beautiful house, Mike. You should build it. Honestly, you should. Gavin deserves to live in a house like that. He could be so happy there."

He held her very close. "And you," he said. "Could you be happy there?"

She felt her heart start doing the June Spoon, without music, without pink lights, without anything but the feel of Mike Frome's arms around her.

"What exactly are you saying?"

"I'm saying I love you. I'm saying I want to marry you. I'm saying I want us to build that house and live in it, happily ever after."

She tried to speak, but there was something big and annoying sticking in her throat. She looked up at him, very much afraid that there were tears in her eyes.

"Dad! Dad!" Gavin came barreling out of the house, with another little boy behind him. He stopped and grinned. "Suzie! You made it!"

Suzie pulled herself free of Mike's arms, brushed at her eyes and reached down to give Gavin a hug.

"Of course I made it," she said. "Do you think I'd miss your play?"

"Naw." Gavin grinned. He pointed to his friend. "This is Boomer. He's Lancelot."

She held out her hand. "Hi, Boomer. I hear you can't hit the—"

Gavin shook her arm. "*Suzie!*"

She grinned back at him. "I heard he can't hit the high note in that Camelot song. I'll bet you can't, either."

"I sure can't," Gavin said without rancor. "Ask Dad. I'm so bad at singing dad said I should just lip-synch 'The Star Spangled Banner' in the mornings at school."

Suzie looked at Mike. He had the painting in his hand, and he had come over to stand beside her.

"Gavin," he said. "Suzie has something to tell you."

She frowned. "I do?"

"Yes. She's got some really great news." He nudged her playfully. "Tell him, Suzie. Go ahead."

She narrowed her eyes. "What?"

"Go on. Say it. *I…*"

Oh…

She rolled her eyes. "You're incorrigible," she said.

"No," he responded with a grin. "That would be you. But come on, the kid's waiting. Say it. *I…*"

She looked at Gavin, who was smiling quizzically, obviously thinking the grown-ups were nuts.

"Umm," she said. She cleared her throat. "I…"

Mike nodded. "That's right. *I lo…lo…*"

"I—l…" She sighed. "I love your dad."

Gavin whooped with pleasure. "Cool!" he said. He

and his friend Boomer bumped chests. "I told you, Boomer," he said. "Way to go, Dad."

"Why, thank you, son," Mike said humbly. "Now if you guys would kindly get lost, I've got something I'd like to say to Suzie."

The boys ran off, giggling. Suzie turned to Mike with her scowl firmly in place.

"Well?" She put her hands on her hips. "What do you have to say to me? After you put me on the spot like that, this had better be good."

"Oh, no, sweetheart," he said, pulling her up against him once more. "This is going to be *great*."

Everything you love about romance...
and more!

Please turn the page for Signature Select™
Bonus Features.

QUIET AS THE
GRAVE

**BONUS
FEATURES
INSIDE**

Behind the Scenes: Clubs
by Kathleen O'Brien

The dictionary defines *club* as "a group of people associated for a common purpose" and "anything used to threaten or coerce."

Coincidence? I'm not so sure.

My own history with clubs has certainly included elements of both.

I joined my first club when I was about eight years old. It was the I Hate Boys Club, and it had only two members, my best friend, Celie, who was vice president, and me, the president.

I'm not sure why I was president, except that I was bossier than Celie (being a few months older, which was important when your years could be counted on both hands), and the fact that our clubhouse stood in my front yard, not hers.

Before we got so lofty, that structure used to be called the dollhouse. It was one large room, about the size of a decent potting shed, and had been built by my father to look like a miniature version of our real house, just a few yards away. It was white wood, with a front porch held up by columns and a bright red door. My mother later told me that my dad hammered it into being in the weeks after his own mother died, pounding off the grief.

But, heady with the power of being self-appointed executives, Celie and I redecorated the dollhouse with everything a club needed. There were cast-off chairs and nicked desks and three rather surreal stiff blotter-paper hands, to which we stapled small boxes labeled "Dues" "Donations" and "Debts." The fact that our club had no funds whatsoever didn't diminish our delight in the bureaucratic alliteration.

I don't remember how long the club lasted. Probably not long. Our only purpose was to spy on my boy cousins, who lived next door. Celie and I would climb to the top of the clubhouse, stretch ourselves out as flat as possible on the hot, sticky roof, and watch their comings and goings. We provided a typical eight-year-old's commentary, heavy on words like *gross, jerk* and *yuck.*

I don't think my cousins ever heard us, so the I Hate Boys Club probably didn't do any real damage to anyone. But two years later, when we started our next club, we had obviously lost a lot of that innocence.

The new club was formed for the purpose of staging a play my father had written for us. Celie and I had the lead roles, of course, because he had written them expressly for us, and the characters were even named Kathleen and Celia.

But we handed out the rest of the roles like political appointments to the classmates who pleased us most. The power went to our heads immediately. "You may be Sister Zulema," we told Connie, but later we retracted it on some trumped-up charge. I think, in fact, that we envied the rag curls her mother wound into her pretty hair each night.

We set up membership requirements, attendance at meetings and rehearsals, and a set number of lines to memorize each week. I cringe now, thinking of how insufferable I must have been, but at the time I saw myself as the captain of the ship, saving us all from ruin, steering us toward the glory of a successful performance.

One day, a girl on whom we'd bestowed a desirable role didn't show up for rehearsal. Celie and I were incensed. My father was a lawyer, so I immediately thought how cool it would be to hold a "trial." We assigned the other classmates parts in the drama—this one would be the defender, this one the prosecutor, another girl the judge. I don't know why someone didn't just tell us to take our control-freak arrogance and stuff it, but they didn't. It's hard being ten.

I don't think it ever occurred to Celie or me that anyone might take the whole theatrical nonsense seriously, but the girl on "trial" absolutely did. The night before the trial, her parents called my parents. Their daughter, they said, was nearly sick with fear and distress.

I will never forget the look on my father's face when he came into my room that night. I adored him, and the realization that I had profoundly disappointed him was almost unbearable. He sat down on the edge of my bed and asked me my side of the story. Then, when he saw that it was all true, he began to talk to me about empathy, about the beauty of "inclusion" and the unnecessary ugliness of "exclusion." The grace of kindness, which brought joy to the giver, and the pettiness of cruelty, which crabbed and soured your own soul.

He took his time. He had a talent with words, and he used it to make me look at myself clearly. Before he was finished, I was limp with shame, and I was finished with clubs forever.

Until it came time to imagine what a self-centered control-freak like Justine Millner Frome might do to ease her burden of boredom. What could she do to keep herself feeling comfortably important, the glittering center of a subservient universe?

A club, I thought, remembering the shame and the pain. Definitely, a club.

Great Moments
in Fictional Caves
by Kathleen O'Brien

1) Tom and Becky explore Injun Joe's Cave. For millions of young readers (including me), this was our first detailed description of a cave, and it imprinted indelibly on our psyches. Forever more the word *cave* conjured up the images Tom and Becky saw—stalactites as big as a man's leg, a spring lined with sparkling crystals and exotic spaces called "The Drawing Room," "The Cathedral" and "Aladdin's Palace." It was Mark Twain's genius that he could make the experience of being lost here both thrilling and terrifying. When I learned that there really was a similar cave near Twain's Hannibal, Missouri, I was so tempted.... The real-life stories rivaled anything in the novel. Apparently a local doctor named McDowell did experiments on corpses in this cave, and rumor had it he kept his dead fourteen-year-old daughter's body in a glass cylinder down there. Exciting stuff. But I'm not as brave as Becky, and, sadly, plain old

claustrophobia kept me from seriously considering a trip of my own.

2) Samuel Taylor Coleridge builds "caves of ice" under Kubla Khan's "sunny pleasure dome." Though I'm still not sure *exactly* what the poem "Kubla Khan" means (with apologies to my long-suffering senior English teacher), I've always found the idea of those ice caves unforgettable. Below the "incense-bearing trees" and the fertile ground, and the gushing fountains, the caves lie waiting. Like a frozen, exquisite hell. That inevitable tension between beauty and danger, between joy and despair, is strangely exciting. So is the idea that the whole Kubla Khan landscape is so hauntingly beautiful that if you ever saw it, and dared to tell anyone what you'd seen, they would lock you up as mad.

3) Count de Almasy carries a broken Katharine Clifton into the Cave of Swimmers. Whether it's the book or the movie, the caves in *The English Patient* are romantic, beautiful and cruel. The idea that images of swimming people had been painted on the cave walls, proving that the land had once known water, was somehow heartbreaking and wonderful. It was as if the caves could immortalize a geography, or a love, that had been doomed from the start.

4) Hawkeye leads Cora and friends into a cave behind a waterfall in *The Last of the Mohicans*. This may be the most romantic cave moment in film history. Hawkeye realizes he'll have to leave Cora in the cave if he's to have any chance of saving her in the end. She'll be captured by the bad guys and taken away. But then he grabs her by the arms and says, "I will find you." His wet hair is streaming in his face, and his voice is hoarse with emotion, half drowned by the thundering waterfall just inches away. I'm sure I heard a dozen women in the movie theater sigh. A few may have whimpered. I may have been one of them, although I'm admitting nothing.

5) In *The Crystal Cave*, Galapas takes Merlin into the crystal cave, and shows him his future. Everyone likes Merlin—he's the best part of the Camelot story, anyhow, once you've realized that Arthur is going to lose the girl. But the mental image of a cave made of crystal is simply too gorgeous to resist. In all that gloomy darkness, a secret stash of glittering magic! Even if I hadn't been a Mary Stewart fan already, the title alone would have made me buy this book, the first of the Merlin trilogy. And, of course, Mary Stewart never disappoints!

TOP FIVE
My Top Five Favorite
Paintings of Children
by Kathleen O'Brien

Suzie Strickland might be eking out a living painting portraits of children, but she's got a long way to go before she can compete with some of these amazing paintings!

1 Carnation, Lily, Lily, Rose, by John Singer Sargent

This picture of two little girls painting paper lanterns is one of the most magical works of art I've ever seen. The girls are in white, absorbed in their creation, seemingly unaware of being observed. In this fantasy garden of white flowers and green grass, blue twilight plays overall, capturing that ephemeral moment when the world holds no work, no struggle, no practicality of any kind...only beauty. The story behind the painting is wonderful, too. Apparently Singer Sargent painted only about ten minutes a day, when the light was perfect, and it took him about two months to complete the work. Dolly and

BONUS FEATURE

Polly, the girls in the picture, must have found that tedious, but it doesn't show!

2 Little Girl Sitting in a Blue Armchair, by Mary Cassatt

Any list like this could include half a dozen of Cassatt's extraordinary paintings, but I've chosen just one to represent them all. In this picture, a little girl lounges in a bold blue armchair, looking disgusted with life and completely unaware of how adorable she is. Cassatt didn't need to romanticize children. She understood that part of their charm was that they didn't care what anyone thought of them. This child is bored, bored, bored, and you can almost feel a tantrum brewing, like the cool air that hits your face before a storm. The puppy in the chair next to her is so small you almost miss him at first, but he knows what's coming and looks loyally resigned to riding it out.

3 Harmony in Grey and Green: Miss Cicely Alexander, by James Abbott McNeill Whistler

Cicely Alexander reportedly had to suffer through seventy sittings before Whistler finished the portrait, and the expression on her face shows that it wasn't easy! She seems to be struggling

not to just toss down her hat and walk away.
Thank goodness she didn't, because this subtle,
unsentimental portrait, with its wonderful interplay
of understated colors, is a beauty. Notice the
stylish dress that Whistler supposedly designed
himself. And don't miss the feather on the hat,
which is so real you can almost feel it tickling
your skin. The butterflies above her were
Whistler's favorite—he frequently used a butterfly
monogram to sign his paintings. And how can
you help loving a painter who had an infamous
feud with an art critic? Critic John Ruskin once
said that a painting of Whistler's was the equivalent
of "flinging a pot of paint in the public's face."

4 Girl in a Red Hat, by Alcide Robaudi

This is a much more romantic look at childhood,
and might even be overly cute if it weren't for the
joyous exuberance of this fantastic hat. This little
girl, painted by a French illustrator from the
late 1800s and early 1900s, has yards of flyaway
copper-silk hair topped with a huge red hat
decorated with leaves, flowers and berries. She
always makes me think of Dylan Thomas's "Fern
Hill," in which the poet remembers a childhood
when "honoured among wagons I was prince of
the apple towns." Here, surely, is the princess.

5 The Boyhood of Raleigh, by Sir John Everett Millais

This picture shows two well-dressed boys of privilege listening to a barefoot sailor telling stories of the sea. Both boys are absorbed, but the young Raleigh is almost feverish with enchantment. We see his whole adventurous, chaotic, tragic future in his eyes, and in the way he clutches his legs, as if he must hold himself together, as if he can only barely keep from jumping up and flying to the water that very moment. The romance of the sailor's tale is evident in the bright, overblown colors of his clothes, and the dramatic sweep of his arm as he points toward the open sea.

Wedding Presents from Quiet as the Grave
by Kathleen O'Brien

The Presents Justine Kept

Towel warmer and matching floor-length, monogrammed his-and-her robes, with a baby-sized robe for Gavin: from her father

Chocolate fondue fountain: from her mother

Louis XIV chaise lounge upholstered in authentic leopard skin: from her paternal grandparents

Diamond navel ring: from her younger sister, Mindy

State-of-the-art mechanical cork remover: from Bourke and Jocelyn Waitely

A painting of Justine dressed as Marie Antoinette: from her maternal grandparents

An Angels vs. Devils chess set, carved from white marble and onyx: from a sexy ski instructor she met one winter in Vermont

A blue Chihuly vase: from Heather and Griffin

A weekend at a bed-and-breakfast on Cape Cod, with babysitting thrown in: from Reed and Faith

A sailboat: from Mike's grandfather, Granville Frome

A pair of ruby earrings, with no card included, however, lots of possibilities were bandied about among the guests

The Presents Justine Exchanged, Returned, Tossed Out or Cashed In

Crystal wind chimes and a hand-made wooden garden bench: from Natalie and Matthew

A library globe, and a smaller globe for Gavin: from Parker and Sarah

Engraved stationery: from Harry and Emma

A $5,000 savings bond: from Mike's parents

A CD collection of doo-wop music: from Boxer Barnes

A set of cocktail glasses decorated with cancan dancers: from Rutledge Coffee

Suzie's Favorite Wedding Presents

A golden retriever puppy: from Reed and Faith, who have bred Suzie's original puppies, and now have a new generation to love

A new Nikon camera: from Heather and Griffin, who have commissioned Suzie to paint portraits of their children

A motorboat: from Granville Frome, who knows Suzie's too impatient for a sailboat

A rustic, wood-burned sign: from Gavin. The sign says, "The Fromes...Mike, Suzie, Gavin and_____"—Gavin secretly hopes they can fill in that last name as soon as possible

A trip to Paris to see all the great old masters: from Mike

A lot in Firefly Glen, big enough to someday build Mike's dream house: from Mike's parents and Suzie's parents, together

And Suzie's present to Mike: a check for one year of college tuition, so that he can begin his architectural degree

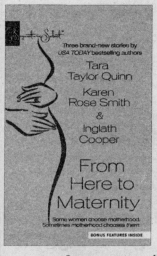

COMING NEXT MONTH

Signature Select Collection
FROM HERE TO MATERNITY by Tara Taylor Quinn,
Karen Rose Smith, Inglath Cooper
Some women choose motherhood. Sometimes motherhood
chooses *them*. Enjoy this heartwarming anthology—just in time
for Mother's Day!

Signature Select Saga
HOT CHOCOLATE ON A COLD DAY by Roz Denny Fox
Despite their high-maintenance families and high-risk jobs, Megan
Benton and Sterling Dodge find plenty of ways to stay warm during
the blustery month of March.

Signature Select Miniseries
A LITTLE BIT NAUGHTY by Janelle Denison
Two sisters find blazing chemistry with the two least likely men of
all in TEMPTED and NAUGHTY—two sizzling page-turning novels
that are editorially connected.

Signature Select Spotlight
HER PERFECT LIFE by Vicki Hinze
Katie Slater's life is perfect. She's a wife, mother of two and a pilot
in the United States Air Force. But then she's shot down by the enemy,
left for dead by a man she trusted and taken as a prisoner of war in
Iraq. Now, six years later, she's back home...only home isn't there
anymore...and her perfect life has become a total mystery.

Signature Select Showcase
SWANSEA DYNASTY by Fayrene Preston
Built on the beautiful, windswept shore of Maine, the great house
of SwanSea was built by Edward Deverell as a monument to himself,
his accomplishments and his family dynasty. Now, more than one
hundred years later, the secrets of past and present converge as his
descendants deal with promises, danger and passion.